The Phoenix Rises

By

Kathy DeMatteis

Table of Contents

NOTE:

When you see a name or business in Bold in the story, please note they are paid contributors that have come into our story line to promote their business or their dreams. You will find a directory in the back of the book with locations and coupons to enjoy!

Writing this book is undoubtedly a test of my faith. Without the voice of God in my ear, guiding me each step of the way, I would not be as far as I am today. The gratitude I have for my father in Heaven is what sustains me through all my uncertainties. Thank you for being the voice that I can count on!

Your daughter in the Universe, Kathy Sue Conrad, this, by far, has been our biggest test of faith, and we are proving every day that our strategy for guiding me each step of the way, I would not be as far as I am today. The gratitude I have for my father in Heaven is what sustains me through all my uncertainties. Thank you for being the voice that I can count on! Keeping our marriage together is working. You are my best friend and the one I count on to get me through everything we do. Dr. Andrew Barrett, you rock, dude! Dr. Donia-Gonzales Copeland, Shonta Gibson, aka Queen G, Eddie Bell, the famous photographer from the Las Vegas Strip.

Ward Whipple, thank you for shaking me up! Pete Denesowicz-your unwavering loyalty to help Conrad and me in the biggest shifts of our lives has been the saving grace to our marriage. You are so much more than our best friends and graphic guy. You are an angel of love. You have always been there to guide the two of us. Thank you, Pete, for everything you have done for us!

Thank you, Big Dennis and Jessica for letting me crash at your places. Sharon Lantz for the Silverton Experience. I could not have done this without your saving grace Mom, thank you for being there when I needed it! Titan, thank you for helping with the horse lingo! Clinton and Wanda Harris of TenderBones Rib Shack, Monique Outterbridge of Velvet Cakes by Gwen, Heather Roemer, Charlie McBride, Shonta Gibson, and Eddie Bell for having our back during the biggest challenge of our lives.

Acknowledgments

Thank you, God, this journey has been so incredible, and I am so thankful and grateful that you chose me to tell it. Thank you for showing me how to see the lesson behind each encounter. How to walk in step with you. How to see the sacred geometry that exists once you understand it's all a numbers game. The world vibrates at a frequency, and the frequency you put out is the frequency you get back. I have learned something from each encounter I have had. There is a reason and a season for each person we meet. Thank you for the opportunity to learn it. Tammi Morrison, you have been my biggest cheerleader during this final push to get The Phoenix Rises out. I could not have done this without you, and I am eternally grateful for our chance encounter that day at Tibbets in Lincoln, Maine. John Pasquarelli from Vibrations Recordings in Hodgson, Maine, has been the honor of my lifetime to be able to work with you to record something I never imagined I was capable of accomplishing. It has been an absolute privilege to work with you, and I am grateful for the opportunity and support you have shown me. Bill Castlelot, thank you for listening to me and running me all around the back Roads of Maine!! Thank you for encouraging me and sharing my skin care products with all your friends. Your support of me and everything you do from the bottom of my heart thank you. Kathy Mushero from the Lincoln Library in Lincoln, Maine. You have been such an amazing support for me, and I am honored to have met you. I always feel so welcomed and loved when I come to the Lincoln Library. You will forever be in my heart as my first paid gig as an author. And the best part is I did write Lincoln long before I knew it existed!! You'll have to read it to find the synchronization!! Natalia at Book Publishing Plus and the team that has put me around the world. Thank you for working with me to give me a cover that means the world to me. The Crooked Spoon on the front cover was hand-carved by Lee Hockeridge from Passadumkeag, Maine. I knew when I saw his ad for his Crooked Spoons that I had to meet him, and boy, am I glad I did. Walking into his workshop and seeing how he takes discarded pieces of wood, meant for the burn pile, and turns them into culinary works of art is mind-blowing. But it's his prior life that is the reason I was there. See, back in the day, Lee traveled the country and networked with businesses to help give people with disabilities employment. It has been my dream to see the majority of my skin care products manufactured by people with disabilities, which I have outlined in detail with the help of a young woman with cerebral palsy who has a dream of walking. Her story is inside the chapter titled Welcome to my World and it is truly the main reason all of these books were birthed. Monique Outerbridge, for your faith in me. I know this was a giant leap of faith, but dreams are meant to take shape, and let's get to baking! Wolfgang Von Baumgardt, what can I say but thank you, sir. It has been the most amazing journey to work with you since putting my bid in for Governor of Delaware. Your relentless dedication and commitment that you have made to not only this project but to the State of Delaware and humanity is beyond the pale. You have dedicated your life to this, and I feel you are not appreciated for what you have done. You are brilliant, and it has been my absolute privilege to be able to work with you throughout the years. I look forward to many more. Sandra Turnberger, if there was a teacher who ever deserved Teacher of the Universe, it is she. It's been over 40 years since my heels walked into her business class, but you would never guess it. She has been the teacher throughout my life who has supported my businesses throughout my career. She still to this day posts on my pages, encouraging me, always telling me never give up, I knew you had it in you. I love you, Mrs Turnberger, you are the best!! Dee Dee Copeland, you inspire me each day to keep teaching. Keep preaching!!! My children for being the best kids any mother could have asked for. Nat said it best when he said, "My hands were meant to hold your soap". Without Dennis, I'd have no tallow or lard or goat's milk, the basc ingredients that go into each bar of soap we make. How my children each played a part, Ellie is the reason I made The Goddess Within. I did it for her. She is my inspiration, and those grandchildren of mine keeping their bodies safe with all-natural resources have been my greatest gift. They are the reasons I work so hard. It's these children that will inherit what we build, so I made sure to build something good. Kim Waterman, since that day in Las Vegas, you have been there for me in more ways than one. You have been our angel, and I thank you. Kim Hodge, I would not have been able to do this without you. You are the only person in the world who took me out to breakfast and celebrated me when I wrote and published my first book. Thank you!!! Heather, I got you, girl!!! Steph S. For everything you have done over the years, you saved me when I needed it. Clinton Harris of TenderBones Rib Shack. Thank you for believing in me enough to be my first paid advertisement. You have challenged me to do something that I have wanted to do all my life, yet I get to do it in a way that doesn't cost me my life. My dream when I was a child was to be a Chef, but God had different plans for me. Thank you for giving me an opportunity to one day have a chance to duke it out with Chef Bones, and may the best pork picnic win! Completing these books and doing what I have done would not have been possible if it were not for my husband Conrad. Thank you, I am who I am for you, built me to be this way. I know this has not been easy, and many couples would have collapsed; we have managed to keep it going, and that counts. Thank you for being by my side through the darkest battles of my life. Now let's get this party started!

About the Author

Kathy is a proven psychic medium who has spent her life trying to understand and embrace her psychic abilities. Having the ability to see the past, present, and future, Kathy has used her unique gifts to bring peace to others while also learning how to improve her own life. She wrote this book in an attempt to help other people recognize their gifts and to help others embrace their natural intuition.

CHAPTER 1

IT IS ALL IN CHARLOTTE'S HANDS

As Clinton and I made our way to the first lake in North Turner, we arrived in Bear Pond, not by mistake. As the plane touched down in the center of the lake in less than twenty minutes from Lovell, I was impressed. We glided right up to a wooden dock, where a Jet Ski and a paddle boat were tethered to the side. The camp that stood up on the hill was more impressive than what I had thought it looked like in the real estate app. There was a massive wall of windows that wrapped around the front and sides from the floor all the way up to the roof line. The reflection of Bear Mountain was virtually staring me in the face as I watched a bald eagle fly behind me. Its majestic wings, spanning eight feet, commanded the winds with ease.

In the center was a stone walkway, where alongside were old wooden boats, painted gray, filled with red geranium, purple sage, basil, parsley, and chives. The more I looked at every tag, reading what each herb was, the more I realized I was reading tags for cannabis plants. One said Purple Kush, then Girl Scout Cookies, and the list of plants grew further the more I walked up the steps. I simply had to laugh at the irony of it all. "You really do not need to go to Mexico to get weed. Heck, it's already on the boats in Maine," I chuckled to myself.

As I made my way to the last step, a whole new world opened to me. A beautiful archway, made to look like a giant white heart of wrought iron, brought me into the space inside the secret garden. I looked all around and realized this was a wedding place. Tall pine trees shaded the sandy beach, and a very large wood-burning fireplace that reminded me of a brick oven was situated across from the kitchen counter.

Adirondack chairs were positioned all around the fire pit. In the center, on a brick-lined patio, stood an open pavilion of stained wood with orange and yellow trumpet vines peeking through. There was also a barbecue pit with bar stools in front. Then, it hit me like a ton of bricks, and I knew in an instant that this was my place.

I stopped right in my tracks, dropped my bags, and ran back to where Clinton was tethering a rope from the plane around the base of one of the trees. "Is this place for sale?" I hollered down to him as I almost fell down the steps. "What are they asking?" I inquired as I landed in his arms.

"Lower than what you think," he replied gladly, as he pulled tightly on the rope, making sure it was secure.

Clinton and I walked back up the steps as he pointed out all the herbs. "What do you think of all this?" he said, bending down, pinching off a piece of a plant, rubbing it in his fingers, and putting it up to my nose.

Smiling and breathing its fragrance in, I flashed my eyes at him and said, "I can make you a heavenly lavender and honey ice cream with this if you would like."

"You will," he responded with a cocky little arrogance as we rounded the bend. Clinton pointed off to where a large white box was sitting. "Do you know what that is?" he asked.

"Oh my God, you read my mind, it's honey!" I exclaimed as I ran over to see if the hive was still intact. Drawing closer, I could see the bees flying in and out while calculating how quickly I could have a lavender and honey body scrub manufactured.

I turned to see Clinton up against the outdoor kitchen counter, standing there in his business suit. He leaned over, and I knew he was watching me.

"Do you like this place?" he asked as his hands rubbed the countertop and pushed away the pine slats that had accumulated.

"What do you think?" I replied. We headed to the back door, where a digital keypad was staring at me. I looked at the keypad and didn't even think anything of it when I hit #7504. Passing the majestic wrought iron gate, I entered the enclosed patio.

"You're really going to like this!" Clinton exclaimed as he opened the first glass door. Redbrick floors with a beautiful, shellacked finish were host to an intricate black wrought iron patio, set conveniently with three matching chairs. The walls were made of artistically carved wood and glass and projected the craftsmanship of the carpenter's energy. I looked up and saw the cedar wood ceiling, where, positioned perfectly, was a wrought iron chandelier with eight beeswax candles, so strong that I could still smell its scent.

I stood there in utter amazement. I looked at the box of numbers some more and wondered how it was that I knew the code. On the wall to my left was a little wooden shelf with a set of keys all lined up, where I fumbled with this one key. Rubbing the plastic for a minute in my hands, I placed it back up on the hook. The fireplace caught my eye first. Flanked between the kitchen and the dining room were two winged-back chairs and a table. That is all it took.

The house that sat on Route 219, with its grand view of the mountain and lake, spoke volumes to me. Clinton brought my Energy Moon table in and set it up in front of the fireplace that overlooked the view of the lake. The mountain loomed in front of me with its giant bald spot. It made me think of Clinton in a certain way and I giggled to myself as I wrestled the cotton and hemp sheets with the Moon table. The more I looked around the living room, the more I wanted this place. I could clearly see the chaffing dishes lining the counters as my Lobster Bisque took center stage.

I clearly saw myself sitting in the chairs, relaxing as each guest was snuggled into bed.

Once I smoothed out the round fitted sheet, making sure it was secure, I went through the stone plaque grids, adhering them to the underside of the table. I decided to go with the grids because they were designed for sexual energy, with orange calcite, carnelian, citrine, fire agate, garnet, and green aventurine just waiting to release their powers. I placed them all along the spine of the table. The more I looked at the height, the more I thought it needed to be lower. I pulled the handle to the table, and, in a flash, it was down. Once I had the half-moon top sheet in place, a smile came upon my face. The table was perfectly positioned right in front of the fireplace. I sat there for a moment and thought about how nice it would be to have a real wood fire going while we massaged each other. The more I stared into the empty fireplace, the more I could see his skin glowing, with my hands slowly sliding up his legs. Now, I really wanted to light a fire.

I got up, headed up the stairs, and turned around the bend. I could hear a rattling sound coming from somewhere. Peeking in, I was wondering where Clinton had gone off to. I heard the toilet flush and, in an instant, smacked right into him.

He turned to me and said, "I've hung your clothes in the closet," as he pointed to a room across from the bed.

I looked around at the pale blue walls with bright white trim and walked around to the bathroom that connected to my own private dressing room. The marble on the floor made me think,

"This must be the honeymoon suite." I came up to a crystal bathtub that looked out to the lake with a glorious mountain view. I began to walk around all the other rooms to see how they were adorned. I knew this place was it. I even chuckled, thinking, "I bet I could sell my Lobster Bisque to the truckers," as I heard the rumble of one passing by.

Clinton looked at me and asked, "Do you think you can write your cookbooks up here?"

Smiling, I said, "Yes," and made my way through the glass sliding door, rubbing up against him and feeling his massive strength. I stepped gracefully onto a porch that wrapped all the way around the entire house, supported by intricate columns, and headed down to the beach, following the brick walkway all the way out to the lake. I pulled up a chair, and as the sun beat down on me, I began to imagine myself writing here.

My home on Lake Kezar catches the morning sun and cools down rapidly by midday. Here, there are fewer trees, allowing the sun's rays to heat the property. The western sun exposure will be an excellent source of energy that we can capture with solar panels.

Clinton unraveled the line of the little rowboat, and we headed out onto the lake. We took turns paddling and pulled up to a large property with an old farmhouse set high and away from the beach. "So, what do you think of the place?" Clinton asked as we pulled the boat up the shoreline.

My toes were inspecting the sandy bed. I let them splash in the water while my eyes scanned the whole view. I looked out onto the lake and began to imagine a large aluminum pier with rows of paddle boats floating in the water, each with its own number assignment. I could see the kids throwing a ball in the lake. Off in the distance, I could see one of those giant inflatable water slides, kids laughing and cheering as they swooshed down the slide and into the water.

"This is the place for the Spiritual Camp for Kids I was telling you about," Clinton said as he started to walk up the hill towards the large house. Looking around, I saw a few goats in the back and chickens seeming to have free range of the yard. "There is even more property for sale once you climb up higher on the mountain," he added. Clinton pulled his phone out and hit the real estate app. "There is plenty of room for expansion, and we could have all different age groups," he said.

Tears welled up in my eyes. Reminiscing back to the days when I was an orphan, I thought this would be a good place to heal. I turned to Clinton and said, "The house we are staying in could be turned into space for teachers and other people who come in to help the students, a place where they can take a break if need be."

"Wow, that is a pretty good idea," he said as we walked down the dirt road to a metal sign that read: Dedicated to Ms. Leslie White. In my mind, I could see her brown curly hair, and I knew she was happy with that thought as we gazed out over the lilies.

An image of a short, balding man wearing green dress pants and a button-down shirt overruled my thoughts. I knew in my heart that this was a good plan. We headed back to the small boat and pushed off the shore. The yellow lilies were in full bloom as I steered the boat into the murky water. Dropping my paddle, I began stirring up the debris. I knew if I got out of the boat, I would sink into the soft earth. One part of me wondered how far I would go; the other part of me could feel the mud, and I envisioned little fish eating my toes. I decided to pull out a few lilies and take them back to the house and put them in a vase.

Clinton laughed and asked, "Afraid of a little mud?"

I looked over at him as I imagined the mud caked all over my body with my face all contorted. I just grinned and said, "I can live without it."

"We'll see about that," he bantered back. Clinton reached over the side of the boat and scooped some mud up in his hands. The smell was awful, and he put it up to my nose. "Just wait, I'll have you encased in this," he said as he grabbed my arm and rubbed it on me, all the while laughing profusely.

The thought of being wrapped in this mud gave me the creeps. "Don't you dare!" I bellowed out as I frantically splashed water on my arm to rinse it off.

As we made our way back across the lake, he looked at me and said, "This is where we will make our own start. Something different from the Center of Love Club but still under the umbrella of the group. Someplace where even a teacher's family could come so that everyone could get a sense of love."

"Would you still teach all the healing arts here?" I asked as I took the oars from him and paddled back, positioning the boat so that I could get a good look at the property.

"I would do that," Clinton proudly stated. "I would get it started at least, and I could teach the children the healing arts."

As he said it, he looked directly into my eyes, and I melted in his chocolate-brown stare. My mind began to wonder about all the kids: bruised, battered, and orphaned with feelings of hopelessness.

"You know, Charlotte, I have been thinking about that. What if we started training kids when they were younger to do reiki and massage? They could learn how to heal themselves," he said.

"Of all of the highly questionable experiments our government has done, I can't imagine this would be looked upon as bad," I said as Clinton took back the oars and rowed across the lake.

The late summer sun was still drawing the crowds, as the long beach and sandy shore got me thinking. I could see campfires and smores as shamans helped children address their fears. I could see them making their own drums and rattles. I looked back up to the house that stood all alone at the top of the beach. The more I looked out, the more I could see all its possibilities.

I looked over at Clinton as we pulled the boat up to the shore. "One or two weeks is great for a camp, but these kids that have been displaced are going to need more time than that," I said.

"I think you're right," he said, "this needs to be a group home of sorts, and in the summer months, we could invite more kids whose parents want them to experience a different kind of camp." He took my hands and said, "We'll see what happens as time goes on, and we've got to look at regulations and zoning laws. If this is meant to be, God will pave the way."

I looked back over at the lake and thought, "I could live here if it were meant to be."

Clinton grabbed the keys from off the hook and said, "Here, come with me." He opened an oak door that led to the garage and grabbed the passenger door of the Escalade, making a gesture with his hand. "My Queen, get in," he said.

I looked up at him as I let the name "Queen" rattle around in my head. He shut the door tightly and got in the driver's seat. He fumbled with a remote control that was inside the arm rest, hit the button, and the garage door opened. Clinton pulled out to Route 219 and the familiarity all came back to me. We went out to the light on Route 4, where he made a right turn.

"The grocery store is not too far away," he said as he pulled into a Lobster Shack on the side of the road. He ordered some clam strips, scallops, and haddock, and we sat down on the picnic table. "This is what life should be like," he said as he popped a scallop in his mouth and savored the taste.

The haddock was dusted with flour and herb finish with plenty of tartar sauce and French fries.

"I could get used to this every Sunday afternoon," I said.

Clinton reached over as he pulled a chunk of fish off my plate. "Yeah, me too," he said. "Now, let's get going," he bellowed as he got up and headed back to the car. He moved to my side and held open the door.

"I rather like this," I thought to myself. Inside the grocery store, I grabbed a few things: some eggs, butter, milk, coconut oil, a whole chicken, celery, onions, rosemary, sage, thyme, parsley, and saltine crackers. We traveled along a side road that cut through the trees and landed right back on Route 219.

As we walked back inside, I put the groceries on the counter and preheated the oven to 335 F. I opened the whole chicken that was wrapped in plastic and ran it under the water to clean it up, using a few paper towels to get all the liquid out of the cavity. I placed the bird in a large cast iron roasting pan and turned to the stove, where a cast iron skillet was sitting on the back burner. I chopped up a whole sweet onion and three stalks of celery and began sautéing them with a whole stick of butter. I walked out the back steps and down to where the herbs were waiting, picked up some chives, parsley, rosemary, sage, and thyme, and came back to the kitchen.

Using a chopping knife and the cutting board, I ran the herbs under the water just to make sure there were no bugs on them and chopped them up right away. With a good handful of parsley and two large pieces of rosemary sprigs that slid right off the limb, I carefully pulled off the little leaves of the thyme until I was satisfied that I had at least 2 tablespoons and at least 20 fresh sage leaves. When they were all minced up, I tossed 3/4 of the herbs into the onions and celery and stirred thoroughly to incorporate them. I looked in the closet, where I found a large bowl and pulled out two packages of the saltine crackers I had just bought. Crunching the bag with my hands until they were about the size of quarters, I placed them in the bowl. Then, I poured the sautéed vegetables and herbs over the crackers and gave them a toss. I cracked two eggs, stirred it up, and then added about half a cup of chicken broth. Stuffing the bird with my savory blend, I mixed the remaining herbs with 3 tablespoons of butter and rubbed it all under the skin, sprinkled it with some sea salt, then placed it in the oven at 335 degrees and set the timer. I just could not pass up the butternut squash, as I let it simmer in some water while I prepared the asparagus.

After washing my hands, I went out to the living room, where the fire was beginning to crackle and pop. The sun was getting ready to set when I thought about massaging Clinton. I became lost in its warmth and dancing flames when I heard Clinton's footsteps come from behind me.

"I found a bottle of *Muscle Ease* with Cannabis," he said as he opened the bottle.

I took a deep breath and inhaled the blend. Closing my eyes as his hands came behind my back and his lips pressed against mine, I felt Clinton's hands lift my shirt up and run past my breasts as he tossed it onto the chair. His warm hands glided from my naval up to the center of my chest. He reached for my black lace bra as his fingers freed each hook. My eyes were completely lost in his eyes as the skimpy material slipped off my shoulders and down my hands. I let him take total control of me. My body began to tremble as Clinton pulled the black latex leggings past my hips, and, in one swift move, I was lying on the round table. I pulled the sheet up over my body to keep me warm as Clinton grabbed the chair from the dining room and set it firmly behind my head. He instructed me to take a few deep breaths and placed his hands around the back of my neck, softly cradling my occipital lobes.

On my third breath, I felt his hands glide along either side of my shoulders as the oil cascaded up and down the side of my neck. My muscle fibers melted under his touch as the stress began to flee from my body. On repeating the gliding stroke, I could feel myself falling deeper and deeper into the innermost recesses of my brain. The blood pumping through Clinton's veins was at just the right pressure to ease away my tension. I drifted away and began to see pieces of information in my mind's eye. Startled by what I was seeing, Navy boats appeared before my eyes. The more I let his fingers run up and down my flesh, the more I could feel my neck release, and I began to wonder if his body was affecting me. I closed my eyes and wished for a moment I had an edible when he laughed and said, "Hold on, they are in my briefcase."

Relieved and excited that he heard my thoughts, he got up and went to the bedroom where his briefcase was waiting. Inside this case were all kinds of wrapped treats from the Center of Love Club, and I was most excited when I saw a jar of coconut oil in a green hue, as well as some lollipops, cookies, and a few tinctures in bottles that had my name in handwriting that I thought was Karissa's. He pulled the tincture out and let the drops run against my lips. The lavender, rose, and honey notes warmed my heart, and I knew this was more of a healing lover's body blend. With a blend of Sativa and Indica, I could feel both effects simultaneously when he softly whispered in my ear, "This is your strain, cultivated just for you; she is called the Naughty Fig, and she is pollinated the old-fashioned way."

A warm smile came over my face, knowing he was looking after me. As the tears started to fill my eyes, I thought about how lucky I was to be as free as I could be when he placed his hands along the sides of my neck again and took a deep breath. The music that was now swirling around the open rafters had a curiously familiar ring to me, and I began to wonder who orchestrated the notes as I drifted peacefully to sleep.

CHAPTER 2

KENNEDY'S TRANSFORMATION

Karissa watched with excitement as the Golden Goddess, otherwise known as the 1979 Pontiac Trans Am, also known as The Phoenix Rises, roared down the driveway of the Center of Love Club with Winslow, otherwise known as the Legend, behind the wheel. The dream of competition is alive with Kennedy in the passenger seat as hemp fuel comes screeching around the lake. Karissa gave one final wave to Kennedy as he and the legend from the NASCAR days rounded the last bend. Safely tucked into the rear secret compartment was Karissa's cannabis-infused edibles, just in time for the private party in Charlotte, North Carolina.

Kennedy turned his head one last time to look at the long red locks of hair on his beautiful bride. He gave one more wave through the T-tops, wrapped his right hand around the Hurst shifter, and stomped hard on the throttle. The fat rear tires screeched, getting a grip on the gravel, as her rear end broke loose. Her back end kicked out to the left as Kennedy let off the gas.

With a sparkle in his eyes he knew deep down inside that these cars were the future to bring the American dream back alive. Then, without a second thought, he hammered the gas pedal. The large opening shaker scoop rocked back and forth as he ripped through all six gears. The torque of the Pontiac motor planted him and the legend in their seats. Karissa's ears perked up as if two antennas were coming out from behind her head. She listened to the roar of the engine through the night air, tuning in as each antenna rotated like a periscope on a submarine. As the exhaust notes echoed off the lake, the 505-cubic inch motor, with the 4.11:1 ring gear, caused a vibration, leaving her breathless as she shook.

The Phoenix squealed to life, rumbling through the woods with her motor so powerful that it sent ripples of energy into the lake as Karissa watched Kennedy handle the curves. The racing legend looked over at Kennedy and said, "We gotta get this bird in flight, and we don't want to get caught with all this weed in the trunk."

"That's a ten-four, good buddy," Kennedy said. As he pointed to the sky, the speedometer took flight, and the needle was buried at 160 MPH. In what seemed like a brilliant explosion of lights, heaven's gates opened as a new bird flew by. Her wings opened wide as her platinum feathers flapped in the air, flying in a gown of opulence with her black lace bra with diamond studs and amethyst door panel trailed to a white pearl finish. Hues of fluffy clouds surrounded her gloss. Her feet and hands were adorned in black diamond radial snowflake wheels. She sported long black locks in tubes of curls as her breasts and womb called out to me to pull her hair and put her on all fours when the new Pontiac Trans Am came into full view.

"Whoa, hot damn, did you just see that?" the legend said as he turned around to catch a glimpse. Kennedy slammed on the brakes and did a 180 as he watched the mystical car flying past him. His breath panted as he gripped the steering wheel, looking over at the legend. "Once again, I find myself in another dimension, and I know this one, as I am familiar with her scent," he said. Kennedy looked out the window as the energy of the woman from long ago reached back to him. He slinked back into his seat, closing his eyes as he remembered that most passionate week with her. Her lacy underwear always wanted to get out of the way. It was not a choice anymore. He reached out to her with her gown of purple sequins. Once again, his mind went back to her that day on the boat. "Oh, Madison!" he thought.

Her arms ripped my dress pants off as I fumbled with the buttons, trying hard to get my lips into her chocolate cupcake. I couldn't help myself anymore as I slid her dress up over her hips. I was lost for a moment as the pink and cocoa confection called for me to taste her moist cupcake filled with a strawberry cream dream. I let my tongue go wild and dove in. Oh my god, she was sweet. Oh, what is it about bakers that gets me so hot?" he reflected.

"Oh, is that the black beauty you were referring to earlier this week?" the legend cooed, "your story just blew me away."

Kennedy turned the car back around as he shook his head back and forth. "It's been years since I had her, so I don't know what I was thinking back then. She was amazing, and I could have had her for real," he stated.

The legend ran his fingers through his hair and ran his tongue along his teeth. "Let's go get her!" he said.

"Oh man!" Kennedy exclaimed, "I would do anything she said, as long as she kept stuffing my face with her frosting."

The legend looked back over. "Tell me you're not talking about her baked goods, man," he said, as his eyes grew wild with excitement.

Kennedy laughed through his nose as he gave a little snort. "I had to make sure her cakes looked good on that display in Bermuda," he said with a wink, "and I even used my fingers to clean up her cream that had spilled out along the table."

The excitement in the car began to go higher as the racing legend fiddled with his hat and began licking his lips. "I can taste them now," he said excitedly, "man, do I have a sweet tooth!" "I'm happy to say I got her cleaned up just in time for the judge's eye, so she won first place that night." His eyes twinkled as he listened to the motor, contemplating in which direction to go next.

The legend glanced back at Kennedy, rubbing his hands along his jeans. "Dude, I don't know where you're going with this, but I like the way you think," he said.

Kennedy knew fully well that the legend was thoroughly hooked as he unraveled another tale. "It was what happened one night when we got back into the cabin that utterly rocked me to my core. Her goodies just sent me through the roof when my teeth latched on to her 'wedding rings.' It was all I could do not to blow my load right then and there. She held her hand on my twinkie as she guided its head inside her sweet confections. I could tell she wanted my recipe as her fingernails dug into my wrapper. I was drooling and could barely hold back. Her muscles clamped down on me, and I was sucked inside her buttercream. I knew that I blew it, but it wasn't my fault. It was the sweetest cupcake I ever felt, and that was all it took."

The legend raised his hands and shouted to the night sky. "Why, Penis? Why? Why do you do that at such the wrong time?" he asked.

Kennedy gave a wink and a nod. "I know, right? Like the finish line of a race, it's all about getting into position, then hitting the pedal to the medal 'til you see the checkered flag. Then, it's champagne exploding and a big fat check," he replied as the legend laughed.

"Yeah, I know. The only problem is they did not say the race took your whole life and a man needs a little something extra. That is where that Purple Kush comes in. I can go for miles with just one cookie," said Kennedy. He pulled one of Karissa's soon-to-be world-famous oatmeal and chocolate chip cookies out of the bag and offered the legend one.

The legend took one bite and savored the flavor. "I can barely taste the weed in here," he said, "are you sure this is going to do anything?"

Kennedy smiled back and said, "Oh yeah, it is deceiving," gripping the wheel harder. "We should go back and find that car, right?" His right hand wrapped tighter around the shifter as he dropped it into first gear and gave her some gas. "We gotta catch her," he said as the car began to take off.

"Nah, nah, sonny," the legend said, as his left-hand slapped down on the gear shift, "you got to get that pecker of yours under control; it's gonna get you in trouble someday."

"I know," Kennedy murmured, as he fell back into his seat. "They are all just so lovely, but I just can't risk losing my wife. A baker I can replace, Karissa; on the other hand, I can't, and she has a secret that keeps her cookies not tasking like a dank weed," he elaborated.

The legend began to laugh. "I know what you mean," he reflected, "been on the track for years with all those sweet little ladies knocking on your trailer door with their all-season radials jumping out of their shirts, and a man eventually learns he can't drive every car along every track." He patted Kennedy on the shoulder. "Come on, let's get going," he said, "we got a long night of driving ahead."

Feeling his senses coming back to him, Kennedy tried desperately to justify himself. "I feel like a camel in the desert, and the only refreshments I want to drink are in the base of a woman's sink," he said.

The legend looked over his shoulder curiously. "You know, Kennedy," he inquired, "what year would you say that Trans Am was, anyway?"

Kennedy began to think for a minute, then he said, "You know, it did look an awful lot like the 1979-81 body style, but she had a different look about her like she was brand new or something."

The legend removed his hat and scratched his head. "Did you ever see a color scheme on that year like that?" he asked, "did you see those black diamond wheels?"

Kennedy looked back and forth between the road and the legend. "Do you think the Trans Am came back, and we don't know, or did we die and go to heaven?" he mused.

The legend began to laugh. "Maybe we're in the desert, and it's all just a mirage," he said.

Laughter roared out of Kennedy's mouth as he connected to the jeweled crown of racing. "Come on. We've got to get to Jamestown and bring this box of chocolates to Clinton for Charlotte before they leave for Rhode Island."

Kennedy's eyes fixated on the trees as their colors went from yellow to orange. He took a deep sigh, remembering that night when he was playing with Charlotte's car. "I promised you some clam chowder, too," he said.

The legend looked at Kennedy and asked, "So, what is with you and Charlotte?"

Kennedy blew the breath from his mouth as his head rested up against the back of the seat. "Man, do I ever regret not tinkering with her carburetor some more," he admitted.

The legend snickered back, "Who are you referring to, Charlotte or the car?"

Kennedy smiled at the legend. "I was talking about Charlotte," he said, "and I should have done it when I had the chance."

"I know what you mean," said the legend, "and I didn't do it either, but man did I want to."

CHAPTER 3

KARISSA'S CALLING

Karissa gazed at the moon as its beams shined through the woods. She walked around the property of the Center of Love Club, sizing her latest accomplishments up. Her smart phone was already in her hand before its chime rang with a text message, "meet me in the middle of Dixie Lane and 2A in Aroostook County, Maine."

There was a definite change in the air as a platinum feather floated down from the sky, landing on her hair as the Moon began to rise. Within seconds, another message appeared: "Hire Olivianna, and you'll need to get Charlotte's Aunt Mabel and bring her to the club! Particularly important you do this. I will send you her information in an email in the morning. I'll see you in a couple of weeks or so. LOVE You..."

Karissa walked back to the club, her dress whirling around her legs as the wind tickled her spine. She typed a message, "OK, I got it. Love you too!" and hit SEND.

The lake had grown choppy, so Karissa headed into the kitchen. The wind was picking up again as her cinnamon curls whirled around her face. Her flowery dress flowed up in the breeze as the cool air sent a shiver over her shoulders. She glanced over at Olivianna as she was piping the frosting onto the cake, mixing the slightly green hue of cannabis with the yellow-gold sponge cake. A sweet mango puree was encased in between each layer. The Purple Kush butter cream frosting was piped along its seams. Karissa watched as Olivianna squirted the creamy confection out of the pastry bag, her hands steadily and exquisitely designing her masterpiece. Karissa put out her finger, waiting for a dollop of frosting to taste. Olivianna half watched Karissa's face while piping the finishing touches on the protégé cake. She looked up to see if her frosting was meeting her approval and continued to pipe out her design.

"Well, this has been an exciting week, hasn't it?" Karissa exclaimed, as she fluttered about the kitchen, her fingers grazing ever so softly on the shoulders of Olivianna. "By the way, your frosting is divine," she said as she licked her lips and put her finger out for another taste. She closed her eyes, savoring the sweet and salty cannabis infusion that is the hallmark of *The Center of Love* confections.

The wind picked up once again and blew the back door open, sounding a crack up against the wood that startled Olivianna.

Running up to the oven, she bent down to inspect her cake. The warm glow of the light assured her that it was going to be fine as she took a deep breath. Just then, Jaxson walked in with a man dressed in what looked like a military flying uniform. His pearly whites smiling bright as his aviator shades flash star lights all around the room. His light cocoa skin and green eyes sparkle, making an even older lady blush. Jaxson walked up to Karissa and put his arms around her. "You were amazing this week," he softly whispered in her ear as he nuzzled against her neck.

She blushed, knowing that the week was a massive success. "Thank you; you were incredible, too," she said with a broad radiant smile. Her love club landed one of the world's largest tycoons bachelors with one of her newest members. Her plan for love was working, and she was beyond excited with herself as she rubbed her hands together and put them up to her heart, thanking God for the miracles this week.

As they breathed together in delight, the group of business partners, so oddly designed to take flight, grew deeper into the love that was guiding their nights. They both pulled away, bowing in Namaste as their eyes met once again. You can see the sparks flying as they both float around the room. Jaxson's wings began to emerge like a ruffled rooster in a hen house as he pulled out a coffee cup. The look of dominance emerged, and it was clear he was leveling up. Everyone felt body chills as the temperature of the room dipped down.

"Officer Ricard Wilcatta," he said as he poured coffee from the carafe, pointing a finger at the man in uniform to make connections.

Ricard dropped his bags on the floor, took his hat off, and high-fived around the room. Then, he hollered, "They call me the 'Wild Cat'," as he slinked up to the kitchen counter, rubbing up against Karissa.

Karissa headed to the refrigerator, pulled out one of the first batches of hard cider of the season, and handed it to "The Wild Cat, aka Ricard Wilcatta. Popping the cap off, he took a long gulp as he grabbed a bar stool and hung out on the counter.

Jaxson hunted through the refrigerator for some heavy cream. "Thank God we planned on staff development," he said to Karissa as he sniffed the quart-size glass bottle that housed the fresh bovine juice. He poured the chilled cream into a silver bowl, heaps a few tablespoons of confectioners' sugar, and a teaspoon of vanilla extract. Then, he began to beat it with a whisk. The sound of the metal clanged and clinged around the aluminum bowl as he beat it with his whole body. He whipped and whapped it hard until it doubled in size, looking like a 'kitchen God,' as the whisk whirled round and round in his strong hands. He dolloped the sweetened bovine substance atop his dark roast Dominican blend, topping the white mountain of sweet love with a sprinkling of cannabis-infused toffee and dark chocolate shavings as the mocha emulsion dream made its way to his overgrown mustache. The cream lingered on his whiskers and made one wonder if he was leaving it there on purpose, until we watched his tongue lick it off.

Then, we knew, without a doubt, what this man's mission in life was.

Just then, Nadia and G'anacia come bursting through the back screen door, excited from the calls they had just received. "Guess what, y'all," G'anacia beamed as she clapped her hands, "I can't believe this, you guys. We just got hired by Clinton to bring our version of soul food down for Charlotte's wedding!"

Israel smiled and said, "I just took final measurements on his tuxedo last night."

Ricard nearly spit out his beer all over the table. "Damn, that was fast," he said.

"Well, if I know Clinton Tuckerman like I think I do, I will say he's got the next ten years for her well planned out," Karissa chimed back in, "that man is on a mission."

"When will Kennedy be back?" asked Israel, "I need to make sure his tuxedo is ready for the wedding." He hugged Karissa and said, "Good to see you again."

"He should be back in about seven to ten days," she said as her hands waved in the air. She pointed to the sky with, her eyes focused deep, as her fingers twirled in the air.

"Are you ready for soul rejuvenation this week?" Jaxson asked, jumping up from his chair in a flurry. He was on the floor as his wings once again emerged. "Who's ready for a night flight?" he inquired as his eyes twinkled, making a bee line for Karissa.

"We have a few aspiring entrepreneurs coming in, Jaxson," Karissa teased, "I think you would be able to do a lot with a few of them."

They begin to dance around the room. Jaxson reached around Karissa's waist and pulled her body ever so tightly to his that her cleavage nearly burst out of her dress. In the brisk movement that made the room shake, his wings emerged as his aerial dominance protruded once again. "You bet I will. We got a lot of good things going on," he replied as he pulled away, kissing her hand. His lips gently caressed her fingers. "My Queen," he whispered, as his cheek nuzzled her palms, "I brought the jogging sets you requested from **FlyDesigns**."

Karissa's face lit up. "They will come in handy with this chilly Maine night air," she said.

"I'll bring them in tomorrow morning when I do my presentation," he said, "this has been moving so fast. We've got a lot to do this week before we begin the drive to Natchez, Mississippi."

"You should see the house in Jamestown," Ricard chimed in, "Clinton's been renovating the hell out of it. It looks nice, though. He's got good taste." Curiously, Ricard extended his hand to Olivianna. "What kind of cake?" he asked.

"You want a piece?" she asked, cutting into the green goddess and handing a piece to him.

"It's made with cannabis, mango, and butter cream," she said.

"Oh, snap!" he said, "let me have that," as he downed a giant slice. Ricard looked around and called out. "Where am I sleeping tonight, by the way?" he asked, "who handles accommodations in here?"

Karissa headed to the roll-back desk, pulled out a set of keys, and made her way to Ricard. The keys were dangling in her hand. They had an owl carved out of wood winking at him. Karissa smiled and said, "Your cabin marked number two," as she dropped the keys in Ricard's hands. She walked over to Olivianna. "Kennedy sent me a message to hire you," she said, "did he say anything to you about that?" Her eyes slanted as she read Olivianna's mind.

"Yeah, he did," she said, "and a bonus if I stay on."

"Hmm," said Karissa as she pondered all of this. "A bonus. I wonder what type of bonus he was referring to?" she thought as she eyed Olivianna up and down. "We need to have a little talk," Karissa said. She took Olivianna's hand, and they sat down. "Clinton and Kennedy are up to something, but I'm not sure all about what's going on," she said, as her fingers tapped on her lips, "now, what does all of this have to do with me getting Charlotte's Aunt Mabel and bringing her to the club?" The only thing she could see in her head was checkered flags. She stopped herself mid-thought and asked herself once again, "What is it with Aunt Mabel?"

The sound of the wood scratched along the floor as G'anacia pulled up a chair. "Well, all I know is that this week up here was incredible. I cannot believe y'all do all this. I feel the best I have ever felt. The body wraps and massages are delightful. I'm singing!" she exclaimed, clapping her hands and smiling. Olivianna washed her hands and dried then with a hand towel that was sitting on the table. "What do you think they are conjuring up?" she asked.

Karissa looked back at Olivianna and G'anacia and asked, "Do you want a permanent job?"

Surprised, the two chefs looked back and forth at each other. The silence of the room could be heard as Karissa wrapped her hands around a cup of tea. "All I want you to do is be advisors to me. I just need a few more sets of eyes that can really see," she said.

The three women reached out their hands as they connected around the table. Their thoughts began to collide as G'anacia said, "I keep seeing Pontiacs and Cadillacs, a large manufacturing plant in Dover, Delaware, and clear blue skies, really clear blue skies."

Karissa nodded her head up and down. "That's what I am seeing too," she said, "and I see a gorgeous Firebird of crimson red fading into a passionate orange."

Nadia was fumbling with the bar stool, making it rock back and forth with her hips as she reached over the counter. Her fingers ran down the shades of tourmaline in her cannabis-infused buttercream dream. "I overheard a conversation with that man in the hat who seemed so mysterious here," she spoke up.

Olivianna's ears perked up as she looked at Nadia, "you mean Winslow, the legend?"

Nadia wasn't paying any attention to the increased tension that she was feeling as she carefully formed her words. "He never talked to me; whenever I said something to him, I began to wonder if he was even real," she said.

Karissa started to smile as her suspicions were starting to confirm. "He's a much more different type of a ghost than what I thought before. He is a shape shifter and is particularly good at what he does. He's dipping in and out of people's bodies. He's like the captain in the Maceral Cove House."

Olivianna smiled and said, "I thought so too, and I was just waiting on confirmation to make sure I was reading the energy right. I keep having a sneaky suspicion that he is a race car driver, but I can't put my finger on it exactly."

"That's the thing," Karissa chimed in, "he is anyone he wants us to believe he is, and the damn ghosts are getting better with this shit," she said, turning to Jaxson.

"They are rising," she said.

"I told you, Karissa, it's happening," Jaxson replied, filling his cup of coffee again.

"What's happening?" G'anacia asked, running her hands along her shoulders, "I'm getting goose pimples all over my arms."

"Ah," Jackson said, looking at her arms and confirming it, "it's the truth, and it's happening."

"What are you talking about?" G'anacia asked, with a look of knowing and disbelief, "you're talking about revelations, right?" The room grew quiet as everyone started to gather around the table. G'anacia's voice turned low. "You know, out in Vegas, we had this thing where grasshoppers were invading the whole town," she said, "You don't think it could really be happening, do you?"

"What, the second coming?" Olivianna said, tapping the side of her coffee mug.

Karissa laughed. "You ain't seen nothing yet," she said, looking over at Jaxson, "what do you think we are talking about?"

"I don't even want to know, but if you want my opinion, it is the revolution," he said, putting his coffee mug down.

"The revolution," mouthed G'anacia as they looked at each other.

"You just wait and see what I teach," Jaxson said, as his wings began to ruffle out, "I'm going to be flying all around this lake."

"Flying? What are you talking about?" G'anacia said, rubbing her sore toes, "I have been flying all week as high as I want." She chuckled some more. "Lord God, I cannot wait to see what this week brings."

"What I'm talking about is a team of angels," said Jaxson, "and hear me out on this." He sat down with the coffee mug wrapped around his hands. "If everything is what we believe, then whatever we read and believe to be true is so," he said, "so, what if we start to believe in something else?"

Nadia looked at Jaxson and asked, "What are you proposing we do?"

Jaxson gave Karissa a look and said, "Shit, I'm ready to head to Vermont myself."

Jackson then turned to Nadia and asked, "Are you up for an angel ride?"

Nadia paced around the room with a look of sheer worry on her face. "Are you talking about the end of the world?" she asked.

"Not on our watch," Karissa and Jaxson chimed in as they stood up in unison with their wings protruding. "Why do you think we're doing all this?" They said, "we're building an army of Angels."

Ricard stepped back into the conversation. "We have got to wake the people of the planet up before it self-destructs in the New Big Bang, so to speak," he stated.

"How long do we have before the whistle blows?" asked Oliviana.

"No one knows," Jaxson answered, "it's not been revealed."

Karissa's wings, all white and fluffy, slowly breathed in and out. "We just need to keep connecting and doing our job. Build our legions and get the word out. We've got to get expansion into other countries and see what's happening over there," she said.

Ricard's wings begin to emerge for the first time, a wingspan so massive, that it almost took up the entire room.

"Show off!" Nadia quipped.

Ricard's wings begin to flutter. "You want to see my fuselage? We need to free the colonies before we are taken over by the machines. It could be tomorrow; it could take another hundred years, but look at all the signs like the hurricanes up the coast, the pests invading, and, heck, who the hell even heard of a stink bug twenty years ago? You ever look at those things?" he said as he began flapping around the room. "They look like an alien space craft," he continued, as he fashioned his hands into an inverted pyramid, "and they stink!"

Karissa started scratching her head. "Honestly, I am a bit perplexed. Why so soon a wedding? And why didn't Clinton opt for them to get married here? We could have done it in less than ten minutes. Why did he take Charlotte away so quickly?" she said.

"I tried to interject," said Ricard, "but Clinton said to follow orders, so I'm just going to do what he says."

Jaxson reached for Nadia. "I don't know, I thought it was rather romantic in a way, Charlotte did the food for her own engagement party. I mean, it felt like a wedding feast, anyway. Did you see the way she put that lobster tail in that portable mushroom cap?" he spoke.

"We have a whole tray in the refrigerator left over if you want me to heat some up," Karissa said as she looked up at the clock, "The crews from the farm will be down to pick up the leftovers for all the workers. I'll just keep baking cookies and make my peanut butter cannabis balls," she said, pointing to the wall ovens. "Heat everything up," she instructed. "I will tell Anastacia to bring everyone down so we can celebrate all night long! All I can say is thank God for James, the head chef," she concluded. Karissa pulled out her phone and sent him a text: "PARTY AT THE CLUB!"

"Ew, Anastacia… she sounds exotic! Is she staying at the farm? Maybe I will take a fly down there," Ricard chimed in, "I heard there's a shortage of wildcats in the area. Maybe she can stroke my fur."

"I'm a messed-up man," he giggled and scooped up another piece of cake, "thank God, I'm not flying tomorrow." Ricard plopped himself down in the lounge chair. "So, what did you guys think of what she cooked?" he asked as he gobbled down the cake. "I take it Clinton was impressed; I heard she is the best," he said.

"That grilled cheese with rosemary focaccia bread was off the hook with the roasted tomato soup; it was like fancy comfort food," Jaxson replied.

"She made him Lobster Raviolis, too," Nadia noted, "there's not much left of that, but it's over there if you want some."

"Oh, snap, man!" Ricard exclaimed. He hopped out of the chair like a frog, grabbed a plate, went through the trays, picked out all the sweet white meat, and piled it on his tongue.

"I thought you were a wild cat, not a frog," Jaxson laughed, "I guess you are here looking for love too." Everyone present bellied over with laughter; who isn't looking for love? The Wildcat laughed. Jaxson fanned out on the velvet crush queen chaise lounge. "You're in the right place then," he said. He brought the mug back up to his lips and adjusted himself as his eyes surveyed the room. "Does anyone know who that guy or spirit was that left with Kennedy?" Jaxson asked.

Karissa pondered as she struggled to regain control of the room. "His name was registered Winslow, but everyone else calls him the Legend. Every time I tried to get his attention, he never answered me," she said, "some racing legend is all I know."

Jaxson gets up and pours another cup of coffee. "Maybe he was just hard of hearing or something," he said. He used his fingers to lick the rest of the cream sitting in the bowl.

"There he goes again, teasing the women in the room," said Olivianna. She looked over at Jaxson as if to say, "Was he not just in this conversation five minutes ago?" "That's who I'm talking about. I think he's a ghost!" she said.

"Yes, but which one?" asked Jaxson as he danced around the room, "and why is he in all of this?"

"Should we try and conjure him up?" asked Olivianna.

Karissa blurted out, "Racing legend," as her mind began to spin. "Damn, I bet I do know what's going on now. Kennedy had this pipe dream of Pontiac racing coming back and he talked about it for years now," she said, "and I wonder if he was just conjuring the Pontiac line of racing to come back."

"Who all drove for Pontiac that is now dead?" Jaxson inquired.

"They're dead in the water if you ask me," Ricard snapped back, "but if he's looking for Pontiac to come back, then no better time than now with hemp coming in and panels made with hemp are supposed to be the strongest ever made."

Jaxson drew the mug to his lips, making sure it was not too hot, and gently let the heavenly elixir go down his throat. His mug hit the table as he said, "It should make body work and car insurance cheaper."

Ricard's ears perked up. "Designed from Hemp engineering, top secret is what I've been hearing round the street," he said.

Karissa looked rather perplexed as if caught up in some whirlwind of information before her mind gently came back to full swing. Her voice lowered to a soft hue as the last of her breath came out in a long full release. "Clinton and Kennedy got me running ragged with all of this, and I suppose they had something going down but kept me out of the loop."

"Speaking of the wedding, when is it happening?" Jaxson asked.

Nadia chirped, "In three weeks, that's what Clinton told me."

"Is Charlotte really going to marry someone that fast? That is crazy if you ask me." Nadia retorted.

"Hey, no judgment," Karissa chimed in.

G'anacia shifted her position in her chair and propped her feet up. "Salem did leave in a huff," she said.

They all giggled under their breath. "Did y'all see how she reacted when Charlotte kissed her?" asked Nadia, that was priceless. Nadia started dancing around the room, giving Jaxson a look as she rubbed her arms all around her body. She danced to the song that was playing in her mind, humming, "all night" …. bah bum bum…. bum…. bum," as she started to rub his neck for him.

When he closed his eyes, his mind contemplated hearing the music from Beyoncé as he downed the rest of his coffee. He grabbed her hand, and out the door, they ran as a flash streaked through the sky like Haley's Comet. He was clearly teaching her to fly.

"I've got another teacher from Philly coming back tomorrow," Karissa said as she put her plate in the sink, "everyone calls him 'Big Willy'."

G'anacia flashed a perceptive look.

Karissa laughed and said, "Well, I ain't seen no proof. Besides, he'll be here tomorrow." She sliced up the cake, offering it to everyone in the room. "He ran down to the farm for a few days," she said, "I think he is high up in the Philadelphia Police Department or something like that." "Well, G'anacia" Karissa said, "looks like it's your turn to learn to fly." She pointed to Ricard. "He might be young, but he's been flying for a while now, and I want you to go over things with him." Karissa sat down in the chair, waiting for the angels at the farm to arrive.

G'anacia looked around. "Well, I don't know if I'm ready to fly yet," she said.

Suddenly, the back door opened and in walked Anastacia with a handful of people from the farm. "You, I'm hungry" she said, "what you got to eat?" She made her way down the center island, picking through the trays. "The Wildcat" came out of nowhere and started rubbing on her leg. She looked up at Ricard, eyeing him up and down. "Down boy, where do you come from?" she inquired, pushing his head away.

Ricard flashed his pearly whites as he extended his hand, "I'm a pilot, able to fly you to your deepest darkest desires with a flip of my switch," he said, as his wings protruded boldly, and his eyebrows began speaking in a language all their own.

"Yeah, well, hold on, kitty cat, I got a boyfriend for that," she replied.

"Ah, not for long," Ricard said. He picked up his fork and grabbed another piece of cake. "Ain't no boyfriend alive that can do what I can," he said, flopping in the chair, "hey baby, can you rub my feet?"

Anastacia just laughed in his face. "Oh yeah, I'll get right on that," she replied sarcastically. She piled up the trays and carried them outside.

Ricard jumped up from his chair. "Hold on, pussy cat, I'll get that for you," he said. He grabbed the stack of trays out of her hand and put them back on the counter. "Come on," he purred to her, "we're supposed to party here tonight."

Anastacia pensively looked over at Karissa, as if to say, "What gives?" She looked back at the pilot, "Whatever, dude, you're still not coming with me," she said, picking up the trays and looking at her crew. She stood there for a few seconds. "Screw it," she said, putting the trays back down, "I don't feel like cleaning up anyway." She made her way to the velvet lounge with her shoulders arched back. "How about you massage my feet, little pussy cat? "She said as she fanned them back and forth.

G'anacia looked at Ricard. "You really got a lot to learn if you wanna find a good woman," she said, handing him the rest of the trays, "you better sign up for another class."

Anastacia made a clicking noise with her tongue, using her finger as a trigger. "Bang, Bang, kitty cat," she laughed.

"You got that right," G'anacia giggled, "and He thinks he's a wildcat."

Chapter 4

The Conductor's Inn

It wasn't long before the Phoenix was on Route 138 when the salty air began to engulf the golden classic from long ago. Kennedy slowly brought the car down Highland as he pulled into the circular drive overlooking Maceral Cove, making his way past the castle and climbing the steps to the newly renovated outdoor kitchen. He placed the wooden box of cannabis confections into the refrigerator. Overlooking the ocean, he thought to himself, "I am once again the crab, as my body is bending back, feeling her spirit enter me. As my eyes flutter open, I am spellbound, spinning under a canopy of lights and stars as sounds of the sea crash all around me. I am supported by millions as they make their way towards me."

"Was Charlotte calling me here as I walked across the property up to the guest house?" he asked himself in his mind. Having accomplished the first delivery of the morning, he was back on the road again as he looked around for the Legend. He scratched his head, wondered where he was, and surmised that the Legend was a grown man as he unlocked the door to the little guest house that stood to the right. He walked in and flipped the switch to the left. The lights came on, and a little couch with two wings back chairs greeted him. He sat down for a minute and began to send Karissa a text. He got up and headed to the kitchen, as he fumbled through the refrigerator, looking for something to eat. Suddenly, he heard a creak.

Looking around, hoping to see the Legend, the door in the hall opened all the way up, revealing a small bedroom. "Damn, this place is creepy," he thought as he cautiously stepped inside the hallway and hollered out, "Winslow, is that you?" Waiting for some specter to jump out and scare the crap out of him, he fumbled with the old crank of the window until enough of a breeze blew in to clear up the musty smell of the old home. He pulled the hand-sewn quilt down and slipped inside the sheets.

Straining to hear if the legend had come in yet, he began to drift off. Within a few minutes, he heard boots clicking on the hard wood floors. "Hey, Winslow, is that you?" he shouted out, "take any room you want … I am going to bed." The only thing Kennedy heard was the faint sounds of boots walking back down the hall. It only took a minute to fall into his dreams as the outline of events was laid out for him.

The Conductor stepped onto the stage, unfurled, taking the lead as he bowed to his Queen. With a ruffle of his tail, he turned around and got the show on the road. With his attention now fully focused on the symphony, he gave the lead violist a nod. As The Center of Love Show was about to commence, his golden baton was rigidly attached to his fingertips. His right-hand flinched as he gave the signal for the musical tale to unfold, precisely commanding his fleet.

The slurry of aromatic notes sounded as the baritones chimed in. The harpist strummed with her nails of gold, taking me further into tails untold. The Garden of Eden exploded in his mind. The brilliance of colors dazzled as the cherubs climbed, and a garden of flowers flourished in his sights. Trumpet vines and fireflies were hidden inside the Purple Kush delights.

His hands flowed over her flesh as the fiddles rose in the air. The plumes of wisteria shadowed the violinist's hands, teasing him. The crescendo struck as the brass horns blew the flurry of angels as they all arose. The trumpets sounded to my delight, as the vibration of the percussion drummed out of sight and he felt the clang of the cymbals vibrate up the spine, as they began to crash with palpitations so strong.

He began to sail away in his mind as the oils penetrated her body while he made love to her on the stage. With each passing swipe of my hands, he watched her tremble under his spell. Her skin glowed as his fingers pulled on each of her ears, feeling the flow of her body as he commanded her to him. Then, his fingers and thumbs ran along the side of her jaw, making little circles from her ears to the center of her mandible. They slid gently along the side of her face as his hands caressed her head. He felt her going deeper into him with each breath she drew. It was then that he knew that he had missed his chance. "Oh, Charlotte!" Kennedy cried out in his sleep.

He awoke to sweat beating off his brow. Then, he got up, headed to the bathroom, and relieved himself before crawling back into the bed, dreaming of Charlotte in his arms. He tried and struggled to let her go, but there was something about her that he wanted to know more of: something that he saw in her as she dashed around the kitchen, the way she handled so many things at once as if they were mere child's play. She danced circles around any of the other chefs, and he began to wonder if the kitchen was the best place for her to be anymore.

He pulled his cell phone off the nightstand and sent off a message to Karissa about where to pick up Aunt Mabel. He scanned through the emails and saw a letter from "The Governor" of Delaware. He squinted and looked for his glasses to read the fine text. The more he scanned the message, the more he knew that her visions for Pontiac to come back had a fighting chance. He confirmed our meeting at the **Foobellas** facility and scheduled the date to look at properties in the Dover, Delaware area, where an auto manufacturing facility could be built with rail access. He took a deep breath, knowing the car he had seen just a few hours earlier wasn't only the car of his dreams but the car of Delaware's Economic Recovery. He lay there looking at the ceiling, envisioning a car manufactured with hemp technology. He imagined the tracks at speed ways all over the United States with the Pontiac line of racing as the Grand Prix ran circles around the ceiling. He took another deep breath as the crickets chirped and the sounds of the water lapped up against the shoreline and drifted back to sleep as the checkered flag waved in front of him.

56

CHAPTER 5

I GOT SOMETHING YOU CAN EAT

The luxurious sheets made of Delaware hemp and Virginia cotton enveloped my body as Clinton put the finishing touches of his massage on my back. I lay there, not able to move, as every chakra spun, and my muscles rejoiced. The heaven I had been in was luring me to stay when I finally stood up and positioned myself so that I was standing facing him. With my hands firmly grasped to his right hand, I ran the oils from his palms up his forearm, rounding around his shoulder blade, then back down his arm as my hands interlaced with his. The electricity began to ignite as his soft lips began to dance around mine. The energy began to spin out of control, as I felt the fire that was burning inside of him start to rise.

With my palm against his palm, I closed my eyes and imagined that our secret sign language was being spoken as I felt our hands mingle. As our fingers wove tighter, I felt a renewed surge of energy surge through me as our wrists bent back and forth when he lay down on the table. "My turn," I said.

I moved over to his other arm and repeated the same strokes as his breathing became shallower. I knew he was even further in. Allowing the music to sway into my soul, the notes lulled me into their dance. I slid the sheet off his legs, from his toes to his fingertips, in one smooth gliding stroke, circling around the other side of his body and putting a ring of protection around him.

Pulling the sheet down to his waist while reveling in his chest, I allowed my fingers to peruse his flesh. My hands continued the journey down to his lower abdomen, circling around his waist as they slid underneath his back. Letting the weight of his body do the work, I reached up to his neck.

Taking his whole torso in my palms, I explored every aspect of him. I changed my position and was standing next to his legs. My fingers trailed up his thighs as I poured the oil into my hands. Starting with his feet, I let the warm emulsion linger up his legs, around his knees, and up over his thighs.

It had been over a year since that night in my house, and this was the first time I had Clinton all to myself. I was taking all the things I had learned and applying them in a new way. I took a deep breath again and allowed my hands to slide back up his leg, past his knee, then I pushed in deeper as I moved up his thighs, then rounded my hands around his hips.

A flurry of emotions suddenly came over me as I slide my hands back down his leg. I took another breath and let my fingers dance up his skin as they lightly feathered his flesh. His breath hastened as he re-positioned himself. I applied more oil to my hand and lowered my body so that my hair was grazing his legs. I could feel our chakras opening further as I ran my fingers up his shank. I was dangerously close to what was now fully engorged as the thumping of my heart matched the beat of what was now throbbing in front of me.

His engorged veins flowed with blood as he inflated like a blow-up water slide at an amusement park. I lightly placed more oil in my hands to caress his mast, starting with the base as my fingers encircled his manhood, slowly gliding up his lingam, marveling at every detail I could feel. The resonant vibration that emitted from his Kamasutra soul teased me like it was a 450-calorie nut-filled chocolate bar encased over rock candy.

As the passionate moans escaped his lips, a feeling of excitement flooded over me, and I became ever more fascinated. I closed my eyes once again and allowed myself to feel everything as I pressed my lips against his flesh. My tongue became my sensory gauge as I explored his cocoa-infused wand. With each kiss I placed on him, I loved him with a gratitude I had never felt before for anyone.

With each push of the fluid that was in his legs, I slid from his toes to his waist, ever so slowly teasing him until I couldn't help it any longer and allowed myself to explore him fully. His veins pulsed in my hands, as I examined every inch of him, allowing my body to run along his as if I were hunting for lost treasure on the bottom of the sea.

I felt torn in that instant, wanting so much to continue to massage him but also wanting him deep inside me. It was a strange form of torture that I knew, and he knew, that I was in. As he smiled, my body started to tremble inside, not knowing which way to proceed.

My excitement continued to build as I let my fingers trace over his skin. I flowed along the length of his legs, trailing up his abdomen and circling around his chest, as I danced my digits around his face.

A passion erupted inside of me, one that wanted so badly to please him, and I dared to open myself up more and let all of him into me. My back arched, and my wings protruded prominently as they fluttered out.

In an instant, he pulled me on top of him from the side. Trembling as my inner Love Goddess dared to take over, I pulled on his lips as his tongue darted in, lingering, as I nuzzled my nose on his neck. Teasing his nipples as I gently bit on them, I felt my hips slide up and down on his shaft as my lotus opened to invite all of him in. With each passing shock wave, a series of explosions shuddered inside of me. I felt his vein pulse with blood as his member swelled to nearly twice its original girth, spurting torrents that penetrated right through my entire being.

I felt the deepest waves of magic ever as he matched each thrust with me. In what felt like a burst of shattering glass, I was entangled in his arms, flying across the lake in the darkness of the night sky. Climbing higher and higher, we soared up the mountain top, our bodies connected as we flew in the star dust. Nestled up against a tree, I felt his force penetrate my innermost depths. My body convulsed with each new sensation as I let him take me further into the recesses of his world.

My lips started to speak in a language I had never known before as I rejoiced in his sexual appetite. In an instant, we were on the ground when his tongue engulfed my neck as I convulsed under the sheer brilliance of the moment. Shrieking wildly with the night owls as my body arched up to the moon, I gazed up at the stars, and they felt so close that I could almost touch them as they twinkled in the galaxy. The crescent moon virtually smiled down upon me, igniting a new inner life force as my wings emerged once again. We swooped down the mountainside like eagles in the night sky, diving into the water not far from where the lilies made their home. The water shone like diamonds as it flickered off the sandy bed. I felt myself lose my footing as he picked me up, wrapping my legs around his waist, hovering high above his head as the moon illuminated his face.

This time in the water, I felt freer and more relaxed, as if the veil of darkness were a protection for me, and I allowed myself to enjoy all of him. I was as free to make love as the deer in the woods without a care in the world —the night was my hideaway, my escape from a world of reality, a special place where I could be as open as could be.

His kisses conveyed a combination of power and gentleness as he took me in deep and then teased with his lips, pulling on my tongue as his saliva mixed with mine. His body was so strong and powerful that I felt safe in his strength, shielded and protected in a way I had never felt before, cocooned as his wings came all around me. In an instant, we were flying across the water without a care in the world.

I did not care; I really did not, as it was the most peaceful moment I had ever felt. All I wanted was to continue to feel this way as I felt him drive deeper inside of me as we approached the shore. Hidden in a cove where no house was near, I felt the sand under my skin as he hovered over me. I never felt anything as delightful as I massaged my hands up and down his chest, utterly astonished at how incredible he was and how easily he took me over the top. I was acutely aware of how my voice echoed across the lake as I started panting to the God inside of his soul, begging him to come out and play. I let myself go completely as I screamed out his name and felt our bodies lifting over the canopy of trees.

Suddenly, we were back again. As I walked through the halls of a library, I stared at each bookshelf. He pulled a particular book of interest off the shelf marked '2025' and opened its spine. Spanning through its pages, I saw my name in bold. I looked up, wondering what was happening, as I took the Book of Life and studied its words. I closed my eyes as I began to realize that everything was already written. Fascinated, I scanned and devoured the pages as I followed the dates and places in a trail of lights as I awoke to the sandy shore.

I gazed around at the glow of the lights of the little boats as I smelled the roasting chicken wafting past my nose. Lying in a heap with his body covering me, I reluctantly said, "I've got a chicken in the oven. Are you hungry?" Laughing at my timing, I crawled onto his back. My arms wrapped around his neck, and I breathed into his trap.

The smell of the chicken was lingering through the air as we walked back into the kitchen. I ran to grab a night dress from the closet upstairs. Then, I made my way back down the back staircase into the kitchen. Thank God for the Yukon Gold potatoes that I had put on. He added a few tablespoons of butter, a splash of heavy cream, and some fresh parsley, with salt and pepper, beat it with a hand masher until it was smooth and fluffy, and offered me a taste. I sat at the bar stool and watched as he pulled the chicken out of the oven and laded some drippings over the bird. "Five more minutes, and it will be perfection," he said as he shut the oven door. I grabbed a large platter and laced it with some sage and rosemary as I prepared the table for him. I found ruby red glasses in the cabinet and placed them on the table. I heard the oven doors open again and watched Clinton as he placed the golden bird onto the plate.

"Do you mind if I make the gravy?" I asked him, while he spooned the stuffing out of the golden bird.

He looked at me and smiled, pulling a piece of the crispy skin off from the neck. He placed the crackled flesh into my mouth and said, "I could get used to that." I must admit that the taste of his fingertips made it hard for me to pull away from him. However, I did and used the pan drippings to make a light gravy with some of the arrowroot powder I found in the cupboards and the rest of the chicken stock. I cracked a few swirls of black pepper and then tasted it to make sure it was seasoned well. I let it bubble, adding a bit more chicken stock until it was the consistency of a lazy river and added a few more minced fresh herbs of sage, thyme, and rosemary to boost the flavor. Then, I took one more taste, sprinkled a teaspoon of sea salt, and gave it another whirl. I could feel Clinton's body up against my back, and I ladled the gravy onto the spoon and asked for his opinion.

"Damn, that's good," he said as he pulled me away from the stove with the lure of his lips against mine.

I did not know what was happening to me. All my life, I had been in pursuit of the stove, and now, there is a new love that is coming into my soul. I felt the tug of war in my heart as I tried to pull away to finish what I had started. I washed my hands at the sink as my engagement ring sparkled under the water. I became entranced in its color spectrum as I ran the name "Charlotte Tuckerman" in my mind. I pulled the asparagus out of the refrigerator and snapped the bottoms off. I turned to him and spoke. "I do not think I can take your name."

He laughed back at me and said, "I don't blame you for that. You have stood on your own name for so long, plus I think it's better this way. You have had your identity since birth, and you wouldn't want to lose it just because you accept a marriage proposal."

"Well, that's one thing out of the way," I said. Frankly, I was surprised at this response but relieved that keeping my birth name was not a big deal for him.

I sautéed the asparagus in a little bit of butter, hit it with a splash of salt, and drizzled some reduced balsamic vinegar on top. I peeled all the seeds and flesh off the buttercup squash, added just a few tablespoons of butter, a pinch of salt and sugar, and handwhipped it up with a slotted masher.

I heard a bottle of wine being uncorked before listening to the tell-tale sound of its liquid as it was poured into the cups. The dining room lights were set down to a low hue as the shadows of the fireplace danced around the room. I tasted his fingers as he dangled the herbed meat inside my mouth, teasing me in a way I never expected. I was hypnotized as I watched his digits trace my skin. I was, in an instant, taken back to the fateful night that I watched Karissa and Kennedy through the windowpanes and knew that what I had wished for then was coming true for me.

He ran the chicken gravy all over my lips, then kissed me so we could both taste it, tempting me as my body began to explode, flooding the table as the fire arose. Our hips arched, and our wings came out, with lightning bolts and thunder, as the whole orchestra thunders amid the roaring applause of the audience as they screamed, "Bravo! Encore! Bravo!"

The conductor turned and bowed. "OK, one more!" he said, as the symphony orchestra began to explode and the cello and violins took up their bows. The passion that was once lying dormant in me began to erupt as I dropped to my knees. I felt my wings protrude again as they reflected in the glass with white billowy feathers, whereupon I knew that I was transforming fast. I looked up to Clinton as I watched his wings of fire emerge, took his hand, and agreed to be his wife. With that, my new life emerged.

CHAPTER 6

FLIGHT CAMP

The morning chill of fall began to descend as the help from the farm assembled down on the lake. The new guy, Kevin, had just checked in as breakfast made its way to the table. Karissa and Jaxson stood in a circle as everyone gathered around. Holding hands and praying as Nadia beamed, looking over at everyone. "You gotta fly with Jaxson... or maybe not," she said, as she pulled her shirt over her head, mumbling, "lord have mercy on me."

Karissa looks over at Jaxson. "Did you make the newspapers again?" she asked.

"Maybe," he laughed.

The scent of the cannabis-infused cinnamon donuts lingered over the water as the hot mulled cider with rings of orange, cinnamon and cloves garnished each mug. It matched the hues of the trees as their leaves began to turn.

G'anacia was working on her fear of water as Jaxson gently took her hand. Taking her no further than a few feet over the water, he looked like an eagle holding its prey. She spanned her hands out in front of her as they scanned the surface of the lake. Within moments, he had her higher up in the canopy as the students watched intently.

A plate of mini breakfast quiches sprinkled with ham came out with James as he made his way to the fire pit, watching what looked like lightning bolts in the sky as Jaxson instructed G'anacia to do spirals in the air.

Kevin wasn't sure what he was seeing as he glanced over to Olivianna and Anastacia. "What's happening here?" he asked. "Yo, dude," he said, turning his attention to James, "what did you put in these donuts, mushrooms?"

James laughed. "No, man," he says, "they didn't tell you this was a flight camp you signed up for this week."

"I guess not," Kevin said, rubbing his balding head, "I've seen a lot of things in my lifetime, but this is some shit." He got up and walked around the fire pit.

Nadia got up and walked over to him, trying to reassure him of what he was seeing. "You don't understand," she said, "we're angels in hiding."

As Kevin looked at her like she was on crack, he grew even more unsettled. "I'm not feeling so good, and I'm feeling dizzy as all get out" he said, holding his head, "can I go lay down somewhere?"

Karissa took him up into the house, pulled out a tincture, and placed a few drops on his lips. "This should calm down your head. Go lay down on the couch for a bit," she said reassuringly, "come back down when you feel up to it. I know this was not what you expected. You're getting a crash course -- you know what I mean? You will understand everything by the end of the week." She rubbed and kissed him on his forehead. Her lips slowly kissed his third eye, sending a message to his soul to come alive. "You will be OK," she concluded. She headed back out to the beach just as Jaxson brought G'anacia in for a landing.

"How do you feel?" Nadia said, jumping out of her seat. "Can I go next, please?" she begged Jaxson to take her back out again.

"Tell you what, I'll take you back out tonight for a private lesson; how about that?" he replied.

Nadia flashed a big smile on her face as she grinned, biting her lip. "OK. I'll wait for that again," she said as she pulled her sweatshirt down over her legs. "I would rather do that again anyway," she said with a smug glance at Anastacia.

Anastacia rolled her eyes as the Wildcat reached out his hand to her and asked, "Can I take you flying?" She batted her eyes and took flight. "I don't need you to teach me," she retorted as she darted high above the canopy.

"Damn, she's a witch," the Wildcat mumbled as he opened his wings, chasing after her in the sky. Creeping up on her faster, he swooped around her, trying to get under her downdraft. "You don't have any boyfriend," he taunted her, "why won't you let me help you?" He jumped on her back.

She did a barrel roll and dropped him like a bomb, watching closely as he plunged into the lake with a splash, causing a roar of laughter on the beach. Slamming his fist in the water, he fumed out of the lake, chasing after her. Her wings took on a new shape, altering her aerodynamics and flight path, when she took an unexpected turn, throwing him off her track.

Karissa looked over at G'anacia and said, "I told you; Lake Kezar is where it's at."

"Hey, what's up?" Big Willy from Philly hollered as he headed to the beach. He gave Jaxson a high five.

"Bro, wazz up? Long time no see; where you have been hiding?" asked Jaxson.

"Man, it's been rough these last few weeks. Been getting Mississippi ready for the boss. He's had me working all kinds of overtime, and the place is looking fine," replied Big Willy.

Karissa introduced him to the crowd, "Hey guys, this is Big Willy from Philly," she said.

Willy heartily shook everyone's hands. He grabbed a doughnut, walked over to G'anacia and picked up her hand. "Who is this sweet chocolate dream?" he asked as he kissed her hand.

"Oh boy! Casanova, I see," she laughed.

Karissa and Jaxson took G'anacia's hands, and together, they lifted off the ground, soaring higher as the sun brooded down on their faces. Swirling around the lake, G'anacia worked up the nerve to fly on her own. The teachers began to loosen their grip as her wings emerged further out of her body. On the count of three, G'anacia looked over at Karissa, and Jaxson told her that he would be flying completely underneath her because, even if she fell, she would land safely on his back.

As Big Willy watched from the side of the lake, he could sense that she was going to need more help, causing him to take off in flight. Flying backwards in front of her, he kept telling her just to focus on his eyes as he penetrated her soul. His eyes virtually became laser pointers, as she became entranced into his energy field, as Karissa and Jaxson slowly let go of her hands.

She flew all over the cove as he steadily took her higher over the mountain tops. It was as if she was caught in his radar guidance that was controlling her flight. As he approached closer to her, his body shimmered under hers, and he slowly enveloped her, taking her safely to the tip of the mountain. Once her feet hit solid ground, she began to shake and cry. "I can't believe I just did that," she said, as she shook in his arms. His energy surged into her, as she felt her feet tremble with his velocity.

"You ready for more?" he asked, taking her hand again, "ready for takeoff?"

She looked over at him as he gently began to flap his wings, then looked towards the shoreline as the cove of angels watched. "I am," she said, closing her eyes. Her wings burst forth in bright, brilliant gold as she took her first solo flight.

Trailing down the mountainside, the wind rushed around, her hair whipping in the breeze; he instructed her to land closer to the shoreline. He took her hand as their bodies became perpendicular to the water and eased her slowly in. Wrapping his body around hers, she was thrilled when her toes began skimming the top of the water. "I got you," he said as he held her tight. "I want you to just breath with me, were going to get through this together." As they danced around the water for what seemed like all afternoon, he taught her how to land, do a barrel roll and dive down into the water. Using her wings to propel her faster, she soon got used to everything. They seemed to be lost in their own world, and as the sun slowly made its way down past the trees, it dawned on them that they had missed dinner.

"Come on, let's head on in," Willy says as they make their way back to the shore. The closer they got, the more she noticed how cold the lake was getting. He placed her by the fireside and, within minutes, had a blanket wrapped around her as the fire warmed her.

Bowls with ham and potato soup warmed up her soul as the scent of apple turnovers baking in the oven lingered down to the lake. Ricard took the hint, picked up a bowl of soup and a spoon and offered it to Anastacia. "Here, let me feed you," he said, sitting on the side of the chair. She looked up into his eyes as he lovingly placed the creamy base in her mouth.

The wind picked up, swirling the embers high up into the air as the group of strangers shared another meal under a blanket of stars and moonlight. As the sound of crickets sang over the lake, a new love story was beginning to take shape. Her strawberry blonde hair draped long past her hips as she let him guide her up into the sky for one last flight of the night. Their passion ignited as streaks of fire burned like wild flames as they flew north to where the Northern lights lit up the sky. Swirling in pink and green lights as the stars twinkled in the sky, it was a glorious expedition as their wings flapped high above the canopy of pine trees. They soared all through the early morning hours until they made their way back down to the Center of Love Club just as a large vehicle pulled down the drive.

CHAPTER 7

KENNEDY'S VISION QUEST

The massive mobile cooking motor home pulled around the bend, tooting the horn as Kennedy shouted out to Karissa, "Honey, come take a look at this thing."

Karissa walked out the back screen door, eyeing the graphics up and down with her hands on her hips, just as Kennedy put it in the park.

"What do you think?" he asked as they met at the side of the mobile monster.

"That's a pretty big motor home you got there; what are we doing with it?" asked Karissa.

"Listen to this, babe… get this dream," said Kennedy, "my 1979 Pontiac Trans Am acts as a special guest pace car taking the first lap in Delaware at Dover Downs Speedway.

"What happened to you?" Karissa cried, putting her hand to his forehead. "Did you get enough

sleep?" she asked as she looked at him perplexed. "You went off with that race car driver, and you've come back a different man," she said, "who are you and what happened to the Kennedy I once knew?"

"You know, honey, I'm learning you just got to trust what happens in a day," he said, smiling back at her.

Karissa laughed back at him. "I have been trying to tell you that for years," she said, whirling her hair in his face,

"*The Center of Love* is making its official debut as one of the sponsors for the resurrection of the Pontiac Trans Am!" exclaimed Kennedy.

She looked at him cross-eyed. "How's that?" she quipped, "I don't see my emblem on this thing -- just some man in a racing uniform holding his helmet."

"That's not just some man holding a helmet, Karissa; he is a legend on the racetrack!" he replied.

"How on God's green earth does that equate to *The Center of Love* making its official debut?" she asked, looking harder at the man in uniform.

"The dream's coming to life," he proclaimed as he rubbed his hands together.

"You don't say," she said, "you're still harping on Pontiac coming back to life?"

"Absolutely," he replied, with fists raising in the air. "I got a lot of money invested in this one, baby," he explained as he whirled Karissa around the driveway like a ballerina, "Daddy's coming home."

"When does all of this happen again?" she asked, "this year or next?"

"In a few weeks, when we head to Dover Downs during the October race, right before Charlotte and Clinton's wedding," he said, "are you listening to me?"

Karissa's eyes squinted down tightly, her arms folded over her chest. "Are you sure about all this?"

"Clinton is handling his end of the deal by negotiating to supply the needs of the recreational Cannabis Nation; the stadium roars, and our stocks will go through the roof while we're the official Love Club for one of the hottest names in racing," Kennedy shouted!

"What stocks?" asked Karissa, "we're not public."

Kennedy counted the money in his pocket and stuffed a few new crisp Benjamins into her bra.

"We've got stocks, baby, trust me on that," he said, "Daddy's working on a plan."

"Kennedy, I don't know what the hell you've been ingesting lately, but I like the way you think," she said with a wink.

"Now, here's the plan," he said; get this: "Aunt Mabel's is the face of the new breakfast sensation, the first official cannabis-infused breakfast cereal. It's called "Weedies," the green breakfast for the golden oldies," he explained. As Kennedy opened the back door, a shiny spectacle greeted them as a large gas stove, a massive refrigerator and a sink ran along the wall.

"You don't think this is going to be a bit over the top, Kennedy?" questioned Karissa.

"What do you mean, a breakfast cereal chock full of vitamins and minerals, enhanced with walnuts, coconut, and honey, sprinkled with a smidge of Sativa? Heck, years ago, there was a movie about old people swimming in a pool full of aliens and getting their life back. For that, they needed to believe in a spaceship flying out of the sky. This just means they eat a bowl of granola. How hard can it be?" he continued.

"So, let me get this straight," said Karissa. "you're trying to convince the older generation that if they consumed a Sativa-based cereal for breakfast, they'd regain the fountain of youth?"

"Well, um ... yes, that, Wilford Brimley and nights of great sex. I think a few people might like that and, by golly, just think about those old folks when they got spring back in their step at the nursing zoo… Oops, I mean home," he said.

"Who's Wilford Brimley?" Karissa asked.

"You know, the Quaker Oats and diabetes guy," he replied, with a "where have you been?" look.

"So, you're boxing up my cereal in the attempt to convince the older generation that a cannabis sativa strand cereal could help them regain their zest for life and their energy back?" she said, bemused.

"Damn, girl, you catch on quick," he said with a wink, "don't forget the whole creative thing -- just imagine all those inventions sitting in those old guys heads just waiting to come out."

Karissa nodded, "Yes, this is your plan, Kennedy," as she slowly inhaled.

"That's what I'm counting on, my sweet little butter cup," Kennedy giggled with delight. "I've got a few more deliveries to make around town, a meeting to attend with a guy about a horse, and then, were off to the races." He stopped for a second, returned to Karissa and wrapped his arms around her, "I'm the one carrying the real prize," he whispered as he gently kissed her forehead. "I love you, Karissa; we're going to make it."

She looked up at him with a smile on her face, "I know it, Kennedy, I know," she said, laying her head on his chest. Karissa gazed up into his deep blue eyes. "I will give you something special tonight," she said as she kissed him fully on the lips, "I think this is the most brilliant plan you have thought of yet, and if anyone can pull this off, you can."

"Don't mention it, but I will hold you to that special offering," said Kennedy as he batted his eyes, "I'm hoping it's one of your world-famous massages." "Trust me on this, Karissa, I've got a plan, and I'm having a meeting with a man by the name of Benny Cohen, a.k.a. 'the Big Tuna," he continued, "We got a crew coming in, and we're going to cook like lighting to pull it all off."

"What team, Kennedy?" asked Karissa.

"You remember G'anacia and Nadia from out west?" he asked.

"Yes, they just left," she replied.

"Yeah, well, Clinton is making them an offer they can't refuse," he said. "Soul food, baby, with some slabs of ribs, barbecue beans, it's a southern thing, and all you got to do is get the cake baked." Kennedy paused. "You hired Olivianna, right?" he said, "and put her down at the farm like I asked?"

"Yes, I did, Kennedy, I did as you asked," replied Karissa.

"Good, just trust me on this baby," said Kennedy, "we've got a few bets to wager in Delaware -- got a man that's been betting a lot on this," as he fumbled in his pocket. I'm just not sure how Charlotte is handling everything" he mouthed as he gazed out to the trees.

"What does Charlotte need to be handling?" as she looked at Kennedy with her suspecting eyes.

“Clinton,” Kennedy mused.

“Kennedy, how would you know that?” asked Karissa.

He smiled back at her. “Baby, I'm the Master at what I do, don’t you worry about that,” he said, “I don’t send any man into battle without knowing they are the best. I got a reputation to protect; I'm the Master of Love!”

“That you are, Kennedy, that you are,” sighed Karissa.

CHAPTER 8

CAMP WERTHEFUKRWE

The whinnying sound of the propeller fired up as I packed my clothes, headed down the steps, and boarded the seaplane when Clinton announced, "You ready to look at more houses"? Charlotte tosses her bag into the back seat as she buckles herself up and says, "To the Maine Woods"! It did not take any longer than twenty minutes before the little plane began to make its descent and touched down in Aroostook County on a lake known as Lake Wytopitlock. The craft floated down to the dock where a few camps stood, and a few more camps dotted around the lake; however, a good half of the lake was not developed, and it was the underdevelopment that caught Clinton's eyes. As we walked along the shoreline, I began to get the feeling that this was where we would be staying when I heard a car horn beeping. I look up as an old Dodge pickup truck pulls up, and a gentleman hollers out, "You Clinton Tuckerman?". "That would be me," Clinton hollers to the man as he turns to me, "our limo is here."

Now, I found myself looking out a truck window that made the bumpy dirt back roads of Maine a delight to drive as we rode over the countryside. We pulled up to the driveway of a large white house, and I was utterly blown away. It was nearly identical to the house that I had previously gone to with Karissa to pick out fresh vegetables. However, this one was different. I knelt on the ground to pet the black tuxedo cat with white paws that were rubbing up against my leg. We walked inside, and I was greeted right away by a beautiful young woman with long red hair. "Welcome home, Ms. Charlotte. My name is Anastacia," she said in her Northern Maine drawl. She turned to Clinton and nodded her head. "Your room is ready, Mr. Tuckerman," she said as she handed him the keys. "Will you be joining us for today's festivities?" she asked.

I laughed and hollered out, "It does exist!" as I pointed to the fireplace where the wooden plaque that read "**CAMP WERTHEFUKRWE**" still sat on top of the mantle.

Clinton looked at Anastacia and said, "We will be there." He took our bags, and we walked up a flight of stairs that overlooked the living room. Clinton unlocked the door and made his way in. "This is where we will stay when we come and check up on our properties. He opened the curtains, inspecting the windows for dust.

I looked out the panes of glass that overlooked the apple orchard and knew the place in an instant. The field of vegetables with cows, goats and chickens gazed up at me as if I was bringing them their next meal when I spied what appeared to be a woman standing by the barn door.

Pointing in the general direction, I whispered, "Clinton, did you just see that?"

"Oh, that's one of the ghosts on the property," Clinton muttered as a matter of fact.

"Ghosts," I questioned back, "no, she wasn't a ghost; she was real; I saw her."

"Relax, Charlotte, you see ghosts, honey, and they look very real," he said, as he opened his suitcase and pulled out his toothbrush and toothpaste.

I closed my eyes and asked myself, "Was the woman in the window a ghost, or was it Anastacia?" I looked through my bag, fumbling for my toothbrush and began to brush my teeth. I was too scared to look in the mirror just in case I would see some waterlogged spirit and her kid when I felt the hair rise on the back of my neck. "Great!" I thought. "Why don't they call this place 'Camp Get the Fuck Out of Here'?" as I wiped my mouth on the hand towel. I stomped back into the bedroom where Clinton was lying on the bed, with his shoes still on and hands behind his head. "I knew I was seeing ghosts! I blurted out, "Was that all just in my head, Clinton?" before storming out of the room.

Clinton chased me down the hall, took my hand, and led me to a painting of a mother and daughter. The child could not have been any older than three or four as she ran through the purple lupines on the side of the mountain. "Who are these people in the picture?" I questioned, staring at the painting, wondering why they resembled me.

"Oh, that is the painting of Anna Belle and her daughter, Anna Bella, before they crossed over to the spirit world -- that's Anastacia's Great-great-great-great-great-Grandmother and great-great-great-grandmother," he explained. I continued to gaze at the painting, wondering why she looked so much like Anastacia, when he pointed to another painting, "That was her great-great grandmother," he said.

"Oh, what happened to them?" I questioned back.

"Back in the day, the women who had special gifts were known as witches. The townsmen had them burned in the center of the apple orchard, on the base of the tree of many varieties. Ever since then, they have haunted this estate." he elaborated.

"Haunted?" I asked.

"Well, I wouldn't say haunted, more like enchanted, or how about we use the word 'guided'?"

My curiosity peaked. "When you said the tree of many varieties, what does that mean?" I inquired.

Clinton grew more serious in his tone as he spread his wings wide, emitting a current of electricity that went from the sky to his hands. "The tree has every variety of seed-bearing plants," he revealed.

In my mind's eye, I watched as the limbs went from barren to leaves of rosemary, cannabis, and thyme, with raspberries and strawberries of every kind. Vines with every type of squash trailed on its limbs as apples, plums and peaches came in. Carrot tops were blowing in the breeze, along with a stalk of broccoli. I walked up to the branch and picked a pea pod from its end. I opened it up and let the baby peas roll in my hand. In an instant, they transformed into little sprites as they danced along the garden.

It took all I had to turn my gaze back to Clinton when he said, "They were all good witches, and their cannabis-infused potions are what we continue to make here. They are all her recipes, handed down through the generations."

I started to focus on the red hair, Karissa's, and Anastacia's. Then, I realized they were all a family. I was really confused now. "They don't seem to have much of a family resemblance," I questioned him further.

"No, and they wouldn't," as he walked us back to our room, "soul families usually don't."

"Soul family? Now, what's that?" I asked, plopping down on the bed.

"Soul families are people that you connect with in an instant, and you know this in your heart as the truth." He pointed his fingers to my chest and lowered his voice. "You knew this about me that day in the dining room," he said. He got back down on the bed, snapped his fingers twice and said, "Come back here."

My left leg began to shake as I swallowed the fear mixed with the incredible excitement that had been accumulating in me. Beginning to learn that there was no secret I could hide from this man, I could feel another spirit enter.

"I know what you are thinking, Charlotte," Clinton said as he put his hand on my abdomen, and a bright light began to emit from his hands.

Waves of tremors came over me as bolts of red mixed with orange and yellow emitted from his fingertips. As he traced his fingers over my sacral chakra, I grew more and more agitated as I rushed out of bed. "I am not doing this," I said as I pulled away from him. Out the door to the hallway, then down the stairs, I ran, knowing there was no way I could ever give him a baby, as the tears rolled down my eyes.

The fireplace caught my attention as the white lights that ran along the open rafters lit up the dining room in an instant. I nearly fell over the bear skin rug by the front door. I wrapped my hands around the doorknob and opened the door in a huff when I heard an angel whisper, "We can repair that."

I looked up to see the sun setting with its brilliant hues of gold and pink when, off in the distance, I heard the violins come in. I stood there, frozen in time as I heard Clinton, in his dress shoes, walking up behind me. My hair stood up on end, as I felt hands wrap around my shoulders. I was thoroughly scared to death to turn around, just in case it wasn't Clinton. I stood still for a moment in silence until I let my guard back down. My tone turned now turned a little shaky as I asked him, "Do they still do weddings here."

"We do; I think we might be here just in time to see another bride get married," he said as the waiters walked around with trays of food in their hands. "You know Charlotte, this place is known to get women pregnant."

I looked back up at him in utter disbelief. "Clinton. I am almost 50 years old, and you want me to run around and be pregnant with a kid baking in the oven," I replied, "are you nuts?"

"The fall harvest is one of the most magical seasons of the year," he said as he rubbed my belly some more, "we'll see what happens, my dear." As he spoke, we walked around the perimeter of **CAMP WERTHFUKRWE** until I saw the field of grass with cars parked in it. "It has been bringing people in from thousands of miles away with cannabis-infused wedded bliss packages. One that keeps you coming, long after the band is done strumming as he airs guitars some notes," he said.

"Oh, is that how this place got its name?" I asked.

He looked at me rather calmly and pointed to my chest. "You go to the **Center of Love Club** to heal, and you come to Camp **WERTHFUKRWE** for something a little more," he said as he cleared his throat.

I blushed and turned around. "Oh, brother!" I replied, "Imagine myself doing the nasty with you on the ground."

"No, not on the ground; we have little bungalows hidden in the woods, all in a circle for that," he said, "we are not that kind of club, Charlotte."

"Oh, you mean, you're just like a nudist camp or something like that?" I said, laughing out loud. "Yeah, what did you think we were?" he said.

"Nothing," I murmured. "I didn't think you were anything," I stated.

Fields of swing sets were to my right, and the hottest man looked no more than 35. The more I looked, the more I realized that they were all just chatting it up, sipping on sparkling wine with cannabis-infused candy flutes. I took a deep breath until I heard an ecstatic sound come from deep in the woods.

Clinton looked back at me. "Now, what happens in the woods, we have no control over," he said.

"What do you mean?" I asked.

"It's a place you can tap into your inner animal or mother nature," he said. Just then, in the blink of an eye, he appeared to morph into a moose for a fleeting moment before just as quickly turning into a janitor. "We don't go in unless something is suspicious," he said with a nod and a toilet bowl plunger in his hand.

In an instant, we were out of the woods as he took me back up the front steps and opened the door. With his arms spread wide again, he further described the place. "Not only do we have apples, cannabis, infused wine, and beer. We also have open vaulted ceilings, filled with white lights that twinkle when you flip the switch," he said. He walked me back into the living room filled with the dinner crowd as a platter of succulent lamb chops went by.

I laughed back at him with a particularly amusing little grin. "So, this is a part of **The Center of Love Club,** too?" I asked.

"Why yes, it is, all this and so much more!" he said. I closed my eyes to feel his kiss as the softness of his swollen lips pulled me back in.

"This is the reason why people want to join us. We got 'em waiting in line to sign up," he said as he clapped his hands. "you got to love the **Center of Love Club."** He kissed me more strongly this time, and I swallowed the spit that had accumulated in my mouth as I listened closely to what he was saying. I began to wonder if we were dead as we walked back to our room, and I felt his heart again just to see if it was beating in his chest. "I am real, Charlotte; I am not dead. I am just a shapeshifter, and I can be anything I want to be," he revealed. He shut the bedroom door, and I watched as his fingers locked the latch.

I took notice of the gift basket on the nightstand that was filled with massage oil, bath salts, a body scrub, some foil-lined wrappers and a bar of soap that read "**Field of Dreams**." Picking up the cleansing bar, I sniffed its wrapper. I turned to Clinton with a sultry look in my eyes. "Whose idea was it to send out the products once a month in the mail?" I inquired.

"Did you like that?" he said with a wink.

"Like it, oh, I loved each package that came. Every month, a new item surprise was waiting for me. I just had to trust the process of what was coming. The handwritten notes from whoever packaged it up. It just felt so much like love, and I looked forward to it."

"Well, I already knew you liked the cannabis-infused *Pineapple Upside Down Cake* body scrub," he said as he went through the gift basket, pulling the purple glass jar out." Do you remember that night in your bathtub?" he asked, as he opened the lid and held it up to my nose.

I blushed and emphasized, "Yes, I remember that night like it happened yesterday." Using my index finger, I dipped it into the glass, taking a small amount out; I made small circles around every inch of his mouth, from the bottom left side all the way to the right, then following up to the top, repeating three times. Teasing me the way, he licks his lips. It was all I could do not to lick it off him as he began circling the emulsion around my mouth. The taste of the pineapple with real maraschino cherry bit my tongue as he slid his fingers into my waiting orifice. That is all it took. I was once again in his spell when I felt his tongue inside me and the fury of his kiss as he sucked passionately on my lips. I struggled to regain my composure as I broke away from his embrace. What was it about this man that would make me forget who I am and succumb to him?

Going through the gift basket, I picked up the massage oil named "The God Within" and flipped the lid open. I was delighted with the scent of sandalwood and patchouli with hints of lime and clove. I could feel the energy of the garnet, orange and yellow citrine stones as my sacral chakra began to engage and my hips began to take center stage. I smoothed the oils along my skin and began to imagine me rubbing him. I turned to Clinton with a look of curiosity and asked, "Is this where they make the **FooBellas Products?**"

"The cannabis-infused body wraps and muscle blends are all done here, and the rest are made in our facility in Delaware. I will be taking you there in a few days as we make our way down the coast," he said.

Clinton hung his suits in the closet. "I've got a copper vessel with your name all over it," he said, giving me a wink. He rubbed his hands on the small refrigerator, pulled out a bottle and handed it to me.

The artwork on the label had me spinning in its fable, running my hands along the ball of energy. "What's inside of this?" I asked as I began to peel the wrapper off the top.

Clinton opened a drawer where the corkscrew was sitting inside when he turned back to me and said, "Intentions."

He took the bottle back from me and began to open it. Filling the two crystal glasses that were hand-painted from the gift basket, he held the glass up to the light as I watched him spin the sediment around the bottom of the glass.

"What type of intentions do you mean?" I asked.

He put the glass to his nose and took a few sniffs before he tasted it. I watched his pride come out and I wondered if he crafted this himself. "**World Peace,**" he said. He sat down in the chair and looked out the window across the field.

My jaw cracked a smile. "**World Peace,** is that the intention you put into this?" I asked. Looking into the wine glass as if it were a crystal ball, I closed my eyes and drank the wine, imagining that **World Peace** was now on my lips. I could taste the love with each little sip. I could feel the feet that crushed the grapes, no doubt in the wooden vat that I thought was a bath when I spied it through my bathroom window out in the field of grapes.

It was Cannabis-infused apple wine in a long-neck brown bottle. "You don't say," I mused, as I let the glass come back and bring his peace in, "you just blow me away."

He took the glass from my hand, filling both goblets back up and said, "Come on, let me show you the real thing."

We walked out of our bedroom and down the hall that led to the back steps. The spiral staircase hugged the wall as it led around and out to the back door. As we made our way to the barn, with each step I took, I began to catalog each little inn. Clinton was talking on his cell phone, scheduling more meetings when I looked out to the woods and breathed it all in. That is when I heard him say: 'Houlton,' and I wondered what was up there.

When we approached the barn, and he opened the doors, I was greeted by lines of plastic barrels that looked like water towers. Glass jars of barley, hops, cannabis, and all kinds of other herbs all lined up on the counter. "This is where we craft our wines and beers," he said, raising his hands to the sky. "What do you think?" he asked.

"Impressive," I replied as he led me into another room where several oak barrels were sitting. Each had names and dates engraved on them. I looked back over at Clinton. "How long did all of this take?" I inquired.

"It's been in motion since I was sixteen. Something this big takes years to realize," he said.

I could hear the commotion as he led me to the taproom. It looked more like a dance hall with a stage in the corner with a set of drums on it. The round tables are all set with linens stamped with the **Made in America with Hemp Ingenuity** label. A line of chafing dishes sat along one wall, with blue flame Strenos keeping things warm. I walked over to the first chafing dish and slid the lid up. Inside was a tray of pasta with medallions of chicken breast and sautéed vegetables. The second one was baked halibut over linguine with lemons and garlic. The third one was stuffed cheese shells when I looked over to Clinton and asked, "Are they all cannabis-infused?"

"All but one," he said, "we do give you a choice." We watched the staff scurry around, placing the freshly baked bread on the table.

Kennedy was not lying. I made my way up to the stage, sat down behind the drum set and began to play, imagining all the people that had walked up on this stage to perform. We left the room just in time. As the wedding guests began to gather, we watched as the staff took care of everything. The band began to assemble, and the boutique wines and beers, hand-crafted in Maine, appeared all along the table.

We slipped behind the back staircase that followed the length of the barn. We made it to the bottom, and Clinton carefully felt the wall. "Be careful which one you go through," he said, as he looked directly into my eyes, "One is a trap that leads to a secret room."

My eyes grew wide with curiosity. "What's in the secret room?" I couldn't help asking. I did not know what I was thinking, but time slowed down as the round door rolled open, and I peered in on the most magical fields I have ever seen. Brilliant cascades of colors dazzled, as purple, pink and periwinkle lupines filled my eyes. The scent of honeysuckles filled the crisp air as angels darted in and out of the apple trees. Fireflies lit up the fields as the stars danced all around the night sky, and apple trees of every variety called out to me. The honeybees were buzzing with so much pollen that they could barely fly. Then, suddenly, they heard their queen speak, "Bring me more honey for my tea," and a cup and saucer appeared in my hand. Their bright white box buzzed from all the commotion as each bee fought for the privilege. Then, off in the distance, I saw his massive rack and knew not to move, as Moose would attack. Clinton made a loud noise with his lips, and away went the moose with his family of kids. I stepped further into the enchanted forest when the lull of the violins began to entice me as the mist enveloped me.

While we made our way back down to the main house, Clinton looked over and said, "When I come into town, I like to check on all my operations. However, I always like to make everyone feel special when I come. So, for that, I like to cook them something over the top."

My mind began to think of a million things to cook when he asked, "You good with that?" "Of course I am," I said, springing into action, "how many people would we be serving?"

"There will be about a hundred staff members coming," he answered.

"A hundred," I said, "that's going to be easy." I made my way back down to the main house, where a "new to me" kitchen was waiting. I became so confused with all the houses we had seen as I opened the drawers, trying to familiarize myself with their contents. I longed for my own bed, my own kitchen, and a sense of being rooted again when I opened the refrigerator, looking for something to drink. Again, I heard Clinton's dress shoes click against the tile floor when he came up behind me.

He placed his right hand on my shoulder and whispered in my ear, "Are you ready to go to the next level?" as he pulled me up. He ran his hands up and down my back, delighting my neck with sweet little kisses that almost made me forget my position.

I turned around to see him dressed in dress slacks and a nice button-down shirt. I was taken aback at how handsome he looked as I viewed my own frumpy wardrobe and wondered, "How the hell am I with him?"

"This place has a professional kitchen, doesn't it?" I muttered as I tried to ignore the obvious, "Where are all the chefs cooking?"

I stared at the buttons on his shirt while I began to count my way up to his eyes when he said, "It's out back."

Oooooh, he looked so good that I began to get weak in the knees as I felt myself falling into his trap of 'I-will-do-anything to please.' "Charlotte, this is your kitchen now," he said, "This is one of my homes. What is mine is now yours, so make yourself at home."

I felt a pain in my back, and, in an instant, my spine snapped into place. My wings began to protrude with my new adrenaline rush. I stood firm, letting my hands graze his pant legs as I made my way up and unzipped it. Feeling inside his pouch until my right hand grasped what I was looking for, pulling it out from its hiding spot. "I will admit it's been fun hopping from one place to the next," I said as I got down on my knees and began sucking on the tip of his amber pale.

"That is the first of our seasons you got in your hands," he said. His hands braced up against the inside frame of the refrigerator. "Do you like how it tastes?" he asked. His right hand tussled the top of my hair, pulling on it just a little. I could barely get my lips off the neck of his bottle when a little bit of his froth came into my mouth. "Delicious!" was my only reply. I continued to nurse his flask with the taste of cinnamon and tart apple when a hint of cannabis hit me in the back of my throat. I heard the smile in his voice when he moaned, "Take all of it in, don't miss a drop and do not forget about my pine nuts." Thrusting himself up over the counter, I thought it was rather funny, considering that they were already in my mouth. I wrapped my lips one more time around the tip of his decanter and let his prized possession go down.

Wiping my lips clean, I stood up and placed the bottle in the recycle bin when I blurted out, "I was thinking that I would use the wine with some chicken and make a risotto for tonight's dinner, when he said, "I want you to cook dinner for the open-mic night on Wednesday."

I rapidly counted the days in my head. "No problem," I said with a smile. I pulled out my phone, making sure of my dates and looked at him as my chef hat came back on. The beer got me thinking of doing something with apples. I pulled out a piece of paper from the shelf and began scribbling notes.

He rattled off some instructions that he wanted me to follow as I wrote feverishly to get it all down. "I want you to pay close attention to me. When I give you an order, you follow exactly, you hear?" he commanded.

"Aye, aye, Captain!" I sarcastically interrupted him. Afterwards, I covered my mouth with my hand, not realizing that I had said it out loud.

With that, he gave me a most piercing look. "Wait right here," he said as he got up and headed out the door.

"That's it, I've blown it for sure," I thought, as I slammed down the pen, "here's my marching orders." Hastily, I twisted off the ring.

Clinton came back with a large fuchsia paper bag in his hand. "Oh no, not another ham!" I thought. Upon further inspection inside, I saw a piece of purple tissue paper and a large box with a gold foil seal, embossed "**Center of Love Club**" in purple.

"Where's the ring I gave you?" he asked.

"Oh," I said, as I pulled it out of my pocket, "I was just getting ready to wash it." I fumbled, getting it back in my hand. Then, I pulled the package out of the bag. Wrapped around purple tissue paper was a black and purple gem dress that glistened when the light caught it. The bra was made of black diamond and purple stardust. I brought it up to my chest and stood up. Its panels of material blew in the breeze as I imagined myself as Clinton's Queen.

Clinton spoke in a voice that was a mix of stern and sexy. "Go back to the room and freshen up," he instructed, "wear everything in this box and the black diamond heels that go with it, then meet me in the enchanted orchard by the tree in the center at seven o'clock."

I nodded my head and said, "Yes," as I turned away. Then, I turned back. "How will I know where the center is?" I asked.

Clinton responded in a very sexy tone, "You will know."

I nearly fell to the ground laughing. "Damn, that was one helluva pickup line," I thought.

Clinton laughed back as good as he got. "Fine, meet me by the fire at 8 pm sharp," he said, clearing his throat. He slipped a piece of cannabis-infused candy into my mouth.

I turned back around with a giggle in my step and swooped inside our suite with a mixture of excitement as I plopped down on the bed, wondering who eats dinner at 8 pm in Northern Maine. Isn't that bedtime?

It took me a few minutes to make my way to the garden tub, stepping inside. I opened the jar of the bath salt labeled "**Goddess Within**" and let it fall in. I felt along the bottom of the tub as the smooth crystals dissolved. Then, I unwrapped the soap that matched its name.

I Imagined myself glittering when the strongest vibration began in my knees as I rubbed the lavender and jasmine blend all along my body. In an instant, the tub was filled with silky, milky-like clouds in the sky with shimmers of gold floating by. Rubbing the fusion along my chest, figuring this must be milk in this line. I closed my eyes and succumbed to the cream and honey as I massaged my thigh. I slid down further in the tub, obeying the command I could hear in my head to open my legs and braced myself up with both my hands. Lighting up my body from the root chakra first, I felt the spirit bursting in, but I couldn't tell anymore if the sensation was human, for it did not matter anyway.

I liked the feeling as it tickled my spine from my pelvic floor to my crown. A band of lights expanded as the red locks emerged. Hints of orange and gold appeared as my new hair-do unfolded, and ringlets of red tubes were highlighted as my new look emerged. Smoothing the Lapis Lazuli & Pearl Face Peel all over my cheeks, allowing for a younger look in just ten minutes, followed by Lavender and Honey Underarm Deodorant, the Crown of Gems squirting on my head, I ecstatically screamed, "Yes! Yes! Yes! It's the White Quartz Implosion balm blend with hints of gold specks!"

When I emerged from the tub, my body was shimmering with gold from the top of my head all the way down to my toes. I looked on the counter as a palate of makeup colors was waiting for me. I carefully followed each instruction as I applied the makeup to my face. Lining my lips with "**Lilac Bliss**" lip color, I blew myself a kiss. I spruced up my hair some more with the hair balm. My eyes began to get that seductive, smokey look as I penned the black liner. My eyes became slanted as I gave it a little hook-up.

Meowing like a pussy cat, I polished my nails. The Mascara made my lashes stand out, full and thick. The strand of black diamonds adorned my ear lobes. The pear-shaped Amethyst rested above my bosom.

I strapped the black diamond heels around my ankles, putting the last loop in place and slipped the black diamond with purple star dust gown over my head. Then, I adjusted my breasts into the sparkling cups, making them look fuller than my natural "C" cups. Finally, I took the crown out of the bag and trembled in anticipation of its implications as I placed it on my head.

I began walking back out to the **"Field of Dreams"** in high heels, wondering what I was getting myself into as the gown blew all around my legs in the breeze. The sun had long set, and the moon now lit up the apple grove as I walked back into the barn and up to the round door. I took three deep breaths and moved the door to my left, down the aisles, making my way to the bright ball of orange light. The sound of wood crackled as I got closer to the fire. It called to me as the scent of cinnamon and apples came through the breeze. I stepped into the center of the apple grove, where the round energy bed had been set up to look like a dinner table. Standing in what appeared to be a place of ceremony, I heard leaves blowing around.

I waited with anticipation, as the sound of the leaves crunched, as they fell victim to his shoes, while I listened to the band echo out of the barn. Standing in my gown of black, as my crown glistened in the fire, I watched intently as he walked toward me, carrying two plates with domed lids. He placed the food on the table and twirled me around as he inspected my black crown. "I like it on you," he said.

He ran his right hand in between the open panels of my dress as he caressed my inner thighs. I felt a little shiver come over me as my breath escaped my lungs when his fingers traced my lips. "Have a seat, my love, in the wrought iron chair," he said, lifting the dome before me. A plate of field greens lay in front of me in a cranberry and cider vinaigrette with feta cheese, walnuts, and sliced apples from the grove. Taking his spot on the other side of the round table, he sat down and spoke a blessing.

The wine poured into my glass from hands that vanished as fast as they appeared startled me. I swirled my fork around the tomato and let the emulsion savor under my nose. I could tell the walnuts had a cannabis crunch with hints of coconut on them. Each little note was a culinary explosion as the baby spinach and arugula ticked my nose. The rich creaminess of the goat cheese lulled me into its space as I savored every bite. Then, Clinton motioned for the waiter to come back and had him whisk my plate away. Glasses filled like magic as crumbs disappeared in an instant.

The waiter mysteriously appeared as he placed China, adorned with a filet of chicken breast stuffed with lobster, scallops and shrimp, on the table in front of me. A white wine and cream reduction cascaded all around the centerpiece. A drizzle of roasted red pepper aioli danced along the plate, making my senses do a backflip with just one bite. Nestled on the plate was Parmesan

Risotto with matchstick zucchini and baby carrots. Before I knew it, I was moaning as each fork fully encased my lips. Lost in his world of culinary delights, he took me easily over the edge. I pulled the fork reluctantly out of my mouth. "This is incredible." I purred, smiling over his dish, "I knew I was in for some sharp competition as I dreamed of Bobby Flay and what he would cook in this situation."

My mind was contemplating what I could serve that would keep them lapping out of my bowl when the thought occurred to me that there was no competition. The more I thought to myself, the more I laughed. I was only fooling myself if I did not think it was about a competition. I began to craft my dinner menu in my head as each bite honed me into him. I knew instinctively that he was testing me as one of his pan-seared scallops melted in my mouth, and I sensed that I was in for a stiff ride. "I'm up for some tight competition," I said, clearing my throat. As I sat there doing my Kegels, I writhed with each bite I put in my mouth, licking my fingers as I savored the last of his cream in his cooked-up scheme.

We talked as we watched for shooting stars in the night sky when the dessert plate caught my eye. A freshly baked apple pie, cannabis-infused butter brickle ice cream with praline topping, and Clinton's signature wine and maple gastrique rounding the edges of the plate.

"I will admit that my aunt's place doesn't have enough property to do anything big with, and we should just sell it," I said.

"Unless we were to go up," he said as the fire began to ignite. "Speaking of tight," he said, "why don't you show me what you were working on before."

Blushing, I looked around. "What, here?" I asked, perplexed.

Clinton took another beer from out of the cooler, and unbuttoned his shirt, throwing his tie and cummerbund on the chair.

I caressed the fabric of my dress, letting the gems move me in a more seductive way, as I climbed on top of the energy table and straddled his waist. My spine became an open sea as my whole body arched back.

My lotus pedals opened eagerly, wanting him all the way in. I could feel my own nectar as it began to churn. Slowly, I slid myself all the way down with each thrust he served up as the spirit of love flowed in with the collision of our hips. I looked up and noticed a brass pyramid, and I was at its point. I knew the energy was stronger this time and that the copper pipes were filled with crushed gemstones. With the murmurs so loud that I could no longer hide, my eyes fluttered as each wave sent me up to the ether again.

The higher the energy was calling me up, the more I felt the power under my feet. The scent of jasmine engulfing the sheets sent me into a sexual energy vortex that intensified its speed. I could feel the rushing of his soul flowing into mine. The slower I gyrated, the more I realized that I was sizing him up. "Did he let me have control this time?" I wondered as I convulsed on his crotch. With each passing wave, our hips swayed as my inner muscles gripped his meat. Bringing him into my own command, I thoroughly capitalized on the switch, brought him to his knees, and made him devour me.

I loved the dance of hot romance as I delighted in his tongue lashing, like a black snake, slithering down into its hole. I went back down on his instrument as I watched my life unfold. The excitement increased the more I knew that he was the one for me. Before I knew it, I was ingesting his sage sausage and assuming the head position at **CAMP WERTHEFUKRWE.**

"Just for breakfast and lunch," he said with a wink as he whisked me into the kitchen sink.

CHAPTER 9

A NEW LIFE

Clinton handed me a shiny purple and black foil bag with the **Center of Love** logo on it. "Brew this; it's from my own private stash," he said.

I opened the sealed bag and took a deep breath in, and the scent of the dark roast with hints of cannabis and spicy vanilla reminded me of the islands. "Where did the beans come from?" I asked

"From the Dominican Republic, my Queen," he said with a smile as his lips grazed mine.

Opening the cupboards, I found the French press and began to pour the hot water over the select beans. I looked out the window at the workers picking apples from the abundantly producing trees in the orchard. I walked down to the grove and plucked a few apples, as I smiled at one of the workers and went over to him. The sun was shining through the trees, throwing beams of light all around the back of his head when he said, "I hear you're marrying the boss."

I was a bit startled, wondering how so many people knew what was happening in my life, when I joked and said, "It was on C-Span. My name is Charlotte," as I extended my hand. He shook my hand, and I was taken aback by the strength of his hand.

"My name is Jermyn," he said as he grabbed another basket and made his way back into the grove.

I followed him further in and began picking the Pink Ladys when I bit into the crisp, sweet flesh and asked him, "Are you a member of the club?"

"Why yes," he said, "I am responsible for the apple wine, and I make sure each day that only the best goes into it." "What do you feel like doing?" he asked as he filled the basket.

I turned around to face him and looked into his eyes. Beads of perspiration were rolling down his face. "I feel like I am getting ready to lead something new, that even though I had made all these plans, something tells me that things are going to change, so I don't have much control over what is happening, and that bothers me."

He placed the next load of apples down into the basket and reached out to me. "Did you ever really think you had control anyway?" he asked, musing a grin. "I can tell by your eyes that

God is doing something special with you, you have just got to trust the process and live each day."

"That's just it, I question everything," I replied, as I handed him the apples that had filled the front of my dress up. He wrapped his hands around my hands, holding the bounty of apples and said, "As you should, I recognize my own kind when I see them," as he wiped the tears that had begun to swell in my eyes.

"What do you mean your own kind?" I asked him.

"I was a Senator back in the day," he said, as my eyes grew wide at his revelation.

"You were?" I gasped, "Why are you not doing it now?"

"Term limits," he said as he smiled back at me.

"Oh yeah, that's right… they did change that," I said.

"Yes, they did, and it was the best thing they could have done; enabling career politicians was the worst thing this country ever did; however, it's been fixed, and that is what counts," he said. He hugged me and said, "I am going to be keeping my eyes on you. I know what God is doing in you; I see it as I look in your eyes that you're going to win."

"Win what?" I asked curiously as I grabbed two more apples from the tree and waved goodbye. "I am going to give it everything I have," I said.

"You already have," he stated in parting.

I walked back in, wondering what I would be winning, as the scent of bacon lingered through the orchard in time to see Clinton pulling the trays of bacon out of the oven.

"I gave you a head start on breakfast," he said, pointing to the crisp bacon on a tray.

I put the burner on the stove and gave my bud spuds a toss, then sliced the apples and sautéed them in a pan with some butter, maple syrup, a sprinkle of cinnamon, cardamom, and some nutmeg. I was immensely proud of myself in the moment when I saw a canister of oatmeal and I knew there was a God! It had been so long since I cooked with this much passion and I began to think I must be falling in love, as the leaves began to turn color, and fall crept its way in early. I made up an oatmeal pancake mix and began flipping my flapjacks on the large cast iron griddle. I was now completely in my zone when I placed breakfast on the dining room table.

"I got to hand it to you, Charlotte; you are very creative in a pinch," said Clinton as he leaned up against the doorway. "I really like your resourcefulness," he said as he sent a message to Anastasia that breakfast was ready. "You put cannabis in this, right"? he asked.

"Yes, I did," I replied, standing firm in my mind.

"Good, just checking," he said as the crew came in and filled up their plates.

All of this I was rumbling through my head, as I diced up a large potato and onion and placed them on the stove with a sprinkle of sesame oil. I couldn't help but rejoice when I sliced the fresh ginger. "Looks like a tablespoon," I said to myself, throwing it in the wok and giving it another toss. I took the zucchini and yellow squash and cut it lengthwise and then in quarters. Then, I turned to the veggies on my board and chopped again, making little half-moons.

I sautéed it for a few minutes while I chopped up about 6 large cloves of garlic. I sliced them thinly; I just couldn't resist sniffing my hands as the aromatic garlic was added in. Next, I added yellow curry, gave it a good tablespoon and tossed it all around with a splash of soy sauce and some local honey to keep seasonal allergies down.

Oh, this is the best part: I just love to shake a can of heavy coconut milk up. I have my favorites, but, by and large, I'm known for making whatever I have taste good, so it does not matter which one -- just make sure it's not sweet, as that would be a disaster. Looking through the briefcase of spices, I found some garlic and onion powder and gave it a little toss with a sprinkling of sea salt. I winked and chopped the fresh cilantro up, sprinkling it on top. Then, I poured the coconut milk all over it. Oh man, it smelled so good as I fanned the scent up to my nose and added a sprinkling of crushed red pepper just to take it up a notch. Hot damn, how I wished for some siracha peppers. "Small towns do not carry everything, so you got to learn to cook with what you got," I thought as I ladled the vegetarian dish inside one of the chaffing dishes and set it up for lunch.

Dinner called me the most, and I wanted to stay in my comfort zone, like Sheppard's pie or chicken and dumplings, but something just kept saying that something special was coming. I tried to think of what it could be. My mind was drawing blanks, and I could not think of anything for dinner when Clinton hollered out to me.

"The driver will arrive to take us back to the plane at 8 am tomorrow morning, so make dinner count," he said, as he placed a set of keys and three hundred dollars on the table. "This place will get about one hundred people tonight for dinner. I know you were thinking of doing something fancy for dinner, but I want you to stay in your comfort zone, okay?" he continued.

I smiled back. "He must have heard my prayer," I thought as I ran outside with my phone and the remote. The nearest grocery store was an hour away when I looked at the time. Fighting with myself to not go full-fledged, it occurred to me that white chicken chili would not be half bad, and I could get that done in under 30 minutes. In a flash, I was in the produce aisle, grabbing everything I would need: 10 pounds of grape tomatoes, plum and beefsteak, jalapenos, garlic, 10 pounds of sweet onions, 12 ears of fresh corn, 6 bunches of sprouted coriander seed (wink, wink). Feeling the avocados, making sure I could just press their flesh in, I grabbed twenty of them and filled up the bag. I took a deep breath and pushed my cart, grabbing another 10 pounds of green and yellow peppers. Selecting 8 pounds of boneless chicken breast that were leaking all over the place, I grabbed a plastic package and tossed them in, "I don't t have any time for this today," I thought, as I high-tailed up to the canned goods, selecting 3 cans each of White, Kidney and Black beans.

Down I ran in a flash to the dairy section for 3 large containers of sour cream, heavy cream, some eggs, 10 blocks of Monterey Jack and cheddar cheese. Scanning through the ethnic food aisle, I located a bottle of cumin and 20 packages of the largest white corn tortillas I could find. I raced to the checkout, and it felt like I was already in a show. That is when it hit me: her name was Flo. Standing there, wondering how fast this girl could go, as I rubbed my legs tighter, I felt like I was ready to explode!

It did not take long before I was back at the camp, and into the kitchen, I flew in a flash. I tossed the bags on the counter and began to chop the chicken breast up into bite-size chunks. I grabbed the largest steel pot, heated it, and swirled a half cup of cannabis-infused coconut oil all along the bottom. I added the cubed chicken and then began chopping up the onions and the peppers. I quartered 3 large beef steak tomatoes with 6 plum tomatoes and threw them all in. I chopped 10 jalapenos, including most of the seeds, and tossed them into the magic pot, giving it a swirl with my Crooked Spoon.

I used a serrated kitchen knife to pop each kernel of corn off and slide it into the pot. I chopped up 20 cloves of garlic and gave it a toss with 10 tablespoons of ground cumin and a good handful of sea salt. Then, I drained and rinsed all the beans before adding them to the mix, performed some more magic (from the secret pouch hidden inside my breast), gave it a final toss, and put the lid on it.

One by one, they all filed in, and the beers began to flow as they filled their bowls. Sour cream and scallions were there for those who wanted to fatten it up. The blending of the cheese as the beer and cheddar-infused dip made its debut, just in case anyone wanted a cheesy, creamy taco, too.

The kettle-cooked tortillas with fresh guacamole nicely complemented the apple salsa. It was not until our host, Rob, took the pole to his throat and started belting out the funniest of jokes that I genuinely appreciated what this place was. I placed the cinnamon and sugar-dusted corn tortillas along the side of the plate with the chilled baked corn custard ice cream. "I can up-sell anything I want," I thought as I eyed up my biggest culinary dreams just as Clinton made his way back in.

"Good save," he said, as he cracked me on the ass, "Now go take the microphone; I wrote your name down on the list."

"What," I replied, as I fumbled over my words, "what do you mean, take the microphone?"

"Just go up on the stage and see what you got," he said. Rob called out, "Let's give it up for Charlotte," as the audience clapped. I made my way up to the stage, grabbed the microphone and looked out to the crowd when a voice in me opened, and the jokes just started flying out. I laughed as I rubbed my chin, mortified that I felt some hair and then it started, as my Chewbacca joke came out. The more the audience laughed, the easier it got, and within five minutes, my set was done. I handed the microphone back to Rob as I got off the stage. I ran up to Clinton with a rush in me that I had never felt before when I hollered, "I did it!"

"See, I knew you could; you just needed a little push," he said, "now get your butt in bed; we have an early plane to catch."

Walking back to our room for the night, after having the time of my life, I collapsed once I hit the bed, and I dreamed of being live on the mic again.

The morning after came in a flash. Clinton took our luggage and placed it outside on the front porch. As I glanced back at the farm, taking it all in, it began to dawn on me that he was taking me to all their locations. I was so excited about what was going to happen next as Anastacia drove us back down to the watercraft that was waiting at the dock on Lake Wytopitlock. I climbed into the back of the plane, and Clinton took the pilot's seat once again.

I closed my eyes and began to wonder how all of this happened when thoughts of Kennedy came flooding into my head, and a tear fell down my cheek, knowing in my heart that he was married. A whimper left my chest, and Clinton looked back at me.

"Are you OK with everything, Charlotte?" he asked softly.

"Yes," I responded, "I am OK with everything." I adjusted my right leg over my left. "I'm just thinking about things, situations in life," I said, as I straightened up my back, "you understand what I mean, right?"

"I'd like to think I know what you're thinking," he said with a chuckle.

I fastened my seat belt as the plane's motor ignited. We glided across the lake as the plane took flight, soaring high above the canopy of trees as shades of red, orange, and yellow dotted the landscape. We experienced the breathtaking views of the mountain range that only Maine could offer. I spent my time eagerly looking out the window as we flew over New Hampshire, then Massachusetts.

"Does the skyline look familiar to you yet," asked Clinton as the plane made a turn and followed the coast.

I could see along I-95, and as the Atlantic Ocean extended down the Eastern Seaboard, I knew we were passing Cape Cod. I turned my gaze to where the horizon started to look more familiar. "Wait, is that the Vanderbilt Mansion?" I asked, "Are we in Rhode Island"?

A broad smile came over his face when he said, "I want you to see what I have been working on for us."

I was puzzled for a moment when he said, "For us." I stared back down at the ring on my left ring finger and turned the band until the large round stone was glittering at me. "Did I somehow attract a man who plans things? I wondered. "Oh man, how I would love some fish n chips from the place with the glass lamps on the front of the street," I exclaimed with delight.

"That's one of my favorite places when I got a hankering for, beer battered cod," he said. Clinton flipped a few switches and radioed our position to the control tower. "Three minutes to final approach," he stated, glancing back at me, "and I'll take you there for dinner tonight if you like."

"I don't know what it is, but Newport, Rhode Island, has the best fish 'n chips," I said, "and I think it's the Newport Storm".

"This is the key that makes it so good," he said, "we're getting ready to land, so make sure you're buckled up because sometimes it's rough landing."

My emotions start to get the best of me as I watch the sun glistening down on the water as the plane lowers altitude on its final descent. I was scared and held my hands tightly to my seat as Clinton guided the plane gently into Mackerel Cove, making the sharp right turn to the final stretch.

It has been over a year since I had been to this location; however, my soul knew it for the last hour as I somehow felt it reaching out to me.

My heart began to skip a few beats as the tremors began to grow in me. My mind took me back to that fateful night when all the men were in dress uniform, enjoying the spirit of the evening. Intoxicating in their Navy Whites with shoes polished to a brilliant shine, it was as if they were all still standing here along the shoreline. Dancing under a moonlit sky, floating in a sea of love as our wings ignited in the night.

I opened my eyes as the plane's engines turned one last time, gliding up to where the cottage stood up high. I saw the fresh look of renovations on Highland Drive. I licked my lips and closed my eyes as I vividly imagined each one of them again in my mind, with their energy so powerful, as I exploded on the dance floor. "Oh my god, they must have thought I was crazy and bladder incontinent," I recalled as I broke out in laughter.

Clinton let the plane glide up to the large metal dock that must have been at least forty feet long. I watched him as he tethered the seaplane with two large straps, securing the fuselage. He opened the plane's door. I stood in the doorway as I looked at the leap I was about to take. I handed him the luggage, and he placed it on the aluminum dock. The wind was blowing briskly, causing the plane to bounce up and down. The thought of falling into the water sent a shiver of fear down my spine when Clinton held his hand out and said, "Hold on, and I'll pull you up." With my left leg on the dock and my right leg still coming off the plane, bridging the water, it was over in a flash.

The Intended

As the violins soared

the tones were music in my ears

as the orchestra surrounds me!

I long to go back.

Back in the symphony.

To hear the man that means so much to me.

To hear his fingers as they grace the stage

the piano sounding in my ears.

I do not know how I know you

but I know that I do

and

I do not know what I can do.

every time I hear a violin

and the orchestra play

I see you looking at me.

I see the smile on your face

I see you in my paintings

as my tears run down my face

I am in amazing grace.

119

CHAPTER 10

THE HIGHLAND INN

"Your wedding gift," Clinton said as my feet hit the grass. My bags hit the ground and my head began spinning, thinking back to the last time I was here. I gasped as I breathed into his armpits, safely cradled in his chest. The scent of sandalwood, patchouli and lime mixed with the scent of his testosterone sent volts of electricity up my legs as I looked up at him, stammering for what seemed like an eternity until I could get my tongue to formulate the words. None seemed to come out other than the mummer of my own ecstasy. I do not remember anything except for what seemed like the most incredible kiss coming my way. I watched as his glasses bounced back to the bell off in the distance as he licked his lips and made his way to mine. The taste of mint that had been lingering on his breath as his tongue danced down my neck.

I moaned out again in anticipation as I felt his beard and hands rubbing against my skin. He came so close to my lips that a shiver went through me as I felt his staff calling for my attention. I looked up at Clinton as I began to convulse in his arms. "You have got to be kidding me," I thought to myself as the energy of the captain called out to me once again. I shivered with the thoughts as goose pimples ran up and down my body. Rubbing my shoulders, I felt the chill as the invisible energy encapsulated me. I could sense him how with his fingers licking up my feet like the fog as he wrapped around my thighs and sent his vibrations up to my playground. The chemistry was so intoxicating that I could no longer hold the fluid in, and I began shivering, caught somewhere between scared and excited, not knowing which way to go as Clinton's eyes stared back at me, smiling and watching intently, as the captain came back to me. I'm not sure what I was feeling or if it was right, when I turned to him. "My wedding gift?" I repeated out loud.

It has been over a year, and the house is looking different. I melted in his arms as we walked up the grass, not realizing what I was getting myself into. The water-soaked lawn gave a tingle down my spine when a cool, salty sensation hit my toes, causing me to shriek. "This place is haunted, you know," I said, looking straight at him. "This place has a ghost that likes to have sex, and I think I had sex with him the last time I was here," I explained.

"Yes, I know," he said, as he licked his lips again, pausing as he rolled the keys in his hands, "I like to watch you with him," he said wryly, as he smiled and slapped my ass.

"Oh God!" I exclaimed as I headed up the lawn, wondering what he meant by that. I stood frozen as I looked up at its high-pitched slate roof. I could feel the captain around me again and smiled, knowing I was up for the challenge.

A large fireplace had been constructed at the base of the gardens that overlooked the front of the estate down the cove. It was dotted with lawn furniture that virtually invited one to relax and bask in its warmth. "I can't wait for you to see what I've been doing with the house," said Clinton as he grabbed my hand, and we sprinted to the porch. The flagstaff adorned the place, where an outdoor kitchen overlooking the ocean had been constructed. Cumberlandite lined over stainless steel complimented the natural landscape of the rocks around the property. It had a sink, stove, grill, under cabinet refrigeration, with a dishwasher and wine cabinet along the back wall overlooking the water.

A handful of wrought iron tables and chairs overlook the whole landscape, taking my breath away with its beauty. "How do you like your new kitchen?" he asked, opening his hands in wide expression.

Large potted plants with ferns and exotic flowers blew in the breeze as chives, parsley and basil rounded out the pot, with red geranium ushering in a bird of paradise.

I ran my hands down the countertops that overlooked the water as rows of sage, thyme, and coriander danced between petunias in wrought iron baskets, with the *Center of Love* emblem forged into place on either side of the grand fireplace.

The chimney is standing in the middle with racks embedded into its frame. I imagined cooking dinner in the outside space as I overlooked the bounty of the sea. My smile must have been a dead giveaway, and I could envision myself pulling up a lobster pot and fishing over the pier.

Clinton walked over to the wall, where he opened a door and flipped a switch. Within seconds, the sound of a motor running signaled a transformation, as the large glass windows between the living room and outdoor garden kitchen opened, doubling the entertainment space in a few seconds.

I walked all around the outdoor space, mesmerized by all the detail. "It's not like anything that I ever imagined, your eminence," I said as I reached out to him. I paused for a second, not realizing what I had just said. Wondering where that came from, I backpeddled, "I mean, it's incredible, Clinton," as I buried my head into his massive chest, embarrassed by what I had just said. I pulled back away, running my hands into the potted plants, rubbing the herbs between my fingers and then smelling them, still pondering at my choice of words.

"I heard what you said," Clinton replied as he pulled me back into his embrace, kissing my neck gingerly, "and I like it because I feel like a King the way you talk to me, so it's why I took the property over and re-did it for you."

Hidden in between the trellis that anchored each end was the Jasmine and Red Rose (called Prince of Peace) clinging as it trailed its way up the arbor built into the structure, with lights suspended. In the center stood a copper water fountain of a Mermaid with Neptune holding his staff, surrounded by open seashells with pearls. Her long, curly hair flowed as her tail cascaded, spanning open with crustaceans perched on her fin. An array of lights reached for the sky as if the sunlight itself had burst out of their feet, as the water flowed between their bodies. The more I looked at the statue in front of me, the more it reminded me of Clinton, and I wondered how he was so sure of everything.

As my fingers slid down the long bar that overlooked the water, all I could see were the guests arriving. My wedding destination yearned for me to tempt our guests' palates while they learned the arts of Maschakra in preparation for their union.Suddenly, I pulled out of my fantasy as I looked back at Clinton and asked him, "Is this place for us?"

"The *Center of Love Club* purchased this facility to host our meet 'n greets; Kennedy and I are business partners, and we own all the properties together. We have several partners and are looking for expansion options as we speak. I took over the renovations of the property after I saw how you reacted that night. I envisioned you here. Then, when I saw what happened with the Captain, I knew you needed this place for yourself," Clinton explained.

Wait, you saw that? I thought it was a dream. It felt so real; I thought at first it was you, and then I thought it was the ghost and then this man came that I remember being a teacher. Jesus Christ, Clinton, no wonder my therapist thinks I'm nuts!" I replied.

"Take a deep breath, Charlotte. You did not imagine anything, and it was not a dream either. You were just experiencing the energy as I was there with you. I just came in a different form. Now, let us get back to catching you up on everything," he said. Clinton opened the refrigerator and took out a wooden box embossed with gold lettering reading *Center of Love Cannabis Confections*.

Inside each space was a confectionery masterpiece. The description of each delight was embossed into the top. After looking at each treat, my eyes settled on the hazelnut butter ball with dark chocolate drizzled with white chocolate and toasted nuts.

Clinton picked up a sugar cookie spread with a thin layer of peanut butter in a milk chocolate dip dotted with salted roasted bits of peanuts. The explosions of flavors took my senses so deep in the South where large trees surrounded by sugar cane as I see birds taking flight. Knowing that I was somehow transported in my mind to some location, I succumbed to the fantasy as I let the cannabis butter with powdered sugar melt down my throat.

Clinton placed the confections back in the refrigerator as he escorted me into the house. "We have several others all around the country. I believe you were in one in Virginia last year. This one, though, is my wedding gift to you. I wanted you to have something personal, something for you and me to grow into our love with," he said softly.

I continued to make my way into the house. As the chocolate melted in my fingers, the construction was still in progress, as my mind tried to make sense of things. I walked into the kitchen that reminded me of the 1970s, then turned back. "How did you know I wanted this?' I asked.

Clinton smiled back at me and said, "I know more about you than what you think, so I have left the indoor kitchen more original to its design, figuring you could do what you want with it after you get to know the house more. Ralph, the foreman, will be here in the morning, and you can give him some ideas then".

I continued to follow Clinton's steps as I ran my hands along the pinewood of the walls. The more I walked the long hall, the more it felt like I was in a tunnel. The sound of a harp played in the background as the mist began to billow all around. A grand staircase opened in front of me as I climbed each step. My hands followed the hammered designs of the wrought iron with engraved detailing as they practically led me to heaven, counting each step as I looked up at Clinton.

"I took over the property when I saw what happened between you and the ghost while you were dancing with him, and I was intrigued,' said Clinton, as his hands wrapped around the glass doorknob.

As the door opened, the mystic fog engulfed me, and I was brought to my knees.

CHAPTER 11

NEPTUNE'S CROSSING

I awoke to the wood-beamed ceiling that arched up to the sky. The fireplace flickered through shadows on the wall, as the music of the violins called out to me. I clearly heard the piano, as the tunes trailed up my ears. The mattress felt like I was nestled on clouds of cotton balls that cocooned my frame. Hemp sheets caressed my body, as I found the tag that read Made in Delaware sewn into the side. The lure of the cove was calling me as I pulled down the sheets and got out of bed. My body was encased in a gown of mother-of-pearl satin that flowed down the floor, and I noticed that my toes were painted to match. I slipped my toes into the matching night slippers, adorned with baby pearls. I stood up and examined my ensemble in the full-length oval mirror standing in front of me. Sewn into the bodice that flowed up the thin spaghetti straps were baby diamonds and pearls that danced around my neck. Sitting on the settee was a matching lace robe with pearls that lined the edges, which I quickly slipped over my shoulders. I stood there examining myself as my ruby lips and kohl eyes stared back at me, trying to figure out if this was real or just a dream, when the moonlight shining in caught my attention.

The bedroom, filled with potted gardenias and palms, brought a heady spell to my nostrils, as I was lured to the window seat overlooking the cove. My eyes strained to see under the moonlight, as the hydrangeas and lavender danced up my nose, and the familiarly of it all came back to me. I watched as the mist danced around the window, inviting me to open the frame. The scent of the prince of peace that was trailing up the trellis teased me with its deep rose scent, beckoning me to step through. The rocks protrude from the lawn down to the shoreline as a buoy bobbed in the water. I spied what looked like a periscope slip back under the Atlantic. A chill went down my spine as flashbacks from my former life came swirling around my head. I tried to push the vivid memories back to the long-dormant recesses of my brain; however, the energy itself was way too persistent to ignore.

His silver-lined hair parted to the side, as the curls of hair peeked through the white terry cloth robe, revealing his hairy chest. He was at least seventy years old, but his muscular body felt no more than fifty-two. I could clearly see his figure as it hovered into the night sky, with his wings flowing with gray sparkle, shooting out in different directions as he beckoned me to let him in. His eyes were stained with tears as he grieved his loss. His image is taller with those blueish eyes and soft smile, trying desperately to keep it all together. Seemingly, his heavy brows and thinning entranced me as his ghostly shape from behind the aqua-lined windowpanes called my heart to open to him.

The gown, wrapped around my breasts with hand-sewn pearls and diamonds into the lace and silk bodice, shimmered like cascading waves onto the floor. I felt like a bride on her wedding night, as I waited for his love to come to me. It seemed like forever since I felt the captain's embrace, but this time, I knew it was him for sure. My hands turned eagerly as I cranked the window open to the night sky.

His ghostly arms wrapped around me as we floated to the bed filled with white and golden pillows of down. The ceiling was dotted with rainbows of lights as the glow of the candle shone on the pine. His wings fluttered as he laid me down. As he looked into my eyes, he simply began to cry.

I held him tight as heaves of sorrow wept out of his mouth into my chest. His cries were loud when he poured out his heart to me, as he sobbed into my chest. I felt his voice quiver underneath the fabric as his hands traced my skin. I knew it was Bob again; the captain of the ship released his soul into mine. The reflection of mirrors lined the room, making it clear to me that I was not alone. A figure became traceable as it watched from the settee. The fog billowed into the room as the moon dared to show its orb. I opened myself even more to him as his hands slid down my waist. I felt his urgency as his ghostly fingers teased up my thigh, raising the fabric far up my waist, just as his energy made its way inside me.

It was a sensation I could not explain, for it was not human, but I felt it penetrate me none the same.

In my mind. I beheld his body naked before me, with his silver wavy hair, as he rubbed his opaque lips down my neck, slowly kissing me as his tongue teased my breasts. His long, slender body shimmered in spectra that reminded me of glass exploding, as rainbows of colors burst like confetti throughout the room. Then, I unquestioningly obeyed the command I heard, not sure if it was my own desire, or Clinton's voice that said, "Open up and let the Angel in".

The temperature of the room dropped as the wind picked up. It seemed that I had lost all sense of time and space, and my head felt like it was disconnected from my body. The fabric of the poster bed billowed as the wind beat against the cliff from miles away, matching the rhythm, as his energy engulfed me. Heaving higher, I counter-matched the rhythm of the invisible ghost, writhing on top of me as I closed my eyes and felt him enter further into me. The energy of his presence intensified as his invisible staff penetrated me, sending shock waves up through my body. Its highly charged glowing energy inside of me expanded all through my spine as if virtual pulses of light flickered on and off, triggering explosions and shock waves, so forcefully beyond my ability to duplicate them on my own. I again succumbed to the energy, as my head expanded into a galaxy of tunnels with shimmering lights that made me cry out in a way I had never felt before.

The love lasted for what seemed like eternity, with the moon beaming into the room, as Clinton watched from the corner. In a flash, the Specter and I flew across the cove, dancing about the water, with my wings spanning the Narragansett as I took flight. I delighted in his kisses, so utterly delirious as we flew up the coast. We settled against a cliff walk, and I felt him in me again. The moon beamed brightly in the night sky, as the stars twinkled their cosmic message to me. The sailboats dotted the waters as we flew past them. With the fall season coming to an end, I floated down on the fluffy white cloud of my bed.

"You'll be filming in the spring," the captain's voice lulled, "on the small Island of Jamestown, Rhode Island, as you take over renovations at Highland."

In what seemed like mere seconds, I was again nestled deep into the four-poster bed. The energy from the flight had my emotions on high, as I felt Clinton's body hover above mine.

His wings spanned out past the bed, with his chest muscles flexed, as his submersible began to guide its way into my cove. I could feel the full weight of his body as his tongue danced into mine, and I wondered what I had become.

The way his hands gripped me tightly as I wrapped my arms around his back, with our legs intertwined, now took me to a realm I had yet to encounter. He took my breath away with how deep he came inside of me. Something was different here in the way he changed, as his energy had somehow magnetized and grown twice in size.

There was something peculiar about him that I simply could not understand. It was as if the power of the ocean transformed him. The force of his hips bore down, with each successive thrust more amazing than the last, sending me to paradise. I had no need for air as my pelvic floor rose and my chest arched up to his mouth.

The fireball of explosions trembled as I writhed and spasmed in ecstasy, flooding the quilt with my emotions, as he took me over the edge of the bed.

Wrestling myself back on top again, I began the slow descent down on him. His chocolate-covered treat was copiously lubricated. I made love to his mast. He utterly blew my mind as he rose to full attention, as my hands slid up and down on him, knowing full well that I was making love to a god. My mind was racing on which way do I go next, when I was on my back in a flash.

My excitement began to grow as I listened to him moan as he bore down on me. I was lost in a flurry of mini explosions, as he feathered his fingers down my abdomen, teasing me as he caressed my inner thighs. The excitement of wanting to feel him back in me was overwhelming when I wrapped my hands around his neck. The temptation was even more exciting, as the thoughts of him penetrating me came full circle. The music began to resound in my ears as if it had tunneled its way into the walls, telling me that I wanted "something just like this".

Like a ravenous lion that had not eaten in weeks, he plunged into me, sending me into orbit as his tongue thrashed, as he ferociously dined. His momentum was unrelenting, and his thirst unquenchable, drinking me in like a water fountain that had just burst. My legs convulsed as I cried out to the cocoa man who had become my God.

Waves of blissful sensations flooded me as I released my well into his mouth, not completely satisfied with my screams of delight as the next wave of tremors came over me. I felt like I was climbing the world's largest roller coaster, as each click of the seat brought me into a higher realm. We were tapping at the doorbell of heaven, as he took me into his trust. This time, I screamed so loud that I could no longer control myself, as I had become a runaway roller coaster that was heading face-first into his spell.

Something happened to me in that moment when I morphed into a cat, sleek and black, as I mauled his body in my attempt to take him back. I totally let myself go as I grunted down on him as my arms pinned his biceps to the bed, flexing my inner muscles and drawing all of him in.

My mind had become focused with laser precision as each orgasm was only a precursor to the next one forming. Suddenly, I became insatiable with desire, screaming out joyously to the God that ruled my life. My body shuddered like an erotic volcano ready to erupt, hot with the knowledge that something even bigger was coming as the intense pressure began to build up. "YES, YES, YES!" I screamed as his shaft vibrated inside of me, and a new transformation began.

My body convulsed as he drank from my breasts, my invisible milk flowing into his mouth as I released into him. It was all I could do to take all of him in as my soul made love to his flesh. Mesmerized at how he intensified as my elixir clung to him. I could taste my essence mixed with the scent of his manhood as he repeatedly thrust himself up into me. In one swift move, I was standing on my feet.

"Down on your knees," he commanded.

I slithered slowly down onto the ground and let my fingers trace his legs as I worked my way up his thighs. The room glowed in a brilliant explosion of lights, as his wings spanned back open and began to flutter as if he was going to take flight. I looked up at him as his wings spanned so wide. The lights blinded me, as if the essence of every creature in the sea was channeling into him, building his momentum. All I knew at this very moment was that he was much more than a man. Dancing ever so slowly as the sea rushed up on me in a synchronization only Neptune could coordinate, we exploded on impact.

A man of his convictions commanded my seas with ease with his marvelous head. His built-in sonar scanned the horizon, taking me to new places and realms that I did not think were possible for me to visit. I panted heavily for breath as I flew under his wings. "What are you?" I asked him

"Shhh," he replied as he placed his fingers on my lips, "do not ask questions you might not want

answered." He wrapped his tentacles around me. "Some things are meant to be a secret," he said.

I do not know why this excited me so much, but it did. My breath was almost on hold, as we traveled at such a fast rate that visions of Baghdad caught my eye. I looked over at him, knowing that he was not mortal, when it suddenly hit me that I. "It's for your own safety," he said, "the less you know proof positive the more it's just speculation."

My eyes grew wide as I took a deep breath and found myself back in bed. I looked around the room as his hands held onto my feet. "What just happened here?" I asked.

"You just Astro planed around the world with me," he explained.

"Astro what?" I stammered, as I sat up in bed and wrapped the down blanket around myself, while trying to understand what I saw and felt.

"Your soul left your body, and I took you for a journey," he said, as he fluffed the blanket around my body and began to walk around the room.

"But," I stammered, how did I leave my body and still be here, and what was my body doing while I was there?"

"Your body was on hold while your soul was out traveling," he elaborated, as he sat back down on the settee and looked into my eyes.

"On hold?" I asked curiously, "You mean I wasn't breathing?"

"It's not death, Charlotte," he said, laughing, "it's like you go on pause with the body and operate in the mind."

"So, is this something I can do without you being with me?" I asked. I watched his face intently as he rubbed the side of his chin. "I've seen your visions, I know your capabilities, I have a job for you, and I want you to run for office," he replied. "What?" I asked, nearly jumping out of my seat.

"Not up for the challenge, Charlotte," he replied, "have I got you stumped?"

"Holy shit, he meant it," I thought as I almost regurgitated my last meal mouth and swallowed it in the nick of time. "I thought you wanted me to cook in the B&Bs," I said, coughing on my words.

"I sense some hesitation," he said. Clinton abruptly turned his head to the right. "Are you not happy with this arrangement, Charlotte?" he asked.

I just laid there, totally surprised, as my world seemed to spin out of control. How did he know? I did not share my fantasies with anyone. How was it that he knew everything that I ever wanted? His arms rubbed his chest, as he put the smack down on me with just one eyebrow. "Why yes, I spy on you," he admitted.

I stammered back in a language I had yet to speak, obviously still reeling from his deliverance. "But why? I asked.

His eyes widened as he pointed at me. "It's what I do, I spy on everyone, and I've been watching you for a long time now," he stated.

I looked around the room to see if there was a hidden camera in the corner, and when he sat back down next to me.

"It's not like that, Charlotte," he said, placing his hand on my head.

I was too scared to look into his eyes, knowing he could read my mind, and there was no escaping him when he put his hands on my chin and raised my eyes up to meet his. "I see a woman who can change the course of history and lead the New Nation," he said.

Stumbling to get dressed, I looked back at him. "Clinton, I asked, not knowing what the answer was going to be, "Are you entirely human?"

"All in perfect timing, my dear," he replied as he pulled out a box from the drawer. A lovely set of earrings with a round diamond that looked like the full moon appeared with a series of amethyst tear drops, in three different sizes, encased in gold. "There's a revolution happening, Charlotte, and you're the bait," he said, "Bait, what do you mean by bait?" I asked, as I hurried to get dressed

"It's too early to tell right now, but I believe you hold some keys," he said.

"Keys? I asked, "Keys to what?" I asked as I followed him down the steps into the kitchen. He stopped for a moment and collected his thoughts, then turned towards me. "Keys to the coming post-political paradigm shift," he said.

"What's that?" I asked, thoroughly perplexed and utterly curious.

"Charlotte, have you ever thought about becoming the President?" he asked seriously.

I broke out in a fit of hysterical laughter that rivaled that of our past Vice President. "No more than another woman ever has," I replied in jest, "why?"

"You know, a woman who has accomplished all that you have can be unbelievably valuable to my administration," he said.

My head started running circles in my mind, as I started calculating things over the last twenty years, waving my hands. "Not enough experience, they would say, and I would not last ten minutes the way everyone complains," I replied, "and you know that I am way too sensitive, Clinton and they would eat me alive."

"Not after I am done training you," he said. Clinton pulled a blue Oxford out of the cedar-lined closet and wrapped it around his chest. A major change is coming soon, and I've bet everything I have on you.

"Well," I crackled back, "you may be betting on the wrong chick."

"No, I don't think so, I am a betting man, but I don't gamble frivolously. Besides, I told you I am the Purple Party," he said. Clinton grabbed a bottled of spring water from the nightstand and handed it to me.

My mind seemed to rattle as visions of the seamen flooded into my head again, as I watched him zip up his pants and wrap the matching suit around him. "Wait, Clinton, I cannot do this, this is not me, I'm not cut out for this." I said, "Besides, I don't even care about politics anymore. I stopped voting a long time ago as the thoughts of the CIA, Watergate, and the Kennedy assassinations came into my head. "They will have a field day with me, Clinton, digging their nose into my business," I said, as a chill went down my spine.

"Relax, Charlotte, I checked you out thoroughly," he reassured me, as he pulled up the black socks and slipped his feet into the polished shoes.

"Really," I said sarcastically, "I have got skeletons in my closet, and they will tear me apart." "'Listen here, Charlotte," he said, as he tied his shoes and stood back up, "over the years there has been no President without something up his sleeve, so no one is squeaky clean".

"What about my use of Cannabis, Clinton? I asked convincingly, "What about that?". I crossed my arms over my chest, thinking I had him cornered.

A smile escaped from his lips as he snickered under his breath. "Why do you think you've been picked?" he countered.

He knows I want Putin!

It is just not fair

That face of steel

In his brilliance

Who would not want

A crack at that

Riding on that horse bareback

I would get down to a size 14 for that.

I still want to remember

Where I came from

I am the Russian

Hiding in between the sheets

They are in me

as is American Indian

I feel Navajo

I feel Serge

The melting Pot

As he stomps around the room

Oh, I always wondered

Who he was?

I have always felt a deep connection

I love how everything is connected

We just learn to conduct differently

It's frustrating testing new equipment

We were the experiment

As it was being written

CHAPTER 12

FOOL'S GOLD

Kennedy took a deep breath as he slowed down to negotiate the turn into the long, winding driveway of the Center of Love Club. "Here we go," he said, as he beeped the horn. Karissa looked up from pulling weeds out of her flower urns, wondering who was coming down her driveway when she realized it was Kennedy. He beeped again as he pulled up next to her. "Did you pick up Charlotte's Aunt Mabel? "He asked, as he put the vehicle in park and jumped out.

Karissa walked up to Kennedy, laughing. "Did I ever," she said in jest, "and I think you bit off more than what you bargained for on this one". She dusted the dirt off her hands.

"Why did you say that?" Kennedy asked as he bent down to give her a kiss.

"Oh, you'll find out soon enough," she giggled.

Kennedy gave her a pensively questioning look. "Are your bags packed? he asked.

"Yes, our bags are packed, she replied, "where is the Trans Am?" Karissa made her way around the monster motor home occupying half of the driveway.

"It's up at the Camp in the barn," he said, wiping the sweat dripping off his face.

Aunt Mabel's loud voice boomed from the kitchen as she poked her cane through the screen door and made her way closer. "Open the door and let me out of here!" her gruff voice bellowed out. A look of utter horror came over Kennedy's face as he watched her cane rip the netting off the screen and the grand old larger-than-life lady attempted to barrel through it. All Kennedy could think about were the hordes of mosquitoes that would be all over the house as he ran to help her out of the door. "Mosquitoes will lift you up out of your chair if you aren't glued to it, so you had better fix this screen," she said as she thrashes her cane at Kennedy's chest.

She used all her strength to rip what was left of the netting, leaving the door hanging on its hinges. "You better fix that screen, sonny," she repeated, as she smacked Kennedy again on the arm for good measure.

"You think," he muttered, rolling his eyes in disgust, trying to keep cool. Momentarily taken aback, Kennedy turned to Karissa. "What the heck," he said, extending his hand to Aunt Mabel. "My name is Kennedy," he said, with a half-smile that fully tested his diplomatic skills.

"I don't give two bean poles who you are, sonny," she scolded, hitting his leg with her cane. She lit up a fat blunt and took a few puffs, and swung her cane. "I'm not riding down in that thing," she protested, rapping the door to the motor home, "I was promised I'd be driving your 'golden witch' to Mississippi!"

Once again, Kennedy felt the sting of her cane on his shin, sent him rubbing his leg when he tried to explain the situation. "What … drive my Trans Am?" he responded, "Oh, no way you could operate her." "Sorry, you're just too old, Aunt Mabel," he said, "besides, I dropped her off to get some work done on her." Kennedy hobbled over to the behemoth and opened the main door. "Look, this motor home is very well equipped with all the comforts of home," he pleaded, "we even have leather seats and air conditioning."

Aunt Mabel raised her cane halfway into the air, getting ready to strike Kennedy on his head. Kennedy turned rapidly and ran to Karissa. "I think it would be better if you drove Aunt Mabel and Olivianna to Mississippi," he said, rubbing himself in pain, "damn, that old lady swings hard".

"I bet you do," Karissa scowled, "you're nuts if you think I'm doing this without you, as it was your idea, Kennedy, so follow it through!".

Furiously, Aunt Mabel got in Kennedy's face again. "I don't do planes, I don't do trains, I don't do ships and don't even get me started on this!" she bellowed. She pulled another long hit on the blunt, choking slightly on the smoke. "I know damn well who I want to drive with," she said, wrapping her arms around Karissa. "Good Kush morning to you," she said, giving Karissa a big grandmotherly hug.

Karissa stared piercingly at Kennedy. "I hope you got a lot of money for this gig," she said. She gave him a smile and started to turn away.

"Oh, I sure did," Kennedy whispered in her ear. He smiled back and pulled a bundle out of his front pocket, and slipped a few hundred into her bra, padding her down, "Don't spend it all in one place now."

Aunt Mabel glared over at him. "Whatcha' gonna do, Sonny?" she sputtered, as she pointed her cane at him. "I'm either going with Karissa or the deal's not going through, boy," she insisted, "who do you think is funding this adventure?"

Karissa jumped back in the fray, putting her arms around Aunt Mabel's shoulders. "Dear Auntie Mabel, let's go back into the kitchen -- I want to hear some more of your stories, plus, I just rolled up some of my word-famous peanut butter balls and really need a taste tester, if you don't mind?"

"Mind, hush, oh no, I don't mind one bit, you're such a sweet girl," Aunt Mabel said with her sweet southern drawl, eyeing Karissa up and down. She cut a mean look at Kennedy and turned her gaze back to Karissa. "Let me just give you one of my famous hugs, child," she said softly as she wrapped her arms around

Karissa, rubbing her back and sliding her hands down ever so slowly towards her buttocks.

Kennedy watched intently as Aunt Mabel buried her head into Karissa's breasts and stroked her hips with her hairy knuckles. "You're creeping me out, Aunt Mabel," she said, attempting to pull Karissa out of her grasp.

Aunt Mabel grinned wryly back at Kennedy, and she took another drag on the blunt. "We'll see about that," she said. Karissa gently took her hand and led Aunt Mabel back into the house. Kennedy followed Karissa into the house and grabbed a peanut butter cookie that was still cooling on the racks.Karissa followed Kennedy to their bedroom.

"Aunt Mabel needs handlers, and it's simply not fair to put her all on Olivianna," Karissa said as Kennedy walked into the bathroom.

He pulled the zipper back up on his jeans and flushed the toilet. "Is she really that bad?" he asked.

Karissa sat down on the commode, struggling to pee. "I think I got a urinary tract infection within three days of handling her," she said, "and she's got you pissed off."

"Damn, she's that bad, I am so sorry Karissa," Kennedy said, "but we need to bring her, its Charlotte's aunt and she has something to do with the big deal in Delaware for the Trans Am."

"Kennedy, just what are you up to?" she asked. Karissa flushed the toilet and looked for the cranberry pills in the bathroom closet.

"Karissa, you will not believe what is happening, but I met with a few people this past week and we are working on a deal to get car manufacturing back in Delaware," he replied.

"Do you really think it's possible to bring Pontiac back asked Karissa as she picked up the picture frame of the Trans Am that sat on his dresser.

"Anything is possible, Karissa, if you put the effort towards it, plus with Industrial Hemp legislation recently passed in Delaware, that paves the way for manufacturing on a whole new level," said Kennedy.

"What about freeing up plant space?" she said, lying down on the bed.

"Get this, Karissa," said Kennedy, "I had meetings with the new Governor of Delaware for a good part of last week, toured Dover, met with other state officials, and it looks like we can break ground by Spring of 2028."

Karissa popped back up from the bed, nearly choking with excitement. "This is very important for the People," she declared, as she ran into the closet, grabbing another suitcase. Clothes flew everywhere as she packed her bags. "Kennedy, this is big," she said, dragging the packed suitcase out of the closet. "Does

Charlotte know about all of this?" she inquired, looking at Kennedy sprawled on the bed.

"Clinton is grooming her now to run for President on the IPUS ticket," he revealed.

"IPUS," Karissa repeated, as she slid on top of Kennedy.

"IPUS is the acronym of ***The Independent Party of the United States***," Kennedy explained as he rubbed her hips and slipped the thong off her thighs.

"WOW, Kennedy," she exclaimed, "the Revolution is really happening!"

You bet it is, Honey," he said. Kennedy rolled Karissa onto her back and gently kissed her neck.

"Why, Kennedy, we've got Aunt Mabel in the kitchen," she giggled under the nuzzle of his beard.

"I know," he whispered," and I'm letting her know just where she stands."

CHAPTER 13

WAIT, HOW DID WE GET HERE?

I walked outside the front door to the Highland Drive Estate with a new set of keys in my hand. Sitting in the circular driveway was a brand-new dark mocha metallic Cadillac XT6. Eagerly, I hit the remote control, unlocked and slipped into the car, as the scent of fresh leather filled my lungs.The black leather seats felt plush, as the headrest cradled my neck, with built-in massage functions, as I laid my head back. Wrapping my hands around the steering wheel, I was magically transported back to 1957 in an instant. With her tail fins running down the back, to the batting of her head lights, boy, was she a sight. As I ran my fingers along her polished coat and marveled at the chrome bumper, I was hooked. Truly, I knew I wanted her back then, as I would sit in the car, rubbing her silver buttons, imagining how I would have it again. When I closed my eyes once again, I envisioned an inspired electric retro '57 Caddy design coming into production. The Diamond Edition beckoned, and, as her glistening white walls and black undercoating with diamond star dust came rolling past my eyes, I could hardly escape my excitement as her headlights burst open, with the lashes flashing me with her sultry eyes. With a flip of a switch, her whole top rolled down, and before I knew, my Cadillac convertible was on the line.I imagined cruising down the street with the rich sound of the engine, as she hugged the streets. The cameras were flashing on both sides as lines of people went past my eyes.

Suddenly, I opened my eyes and realized it was just a dream. "Wouldn't that be something," I thought as I pressed the button and the XT6 started up. "You better believe I want it, and I want it right now!" I wished, as I writhed against the strong back that vibrated at the flip of a switch. I watched the clouds begin to form on the way over the bridge from Jamestown to Newport. The power under the hood made it hard to keep it under twenty-five miles per hour in town, but once I hit the Pell Port Bridge, I let her flex her muscles. Gazing over the Narragansett, I opened the moon roof with a flip of a switch. My hair whipped and waved in the breeze, but for a moment, I could have sworn that Marilyn Monroe was sitting next to me. The familiar tug in my gut told me to turn right to America's Cup. The old train cart appeared to my right, and within seconds, I was parked on Long Wharf, overlooking the marina. I walked down to the bar that I loved so much when I used to work here in town.

The wooden doors opened to the Pub, where, standing at the bar with a beer flowing down his throat, was the Wildcat. "Ricard, right," I said, reaching out my hand.

"Yes, that's me," he said, somewhat startled as he turned around and pointed his fingers in my direction. "You're Charlotte, right -- Clinton's soon to be wife," he observed, as he brought the bottle of beer up to his mouth, letting the tip of the bottle dance on his lips.

I was a bit taken aback. "How do you know that?" I asked.

"I flew the plane into your camp the other week," he replied.

"Oh, you're the pilot," I said, as my voice dropped down a notch with my eyes squinting to read his mind. "I remember you from last year at the *Center of Love* Grand Gala. What are you doing here?"I am a private pilot for hire, and I was chartered by **ImagineNat** bringing his artwork up here for some auction at one of the mansions". He was tall, milk chocolaty and charming with sparkling green eyes and a smile that could make any girl swoon, even without a uniform."You know, **ImagineNat, a**s my eyes got wide, I have one of his prints on a shirt, oh my goodness, he is one of my favorite artists!"

"I should introduce you to him," Ricard says, as he finished his pale ale, "give me a few weeks to set it up -- he is a very sought-after guy these days, or why don't you get Clinton to get you tickets and go to the auction and meet him yourself."

"What, are you kidding me, I shrieked! Why not? It is a charity event, bound to be a lot of bigwigs as he orders another drink. I wanted to get back to Jamestown, I was eager to talk to Clinton about this, when I felt a hand wrap around my shoulders. Startled, I turned around to see Clinton, when he reached out to shake Ricard's hand. "We have got an early flight tomorrow,"

Clinton said as he took my hand, whispering, "come on, honey, we need to get you home."

We waved goodbye and walked out of the car just as the rain pelted down. Clinton took the remote from me and opened the passenger door for me to get in. I was puzzled and asked, "How did you get here?" as I scanned through the boats to see if his was docked.

"I flew," was all he said, as he shut my door and got behind the wheel. The drive back over to Jamestown was a bit somber, and I had a feeling I had done something wrong, when Clinton popped a question. "I want to know what you see in him -- meaning, who do you really think he is?" he asked.

I swallowed my breath for a moment, as my mind began to go back in time. "OK, I do admit that I do think he is working for some type of intelligence agency," I said, "at least it is what I thought when I saw him last year.

"Really?" he said, as he looked out to the water, "I know I have not revealed that much to you as to who I am, but now that you have agreed to be my wife, we need to get some rules straight".

My hands gripped the bag of my purse. I hadn't thought about having to answer to a man when I agreed to marry him and began to wonder if I could even do that. I had not had to answer to anyone in many years, and I had become used to my freedom in that way. I looked back over to him as I began digging my nails into the purse's casing, "I agree, we need to have a talk if this is going to work," I replied, as my eyes cut him a new look.

"Charlotte," he spoke in a sterner voice, "you're just going to have to learn to trust me on some things." Clinton paused for a moment, deep in thought. "I am more than what you know. I have plans that I believe you are a part of, and you are going to have to learn to listen to me! You just can't go off running as you please, there are rules in this relationship if you're going to achieve what you're meant to be".

"What are you talking about?" I asked incredulously?

His tone now firmer, "Charlotte, you're not understanding what I am trying to say," he said, as his right hand pounded on the steering wheel. Clinton turned and pointed his finger at me, "What I'm trying to tell you is that you are going to be the one, it's you, you're the revolution!" he exclaimed, as he slammed his fist down on the armrest to finalize the point.

"Have you lost your ever-loving mind? I am no queen of any nation or future President, I said firmly, "and I do not want any involvement with any of this." His words struck me with shock and awe, I know I have always had this deep buried feeling that I would someday be involved in politics, but I did not spend my career in politics when I looked back at Clinton and asked, "Is this what this marriage is all about, how you are going to groom me to be the mouthpiece for some political agenda?"

Clinton pulled the car into the circular driveway, kicking the gravel, leaving a trail of dust, when he said, "Do you mean to tell me you do not have some deep-rooted desire to change the way this country is going? Is that what you're trying to tell me?No, that is not what I am saying, I know I have always had an interest, I just, well, as I fumbled over my words, I have been trying to run away from it.You can't run away from your destiny, Charlotte; it's going to catch up with you no matter what you try to do it avoid it. "You're crazy if you think I am doing that," I yelled, as I slammed the car door shut and ran into the house.

Undaunted, Clinton followed behind me with the look of a senior adviser and voice of a state trooper. "You need to get under control, Charlotte, a President can't be acting like this!" he yelled back even louder. He slammed the front door shut, rattling a picture of Abraham Lincoln that seemed to appear out of nowhere on the wall.

The walls went from white to pine paneling, and it felt like I just went into a time warp as I walked into the kitchen. I ran my fingers through my hair. Flustered, I opened the refrigerator and pulled out a carton of eggs, staring at the contents of the cold box as if the sour cream were going to answer me. Irritated, I grumbled, "Do you want anything to eat?" I listened while he fumbled with his belt, not paying him the slighted attention as I slammed the refrigerator door shut. My mind began to race when I felt his hand grab my arm, and out the back door we went.

The carton of eggs hit the flagstone by the side door where the outdoor kitchen meets the sea, as Clinton bent me over the hard wrought iron table. I felt his hand on my ass as he ripped my underwear off. In my mind, I prepared for the sting of the belt, as flashbacks to the many years earlier came in front of my eyes. I tensed up, ready for this first strike, when I felt the thrust of his manhood drive deep inside.The wind howled, the rain pelted down, and lightning bolts filled the sky. While the thunder rumbled, his passion grew, as he whispered in my ears, "I know it's you". I watched as the storm encased the night sky and succumbed to the force of his thighs. The intensity was the most exciting feeling I had, but I am not going to lie, there was something about those first fleeting moments when we first went outside. Oh, how I longed to feel the leather up against my skin, knowing that I wanted a good licking. I didn't know whether it was the thunder in his voice when he bellowed, "will you run" or the sound of his hand slapping against my ass, but whatever it was, I liked it. I looked out at the sea, instinctively knew that it was about the submarine, about the government, about everything, and when it all finally hit me, I turned around to face him.

"I saw the submarine hovering in the water last night," I shrieked out loud, "you're a spy!".

"Be quiet, my dear," Clinton whispered into my ear. The depth of his vocal cords played havoc on my spine when he looked me in my eyes and said, "You will obey," ripping off his shirt as the buttons flew everywhere. I watched him morph into a God right before my eyes, intoxicated with his raw power. His sheer strength was overwhelming as he climaxed in me. As the hard-

pelting rain mingled with my own secretions, a bolt of lightning
cracked across the sky and in that moment, I knew I would do it.

CHAPTER 14

DO NOT BLOW YOUR ROD!

Kennedy pulled back into the driveway of the white house and could hear laughter coming up from inside. He walked in the back door of *Camp Wherethefukrwe*, where Olivianna sat at the table, looking good as her hair fell down her face. "How do you like it working up here so far?" he asked, as she offered him a fried egg sandwich with Canadian bacon.

Laughing back, she tossed her hair to the side, "Well, it's something, I'm almost done with the cake, but I think it would be better if we just cooked all the food in Mississippi," she replied.

"Yeah, I think you're right," he said, as he put the last bite in his mouth. "I talked to G'anacia and Nadia, and they will be heading over from Las Vegas in a week," he said.

Olivianna opened the walk-in fridge and pulled out the top of the cake. "I'm going to do most of it here and then put it together when we get there," she said.

Kennedy watched Olivianna as her hair spun around the room. "I had made plans to hit Atlantic City on the way down," he said. "The deal for expansion is all over the country, so when we arrive in Delaware, we will be there for a few weeks while we close some deals," he stated. "You might want to freeze that cake," he concluded, as she put it back in the refrigerator."How's the new guy doing, Kevin?" he asked, as his hands lingered through her hair.

"He's shy, but I think he's doing well," she replied, as she washed the last of the dishes by hand and put them on the rack to dry. As Olivianna wiped the counters down, Anastacia came in, glowing from head to toe.

Kennedy gazed upon her with a wondering look. He then set his sights upon Olivianna and rubbed his belly. "Is she pregnant?" he asked.

No sooner than he asked, Anastacia began running for the powder room. Olivianna looked back at Kennedy, "By the sounds coming out of that room, I would say she is," she replied.

"I'm heading to the shed … want to help me wash the *Trans Am* again?" he asked, with a sly smile.

"James, the sous chef, will be here in ten minutes," she said with a wink, "I'll meet you in the barn".

Kennedy made his way out to the barn, where he heard a ratchet turning as he pulled the doors open. All he could see was his mechanic's red high-heeled shoes dangling out of the front of the car, when he heard Olivianna singing as she walked towards the barn. Realizing that he was at a crossroads and wanting the attention of both women, he began contemplating his next moves.

Olivianna's eyes tightened up, pulling hard on the joint hanging out of her mouth, when she offered Kennedy a hit, whereupon he laughed.

"Good thing!" he exclaimed. Making his way back into the barn, he shut the door and pulled up a chair so he could watch the show unfold. The sound of the metal wheels scraping the concrete floor captured his full attention as the creeper slid out from under the Pontiac emblem. Long slender legs, in black leather pants that clung to her like they were painted on, appeared when Olivianna got down on her hands and knees, and he nearly blew it right there.Kennedy jumped up so excited to be her oil boy, gathered what she asked for and got back down on his knees. She put out her right hand and snapped her fingers. "Hand me the wire strippers," she commanded. He looked at his hands, and it wasn't wiring strippers. Instead, it was shrink wrap on his rod.

"You're such a carny, Kennedy," Olivianna giggled, as she handed Blondie the soldering gun and wire strippers off from the hemp plastic rolling cart.

"What the hell was I thinking?" Kennedy asked himself, waking from his nap. "I must have been dreaming he mused as he fumbled through the toolbox until he found what she was looking for.Crawling back under the car, Kennedy watched as Olivianna pulled out a set of sockets.

"Your fan wires are fried," Blondie said, as she examined the wires and handed them to Kennedy. "Who wired them up last?" she asked caustically.

Not wanting her to know it was he who had screwed up, Kennedy tossed them in the trash and said, "Oh, I took it to some guy down the street".

"You mean, Harvey's Car Corral?" she asked, as she rolled the cart back under the front end.

Not knowing who the hell Harvey was, he uttered, "Yeah, I think it was him". "Just what the hell am I thinking?" he said to himself, "if I could just be like David Lee Roth and have both these women down on their knees, begging for me to take care of their sexual needs!".

It only took a few minutes before she had the wiring fully corrected. Her hands wrapped around the front bumper as the creeper made its way out. She stood up as her long blonde wavy hair swirled around. Her name tag hand was sewn up over her left breast, keeping Kennedy's eyes glued to her cleavage. Once she was clear of the car, Kennedy hit the button on the lift as it made its way down.

Olivianna quickly slid behind the steering wheel and turned the ignition. The Phoenix barley grumbled as she pumped the gas pedal. Blondie placed her hands on her hips, knowing this was going to take some more time she cocked her head to the right, and asked Kennedy to get her something to eat.

Obliging her request, he gladly ran to the kitchen. To his delight, there were several boxes of cupcakes on the kitchen table. He opened one of the boxes and saw two dozen assorted varieties. Grabbing one of the large boxes, he quickly ran back to the barn just in time to see Blondie bending over the left fender, with one leg cocked to the right.

Olivianna straddled to the other side of the fender panel, and Kennedy knew that he was in trouble when he mumbled, "Oh, dear Lord." Blondie's right hand quickly reached back out as she hollered, "I need a screwdriver".

"I bet you do," Kennedy said, as he rubbed his jaw and asked her what size she needed.

"A thin, flat head screwdriver will work," said Blondie, as she reached her right hand back out again.

Hearing her choice of words, Kennedy put the box of cupcakes down, fumbled through the drawer until he found what she needed. Jokingly, he said, "Well, I do not know if it's thin, but it's long" as he placed the driver in her hands. Kennedy picked up the box of cupcakes and sat back down in his chair as he watched Blondie writhing over the fender, making him want to smack her and tell her to get down. He ordinarily would never allow anyone to lean on his car like that, or so he thought, as he peeled the wrapper off what looked like Devil's Food and stuffed it in his mouth. Blondie had a way of making him bend on his rules as he watched her hips massage the front panel. Kennedy watched the two women intently as he popped each confection in his mouth.

He reached his hand between Blondie's leather pants, placing the sweet cake down on the machine. "I don't want your button scratching my paint," he scolded.

Blondie slid back down and said, "Then put some protection on it".

"Damn this one was easy," he thought, as he put the fender cover up against her tight leather pants, while watching her nibble on the baked goods he was now stuffing in her hands.

Olivianna pulled out a fat-handled screwdriver and began to give it a few turns, when she asked me for a taste of the cream-filled one. He was so happy to give her what she wanted. Before he knew it, the whole box of treats was gone when Olivianna pouted and said, "I only got one".

"I'll be right back," Kennedy said as he again ran to the kitchen to see what was next. He quickly opened the door, and on the table was a tier of cupcakes that looked like a set of stairs. He was so excited as he figured that these were for the guests, and knowing Blondie was a guest made the decision to take them a no-brainer, so out the door he went.

Within seconds, Kennedy was back in the barn, and there was Blondie spread over the top of the engine as her legs dangled over the side. He nearly bit his lip as the cupcakes fell when Olivianna pulled the red velvet off her legs, mesmerizing him once again.

Trying to finesse the piston into the connecting rod, she cranked her hard. Blondie started wailing as she lubed the bearings and caps. "Yes, ma'am," Kennedy sighed, obeying the command. He reached for some hemp wonder lube and squirted it in her hands. She slid her fingers up and down, making sure he had her all greased up before she connected the rod to her crankshaft and tightened it up. It was not long before she had her carburetor squirting with her cannabis infused fuel when she got back into the car and started it up.

Olivianna shrieked as the motor turned over, the sound of the I.A. II 505-cubic-inch motor with Edelbrock round port heads flowing 325 cfm of air as she bellowed, "Ladies and gentlemen, introducing the 'Road Paver' Roller Cam, giving it a rough and tough idle as she purrs. Topped with a ported Victor intake by Edelbrock on top, are the Holley Sniper EFI Hedman Headers with their 2-inch Primary tubes down to the 3-inch exhaust. "X" pipe to Race Pro Mufflers to 3-inch tail pipes to the 3-inch Trans Am splitters that made the car roar like some badass boy".

Kennedy looked at her and said, "How you managed to make me swoon over car parts, I don't know," as he handed Olivianna the keys. He washed the frosting off his beard, handed Blondie five thousand dollars in cash and told her that he would see her in a few weeks. His whole body was shaking as he headed back down to the house. He knew that his blood sugar was out of whack and was hoping to get another snack when he opened the back kitchen door, and standing there was Cupcakes by Kat with **Monique Outerbridge.** That's when he realized he had eaten the desserts for the wedding guests.

CHAPTER 15

THOSE MOLYNMINIS ARE SOMETHING ELSE.

Standing at the table was **Monique Outterbridge from Velvet Cakes by Gwen,** in her purple jacket with high heels to match.

"Oh my God, where have you been?" Kennedy asked as he reached out to give her a hug. "The last time I saw you was at the Grand Gala in Rhode Island last year. I remember you, you're **Monique Outterbridge**, right?"

"Yes, that's me," said Monique, looking back at Kennedy perplexed, "I just brought in about ten dozen cupcakes for a wedding reception between tonight and tomorrow, but they disappeared on me".

Kennedy slunk down in the chair and said, "Oh, my God, whose cupcakes were these for?"

Monique stood there with her mouth agape. "They were for the Alderman wedding, and I was asked to make a special delivery, so here I am. I was paid a lot of money to drive them up here!" she said, exasperated.

"Oh, my bad," Kennedy gasped. "Do not worry, I can smooth this all out, I am going to do you a solid and just team up from the start," he said, pulling hundreds out of his pocket. Frantically, he looks around the room and pins his eyes on Cupcakes by Kat and says, "You work here, right?" I've been here every week for the last three years as the Sous chef, Kennedy. Who do you think has been cooking your meals?"

Kennedy stood there for a moment, utterly speechless, as he began to think, rethink and think some more, then suddenly, he said, "I got an idea". "I want you to spend the next few days here, on me as my guest. As an apology for all the mix-ups. Give me the night to get something worked out. In fact, stay next week on us and enjoy the facilities at the Center of Love Club. I am going to work something out for you, hold tight and let me see what gets worked out, alright?" he said apologetically as he looked back at Cupcakes by Kat and said, "You can bake, right?"

"OK," said Monique, as she laughs at Kennedy, "I will give you a chance and see what you can do.

Monique, please enjoy some dinner in the dining room on me," he said, as he escorted her to the main dining hall that was already filled up. "We are having one of our specialties tonight, Lobster Ravioli with pan-seared sea scallops in a lobster champagne drizzle," as he looked back at Cupcakes by Kat and said, "fix her a plate".

"Oh my gosh, that sounds amazing," said Monique, "is that the only thing on the menu?".

"Oh, why no, we also have Osso Bucco with a creamy risotto with grilled zucchini and squash," Kat replied.

"Oh, my, that does sound good, I am already sold, but what is the third thing on the menu tonight?" inquired Monique.

"Our third entrée for this evening is thinly sliced chicken breast stuffed with crab and Shrimp Imperial in a roasted red tomato cream sauce, topped with fresh basil over vegetable pasta," Kat informed her, rather nonchalantly.

"Oh my God, that is going to be so tough to decide," said Monique, as she sat down and placed the napkin across her lap.

"Do not decide," said Kennedy as he looked into Kat's eyes, "Give her anything she wants, and drinks are on the house," he directed. "Trust me, Monique, I will make this worth your while," he said, "we have some special guests coming over tomorrow night". Kennedy ran to the front desk and pulled a set of keys off the shelf, and handed her a key in the shape of a heart. "It's my favorite guest room down the hall and prepare for a show of a lifetime," he said as he panted, breaking into a sweat.

"OK," Monique said, "then, I will see where the night takes me" as she buttered the bread that Kat had placed on the table. By the time dinner was over, she had five courses come her way, the glow of the fireplace and the long day made it easy for her to slip up to her suite. The quaint bedroom with the hand-carved four-poster bed had red velvet curtains that hung like tapestry over the rails and oval chairs with velvet crush back. She took a deep breath, poured some bath salts into the sunken garden tub and turned on the jets. "Trust the process," she thought to herself, as she slipped under the sheets and got ready for the long day ahead.

CHAPTER 16

CHARLOTTE'S CONTEMPLATION

My mind went back to when I was mingling with the men in the city all those years back. The secret lives that I could read in their eyes. I had forgotten what loving was like with spies, leaving me there standing in the cold rain as I picked up the shattered remains of the eggs broken on the flagstone.

My mind began to relive the many years of previous events as I looked out over the sea. Secrets I had kept quiet all these years now seem to be haunting me.I closed my eyes as I relived the moments in my mind, as I felt a tingle inside my thighs. Standing out overlooking the bay as I relived the feeling of him taking me over the wrought iron table again. I could almost smell his salty scent on me as I rubbed myself with a velocity that would cause a piece of wood to ignite, when, in a flash, he was beside me.

"I'm sorry, Charlotte, I did not mean to handle you like that. Something came over me when I saw you bending over the refrigerator, and I could not control myself," said Clinton softly.

"You were only reading my mind." I confessed, I like it like that, sometimes," as I winked. "I am so sorry, Clinton, this is just exciting and challenging, and I am not good at taking orders from anyone," I explained as I put my hands across my chest. "I have my own mind -- you know what I mean? I also did not realize you could read my thoughts that easily. You were only giving me what I secretly wanted, but I was too scared to say," I said as I buried my hands in my face, embarrassed by what could come out of me next.

"I knew this was going to be a challenge, Charlotte, but I am determined that I am going to stick this

through with you. I did not need to marry you to do all of this. I am marrying you because I love you, and I am the best one to guide you through what has already been determined that you are to do.I am your protector, but you need to trust me; it is for your own good."

"Where have I heard that before?" I replied as his words hung in the air. For the first time in a long time, I knew again what fear was. My mind went racing back to the oracle I had talked to one day when he asked, "Do you remember your orders?". I looked at him like he was crazy as I tried to pull away from the reading when the mystic called back out to me, "You can't run away from your destiny".

I took a deep breath, and I knew I trusted him. I knew what was in my past. I knew I saw the submarine last night. I knew deep down what all of this meant. "I thought this was all in the past," I said as I looked up at him.

He looked up into my eyes more deeply this time as he whispered into my ears. "I know who you were back then," as a bolt of lightning flashed across the sky, "you have a file, intelligence, CIA".

I closed my eyes as the breath fell out of my chest. "I don't know what you're talking about, Clinton," I tried to say.

"The look in your eyes said something else, Charlotte," he said, "let me ask you something, why did you get out of the game?".

Taking another deep breath, I stared blankly back at him, "The baby," is all I said. As I ran back out to the sea with the rain still pelting down on me, holding my stomach as it brought me down to my knees, I sobbed away for my lost baby.

Clinton came down next to me with a blanket and wrapped it around me. "Everything is going to be OK, Charlotte," he said softly.

"OK, Clinton, to tell you the truth, the torture was easy to deal with, in fact, I rather liked that they couldn't get anything out of me," I explained. "I would just laugh the way they would torture me, close my eyes and just pretend it was a game and learned to laugh at the pain, "then I found out I was pregnant, knew my life was going to change".

Clinton just looked out at the sea. "Come back up to the house and get a bath," he said as he helped me up from the ground. "The sun is getting ready to come up, and the work crew will be here soon," he said in a loving tone.

I wiped away my tears as I walked back up the steps. "Do you want me to cook you some breakfast?" I asked, in a deflated, halfhearted attempt to put aside my anguish.

"Not now, thanks," he said, "go take a bath and get some rest, we're going to be leaving for Delaware for a few weeks and we have a lot of business that we do in that state, and then, it's off to Mississippi for some training".

"What's in Mississippi?" I mumbled as I wiped my eyes of the mascara that had run down my cheeks.

"One of the *Center of Love* retreats – it's an old sugar plantation that does weddings in a barbecue theme – a beautiful antebellum mansion that speaks volumes to me," he said, as we walked into the back kitchen door.

"How many places do you guys have?" I asked as I walked up the steps and headed to the bathroom.

"Seven as of right now and I just picked up another one," he said with a wink.

My eyes lit up when I asked about Bear Pond.

"Maybe, if you're a good girl," he said in jest, maybe Lake Wytopitlock too if you're good!

I started to jump up and down and twirl about. "You're kidding me, right?

"The goal is to be the best cannabis themed all-inclusive healing retreats in the United States, and I want you to be the mother of it – the mother of all Cannabis Healing!" he beamed.

"And this place is ours too, Clinton?" I asked.

"Yes, Charlotte, this one is ours, but in all reality, it's all yours," he replied.

I ran up the steps, not sure what I should do: sneak out the side door and run away or go to the tub and accept everything. Walking back to the room where the garden tub overlooked the bay. I put the plug in and opened the "Ocean Hot" valve and let the saltwater come in. Sitting down as the water came up to my legs, I heard his voice behind my ear as he poured the water over my hair.

"Charlotte, can I ask you a question about your delivery?" asked Clinton.

I put my hands up around my face, hoping he did not expect an answer to the inquisition he had just placed on me. I began to go back to what happened that day as I slid under the water and held onto the scar that reminded me of what was once inside of me.

"I never even saw him," I began to say, "one minute I had something kicking inside of me and hours later I had nothing to show for it, as if he never existed," as the tears filled my eyes. "I never got to hold him; they just said he did not make it, and that was that," I concluded. Clinton sat on the edge of the tub as he rubbed my leg.

"I am sorry, Charlotte," he said, "I did not realize that happened to you".

"It is very strange when you can feel a heartbeat or a kick, then wake up with your leg in a cast and nothing inside of you with no explanation of anything. That is when I went to Maine. Aunt Mable and my Aunt Betty were friends. They lived together for years; they took care of me while I healed. Then I got back up on my feet, and I forgot all about everything. I just dove into my work and stayed to myself," I explained. I slipped back under the water and let it swallow all of me up, hoping the salt would wash my wounds away. When I came back up, Clinton was still there.

"Who was the father of your baby?" he asked.

I felt like a rat in a cage as I slid back under the water, trying to pretend that I didn't hear anything. I came back up, embarrassed by his request, "I don't know … some foreign diplomat." I mumbled.I slid back under the sea, hoping he would leave me alone and not question me on anything anymore. I could feel him as he walked away, and I was relieved that he heard me inside my head.

I did my hair and makeup and put on a new purple dress and a pair of heels that had mysteriously found their way into my suitcase. Feeling better, I walked back to the outdoor kitchen and wrapped the apron around my waist, whipped up some eggs and sprinkled them with some cheese. Sitting under the canopy as the coffee began to percolate, I tried to block everything that had just happened out of my mind.

It didn't matter anyway, as my mind went back to the past. I was just helping. He was so strong and powerful that I got all caught up way too fast, playing a game I had no business in, as I fumbled with my coffee cup, hoping he could hear my confession in his head. I did not dare repeat any more of it and closed my eyes as I heard footsteps approaching, when I looked to my right and saw two men in hard hats coming in.

I took a deep breath, grateful that my thoughts were interrupted, as I extended my hand. "I'm Charlotte," I said.

Clinton introduced us, "This is Ralph, and you're in good hands," he said.

"So, you are the one who snagged Mr. Tuckerman," Ralph said, as he handed me some blueprints. "Do you have a few moments to talk to me about the indoor kitchen?" he asked.

Relieved that my wishes had been granted so fast, I walked into the kitchen with the blueprints in hand. The more I thought about it, the more I couldn't help but think of one kitchen with moss-colored painted cabinets that I had seen in one of the houses we looked at last week. The pink and black granite with veins large and thick, and the bull nose design around the center island, stood out in my mind. "Keep the sink and refinish with white porcelain," I specified. I then asked for a wall of glass that looked over the cove, with a stretch of counter tops, from one side to the end and went out the side door to a room that did not have much of anything going on when I scribbled 'Butler's Pantry' on the floor plan. "Viking stove and the two side by side, refrigerators and freezers, plus commercial dishwashers, in the center island and sunken lights in the ceiling," I continued.

"Oh, and what about the smaller house, Mrs. Tuckerman?" he asked.

I was startled for a moment when I heard the name in the air, not sure if I wanted that name, but then again, I was known as "Eggs" Benedict for years. I stood on the patio overlooking the water, as I closed my eyes, listening intently to our itinerary. "I'll let you know," I replied.

"We have a meeting with the Governor of Delaware, who is coming for a scheduled tour of our skin care manufacturing plant in Newark. The newspapers, WDEL radio, and Channel 6 will be there. Our company is getting ready to go public, and this is an excellent time for you to meet all the other angels who are a part of our team," Clinton briefed.

"I took the liberty of having a wardrobe for you ordered," said Clinton, "and see that you are fond of the purple dress". "It looks beautiful on you," he said, as he kissed my cheek.

I smiled as I looked back up at him. He was wearing a black pin-striped suit and a lavender dress shirt with a diamond pattern print of deep purple in the tie. His shiny black dress shoes caught the sun. He looked so incredible in that moment, standing up next to the God of the Sea fountain, and, for a moment, I wondered if they were one and the same. I stood back up and flattened out my dress, admiring the way that I looked. As my purple heels clicked with each step, I began to feel a bit more important. The day seemed to disappear as I relaxed on the patio chairs. For dinner, we took the boat and headed across the water for the fish and chips I was promised before we let the night fade.

CHAPTER 17

THE BIG TUNA CALLS

The end of September is marked with its chilly nights as Kennedy breathed in the scent of the smoke swirling out of the chimney, and he knew Karissa would have some pot of something on the back burner simmering. Walking inside the house, where Karissa sat at the kitchen table, sipping on hot tea.He leaned down, gave her a kiss and said, "honey, I had a royal screw up at Camp Werthefukrwe tonight".

Karissa looked up at him, knowing that he was lying through his teeth. "Which was it Kennedy: you screwed someone tonight or you screwed something up tonight?" she asked, perceptively.

The temperature of the room went up twenty degrees, and Kennedy knew she had him pegged. In a matter-of-fact kind of tone, Kennedy says, "Well, I ate all of Monique Outerbridge's cupcakes! With a look of utter horror, Karrissa gasped, "You did what!?It's not my fault, I did not tell you **Velvet Cakes by Gwen** was going to be here, it's not my fault, you know I have a weakness for her cupcakes!

"Oh, no, Kennedy, you have got to be kidding me," she said, noticeably irritated, as she rubbed her head with her hands, trying to get her brain to calculate when she looked up at him and said, "Do you have any idea what this means?"

"I know Karissa, but you know I told you **Velvet Cakes by Gwen** are the best, and then I saw them sitting on the table, you know me, I had the munchies!" he exclaimed.

As much as I want to freak out right now, I think I understand what's going on, Karissa mouthed. Trying to embrace what was going to be the ultimate challenge of the year is blowing my mind right now. You do know, you must replace and follow Her recipes to a T and on top of all that, The Center of Love Club kitchens must have 420 Cannabis infused Cupcakes, in six different assorted flavors, in less than 6 hours for the fundraiser happening on Saturday night, she shouted!

"Piece of cake, Kennedy scoffs, I got it all figured out and I already talked to Kat and made a few phone calls".

"So now what?" Karissa said, as she got up from her chair and went to the refrigerator, pulled out ten pounds of butter and put it on the counter.

"Well, this is the deal: tomorrow morning we get Olivianna, Anastacia and Kat, and we have them do a bake off," he said.

"What, you mean like a contest?" asked Karissa as she walked into the pantry, pulled out a fifty-pound bag of confectioners' sugar and threw it upon the counter.

"Yes… Exactly, it's about who makes the best cannabis infused cupcakes," he said.

"Who are we going to get to judge that on such short notice?" asked Karissa as she fumbled through the magazines on the shelf. "What do you think the chances are of getting the editor of High Times to come as Kennedy? Rubbed his forehead. Thoughts of the Badd Dabber raced through his head as he opened a box of Corn Pops and poured them into his hand. Suddenly, the back kitchen door opened and in walked Aunt Mabel with her cane in hand. Kennedy shrieked as the Corn Pops went flying in the air!

"What are you guys smoking and why did you summon us like that?" asked Aunt Mabel indignantly, as she cracked her cane on the kitchen chair.

Karissa laughed at Kennedy as he looked for a broom to defend himself with, when, in walked the Badd Dabber himself and his entourage of friends.

Karissa looked up from her spell book and gave Kennedy a wink. "Here you go, gentleman, you can either stay here or go down to *Camp Werthefukrwe*," she said, "it's your call".

"Well, where is the party at?" asked the Badd Dabber.

"The parties are everywhere, you just get to choose what type of party you like," Kennedy replied. "It is all inside *The Secret Life*," Kennedy said with a smile as he took Karissa's hand. "Do you feel like going out for a flight tonight?" he asked.

Smiling, she looked up at him and said, "Is this your way of trying to recover your fumble?".

Aunt Mabel gazed at the stack of baking supplies that was sitting on the counter, then looked over at Karissa.

"I told you he would eat those cupcakes," she said.

"It is not all he ate," Karissa added, as she crossed her arms across her chest and glared back down at Kennedy.

Aunt Mabel rolled her eyes and gave Kennedy a look of disgust. "I hope they were good," she said.

"Uh huh," as Kennedy smugly grinned.

With a look of horror, Karissa turned to Kennedy and said, "Don't tell me you have been hanging out with politicians again, you know how dirty they are!" as she reached for a bottle of **Anti-Corruption Mist** and began spraying him down.

A look of relief suddenly came over Kennedy's face when he took a deep breath and knew he was safe. Aunt Mabel waved goodbye and headed off to bed, while the Badd Dabber and his entourage took flight to the camp.

Flying in the night sky high above the trees, Kennedy and Karissa watched as the Badd Dabber and his entourage landed at the camp. They made sure that they were taken care of, then took off for a walk along the water's edge. Kennedy held her in his arms, then opened his wings, and off they went to scan the surface of the lake. The playfulness bubbled with joy as they bantered in flight on the way to the mountains that had become their natural habitat in the moonlight. His wings expanded in the night sky, the reflection on the lake as he watched a bass jump out and take flight. He could feel his eagle eyes open as he spied a family of moose off in the distance, as the glow of *Camp WERTHEFUKRWE* came into view.

The fire pit outside burned brightly into the night, and they watched in the distance as the guests danced on the shore. They looked at the people who were now recovering from life's challenges, as they carefully surveyed everything they had accomplished. Standing with their wings outstretched, they caught a glimpse of our newest angel, Kevin, not yet sure of his role, as Olivianna took him under her wing.

Kennedy looked over at Karissa with a surprised look. "She can fly?" he said.

"Yeah, turns out she just needed a family that accepted her," said Karissa, as her wings spread out before taking flight.

As Kevin's wings spanned open, trying to catch up, his feathers began taking on a different hue as they went from dark black to a gray. "I think that's going to be good for him, you can tell he is so lost in his thoughts still," said Kennedy as Kevin flapped his wings harder.

Karissa landed near the edge, not wanting to get her feathers wet. "I have a feeling he is going to make it through; he just needs a different teacher," she said.

Within seconds, they heard Olivianna's distinct voice, as she wrapped her wings around Kevin and led him into flight. Standing back and watching, as he clung to her belly, one could tell he was scared as she swooped up over the canopy.

"There is something about how Maine brings out the angels," Kennedy said, as he looked over at Kevin howling through the night air, clinging tightly to Olivianna.

"He seems to trust her," said Karissa. "Should we bring him down to keep him with her?" she asked.

Kennedy looked at Karissa and said, "That is a particularly good idea, see if they can hear our thoughts and let us call them to us". Within seconds, Olivianna had Kevin at our feet. "You called? she laughed.

Standing there like a baby deer caught in headlights, Kevin looked at us with our wings still outstretched, and Kennedy put his hand on his shoulder and said, "Now that's telepathy!" "You up for a drive, son?" he asked.

Karissa stepped in between the two of them, "We could use someone with restaurant experience for a wedding in Mississippi, a strong man like you who could help with chairs and tables," she said.

Scratching his head, still not knowing what he was supposed to say, thinking back to the day when he placed rolled napkins on linen tablecloths, Kevin thought to himself that he could do that.

He nodded and said, "I did serve Clinton and Charlotte out in the enchanted forest the other day".

"I hear you're a good cook, too," said Kennedy, as he wrapped his arms around him. "You are going to be alright, son," he said, "I can tell you will be getting your wings soon".

Kevin looked up at Kennedy, as if he had two heads coming out of his body. "I don't know about all that, but it was sure fun riding her," he said.

"Say, do you play poker, son? I've got a bet to place in Delaware Park over the next couple of days," said Kennedy, as his phone rang. Kennedy pulled out his phone and as the flashing tone read Benny Cohen, he answered the call, putting it on speaker so they could all listen in.

"Kennedy, this is Benny Cohen. How are you doing?I got everything all set up for you when you get to Delaware. You remember the new party that I was telling you about last week?" he said.

"Yes, I do," Kennedy replied, as he looked at the fleet of angels before him, flapping their wings, "IPUS, is what you're calling it, right?".

"Yes, that is it, it is all going through, we've got a Grand Gala happening, and that is just the start. Be prepared for the party of your life, and do not forget when you get to the gate, tell them the Big Tuna sent you," said Benny.

With that, the phone went dead, and Kennedy just stared into the eyes of the fleet of angels before him with their wings now fully splayed.

"I can do that, sir," said Kevin, as he looked up to Kennedy with his wings protruding. "I mean, I can play poker if that's what you want," he said, "but I don't know anything about politics, though some say that politics is a lot like a poker game".

"Me, neither," said Kennedy, "and I don't know how to play Poker, too, but I need a man who can play the game while we negotiate a few things". It's Owner's Day at Delaware Park, and the purses are big. Our contact is referred to as 'The Big Tuna', but his real name is Benjamin Cohen.

"You mean the guy who just called?" said Kevin, as he strained to remember the sounds of the man's voice. He walked around the shoreline, taking it all in, knowing he was getting involved in something that felt right to him.

"Yes, that's him," said Kennedy, "our manufacturing facility is in Delaware, where the Revolution started. This is where all our other angels make our all-natural skin care line. I think it might not be a bad idea to get a jump start on things and see how the team is doing. I know Clinton is having the Governor of Delaware tour the facilities in a few days.

Karissa looked to Kennedy and said, "Well, we better get this show on the road". She turned to Kevin. "Can you roll with the punches?" she asked.

"I guess so," replied Kevin, as he cracked his jaw and fluffed out his wings. "I thought I was the crazy one all these years, but it looks like I am not the only one," he said, laughing, as he took off in flight.

Kennedy's wings emerged as he sprinted across the lake, concentrating on sending his message to Kevin telepathically. "You'll be witnessing lots of stranger things, I can see it already in your eyes that you are one of us. It's just going to take some time for you to figure it all out, all in due time, my son, in due time," as his wingtip rubbed Kevin's head in flight.

Karissa outstretched her arms to Kevin as he flew across the Northern Sky with hues of green and pink.She looked to him with her most beautiful eyes and said, "Once you realize you can do anything your imagination dreams up, the Universe supports you and provides for you with the tools to achieve your dreams. You must believe, as your mind is limitless".

"I can already see it," Olivianna chimed in, "you've got management experience, don't you?" She flew across the sky doing all kinds of tricks in the air, from back flips to swooping down to the water, then springing high up to the trees, where she ruffled a night owl to fly with her.

"Well, yes ma'am," I also like to fish," he said, as he dove into the water and grabbed a large Bass with the talons that had just emerged from his legs.

Kennedy looked at Kevin as he tore the fish apart and ate it raw. "I take it you like Sushi," he said.

The fleet of angels began to laugh when Karissa said, "We have another property in Rhode Island where we will be having weddings, starting in the summer season. That just might be the place for you, so let us see what you can do over the next few weeks. Plus, when we seal the deal in Delaware, it will cause a shift like nothing we have ever seen. Are you ready for your life to change, son?" said Kennedy.

Taking a deep breath, Kevin looked at the fleet of angels flying in the sky and said, "Yeah, yeah, I am ready for my life to change".

"Good, go get some sleep," Karissa said, and we'll see you both in the morning in the kitchen. Kennedy and Karissa flew back to Lake Kezar, while Kevin put on another show and let himself emerge. Like a shooting star, he whirled through the treetops at lightning speed, as the spectators down below gazed at him.

CHAPTER 18

GOING DOWN ON THE FARM

The morning approached as Charlotte went through the clothes and found a red suit that flattered her figure, and put it on. She walked back through the house as her eyes met the portrait of Abraham Lincoln in what appeared to be an oil print, not realizing that Clinton was right behind her with the suitcases packed.

"We have got another plane to catch, and we will be landing in Maine," as he slipped his hands around her waist and brought her close to him.

Taking a deep breath, Charlotte looked into Abe Lincoln's eyes, "I'll see you later," she said, as she took Clinton's hand. "Where to next?" she asked.

Smiling, Clinton said, "Daddy's got a sweet tooth today, and a little surprise up my sleeve". Outside, sitting in the driveway was a black Cadillac. The driver got out and took the luggage into the back of the sedan. Clinton opened the door to the back seat of the car and let me slide in before sitting next to me. We pulled away, heading for the small field where a private plane was waiting. I looked up to see "the Wildcat" in the pilot's seat and knew instinctively that today would be a good day.

The view from the plane of red, orange, and yellow foliage and the abundant number of lakes came into full view, and I sighed, knowing I was back in Maine once again. The plane landed, and another black Cadillac pulled up to the tarmac. Within twenty minutes, we were pulling back up the driveway to the very farm that had called to me once again. As we walked into the kitchen of *Camp Werthefukrwe, the one in Aroostook County,* the line of chefs stood in a row, each in colored vests. I nodded at Olivianna in red when Karissa handed me a purple vest with my name in gold, embroidered into the left breast. I shook Monique Outterbridge's hand, remembering her from the Meet 'n Greet in her purple jacket and knew that something special was happening. I shook the hand of the young gentleman and saw that his name was Kevin. There was another team in blue with Anastacia and James with the *Center of Love* Logo embroidered in flames, and I knew this was going to be an amazing competition.

Clinton took the lead. "Look, we have some incredibly special guests coming in tonight and we are being judged by not only top cannabis professionals, but the top names in the baking industry with some high-end celebrity chefs in attendance, if you know what I mean," he said, "are you ready for a fight of a lifetime?".

We all looked at each other as we started clapping and high-fiving it all around, when Kennedy said, "Let's take a walk out to the barn where we have a special kitchen set up for you all". We walked into another door, and I looked over at Clinton, knowing that this was the very room he was talking about before.

Once inside, it was like a dream, with three separate stations all in matching formation, when I recognized a chef from my past as Cupcakes by Kat stood at the purple station, and I knew this would be on blast as Kennedy walked to the left, over to the blue portable oven on wheels. He gave it a whirl and said, "Anastacia and James, these are for you". "Olivianna and Kevin, your station is to the right," he continued, as he pulled out a stainless-steel cart with a bright red Kitchen Mixer with stainless steel bowls and matching red spatulas.

"Can I take these home when I win?" mused Kevin.

"Yes," Kennedy laughed, "you get to keep everything". He then walked over to Charlotte and Kat. "My dear ladies, you are in the middle," just as Monique entered the building.

I looked at the stainless-steel cart with the purple mixer and matching bowls. I looked over to Monique and said, "You know, we're going to blow them out of the barn".

"You got that right," said Monique as she took out her phone and took a few photos. I'm posting the announcement now, on Instagram, Twitter and Facebook".

Karissa pointed over to the pantry. "The pantry is full and has everything that you could possibly need, the walk-ins are stocked, and you have access to every cannabis strain that we grow on the property that is already infused inside a butter base," she said, "and you are being judged on taste, infusion, presentation and over all cosmic effect". "May the best baker win!" she exclaimed.

With that, the ovens were turned on, and the butter was dropped into the stainless-steel bowls, while a flurry of colors ran around the secret room when things began to ignite. A cloud of confectioners' sugar filled the air when Charlotte dropped the bag on the floor. Kennedy laughed hysterically when she stood up with sugar all over her face. He walked over to her with a wet towel and began to wipe her face down. Clinton cleared his throat, and she knew that she had better settle down. The mixers were spinning, as the distinct scent of sweet potatoes and cinnamon filled the room, when the first batch of cupcakes was showcased on Zoom.

By 12 Noon, the first round was plated and submitted to the judges. The bridal party was beyond thrilled as they popped each creation into their mouths. The wedding this weekend, as Kennedy took center stage, was for none other than the chief editor of the Cannabis Parade. We watched the smile that came upon his face, and before we knew it, the founder of the Cannabis Awards Show was nibbling on his plate, with judges from all over the country walking up to toast the bride. The Center of Love Club was proving to be one green surprise.

As each confection came rolling across the lawn, the party that had been brewing was reaching maximum form. It was not long before the bride and groom walked up to the altar, tied the hemp knot, and announced the winner for the Cannabis Cup Cake Award. Monique stood high, brimming with pride, holding onto her Molyn Minis and the award she did not even know she was after, when, out of the crowd, CupCakes by Kat, otherwise known as Kathy DeMatteis, appeared with a check for ten thousand dollars. Man, did the crowd cheer when she made her an offer for a guest appearance in Delaware!

CHAPTER 19

SOUTHERN BOUND

It was nearly 6 pm as Karissa and Aunt Mabel heard the rumble of the engine of the Trans Am as she rolled up on the trailer. Olivianna and Kevin were running around bringing in the cakes, as the staff received all the last-minute instructions for the week. This week would be easy, as the cabins were being rented for a large family gathering. Kennedy walked down the steps with his suitcase and turned to Aunt Mabel. "I have your stable – oops, I mean your chariot awaits you," he said, as he giggled at his last attack. Picking up the pace, he ran back in to grab Karissa's suitcase. "Let's go!" he hollered.

Aunt Mabel came around the side of the mobile home, complaining, "It's time for bed, I didn't get any sleep last night with all the partying".

Kennedy looked over at Aunt Mabel, who was wearing a flannel night gown with socks that lost their elastic at least three years ago in what looked like moose-shaped bed slippers and an old blue sweater with what looked like a ketchup stain, as

Kennedy laughed to himself. "Whoop, whoop, Fashion Police," he mocked, twirling around the driveway, with his fingers mimicking the lights of a police car."I thought of everything, Aunt Mabel," he said, as he started to snicker, handing her some rolled oats from out of a brown bag.

Karissa glared at Kennedy, scowling she quickly grabbed the bag of oats out of his hand and stuffed it in her pocket as she hollered "I took a nap already, so I'll start the first leg," she said, "so, why don't you get some rest and let me take care of the driving as she hoped up in the Captain's chair and buckled up.

Kennedy looked at his charming wife with a smile on his face, "I knew I picked the best woman," as he plopped down in the passenger seat and buckled up.

She looked back at him and mumbled, "You bet you did".

As the moon hovered over the night sky, the cannabis food truck in disguise went quietly down the road. "Wake me up when we get to New York," Kennedy hollered out, putting in his earplugs and a towel over his head and conked out as Karissa started the first leg south.

It was not much past a quarter to eleven when the sounds of "Pull over… this is the ball buried police" awakened me out of my dream. Looking over my shoulder to see Olivianna sleeping, as Aunt Mabel was slumped in her chair. "I gotta go to the bathroom, Karissa," Kennedy said, "where are we at?"

"New York," replied Karissa, "you just missed the Tappan Zee Bridge, give me five minutes and we'll be on the Garden State Parkway".

The rest stop was fast approaching, and we pulled up for some gas. As Kennedy made his way back from the bathroom, a couple of young men who looked like they were looking for a hit were talking with Karissa about the Trans Am. Kennedy pulled the nozzle out of the tank and told Karissa to get back in the motor home.

Karissa exclaimed, "We can't leave right now, Aunt Mabel's not back!"

"What?" shouted Kennedy with his arms waving in the air. "Where did the old bat get to now?" he asked, as he went looking around the back.

Karissa glared at Kennedy, "She's an old lady, please have some respect".

Olivianna came, walking around the front of the motor home, when she went up to Kennedy and whispered, "Aunt Mabel is talking with some young men at the back, and I think she thinks she's twenty-three again".

Kennedy and Karissa started walking around the back of the mobile home, when out of the corner of his eyes, came more young guys, ogling over the Golden Trans Am. "Let me do the talking … understand?" Kennedy said, as Karissa adjusted her bra straps. Kennedy wiped the sweat that was beading up on his head, as Karissa hollered out, "Aunt Mabel, where you at?"

"Back here, dear," replied Aunt Mabel, as she waved 'come back here".

"Damn it Karissa, Kennedy sputtered, "what part of get in the motor home did you not understand?

"I don't know, maybe it is the part where I know I am better at this," she replied, as they reached the back of the motor home.

Aunt Mabel's whole belly laughs echoed throughout the parking lot when she bellows out, "These fine gentlemen here were asking me all kinds of questions on this car, I thought you could answer them best," she said triumphantly, as she gave Kennedy the finger, holding it close to her chest.

Kennedy clapped his hands together. "Well, gentlemen, as you can see, my old Aunt Mabel is a bit crazy," he said coldly, as he tried to drag her by the old blue sweater and get her into the motor home.

The tall, skinny young man with greased-back hair chimed in with, "What are you doing out this time of night, grandpa?" as the young men laughed.

"Sir, excuse me, but that woman told us you were her husband," the gas attendant asked, "what's it like to have sex with old ladies?" he asked, as the group of young men laughed.

Just then, Karissa came walking back around the bend, wearing her leopard print curve-fitting dress with her cleavage bursting out of the top. With her black purse dangling from her shoulder, she leaned over the wooden split rail. Just then, a Ferrari came whizzing by, as the wind blew her hair, her bronze lips stared us down through the split rails. "I can't find my ring!" she yelled.

"How do you handle that?" the taller young man asked Kennedy.

"Carefully, very carefully," he replied, handing him his business card, "you might need me someday," as Kennedy winked and walked away.

The kid holding the black card with gold embossing read it out loud. "Kennedy McCormick, President of **What's Your Fantasy?**".

Kennedy walked over to where Karissa was dangling over the wood, helped her back up and said, "OK, I get it … you do good work" as they walked together back into the motor home. Kennedy sat down in the driver's seat.

The young man watched in disbelief as the motor home pulled out onto the Garden State Parkway, kissing the card before putting it in his wallet, as Aunt Mabel waved goodbye from the bedroom window.

"That was close, Kennedy," Olivianna chimed out, as she pulled a breakfast sandwich from the refrigerator and heated it up in the microwave.

"I know," said Kevin, as he continued to pretend he was still asleep under the blankets, "I thought they were going to rob us, thinking we were rich or something".

Kennedy was now thoroughly fired up. "Let us forget about him for now, it's on to Atlantic City, where I rented a room along the shore," he said. "One coin in a slot machine and I promise we will be out there in less than four hours," he continued, "take a shower or a bath, I got a babysitter for Aunt Mabel, and Olivianna is hanging in for the ride".

"Wait, Kennedy … What did you do?" questioned Karissa.

"I arranged a date for Aunt Mabel and, if all goes according to plan, I just got her laid for the weekend and out of my hair," he said wryly.

"You know, she likes women, don't you?" replied Karissa.

"Of course, I do, I'm not blind and I see how's she been drooling over you," said Kennedy, "trust me, she'll be happy with this pick, then we'll have a nice little drive over to Delaware, where Kevin and I are placing a bet at the racetrack". He turned his attention to Kevin. "Got some Tuna on the menu?" he asked with a wink.

A brilliant display greeted us as we walked into the atrium. After checking in, we headed all the way up the elevator. The door opened to the Presidential Suite, overlooking the Atlantic City shoreline. Dinner was already on the table, and our guest would be arriving in a moment. The door opened and in walked Rebecca, a hot brunette with a heart shaped ass, who had just buried her last rich woman.

"I got this, Kennedy," she said as she poured the old woman a drink. "I'm a few years younger and I carry my own gun," she stated, pointing to a duffle bag of toys.

"Perfect," said Kennedy, as he grabbed Karissa and told Kevin to follow suit. "We've got to get out of here," as he ran back to the motor home. Pulling out on the Atlantic City Expressway, he high-tailed it to the Delaware Memorial Bridge.

CHAPTER 20

ANGELS IN MY DREAM

The plane touched down at the New Castle County Airport, and it made its way to a large hangar, where a limousine picked us up. "I did a book signing at the Christiana Mall last year," I told Clinton, as I looked out the window, tapping on the glass.

"I know," he responded, "I kept tabs on you". Soon, we pulled into The Inn at Christiana, a charming old home that sat along the banks of the Christiana River.

"One of the old stomping grounds for President George Washington back in the day", I heard a voice say.

"You don't say," I replied, as I turned the corner to see Thomas Jefferson staring back at me, with his belly a bit swollen by all the food he ate, hovering before me in his ghostly shape.

"Boy, did he love his cannabis," said one of his maids, as her image flashed past me so quickly before they all disappeared through the bookcase.

All of this happened before I even set foot on the staircase of this beautiful estate. I looked up and was greeted by Antonio, the innkeeper, who handed Clinton an envelope with a set of keys. I briefly stared back at him, with the way of his dark hair and olive complexion that could make any woman fall. I quickly turned my eyes away and focused on the little gift shop that was filled with all the products that the *Center of Love* manufactures. I saw a mannequin with a plush robe, with the Center of Love embroidered with purple thread. I saw rows of all-natural deodorants, and I picked up a bottle that read, **"Heart Chakra, Energy Mist,"** and pumped it through the air so I could smell it.

Clinton started going over all the things we needed to know about the manufacturing of our products, as he took me into a bedroom on the second floor. "I take it you own this house, too," I said, as I looked outside at the collection of trees, bearing fruit.

"Yes, this is another property associated with the *Center of Love*. His arms encircled my waist as he drew me in closer. "Do you remember the edible cannabis sugar scrub you massaged into me on our first date?" he asked.

"Yes, I do," I said, blushing.

"Well, that's not made here," he chuckled.

"Why not?" I asked, annoyed.

"Delaware has not freed the cannabis plant to its people yet," he replied informatively.

"What are they waiting for?" I asked.

"I don't know, you would think that the State of Delaware would also want the title of being the First State in the Union that set the cannabis plant free to its people," he said.

Clinton pulled the chair out from the desk and sat down, looking up at me. "Without a doubt in my mind, this is about a deal that they made long ago. You know, so much is done with good intentions; however, when you see the epic failure this has wrought, you need to rise and stand for a cause".

"With the overwhelming evidence by our own government studies, it proves the plant is not only safe, but healing, and you know, Clinton, this is what frosts me so much about this," I said, as I began to stomp around the room, thoroughly infuriated."It makes me wonder why the holdup?" I continued."Why don't they want healing for the People?" I finally asked, as I slammed my fist down on the desk, "just because the wood pulp, paper, plastics, and nylon rope lobbies couldn't stand the competition from natural hemp and wanted to corner the market, and drug companies couldn't patent it." I sat there for a moment, realizing how heated and perceptive I had become, when I looked over at Clinton and asked, "So, this is why you want me to run?".

"Well, that was easy enough," he said, as he got up from the chair and put his jacket back on, "there's way too much money in keeping you sick".

"That's right, Big Pharma hates it, too," I replied calmly.

"Grab your purse and let's go," instructed Clinton, "I have something I want to show you".

I let our words ring in my ears when I began cataloging all the pills I had been taking for years. It's no secret that the restaurant industry is known for way bigger drugs than cannabis. Ending the night with a bottle of vodka, just to drown out all of it, and the staff addicted to pain killers, when something safe, natural, non-addictive was sitting right there in front of our noses.

"That is where you come in, Charlotte," he said, gazing deeply into my eyes.

I looked up to see Thomas Jefferson again, standing there at the top of the steps, before looking back at Clinton. "What do you mean that I don't understand?" I asked. I turned again to stare at the ghost that penned the Constitution with a quill in hand, when I quickly turned away.

"The government does not deserve any piece of this pie," he said, as Clinton laid out his reasons why."They have destroyed many people's lives by making this plant illegal. State legislators do not deserve to capitalize on this. We will never be able to make restitution to all the families that bad legislation has ruined, but we can begin to heal them by giving them back their freedom," he elaborated.

We walked outside the front door, where I looked up the street and saw George Washington on his horse as he led a charge running off into the woods. The door to the limousine was shut as I looked back out to the smoke that was misting in the air, and spied Thomas Jefferson dragging on his pipe. "Tobacco, my ass," I laughed.

Clinton continued: "So many men and women, growing in secret as they could," he said, "They are the real heroes, and they sacrificed for all of us."It's just like the government to come in and steal what others have worked hard for and sacrificed for. With your help, Charlotte, your signatures will secure what many of us have fought and died for in this country. That all people have the right to Life, Liberty, and the Pursuit of Happiness," he concluded.

"What a minute, Clinton, I have a burning question," I said, looking straight ahead. "The Declaration of Independence says that we have the right to be in pursuit of happiness, and we know that happiness is achieved when the human body is in homeostasis."

"That is correct, Charlotte, and now we know that science has already proven homeostasis happens when the endocannabinoid system is being fed, thus creating balance in the body," he specified.

"In summary, based on what Thomas Jefferson wrote then, is not the prohibition of cannabis essentially against the principles upon which our country was founded?" I asked.

"Yes, my dear, it is a good argument," Clinton replied as he patted my knee, "are you sure there is not a lawyer tucked somewhere inside that pretty head of yours?".

All this revelation happened before the car door shut, and I was simply blown away by this man. "Clinton, why aren't you running?" I asked in awe.

"Clinton looked at me inquisitively. "Really, Charlotte, did you forget what my name is? Plus, this is not how I operate; what I do is show people what is inside of them, and you can do this, Charlotte – I know you can," he explained. "Holding a natural plant hostage is unconstitutional and, in time, the leaders will see that no state or government has the right to deny the happiness of the people by starving the body of vital nutrients". He began to glow as his voice resonated further. "Some of our employees have Down syndrome, some are in wheelchairs, and some are labeled 'bipolar'.This plant has been proving its value for thousands of years. These last one hundred is just a little blip on the radar in the overall picture, however, it is imperative to the survival of our nation that we put our red and blue, black and white differences aside and go PURPLE".

As we pulled into the parking lot of the Christiana Mall, I smiled, remembering that day last year. I looked at my suit and said, "Clinton, shouldn't I be wearing purple instead of red, then?".

"Yeah, I was just waiting on you," he said as he took my hand and got out of the car. We walked down the main courts until he took me into a shop with a large butterfly that said *Foobellas* on top. In the front window, there was a small kitchen where you could watch a soap crafter measuring out ingredients."Do you make all the products here in the mall?" I asked?

"No, we just do this as a form of advertising," he replied, "most of our soaps are made inside the state prison as an exit program for those wanting to participate". He handed me a little sliver of soap that was sitting in a bowl. "See how it feels," he said. I rolled up my sleeves and put my hands under the running water, and let the bar called "Field of Visions" lather up in my hands.

Clinton took center stage and said, "We have incentive programs for productivity where our employees earn gift cards at the end of each day from area businesses. We work with a broad spectrum of people and have managed through our programs to have a family of sorts. There will be a lot of press today. Jason, the plant manager, will be showing you around and introducing you to everyone. We have a few group homes in nearby neighborhoods where people who have no family can stay. It's modeled like the farm in Maine, except we only manufacture non-cannabis products here, for the time being, that is. We've got our eye on a property downstate in Sussex County where we want to build the same type of holistic drug treatment facility, if we can get past Planning and Zoning and the County Council. We have a new cereal we are getting ready to introduce. It's cannabis infused and manufactured in Maine, where we have outdoor grow; however, once legalization in Delaware is done, then production will begin here as well".

"Why outdoor grow?" I asked Clinton as I wiped my hands dry and continued to look around at all the other products in the store.

Clinton perked up and became very serious, based on research into the science of plants. "A few years back, they did a study on how plants react to their environment. The emergent book that was published is called The Intention Experiment by Lynne McTaggart. A happy plant leads to happy food or medicine. Based on our philosophy of plant and body harmony, we allow our plants to be naturally pollinated. You see, when the female plant is nearing the end of her life cycle, she analogously starts to call to a mate to reproduce so she can make babies, thus continuing her life cycle. When the plant is denied her rights to reproduce, she becomes frantic and starts screaming for pollination. That scream is essentially the sticky substance that a lot of people like on their weed. However, that sticky substance has her energy, and it is the energy that she will be dying, and her lineage lost. She has no idea she has been cloned; all she knows is she is dying with no propagation, and that stresses out the plant incredibly," he said.

"Could that be the reason a lot of people report that cannabis makes them paranoid or gives them anxiety?" I asked.

"I think so, Charlotte. Everything has energy. What this female plant has been asked to do is forgo her natural life process so she can pump out stronger medicine. Does that even make any sense? Can a woman make a baby without a man? We need both, Charlotte, and it is as if they are trying to eliminate the male together," Clinton continued.

"I had not thought about it that way, however, you bring up a very good point," I replied. I continued to look down the aisles at all the products on the shelf and smelled each one to see what I liked.

"When a woman is pregnant, any nutrient she takes in goes to her babies. Those babies then have a life cycle of their own; those seeds are unbelievably valuable as well. That male energy in the form of the seeds is then extracted through our process. We believe this is balanced plant food: the stems, the leaves, the roots. All of this is what we call whole plant medicine, and this is what our bodies are asking for inside our endocannabinoid system. To deny our people this vital plant for almost one hundred years is something our founding fathers, some of whom were farmers, would be ashamed of now. As we believe in homeostasis, we want our products to be made in the same way nature intended," he said.

"What is homeostasis anyway, Clinton?" I asked.

"It is the tendency towards a stable equilibrium," he answered, as he tied his shoe. I walked around, smiling at the women who were helping the other customers with their products. For a moment, I pondered what he meant by that.

He laughed and said, "Our equilibrium is a state in which opposing forces or influences are balanced".

"So, do you mean to say that if our bodies are not in homeostasis, this could be the reason for the imbalance –things like mood swings and temperament?" I said, scratching my head,

"That is what the definition of homeostasis would suggest, if you understand the definition, anyway," He replied. Clinton picked up a gift box of products and asked a young woman with Down syndrome, named Clara, to ring it up.

"So, what does that have to do with the endocannabinoid system inside our body?" I asked, as we went out of the shop and continued down the walkway.

"Oh, great question, Charlotte," said Clinton. "The endocannabinoid system plays a crucial role in maintaining homeostasis inside the body. Through research, we know that the cannabis plant has the highest number of cannabinols of any other food source, thus making it the number one source for the body to maintain homeostasis," he elaborated.

The light bulbs started to go off in my head. "Is that why I feel so much better when I eat an edible with cannabis in it from the *Center of Love*?" I asked excitedly.

"That would be the reason, my dear," said Clinton, as he opened his briefcase, "here, have one".As he handed me one of the candies, it all started to make so much more sense.

"Elementary, my dear, this is tenth-grade science material between the biology of plants and how the systems of the body work. We know from our own experiences that when we are stressed out, a walk in nature restores our soul. Can you imagine what type of response a plant is feeling when it does not hear nature, does not have a mate, and is forced to work like a slave?" he said.

"That makes a lot of sense to me, it is like a slave to humans, no different than what they do to cattle. Then they feed it to us and wonder why we are all sick," I replied.

"Some people disagree with the Center of Love's philosophy, and that is OK. The consumer base is big enough, so we can all have our place. You have got to know what you stand for," he said. Clinton turned to me and looked right into my eyes. "It's why I had such an interest in you, I loved the passion you put into your food. I knew if I could harness that same love and put it into our food. Then in time, the nation would heal," he explained.

"Holy cow, that is a very big thing to be asked to do," I said, as we continued to walk down the mall, "this is a big freaking deal, Clinton".

"Exactly," he said, "it's why I had such an interest in you when I first tried your food and knew you could develop this further".

A look of excitement came over my face, and when I said, "So, you want me to develop more recipes with cannabis?".This is when things really got serious.

He turned to me, intensified his gaze into my eyes. "I want you to develop an entire line of holistic cannabis infused products for consumption at the White House!" he exclaimed.

I smiled at the thought of me developing food products inside the White House, as I walked down the hallway, looking for a dress shop. The red suit reminded me of Chris De Burgh's song, *The Lady in Red*, as I pressed it down my body and started to sing the words. I thought back to when I was dancing around the house in Jamestown in my red chiffon dress and got lost in my fairy tale.

Blushing forth, he caught me in my moment when he pressed the play button on his phone and showed me the video of me dancing. I smiled, knowing he was watching me and really mattered to him, as he kissed me on the lips. "You look amazing, and I really love you in red," said Clinton.

I walked into an upscale boutique, wherein business suits lined the floors, and started pulling through the racks, until I came across a purple suit. The more I looked at its design, the more I knew it was mine, so I grabbed the hanger and went over to the changing room to try it on. My legs were beginning to look slenderer as I flattened out the suit, and I smiled, as the thoughts of me being the President of the United States began to glow on my face. Then, I heard a noise and looked up to see a handful of purple outfits.

"Here, try these on," the saleslady said eagerly.

After about twenty dresses, I was so exhausted. "Can I do this later?" I said, "I can't pick right now."

"Did they all fit?" she asked.

"Yes, I just don't know which one I like best," I replied.

"OK, give it some thought and come back when you're ready," she said empathetically.

I opened the dressing room door and handed the bundle of their latest fashions to the lady. "Sorry," I said, "your selection is overwhelming". I put my red suit back on and fluffed up my breasts, adjusted my makeup, and spruced up my hair. I walked out and there was Clinton standing, with more bags in his hands than I could count, and I knew in that moment he had bought every single one.

He paid attention as we walked back to where the limousine was waiting and opened the door for me. For a fleeting moment, my life flashed in front of me. I saw myself as the President as I sat down. When I crossed my right leg over my left with my shoe pointing to the driver, I could feel the businesswoman come alive inside of me once again, and in that moment, I knew it was possible.

CHAPTER 21

WELCOME TO MY WORLD

It was a short drive as we made our way to the building on Ruthar Drive right next to the UPS Distribution Center in Newark, Delaware. The side wall was painted to look like we were walking into an enchanted cannabis garden that looked like an enchanted giant green gingerbread house. I saw a trail of lollipops lining the winding path that led to stained glass cannabis infused windows where magic happened behind them. The shutters were colorfully decorated with three tiers of hearts, and we just knew that love was happening behind the walls. The Center of Love logo appeared in bright letters with a large orange and black Monarch Butterfly, resting in a purple hand that takes you to the Promised Land.

We walked into the front entrance where a beautiful young woman, with hair that came down her back, sat at the reception desk. Her bright, shiny name tag read "Shayla," and a handful of reporters and television crews were standing around, talking in the front lobby.

Clinton walked up to the desk and addressed Shayla, "Allow me to introduce you to the new acting President of *Foobellas*, Celebrity Cannabis Chef Charlotte Bennett".

I looked over at Clinton, with a smile across my face, when I reached over and firmly shook her hand, "Good to meet you,

Shayla," I said, "I am looking forward to taking **Foobellas** global".

A moment later, another man came out from behind a door. Clinton extended his hand and said, "Jason, so good to see you".

"Mr. Tuckerman, it is good to have you here today, and we are so excited about today's tour of the facility," he said. Jason handed us all booties for our shoes. "Please put these on while you tour," he said, Kennedy just called and said that they would be getting here within the next few minutes".

"Excellent!" said Clinton, "just waiting on the Governor, I take it?".

Shayla spoke up, "Yes, her assistant just called and said that the Governor is about five minutes away. A reporter from the local newspaper came over, introduced himself, and asked if it was OK, to take our picture.

"Of course it is, Charlotte," Clinton said, "come over here and get in the picture".

I walked over to Clinton as the flash of lights began, and Kennedy, Karissa, and Kevin followed right after. Then, the commotion reached a higher level as the front doors opened and in walked the Governor of Delaware, her Chief of Staff, and her Chief Executive Assistant, Bonnie. The press came alive as the microphones and cameras appeared, flashing lights all around, reminding me of Hollywood's Red Carpet.

Jason led us through a set of doors, where, over in the corner, was a long line of empty wheelchairs. Once I walked through the set of double doors, I saw a group of people suspended in suits that were tethered to giant robot arms that allowed them to work. I watched one woman with auburn hair glide down the floor with her wings proudly protruding, as she flew from station to station. I could not help but put my hand on her sleeve. Intrigued by her, I followed her around, asking her questions when she smiled back at me and said, "Let me tell you my story".

"I have not worked in an exceptionally long time, as today is my seventh day on the job," she said, "and my name is Jaeden, and I am 38 years old. I was born with Cerebral Palsy, and I am excited to finally find a place where I fit in. They have a robot that can help me be more productive. They have this ergonomic suit that can help me do activities and get things done on the job more efficiently. While in the suit, I forget about my disability. It is nice to work in a place where people have all kinds of disabilities, and they are willing to work with your weaknesses and turn them into your strengths. Rory, my service dog, gets to come with me. She just lies quietly at my feet until I need her to do something, like pick up an object from the floor that I dropped. She is very friendly and loves people and is very in tune with everyone's feelings. Even though she is my service dog, I feel like she gives everyone a sense of peace when she is around," she stated.

I knelt and looked in the dog's eyes and told her she was a good dog while she licked my hand. I stood back up and looked at Jaeden, and asked her to tell me more about herself.

"For years, I have struggled to find my place in this world. It is nice to work for a company that embraces differences, and they do not mind helping you become the best person you can be. While in the suit, I get to experience things that I cannot do on my own. It allows me to move my legs in a way that I cannot do in less I am not in the water. My brain does not have to work so hard to get my legs to move the way that I want them to. Even though I have certain tasks to do on the job, being in this suit takes my mind to different places. I allow it to go there so that I can have the freedom that I have always wanted to have. I enjoy going to work. I enjoy working with people with different disabilities in helping them realize their true potential. Everyone has the right to live their best life possible. Everyone has value in this company, and the people who run it realize that. They look at our abilities as their assets, not at what we cannot do. That is very refreshing in a world that does not like broken things. This company allows your brokenness to become something beautiful," she said with all her heart.

"I love how you said that, and you speak with such a passion that I am blown away," I said. "You spoke of brokenness. You know I always like to believe that we can achieve anything we set our minds to do, that the opposite of broken is whole, I continued. "Tell me, if you had a fantasy, a wish right now, what would it look like and what do you see for yourself?" I asked

"Jaeden's face lit up. "On the hard days when I put on the suit, I imagine I am at the beach running along the sand, letting the waves hit my toes. Rory is with me, and we play fetch in the water, and she runs free. Helping me with the occasional task, but she gets to be a regular dog and frolic about. I can go on vacation anywhere and not have to worry about whether it is accessible or not, or if I am not going to be able to participate with my family. I do not have to worry about them worrying about me not being included in something that we have going on. In the suit, I do not have to worry about speaking my truth. I am understood, and even when I am not, people are OK with it. I can tell my story without shame, knowing that it will help someone else ease their pain. That way, what I have been through will not be wasted," she said.

"What have you learned from life so far?" I asked, as I watched all the other people in flying suits work around the floor.

"I have just started to learn the value of my true worth. My brain always knew it, but to tell my heart that. I had a hard time really believing it, and it has been a struggle. In my family, we have had many different troubles, and so when it came to my disability, as I grew up, I thought I could do anything. I am so thankful that my family believed in me and treated me as if there was nothing wrong. Everyone adapted as much as possible, so I was included in as many activities as I could be. I am not knocking my family when I say this, but I was not prepared for the real world. Some family members would say that because I was sheltered, but that is not it. It puts it in a whole new perspective when you grow up with a disability. Where I fall on the spectrum with my cerebral palsy, most people do not know how to take me. Although my physical body does what it wants and does not cooperate, my brain is fine. Often people with cerebral palsy have a lot more physical issues and mental deficiencies just because of the lack of oxygen that you get when you are born with cerebral palsy".

I was beyond intrigued with this woman when I asked her, "What do you see yourself doing in the next five years?".

Jayden responded, "Some of what I see myself doing working at **Foobellas** is being able to be my true self. Having a company that would allow me the right equipment so I could do the job most efficiently would give me the most freedom I could ever feel on this side of Earth. When you have a company that is willing to work with your weaknesses and turn them into strengths, anybody can soar. My wings have been broken for so long that I want to know what it is like to fly. To take all the truth that I know in the skills that I have and not let the world tell me what I cannot do any longer".

"Well, Jayden, I can attest to that when you are working with Foobellas, it is to restore those broken wings because we realized something along the way. It took a long time to figure this out, but there are so many kinds of people out there. There is no one out there any more different than anyone else, and just because you might not have what you think you need to succeed, I am here to tell you that you have everything that you need for the mission you came here to do. You are so beyond equipped for this that we could not have handpicked anyone better than you to do it. It is your passion and your knowledge of the truth that brings you here today. I am so beyond grateful to have you as a member of the Foobellas Family," I said."Let me ask you something else, how do you see yourself evolving at Foobellas?" I asked.

"Working in **Foobellas,** I would look forward to helping people with all kinds of disabilities. Realize their potential and how far they can go. We need more companies to take the time to show their employees other things besides skills that would keep the business going. Yes, that is especially important, but sometimes with a disability, a lot of other things come up that you are not planning on. Even if the workplace does not help with some of the other things, it can help connect people to find the right resources. Social workers do not always have those resources, even though they want to help, as they are limited," she answered.

"For example, someone is having a bad day because of their disability, and they need someone to talk to and are having trouble focusing on the job. Now, they need to be able to talk about it and not feel guilty. Workplaces need to have spaces where people need help doing their daily activities, such as going to the bathroom. I know this sounds like a pipe dream, but these are the things that I think about to make everyone able to do their job no matter the disability," she said.

"You know, Jayden, I am a big believer in pipe dreams, and if we can use a pipe as the example, we know that if we put an elbow on a pipe, we can get something to move in a different direction. So no, it is not just a pipe dream; it is your dream, and you deserve to be heard. This is your mission; therefore, this is your gift. There is not one person who understands the relationship between you and that chair but someone else who is sitting in it right now," I said.

"I would like to provide training for staff and other volunteers," replied Jayden. "When they have questions or concerns about helping another employee or client, we will work it out within the company. I will make sure that everyone knows they are valued and loved," she continued."Not so corporate-like, for lack of a better word," she laughed."Once we got it established, I would love for other companies to come in and use our model to help other businesses hire more people with disabilities," she concluded.

The doors opened into a large room with rows of tables and chairs, reminding you of a school classroom. Each table had a team of four members plus a team leader. I walked up to the first table, where I was introduced to a young woman named Brianne, who was pouring what looked like salt into a large silver mixing bowl. I watched as she carefully measured out her salt and checked it off the list. Her mentor gave her a high five and urged her to keep going. As the large bowl went down to the next person, a man, by the name of Terry, started pouring an oil mixture in from a large bucket labeled 'Body Scrub Base'.He got up and hugged me. "Well, well, welcome to my workplace," he said with a big grin. "My, my, my, my name is Terry," he stated, beaming with pride while he clapped his hands.

My heart started to swell as I took all of it in, and I watched as the bowl slid down to the next woman, as she poured the honey in.

"My favorite," she yelled out, laughing band squirming in her chair, as the photographer snapped pictures and the video cams rolled in for close-ups, whereupon she whipped her hair back, striking a pose like a runway model.

The bowl then made its way to the next young man, where he opened a bottle of essential oils blend and poured in the contents. Each angel started stirring with their spoons as they all beamed with pride. The table leader took the bowl to the next table, where containers and lids are ready to be filled.

I looked over at Clinton and said, "This is all a hands-on operation …No machinery?"

"No," Jason jumped in, "we do not believe in that here. It is our belief that when our angels use their own hands to make our products that their happiness goes into it. Sure, we could use automation to maximize cost efficiency, but then, we would not have any jobs for our people to do. We do business the old-fashioned way here for the sake of our people and our customers," he elaborated, much to my pleasure.

Once the containers were filled and weighed, they were wiped down, and the labels were affixed; then, the boxes were filled and ready for shipment to our retreat centers as well as private mail order.

I saw the Governor off in the distance, talking with some of the people. She had a familiar face with a glow to her, and, by the way she shook everyone's hands and hugged them, I knew I wanted to feel her heart, too. When she came and shook my hand, I felt something go inside of me that I at first did not understand. However, it was in her eyes – the window to her soul – that I knew in an instant she was the right woman for the job. The strange thing i that I wanted much more of her attention and began to calculate how closely I could get to know her.

The tour continued into a room, where people were arranging the body products into gift baskets. Jason spoke up. "Making real soap can be hazardous with caustic lye; therefore, our safety training programs start in the prison system as part of our state's exit programs, created by the Governor," he said, as he gave her a nod. "Once our soaps cure for the full six weeks, there is no lye present, and it is perfectly safe for our angels to handle. Our process of hand-crafted products in the age of mass production is what makes us different. We make a good living, and we give back to our community in more ways than one," he explained.

I was so impressed with what I had just witnessed, and was enthusiastically conveying my feelings to the reporters, when it came over the loudspeaker that lunch was ready. As everyone finished up their tasks, we were ushered into the cafeteria, where I could see a few staff members whom I recognized from some of the classes I took. I could not believe what I was seeing as I walked around the room. I sat down next to Rose, the young woman with Down syndrome, and asked if I could eat lunch with her.

"Sure," she said as she smiled back at me. She started to tell me about her daddy in heaven and that he was a policeman. A newspaper photographer came up to us and asked to take our picture. Wrapping our arms around each other, we posed for the shot. Whipping her hair back again, she also gave a seductive smile to the TV cameraman."Ah, thanks, Rose said, as she gave me a hug.

I was so overwhelmed with everything I was seeing and the sheer happiness in the room that I couldn't help but be touched by everything as the tears formed in my eyes. As I looked over to my right, there in the corner was a massage therapist doing chair massages.

"Come on," said Rose, as she grabbed my hand, "I love massage,". She shook her hips as she hopped into the chair. "Oh, yeah, baby," she beamed with wide eyes.

"OK," the therapist said as he started massaging her neck.

"That feels so good", said Rose, sighing with delight.

Jason came up and said that this was another part of our employee reward system. "We also have a group meditation that we do at the end of the shift. That is when we give out our rewards for the day. A voucher to a restaurant or grocery store, nail salon, and even clothing stores. We know what each person prefers, so we try to make sure they are happy with their rewards," he explained.

"This is amazing," I said, as we continued our tour. Looking around the room, I could see massage oils being filled, deodorants, lip balms, bath salts, and bath bombs. To see how each team worked together in harmony was a joy unto itself.

Jason got up on the stage with the Governor. After a brief introduction, the Governor eagerly took the microphone. As I listened to her speak from her heart, I looked over at Clinton and asked where they found her.

He smiled and said, "She got her start with me ... keep listening".

I sat there and listened as she spoke, and, with the things she said, I knew she worked from her heart. I turned to Clinton and whispered, "I really want to have lunch with her someday".

"That can be easily arranged. In fact, we will be staying at the Governor's house in just a few weeks. We already have an official invitation to a major celebration.

I looked at Clinton with excitement in my eyes, for I could not wait to do that, and I began to play it all out in my head. The Governor finished her speech, then went around hugging all the employees. I wanted so badly to have her hug me when she walked up, smiled, and said, "You're next". She wrapped her arms around me, and I fell into her embrace. I simply do not know how to explain it, but whatever it was, it felt like heaven, and I did not want to pull away. On the third breath, we released. She looked me in the eyes and said, "It's so good to finally meet you," and then, she went on her way.

Jason announced that it was reward time. "Please clean up your stations and come to the meditation room," he requested. The whole team gathered, and we were led into a brief but powerful meditation. "In a few short minutes, we will be dismissing for the day. Please give a warm thank you and round of applause for our owners and the Governor who came in today to see how we are all doing", he said. It was a symphony of angels, as each one clapped, danced, and whistled. Watching them jumping up and down, we could tell that they loved working at the Center of Love Club!

Jason handed me the stack of gift cards as he called up each name. I handed them their gift cards and hugged each one goodbye. As I thanked them for being one of our angels, one after the other thanked me for being an angel, too. It was beyond amazing, as I looked over at the Governor, who stood back in awe, shaking Clinton's and Kennedy's hands. "I got to admit, you guys do amazing work here in Delaware," she said.

A sense of pride suddenly came over me that this is the organization I am now an integral part of. As my heart filled with joy, I beamed with a smile so wide that I could not believe what I was hearing. I overheard Clinton say the angels will be celebrating our wedding. They are being invited along with all the people from our Maine facility, who will all be flying down. I looked over at Clinton in utter amazement. When I realized I was getting a new family, I started to cry with tears of joy.

Clinton came over and wrapped his arms around me. "Do not cry, love, I told you, you would have people to take care of – just not exactly the way you thought you would be," he said softly.

I continued to cry with a mix of emotions, as we waved to each person as the golf carts pulled onto their parkways.

"It is not over yet," said Clinton, "we have a tour of the prisons scheduled for this week, the changes this Governor has implemented are remarkable. The transformations inside our prisons have now made Delaware the new model for the entire United States," he added.

"When do we tour?" I asked, as I walked up to the stretch Cadillac.

Clinton opened the door and waited until I got in. "In a few days, we will be there. We have got a few more things on the schedule for now, so let's go back to the inn and rest for the night," he said.

CHAPTER 22

OFF TO THE RACES

The sun was shining brightly on a beautiful October morning, as Kennedy looked through the red and orange leaves that were dropping off the trees. He heard a diesel truck idling along the front of the Inn, as his phone beeped with a message from the graphics guy, Pete, "Hey, my guy, I'm here to get the Trans Am", he texted from his heavy-duty pickup truck.

He wiped his mouth clean with the napkin on the table and asked Karissa to save his breakfast. He took the keys of the Trans Am out of his pocket and walked out front.

"Hey, what do you say?" greeted the man whose dark hair ran down his back, "My name is Andy". The two men shook hands."The deal will be ready by next Sunday," he said with a wink. He hitched his truck up to the trailer of the Trans Am, and Kennedy watched as she rolled away to get her new coat on.

Kennedy headed back out to the small dining room that overlooked our wedding destination and began to sip his coffee again. He looked up to Karissa, who was working on something in her book, when he asked what time she was officiating today.

Karissa looked up at him and said that there is a wedding and small reception scheduled for 11 am."It will only be for an hour or so at best, then I'll be ready for tonight," she replied, "and I scheduled a manicure and pedicure at the spa around the corner for Charlotte and me".

"Oh, that sounds like you are going to have fun," he said as I examined my toes, "and I need one of those too".

"It will be," said Karissa as she got up from the table, "and Charlotte's already there, getting a slimming wrap done".

A look of excitement came over Kennedy's face as he got a good look from Karissa, and he knew that he could not get one over on her."I am a weak man, Karissa," he said, "and I never said I was perfect".

"I know," she said, "trust me. I've been on to you for some time, now. "I knew exactly who you were when I married you. Besides, I am cool with how my life is and, if I want something, I will go after it," she proclaimed, as she slapped her book on the table.

Kennedy knew that he had just been had. "Wow! What happened to my wife, and where did you come from?" he laughed."Clinton, Kevin, and I will be heading over to Delaware Park to start our shenanigans by 10 am. What time will you be there?" he asked.

"I do not know, she replied with a hint of irritation, like a wool tie around the neckline. "Depends on how my day goes," she said, as she crossed her wrists and flashed her long fingernails.

"Whatever you do, don't forget we've got a big party tonight in Wilmington, so make sure you look good," said Kennedy.

Karissa turned back at him with a look that could kill, and he knew that he would be a dead man later.

He slipped inside the limousine and said, "Gentlemen, let's go!". They pulled up to a big building and walked down a ramp and then up the staircase, to where a poker table stood in the middle of the backroom. Out of the door came a short and skinny man, wearing a large fur coat and a wide-brimmed hat, gesturing with his hands.

"Are you the Big Tuna?" Kennedy asked as he extended his hand.

"That I am," he said with a hearty laugh, "but everyone else calls me Ben"."Hey, doll," he said to the tall blonde hanging on his hand, "can you go get daddy a drink?" She stood there for a moment in a smoldering maroon dress with her ample cleavage protruding out of the top nodded affirmatively and walked out.

Kevin blushed as he watched her moving, curvaceous body, wondering to himself how on earth this little man got a beauty like that.

Ben perceptively gave him a laugh. "Don't get too impressed, she's only here for the money. She does not love me. One bad break and I'll be lucky to get a dime out of her with a cup in my hand on a street corner," he said. Kennedy and Clinton looked back at him as they sat down at the table.

"Well, then… looks like we have more business with you," Kennedy said, as he handed him one of his cards, "love is my specialty". The dealer walked in and introduced herself as

Claudine. The blonde came back in with a wooden box of cannabis smokes of several different varieties, and we all picked one up.

A man dressed in a suit, tie, and black round glasses walked in and briskly shook Kennedy's hand. "Say, it's good to finally meet you, Kennedy," he said, "my name is Anthony DeLucas". Anthony turned to Clinton. "The real money is in the contract," he said, "and your stallion came in the other day, so, good job on that pick, Clinton,". He pulled the fattest joint out of the box, and the blonde lit him up.

"I just used a connection I had," said Clinton as he walked over to the window and pointed to where the horse was with the trainers. "He is also expected to win here, today," he added, rapping on the glass, "and we have been incredibly pleased with his performance so far." "A big purse is expected," said Ben, as he picked up the cards the dealer shuffled out. "We give away over a million on Owner's Day," he continued, as the cards went across the table, and asked, "Clinton, what about the mares in Mississippi, how are they doing?"

"They are doing very well and are expected to be coming up soon for delivery," replied Clinton, as Kevin puts down a full house.

"Ah, the kid can play," Ben said, as he continued to draw cards. He slid a bottle of golden whiskey from inside his side pocket. "I only drink the good stuff," he proclaimed, as he offered his flask to us. The game lasted for about an hour, and when the announcement came over the loudspeaker that the horse race was ready to start.

Kennedy got up first and headed over to the VIP section, where he could not help but notice a woman in a flowery print dress who had her back to him. She was wearing a large, brimmed hat with butterflies all over it, as she stood by the rail. He watched her intently as she talked with several men who seemed to be as mesmerized as he was, and he wondered who she was. Kennedy could not see her face, but something about the way she emitted her energy intrigued him. He looked at Clinton, nudging his arm. "Who is that?" he asked eagerly.

Clinton looked right back at him and said, "It's Karissa, you fool", as he shook his head in amusement.

"Oh no, that IS my wife," gasped Kennedy in shock, as he bit down hard on his hand. He walked over and nodded to the gentleman as he took Karissa's hand. "You look amazing," he said. The voice of the announcer came over the loudspeaker, encouraging us all to place our bets and head to our seats.

Karissa looked over at Kennedy and, for a fleeting moment, knew by the look in her eyes that she was on to him. He noticed that her wedding rings were not on and wondered about it. "Where are your rings?" he asked.

Karissa looked down at her left hand, utterly horrified. "Oh my God! I don't know, I had a slimming wrap at the spa, and they must have fallen off," she gasped in shock as she reached for her phone.

"Is that why you look so incredible?" Kennedy asked, as he backed up for another look at her. "Wait here, I will be right back," he said, as he went to place his bet. As he approached the window, he saw a woman with diamonds all on her hands, and that is when the idea struck him, like a bolt from the blue. "I should buy my wife a new ring," he thought. Then, he put down ten thousand dollars on Purple Passion and went back to his seat.

"The Big Tuna", a.k.a. Benny Cohen, turned to Kevin and said, "We have a black tie tonight in Greenville, would you like to come?".

Kevin shook his head. "Thanks, but I'll sit this one out. My nerves are bad, and I just want to rest.

"Not a problem… Good playing poker with you, kid," said Benny with a smile, patting him on the back.

Kevin smiled back at him and warmly shook Ben's hand. Surprisingly, it felt like paper. When he pulled his hand back, he saw that "The Big Tuna" had slipped a thousand dollars into his palm. Puzzled, he looked back up at his new benefactor in utter amazement.

Ben smiled and said, "You deserve it, kid".

Kevin thanked him profusely and looked up at Kennedy. "What was that all about?" he asked, showing him the money.

"Beats me," Kennedy said, "just take it and be grateful that you got a gift".

Kevin slid the money into his front pocket as a smile lit up his face.

Place your Bet

Wide Brimmed Hat

Flowery Dress

Midsize Heel

Suit and Tie

Galloping Horses

Training Stables

Delaware Park Racing Casino

Roulette Wheels

Poker Tables

Slot Machines

Fields of Green

Biggest Purse you will ever see

Gun Bangs

Gates Clang

Mounted Men

Checkered Vest

Majestic Stallions

Racing the Track

Hooves of Steel

Leads the Pack

Daddy's Pride

Right behind

Neck to Neck

Place your Bets

Oh, But Wait

Who is this?

Daddy's Pride right on time

Purple Passion

Takes the lead

Bets are locked

Independents

On the track

Gets a crack

High Tails It

neck to neck

Beating the incumbents

Where did she come from?

No one knows

The Rumor Mill

She pants, she grunts

She kicks up her heels

Then bows to the King

Knowing he got her here

The hats go up

The roses

Fall

The irony of it all

Chapter 23

Desserts on Me

Stuffing the money he just won in every pocket he could find, as the teller kept counting hundred-dollar bills behind the glass wall, Kennedy looked at Clinton, smiling with his latest win. Walking out the back gate, the "Big Tuna" turned to Kevin. "You did good, Kevin," as they walked towards the waiting limousine. He looked at the clock, and it was 4:20 pm on the dot.

They pulled into the parking lot at the Inn at Christiana, where the last stragglers from the wedding reception were just leaving. Ever Kevin's eye caught an angel standing in a pink bridesmaid's dress. She was the most beautiful woman he had seen in ages, and she couldn't have been more than twenty-seven at most. With long blonde hair braided down the sides, she was the most perfect creature he had ever seen. As soon as he saw her, it was love at first sight.

Kennedy walked over to Kevin. "I'm taking Karissa to that private party tonight with Clinton and Charlotte," he said, "are you sure you do not want to go and mingle?"

"Nah, I'm sure," replied Kevin, "you guys go have fun".He gazed back at the woman with the golden hair, who had by now thoroughly bewitched him."Yeah, yeah, I will, too," he thought,

She looked up at him as she began to take the braids out of her hair. As she twirled it all around her head, she smiled and asked, "Do you want to go get some coffee?".

Kevin's eyes were now totally lit up. "How about if I fix you a cup myself?" he asked.

She smiled back and said, "I would like that very much," as they walked to the back of the kitchen.

Kennedy did not mean to interrupt that most magical moment, as Kevin tried to pour the coffee into the cup.

"What's your name, again?" Kevin asked, as he giggled under his breath.

She took his hand and whispered in his ear. "My name is Miandra," she said softly. The sweet sound rolled off her lips and floated around the room in its own unique tune. She led him to the pantry room and shut the door.

"Are you real or just a figment of my imagination?" he asked, as his hand caressed her porcelain face.

"Does it matter?" she questioned, as she reached up and let her lips dance up against his, in a kiss that could stand the test of time, as a love of a lifetime began to bloom.

Kennedy left the kitchen and took the stairway up to his floor, walked down the hall, inserted his skeleton key into the doorknob, gave it a little wiggle, and opened the door. Stepping in, he turned around and looked up. The room had taken on a crimson hue of its own, as if fire and brimstone were getting ready to rain down. The fireplace was roaring, as the candles burned on the mantle. He heard the string instruments make their way in as the flurry of aphrodisiacs tickled his spine, as lively notes of Jasmine and Lavender danced in front of his eyes.

Standing in the bathroom doorway, with her arms outstretched against the frame, was the hottest version of Karissa that he had ever seen. Kennedy was hypnotized by her beauty, as the gold glistened on her skin. Her bright red hair was fashioned up, with springs of curls flowing around her face. Her warm cocoa lips were just begging to be tasted. Karissa's green eyes pierced through his soul as she cracked her whip with her right hand. With but one

flash of her alluring lash, Kennedy was down on his knees.

She was wearing a chocolate sheer robe that flowed behind her as if a windstorm blew in, and her coral bra, with fabric that looked like two horizontal crescent moons, clearly exposed her golden dollars. Kennedy jumped on her milk jugs like a carny in a side show, bouncing his tongue back and forth on her nipples, while he listened to her explode with delight.

Her shawl did little to obscure her golden dollars, as her ruby hair strands went down to her navel; thus, revealing enough to make him want to get down on his knees and beg his love goddess for her forgiveness.

She stood in black high heels adorned with cocoa rhinestones and a brown puff of feathers at the top of her open-toed shoes. Her toes were freshly painted in gold, shining through her open heels.

"Oh no, she knows I have a foot fetish," thought Kennedy as he imagined starting there.

With a snap of her fingers, she firmly commanded him to get down on his knees, as the tip of her whip struck his back. Kennedy was so turned on to hear this coming from his sweet wife, and he had no idea about who she had just turned into. He did not care and readily thought that she could turn into whoever she liked if she wore that dress for him that night.

Kennedy took her left shoe off first and began caressing her foot, teasing her with little kisses as he sucked on each toe. He took the other shoe off and gave her feet the attention they so richly deserved. Kennedy, the mechanic, deftly caused Karrissa to be well-lubricated. He tickled her thighs with his mustache and escorted her to the bed, where he adjusted the pillows to bring up her hips. He got back down on his knees, licking each perfectly painted digit before placing each one in his mouth and sucking on them again.

Kennedy pulled the purple-ribbed bottle of massage oil named "Passion" off the nightstand. He begins to massage her legs, and his hands flowed ever so softly, as he made his way up to her pink quartz. He taunted her as his fingers barely grazed her lips before he made his way back down to her toes.

Using his golden tongue, Kennedy slithered his way up her legs as his warm hands caressed her flesh. The closer he got to her buttercup, the more she moaned. Her hips bucked wildly as he heard her pant and instinctively knew that Karissa was rapidly approaching the first of her many orgasms to come.

"Oh! Kennedy," she moaned, with her legs shaking harder and harder, the closer he got to her love canal.

Kennedy could tell that she craved his tongue on her rosebud, but he was going to make her beg for it some more. He reveled in her writhing and thrashing as she convulsed under his touch. Her crescendo of spasms began to flood the pillowcase, and he knew her motor was primed up. He teased her pulsing rose quartz with a gentle little rub with two fingers; by sliding them back and forth, and knew she wanted him boring deep inside her tunnel, as he kept fingering her love channel. He flicked her rosebud at the same time, until he felt the surge of her next wave come on with a bit of her love juice trickling out.

Not satisfied with that little drop, Kennedy grabbed Karissa by her hips and rolled her over on all fours. He pulled her panties to the side as she pulled her robe up over her hips, teasing him with slaps to her ass. Using more of the Passion massage oil, he began dripping the erotic blend between her cheeks as he let the oil squirt down her crack and massaged her walls with his left middle finger. He used his right hand to crack her cheek hard, making sure that she knew who the top dog was. Her love nectar squirted out in torrents, quenching his thirst for her feminine essence.

As much as he wanted to pull on her hair, Kennedy knew that she had just had it done at an expensive salon and hated to waste the money, but then, the urge suddenly overcame him. "SCREW IT!" he thought, "and I just love the tousled look on a woman". He grabbed her by the hair with his left hand and pulled the butterfly out.

Karissa began to quiver as her elixir flooded him once again. She begged for mercy when he flipped her over on her back.

Kennedy just loved the way Karissa inserted her long fingernails inside her love passage, but told her that it was his job, as he pulled her hands away and scolded her not to touch. As he reached up and suckled on her breasts, he let his fingers flutter in her nest until he felt her tremors building up to the next level.

Tiny explosions were happening inside her, one after another, turning her lazy river into wet and wild rapids. Kennedy fancied himself on Noah's Ark as his boat began to inflate, getting ready to ride the wave of the Great Flood that inevitably was to come. The louder she raised her voice, the more he knew that the dam was about to burst. Not until she was screaming did he dare pull his digits out. Her long legs thrashed, wildly begging for his craft. He gave her a couple more licks in preparation before guiding his big barge inside her and hitting the throttle up.

Her Sea of Eros swelled as if a typhoon were coming. All Kennedy could do to ride the wave of tremors that were pushing his vessel out of her port. He could hold on no longer before being swept out by her tsunami. Karissa shook the bed seismically in her final release. "Thank you," she moaned in ecstasy. "You're welcome," Kennedy replied, as he kissed her on the lips.

He got out of bed while she panted to catch her breath, knowing damn well that she wasn't going anywhere. "Nobody does it like I do," he thought, as he spanked her once more. Kennedy made his way to the bath, hopped in the shower, trimmed his beard, and brushed his hair. He quickly put his clothes back on and returned to the bed, where Karissa was still coming back down to reality, and patted her on her hips, "Get dressed and I will meet you downstairs in twenty minutes," he instructed. Kennedy made his way back down to the kitchen to grab a bite to eat. Making a ham sandwich on rye, with a touch of sauerkraut and a dab of Dijon mustard, he sat down thinking that he would take a little catnap on the back deck before getting ready for the party in Wilmington. That was until he looked out the original glass windows and couldn't believe his eyes. Kennedy put his snack down and ran out the front door. "Rebecaa, what are you doing here?" he asked, thoroughly surprised.

"Lesbian, my ass," she said, "you know, Aunt Mabel is on you, Kennedy".She quickly pats him on the back, gets in her car, and takes off.

"Right… you had to be kidding me," he yelled out loud, just before he turned around and witnessed the most frightening thing I've ever seen. Just as Karissa was making her way out of the motor home, wearing nothing but her little sheer ensemble and high heels, Aunt Mabel came out and gave her a big hug.

Olivianna laughed as she looked straight at Kennedy.

"Man, do I ever want to dump her in the sea," thought Kennedy. "In all my years, I have never had a woman pull a stunt on me like that, and while she's almost eighty, the woman has a grip like a linebacker".Kennedy looked over at Olivianna. "Was she really that bad?" he asked, shaking his head.

"You have no idea, unless you keep her on a gummy, she is like a bulldog on speed with energy like you won't believe," she replied, "it's all good, I found out that she used to decorate cakes back in her twenties and she's a real hoot if you just give her some space".

"Great," Kennedy said as he opened the door, "No Sativa for her then. What kind of cannabis did you use to bake the cake"?

"I used an Indica blend, as I thought it would be better," Olivianna said, as she headed into the motor home.

"Good thinking, can you give her some?" asked Kennedy.

"No, Kennedy!" exclaimed Karissa, "I've got some hard candy I can give her".

Just then, Charlotte came walking outside. "Hi, Aunt Mabel, how was your trip?" she said, as she hugged her tightly, "I missed you".

"It would have been really good if it were not for this jerk, you like so much," Aunt Mabel responded, pointing her cane at Kennedy, "and I simply do not know what you see in him".

"Auntie, Kennedy is a genuinely nice man, you'll see, just give him a chance, please," replied Charlotte.

"Oh, dear, I do not know how you talk me into this stuff, and I do not know why you just could not marry someone else," said Aunt Mabel, plainly.

"Auntie, I am not marrying Kennedy," said Charlotte, giving her a stern look. She gave her favorite aunt another hug and whispered in her ear, "I told you that in private months ago that I'm marrying Clinton Tuckerman," just as he happened to come outside.

Aunt Mabel took one good look at Clinton, "Well, that's better, dear, but you could have fooled me," she said, "now, what's for dinner?"

CHAPTER 24

I NEED ME SOME TENDERBONES

Aunt Mabel began her picking by pointing her cane at Kennedy, "What's for dinner, Sonny?" she crowed.

Kennedy climbed into the driver's seat of the motor home and shouted, "I'm thinking pizza, who's coming with?"

"Pizza," Aunt Mabel responded, disgusted at his choice. "Why the hell would we eat pizza when we are this close to that famous barbecue joint?" "I'm thinking ribs, cornbread, collard greens, and some macaroni and cheese, sonny boy," she added cantankerously, before Kennedy cut her off.

"Not today, Aunt Mabel," he interjected.

"I thought you were taking me to a restaurant," she huffed with contempt.

"Kennedy turned around and said, "We have plans in Wilmington tonight and I'm not taking the time to go all the way to Bear right now".

Karissa looked over at Kennedy, batting her eyes. "Please just let her get her barbecued pork, big Daddy," as she rubbed her hands up and down his chest, as Olivianna rolled her eyes.

"Kennedy's jaw dropped as he stood there looking at his wife's breast in her alluring ensemble. "Damn, if I wouldn't give her the world," he thought as he told her to change her clothes.

Charlotte chimed in, "Are you talking about **TenderBones Rib Shack**?" she asked.

"Yeah, that's the one," answered Kennedy,

"Oh my Gosh, he makes the best ribs, Clinton," said Charlotte, "let's go and get an early dinner before the rush," she said, as she climbed into the motor home, with Kevin and Aunt Mabel eagerly trailing.

Clinton looked at Charlotte, shaking his head, "You think Chef Bones got it going on?" he said, "Just wait till you wrap those lips of yours around my pork".

Charlotte stared directly into Clinton's eyes. "What… you want a showdown with Chef Bones?" she said, laughing out loud, "that's going to be a really good episode".

"You just wait to taste my sauce, baby," Clinton snorted back, "that Chef Bones ain't got nothing on me".

Charlotte giggled under her breath, "Yeah, well you just wait till those TenderBones and his amazing sauce is all over your lips," she said, "then we will see how that smack talk of yours is really working".

Karissa climbed into the front seat, wearing a pair of blue jeans and a flannel shirt. "You know Kennedy," she said, "according to the **TenderBones** web page, today is 'Fresh Fish

Friday' and this could be over so much faster if you just play nice". She rubbed his thighs and batted her eyes.

Kennedy looked back at Karissa and slammed his fist on the steering wheel. "OK… Fine, if y'all need some TenderBones, then so do I," he said, as he started the motor home and headed to the Route 1 interchange.

"You're driving way too fast," Karissa complained, "we're bound to get a ticket and have a cop up our ass".

"Boy, would I really like that," shouted Aunt Mabel, with her hands in the air. She got up and positioned herself between Kennedy and Karissa.

"Do NOT make me think that," said Kennedy, gagging.

"Well, there, Sonny, you think you are the best?" said Aunt Mabel, licking her finger and sticking it in Kennedy's ear, "bet I could tell you stories that would make you blush".

"Aunt Mabel, what the hell is with you?" said Kennedy, as he rubbed the side of his face after nearly crashing into a guardrail. "What's the matter with you, at least I know where to stick my fingers, your old bat, "said Kennedy, as he flipped her the bird.

"Kennedy!" Karissa shouted as the motor home erupted in screams, "Please stop it".

"Oh dear, I am so sorry," Aunt Mabel said, as she ran her fingers through Karissa's long red hair.

"Great!" Kennedy thought to himself as he carefully watched Aunt Mabel's right hand grabbing Karissa's hair, giving her lovely locks a little tug. "I should have kept the Trans Am with me and could have thrown her in the driver seat on the back of the trailer and watched her from my rear-view mirror with her fake wig blowing in the breeze …But NO, not me!" he thought some more as he floored the gas pedal.

"A cop, Kennedy!"Olivianna shouted.

"Oh God!" the passengers shouted in unison as Kennedy slammed on the brakes. Everyone in the back held onto the kitchen table for dear life.

Did you miss him?" Aunt Mabel snickered, "you jackass".

"I don't know," said Kennedy, as he pulled the RV over to the shoulder of the highway. The Delaware State Police cruiser blew past them as he threw it into park. "Screw it!" he exclaimed, "order some pizza and I don't care… screw the barbecue stand".

Olivianna yanked Kennedy out of the driver's seat. "Oh no … I don't think so, buddy boy," she said firmly, we all want us some TenderBones tonight after what we had to put up with".

Kennedy climbed in the back and sat down at the kitchen table, fuming. He fumbling with the jar of cannabis infused gummies, popped two in his mouth, and chewed them up. He took a few deep breathes and centered himself."Aunt Mabel, may I ask you a question?" he said calmly.

Aunt Mabel looked at him squarely in the face."Yes," she said.

"Why don't you like me? He asked, I don't know why we're not getting along".

"So, you think I don't like you, Sonny," she replied, "ha, you're funny, this is me not liking you". She pulled out a deck of cards and slammed it down on the table. "Do you play poker, Sonny?" she asked.

"Only if I bet," said Kennedy, looking over at Kevin.

"OK," Aunt Mabel yelled gleefully, "loser gets your wife under the sheets!".

Karissa turned around, looking at the entire scene. Clinton looked over at Charlotte, then at Kennedy, wondering what was going to happen next, while Kevin just continued to shuffle the deck. You could hear a pin drop when Kennedy said flatly, "I do not bet on my wife".

"Bullshit!" Aunt Mabel yelled back, "You bet on her cooking".

Karissa's drink sprayed out of her mouth as Clinton shouted, "Dear Lord, how did I get myself into this mess?" as the motor home exited onto Route 72.

Within minutes, they pulled into the shop at 2504, Red Lion Road in Bear, Delaware, where you could smell the pork from the parking lot. "I'll see about this," said Clinton, as he opened the door letting us all in. Within seconds, about ten more people walked in, and before we had our order placed, the line of patrons stretched around the building.

Charlotte looked over at Clinton with a smile on her face, "See, I told you so," she said, "Chef Bones has got a reputation," she said. Just then, the main man himself put his head in the window and hollered. "I got an order for Frank for the Chef Philly Cheese steak," as he signed the box and called out "number fifty-seven thousand two hundred and three!".

Chef Bones looked up he saw Charlotte waiting in the wings. "Well, I'll be darned," he shouted out the window, "hey Wanda, come take a look at who's in our shack... it's the famous Cannabis Chef Charlotte Bennett".

He opened the side door up, gave her a big hug. "I just ordered your third book," he said, "you trying to take a run for my ribs, girl?"

Charlotte laughed back. "Oh, I see you never change," she said," you know I beat you that day, so don't even try to play me!".

"Oh, is that what you think?" he asked, chuckling, "and I think you're coming back to get your butt whipped again, Charlotte".

"Always a comedian," Charlotte jabbed back, "you know I was the one that won that night," she said, when out from around the corner came the woman whose recipe for macaroni and cheese will make any man drop to his knees and beg for mercy.

Charlotte turned to face Clinton. "Clinton Tuckerman, let me introduce you to the other Clinton, the Master of Pork in Delaware, otherwise known as Chef Bones, and his amazing partner and wife, Wanda Harri," she said enthusiastically.

Clinton extended his hand. "Wait, your name is Clinton too?" he said, "now ain't that something?". He rubbed his chin and said, "I can't wait to sink my teeth into your tender bones and see if you beat my recipes".

Laughing in jest, Chef Bones asked, "Are you wagering a bet?" while Clinton nodded affirmatively.

"OK, I'll call you on that, I got the sweetest barbecue in the whole Eastern Seaboard," he said, before hollering to the kitchen," order up for Tuckerman!"

"You don't say," said Clinton, as he grabbed the bags of food and took a deep breath, "we'll see about that". Chef Bones laughed. "Now, you're talking some real smack," he replied. "Care to wager a little bet on that?" he asked as he folded his arms across his chest.

Strangely, the culinary tension in the air was as palatable as the smoke swirling around the building when Clinton Tuckerman pointed to his chest and proclaimed, "Bones, you're on!"

We all pulled out our phones and began snapping pictures or videos, not knowing what was going to happen next, while posting everything live to Facebook and Instagram. Then we headed outside to the picnic tables, where the lines grew longer as news began to spread.

While devouring the vittles that Chef Bones and his amazing crew fired up, it became clear that this was going to be the ultimate showdown in the First State between two restaurateurs over who makes the best ribs, Clinton Tuckerman of the *Center of Love Club*, or Chef Bones from **TenderBones Rib Shack**.

CHAPTER 25

A PRIVATE AFFAIR

We pull back into the Inn as everyone exits and goes about their way. I make my way up the stairs to our suite and lie down while Clinton gets ready. The pile of shop bags hung in the corner, calling me to rummage through them. I looked through all the dress boxes and pulled each gown out, trying to figure out what to wear tonight when Clinton walked out of the bathroom. He was wearing a black suit with a sequined purple vest, "We have something special going on tonight," he said, "go freshen up, do not wash your hair".

I watched him go through the bags carefully, placing each one on the hook, when I heard a knock at the door and wondered what was now going on. I took a deep breath and sighed, realizing I was being commanded again, and wondered what exactly I was doing with him when I walked back out and saw a woman unpacking a bag of makeup and styling products. My skin felt "sun kissed" as the moisturizer ran along my jawline, as her hands gently caressed my face. The mineral make-up as it enveloped over my flesh with the fluff of feathers as they tickled my nose, "Translucent," I supposed. I laughed it away, thinking that it was a fly, giggling inside, that I was trying to hide. Then, I opened my eyes and saw my new face. The amethyst cat's eyes are on the prowl. I looked up to the makeup artist who weaves magic with her hands, watched as she tussled my hair, and wondered who this person really was.

"Your eye makeup is, in a black and purple," as she said, "lower your eyes. My lashes looked down to the floor, mesmerized by the long trails of black lace with feathers, and I knew then that I was stepping into a new world. The brilliant white baby diamonds, of no more than nine points each, were woven together with material over the satin body of black. I stood up and took a deep breath. "Are you sure about this?" I asked.

That was when Clinton came from around the bend, in his jet-black tuxedo with purple tie to match. Never did I think at that moment that 007 would pass by me, as images of Sean Connery flashed in my mind. Oh, how he looked like a spy! "Oh my God!" I gasped as the gown opened to baby purple amethysts as the gemstones faded from white, to lavender, to Smokey Quartz, to Black Onyx, to a dotted trail of Black Diamonds. It was both mind-blowing to behold and electrifying to walk in as currents of energy went through me as it glistened in the sunlight.

I was not expecting all this as the limo exited route 141 and headed up route 100 to what they call Chateau County, with Benny, at the door with a cigar in his mouth, said, "Come in, come in, the party's just starting".

As we made our way around the room, very famous people, whom I had seen on television, were walking around with glasses of champagne, as they eyed me up and down. Clinton walks me to the head of the Democratic Party in Delaware and whispers in my ear, "You do not even want to know, just shake his hand, let him think that you're one of him and see how he takes the bait and how far he strings it out on a line," he said.

As I shook his hand, I had a strange feeling come over me that he was a Republican in disguise. It looked like he had a giant R stamped to his forehead as if political affiliated was a determinant that one should be ultimately judged upon, when I realized he was fishing for information and through him a line. He said that he was in the Purple Party once upon a time. At first, I thought this was some lofty idea of a revolution or a pipe dream, and didn't question him any further. I searched for a few moments as I continued to walk around the room, trying desperately to see if any of the people here were like me.

The air felt stuffy as one little blonde started to talk to me, and it felt like I was in the politest interrogation room imaginable. I longed for some cannabis instead to get me through this, when from around the corner, a little bear caught my eye. I looked closer and saw it was an excellent wood carving, and spied Karissa chatting with a retired Senator, when I came to join them.

Smiling at me, she said, "You are going to have to get used to this"."Yeah," I said, smiling back."Come with me," she said, discreetly. We walked along the back, beside the pool, as the sounds of deals were being struck. Then, I realized I had walked into a political fundraiser. In an instant, my mind was back in Newport, where I remembered all the deals that had been made, as Karissa handed me a breath mint from her purse. This will help you get through this, as she popped one in her mouth. "Now, get out there and mingle, kid," she said with a smile and walked away.

I took a deep breath and started to walk around and get my footing. Then, I looked up and saw a thin man in a dark gray suit, blue shirt with a navy-blue tie. I sat down with him on a bench under a canopy of cypress trees that ran along the back length of the property as we talked about his political dreams. His pearly white smile glistened as he ran his fingers along the side of his light brown head. I liked his boyish smile and blue eyes that had an enchantment all their own. We talked about his dreams of being the President one day and how he centered his career around that one goal.

I laughed when I said that I had never given a thought to being President. I did fancy being a State Representative when I was a kid, but it was just a passing thought that I let flow out as quick as it came in. Just then, a little gnat flew into my eye, and I blotted it with a napkin, trying not to disturb my makeup or rip off my fake eyelashes. Just then, a bright light emerged from the billowing atmosphere flying above my head – a light so bright and pure I wanted to get into it immediately. I closed my eyes and took a deep breath, feeling the invisible cord start to pull me, wishing that this energy would whisk me away from here, hiding in plain sight. Suddenly, a reporter's microphone and a cameraman were right in my face, and in an instant, I was in the spotlight.

The Crescent Moon hung in the sky, winking as the newscaster kept asking me questions. Turning back to get his name, I saw that he had vanished into the crowd. "Now that was awkward," I thought, as I continued to fumble with the half glass of sour grapes that tasted more like vinegar to me. Making my way to the outdoor bar where a gentleman was pouring drinks, I traded my wine glass for a brandy snifter. After a few sips, it warmed up my chest. I found myself in the conversation of a man closer to my own age. I glanced over at Clinton as he tipped his glass to me. Smiling back, I turned to the man and told him that he was my fiancé, as I walked away.

Clinton took my glass and gave it a sniff. "Moonshine," he said, "Is it that bad?" he asked, as he handed it back to me. "This party is that bad," I thought as I faked a smile through my teeth. "I guess of all the things we talked about these past weeks, we forgot to ask which political party we were affiliated with, too," I said.

Clinton drew in his breath. "Oh, I'm sorry, Charlotte, I thought you knew," he said.

"Wait, how would I know that – I mean, you told me you were in the Purple Party," I replied.

"I am the Purple Party," he said, as he reached his hand around me and whispered in my ear, "don't worry darling, we have other parties to attend, too, and we have a lot to do in the next few years".

"We are building alliances along both sides of the aisle," he explained as he took my hand. Looking back at him, I got the distinct feeling that our Union was bigger than what I had originally thought. "Charlotte, face facts: you do not act like a Republican any more than I act like a Democrat," he said.

Looking back at him, I asked, "Is this really just an arranged marriage that I am entering into?" as a chill went down my spine.

"Yes and No," he said, as he took a sip of lemonade, gazing out to the back of the yard. "Look, I know this is a lot for you to understand, and I am taking you as slow as I can. I checked you out completely. I know where you stand. I know we can complement each other, but we're going to see how well we work together. I am making sure you can handle commands as I set forth. Do you understand?" he continued,

I looked up at him, and my first thought was that I was a little girl being reprimanded by my boss. When the second wave came over me, I felt comforted that he had that much faith in me. I laughed for a moment as I looked back at Clinton. "Thank God this place is full of people," I said, "and I doubt that I will be submitting to your demands right here".

"Careful, Charlotte," Clinton said as he smiled back at me, "I saw you and the ghost out by the cypress trees talking back there".

"You know, I thought that was a ghost by the way the mist appeared," I replied, laughing back at him. I took his hand and said, "Let's go for a walk". Walking along the side of the pool, I asked him what he thought of all of this.

"If you listen carefully, you can hear the river not far from here, and this is very close to the original DuPont site where they made gun powder for the American Revolution, back in the day," he said, as we strode along the winding path.

"Well, that explains all the ghosts I was sensing," I said, as we continued our walk along the property.

"Politics is just a part of this country," he said, "it's the way it is; you've got to be willing to play in the game if you want your agenda to be arranged".Clinton turned to me with a serious tone in his voice. I am working on the Cannabis Freedom Act of America," For us to build our alternative healing retreats all around the country, the way we planned, it's going to take a few law changes, if you know what I mean".

I fully understood that the law needed to change, as I wondered again where I fit into all these plans.

"I know, Charlotte, that with you being a cannabis chef, you clearly see the importance of this," as we continued to talk of its implications. "You are very lucky that you have been in Maine, and we voted on this in our elections," he continued."Delaware and many other states are spending millions of dollars on how they are trying to regulate and capitalize on cannabis. Do we spend this much time talking about tomatoes? What will it take to get them to understand that when we all have an equal stake in the game, is when we are all truly equal in the eyes of the Constitution?" he concluded.

Don't you think it won't take some green persuasion, as they handed me another glass of Chardonnay? "Again, Charlotte, it's why I want you to do the cooking for them, butter them up and see what you can get out of them," as he tips his wine glass to me, "drink up".

"Come again, what?" I replied, "Oh, I know what's going on here – you want me to spy on them!" as I came very close to throwing my glass hand against the wall. "I know what's happening here," I said firmly, "you're trying to bring me in again," as I stood there for a moment tapping my heels. "I'm not getting caught up in this damn drama, do you understand me?" I retorted, growling at Clinton, "and I will not be a spy again".

Clinton, sensing this was not going down as easy as he would have liked, reached his hand around my waist and said, "I want you to run for office".He took a pin in the shape of the state of Delaware from his pocket. It had a Ruby in the heart of Sussex County, with an Amethyst in Dover, topped with a Salon Sapphire to represent New Castle County, and pinned it to my dress, over my heart."I told you this before, I want you to cook for our guests," as he tipped his glass to a portrait of one of the Presidents of past presidents.

"So, you mean I get to cook the food for Senators and diplomats at our gatherings at the White House," I said incredulously, as I squinted my eyes, not believing a word he said."So, I'll get to dazzle them with cannabis- infused culinary delights and I'll get to have a heart-to-heart with ol' Putin himself over some cannabis infused vodka," I quipped as I laughed out loud, boosted by the moonshine brandy.

"If and when you decide to do that, Charlotte, you will have my full support, but you've got to understand that we're just following the protocol according to plan," he said.

Blushing, I thought this would be crazy for me to pass up, and I could have it all if I just followed the next logical step. "You know, I guess I had not thought about that, I thought this part of my life was in the past, but y'all make it all sound like so much fun," I replied, "like I can be anything I want to be".

Pulling me in tight again to his chest, not realizing that all eyes were now upon us, he played with the hair around my face and said, "You can be anything you set yourself to be".

Looking back up at him, it suddenly became much clearer to me what I needed to do, as I looked down at the pin, "So, you want to rule the Free World with me?"

Clinton again pulled me tight and wrapped his arms around me and whispered, "I'll take you there".

"Just how do you propose that I do that?"

"That's easy, let me take you away for a week, I want to prepare you for the Office of President of the United States of America as an Independent candidate of the 'Purple Party', officially known as the Independent Party of the United States or IPUS for short; and your training starts next week in Mississippi".

"Maybe you should change the acronym to IPotUS," I said, unable to resist a good pun.

Clinton, now deadly serious, looked at me cross-eyed. "I want you to run as President. Charlotte," he said coldly, "did you hear what I said?".

I coolly took another swill of the bitter drink that was twirling around my glass, pulled away from him, looked him sternly in the face, and said, "I will give this due consideration," as I placed the empty glass into the pot of mums and walked away.

"You just got to believe, Charlotte," replied Clinton as he quickly held his arm out for me to grab.

I looked back up to him, closed my eyes, and took a few deep breaths, and then knew it was all true. Walking back to the party with my hand under his arm, the perfect gentleman that he was, I looked up and asked, "Do I have to decide about this right now?

"No, you'll know when you're up to bat".

"How will I know, Clinton?" I asked, turning back to him.

"You'll be written in," he said, offering me his right arm.

Is the **Center of Love** looking to have cannabis manufacturing in Delaware, too?" I asked as I looked around the party, as every eye was now glued to me.

Clinton patted my arms and said, "Yes, we would like outdoor grows down in Kent County. I have my eye on a piece of property that used to be a part of the Underground Railroad back when Harriet Tubman was smuggling slaves to freedom. I've been thinking that property, with its historic importance, would have an incredible story to tell. I just love the idea of a cannabis farm on it, and I have been picturing it for years. I also think it would make another great rehabilitation place, centrally located for easy access to all the residents of Delaware. The grand white house has over eight bedrooms and a pool out back. It would also make a wonderful cannabis themed wedding destination, and I want to call it the Canterbury Inn," he elaborated.

"I really love that your heart is in this for helping people," Kennedy said, as he thumped his hand to his chest."A hundred years to fix one mistake, but we're going to make it," he added.

As we emerged from the back of the estate, we saw two men exchange a white envelope. I seductively blushed at Kennedy as I looked him in the eye. Clinton got my attention as he pointed with his wine glass across the lawn and looked at me. "See what you can get out of the short one," he instructed.

I looked straight back at Clinton with a slight tick of my eye and knew I was all the way in this time."Why does my past keep catching up with me?" I asked myself, as I smiled outwardly and made small talk with the blue-eyed gentleman Clinton was having me impress.

The ghost dressed in a navy-blue coat materialized in front of me, grinned and whispered, "Because you volunteered, my dear," as his cool breath tickled my right ear.

CHAPTER 26

THE GOVERNORS INN

We walked out of the party into the waiting limousine, and the chauffeur drove us down to Dover. As we turned onto Loockerman, I looked over to Clinton. "Are we staying at the Governor's place tonight? "I asked curiously.

He patted me on my knee, keeping his eyes straight ahead. "You are going to like this," he said.

"Oh, Clinton, don't make me wait," I said, as I hit the button on the window and rolled it down. We drove past Silver Lake and made a left. After a few more turns, the car reached Woodburn and pulled into the driveway. The Capital Police on duty walked up to the car, and one officer poked his head in the open window. "Good evening, Mr. Tuckerman and Ms. Bennett," he said, "go on in, the Governor is expecting you".

"Thank you, Sergeant, said Clinton in the voice of a DSP trooper.

We walked in through the front door as the Governor opened it up and gave us both hugs. "Let me take you up to your room," she said as we began to walk up the steps. Down the hall on the right was a beautiful guest room in Queen Anne Style, and we stepped in.

"Take your time and freshen up, then come join me out on the front porch, I had our cannabis chef prepare us a little sleepy time dessert", said the Governor.

We hung our clothes up and headed down the steps and out to the front porch, where the Governor and First Gentleman were sitting on the black iron chairs. We sat down just as a man in a white chef jacket came out with a cannabis infused chocolate molten lava cake and placed it down. It was followed by a white chocolate and orange liquor coffee nightcap, when she laid out the schedule for tomorrow's events.

It looks like I won't get any sleep tonight," I thought, as I slinked up the steps and into the bathroom, took off my clothes, and rubbed the heels of my feet.

"No, no, you got to wait," said Clinton, "until then, I got a vessel you can play with". He drew us a bath and handed me a lollipop that was infused with cannabis and pineapple, then I slipped into his dream.

The Jacuzzi was running as he poured in some bubble bath. "The Naughty Fig line from Foobellas," he laughed, "this one is called Temptress". As I let my nose run under its bouquet, I could smell hints of Bergamot, Neroli, Lavender, Jasmine, Ylang, and Sandalwood that immediately took me onto an island getaway cruise. As the bubbles mingled around his neck, I massaged his feet with the oil that matched the blend. Marveling at his splendor, I was just struck by him. I took my time to feel every fiber of his leg, the way his hair clung tight to his skin, and the way his kneecaps made these little clicks as my fingers rolled around his gastrocnemius.

I watched as he stood up before me. The sudsy water slowly slid down his perfectly chiseled bod as he glowed in the candlelight. The more I looked at him, the more he looked like a God, and I was lost in him as he sat back down, resting his back against me, as I massaged his neck. I began to see a ball of red light hovering over us as it slowly descended into our souls. Then, in a flutter of excitement, I was swirling and reveling in how everything seemed to move so fast as the ball of red light wrapped around us, as the rush of the cannabis came in as waves of sensations fluttered inside of me.

The slow rhythmic dance settled into our root chakras, as I unwrapped the first soap in the **Chakra** line. The Red Jasper sat high up in the soap. The scent of Vetiver permeated my skin, tethering me to him as I ran the soap up and down his legs. I could feel myself moving deeper into the experience with each new breath, as I let the soap in my hands caress him.

I reached over to the next soap and peeled off the label that read **Sacral**. I remembered back to when I had that first chocolate that melted in my mouth, as its hints of orange engulfed me. I rounded the soap around his waist as I felt my sacral chakra begin to spin, as the Orange Calcite ignited me from within. I could feel as if his heart were beating in his waist, as I massaged the soap into him. My mind and body were now placed directly in front of him as I circled my hands around his back, massaging the aphrodisiacs into his flesh.

The vessel that Clinton spoke of just a few moments ago was now leaning on a barge, as I unwrapped the Power soap, as the lemon brought me in. The Yellow Citrine that reminded me of my own prowlers as I massage around his abdomen. Gliding my hand around his stomach in slow circles, I imagined myself drawing deeper into his own superpowers. Then, I suddenly felt a spark of energy as I drew my breath in and felt the spirit come through my soul, knowing that I was tethered to it.

The Green Jade **Heart** soap invited me in with the scent of the Bergamot and Neroli, as I connect my hand to his heart chakra and begin to breathe in unison. I felt myself fall into his chest, through the small cavities, as I slipped behind his veil and was safely tucked inside his chest, as his arms wrapped around me. I breathed deeper into what seemed like magic, when the violins called out to me, with each note driving me further into his inner chamber, as his heartstrings wrapped around me.

His luscious kisses started to take my mind into another dimension as I felt the Chamomile and Sodalite wrap around my throat as I was pulled into his nest. Moans of ecstasy escaped my throat as I felt his raw power as he piloted his love ship deeply into my harbor, taking my breath away as each rising wave of desire soared and surged inside me.

The **Third Eye** soap was suffused with an Amethyst and Lavender as the purple energy rained down on me. I felt the rumble in my soul, closed my eyes, and found myself traveling again along a rainbow of colors as we sprinted in a Tunnel of

Love. It all floated down on me and sent my chakras spinning in a harmonious masterpiece as tiny tremors began to shake my body.

In what could only be described as a walk into heaven's realms, I felt Clinton entwined within as we propelled into time. The Crown Blend with the white crystal, drenched in Frankincense and Myrrh enveloped us as our wings emerged, taking me back in time to when we were on the boat floating in the lake. I remembered the flashes and bullets whizzing by, and I knew then what I know now: that I, Charlotte Bennett, will be the President of the United States.

The Love of all Loves unfolded, as the master plans were downloaded inside of me. My mind was no longer aware of anything as he imprinted inside of me. I was drowning in a virtual sea of love, as the essential oils brought my soul to flight. We flew down to the Hall of Records as I pulled out each volume and scanned the pages of what was written before I came into this incantation.

I took another breath, as my fingers were led to the next book, with a date inscribed in Gold, divining the future. The angel to my right told me it was OK to open the book and read the lines. My mind was virtually incoherent as Clinton continued to deliver multiple shock waves into my system, sending me further into his heavenly dimension. I scanned the pages as I read the Plan. It was clearly and unambiguously ordained that I would be running for President, and its full impact hit me. I took another deep breath as if I had not breathed fresh air in a week. In a flash, my soul was returning to my body, arching over the bed.

Successive revolutions spun out of control as I screamed out to the glistening Love god, nestled between my legs, sensing that it was not all the way back in, "This can't be me," I thought, panting as I tried to renegotiate when some doubt began to creep back in.

Clinton changed his position and mounted me. I was totally under his spell, as the weight of his body as he pinned me to the bed, and he knew it as he cried out my name, telling me that I could do it, I needed to do it, that it was in the Plan and he was the angel in heaven who opened the book for me.

"Oh God!" I screamed out.

"YES!" he shouted, driving his dreams even harder into me. "YOU are going to do it!" he compelled with his stern voice, grunting as he churned the vast seas inside me.

In a flash, I took Chief Executive control, mounting his staff, riding him like the wild temptress with the full personal force of "mover and shaker" that I was chosen to be; knowing that I would make an incredibly good President as my love of People, Freedom, and Country, was what I had really planned. "Could I rule him? No, not yet, as I am not strong enough to overpower him," I thought, as he flipped me around on my back again. "I can tell you it is going to take some time to get me there," I said to him, as he kissed my lips.

"I've got all the time in the world, Charlotte, and I'm not going anywhere," he said as he began to shimmer.

Lo and behold! A brilliant white spectacle of light shined above his head, as the energy came in. The white light tingled as it vibrated up my spine, and the spiritual Nile flooded my mind. As my arms wrapped around his neck, I whispered back, "I will do it, Clinton, I will run in your pack".

"Excellent," he said, as he wrapped the purple robe around my shoulders and led me down to the dining room.

"Your dinner awaits you, my dear," he said as he kissed me on the lips and filled my glass with wine. The platters of food on the table enticed us as he candlelight set shadows on the walls and the sounds of smooth jazz played at the touch of his fingertips. The creamy dream of crab and creamed cheese, in a crock with French bread toasted points, was utterly delightful. Oh, how I savored the taste of seafood as I dolloped up each piece. The cayenne pepper with a hint of mustard seed gave me the distinct impression that something wonderful was growing inside me.

Nestled on the plate fashioned from the sea, a French delicacy of scallops, lobster, and shrimp in a creamy base with a splash of Port Sherry rounded out the baked plate. I looked up at Clinton as I put my fork down. "You treat me like a queen, and I was not expecting anything like this," I said gratefully, as a tear fell from my face.

"Toughen up, buttercup, you just wait," he said softly. "We have a meeting with a lawyer tomorrow up at Diamond State, signing some papers for you to be brought in as a managing partner in the Center of Love." The incorporating lawyer will explain everything. We're already an S-Corp, and we're just adding you to the lineup," he explained, as he pulled out his briefcase. "I want you to read over these papers tonight to understand what you are getting involved in," he said.

As I looked at the stack of incorporating papers, everything became clearer. I was more than a wife or some dream as the first woman President – I was a managing partner in all his investments and already knew about some of them as I ran through the papers: the manufacturing facility on Ruthar Drive in Newark, the farm up in Maine, the B&B in Jamestown, among others. As I began to read the last paper, I suddenly heard a telltale sound. "Did somebody knock?" I asked. I looked up from the papers as a dark chocolate soufflé took me by surprise. Standing there was the cannabis chef of the Governor's Mansion.

CHAPTER 27

WHAT IS YOUR FANTASY?

"So, tell me," I said, as I let the last drop of chocolate dessert go down my throat, "how did you get the job here at the Governor's Mansion?".

He pulled up a chair, sat down, and said, "It happened one day, out of the blue, as I was cooking a smoked pork quesadilla," he said. "I got a message from the lady when she was running for Governor. She had heard about my culinary experience. I proceeded to tell her that I have no formal learning, and I am pretty much self-taught from on-the-job experiences and have been working in kitchens for over five years, he continued. She asked me what some of my aspirations were, and I told her that my dream is to have a cannabis-based farm-to-table restaurant. She asked me what type of food I liked to make, and the first thing that came to mind was a quesadilla. She said that it sounded wonderful and asked if I had any extra. I was a bit hesitant, but I told her that I had enough leftover and could make a few more. She asked if I would be willing to bring them over and tell her more about my restaurant idea. I said, 'hell yeah', fired up my stove and brought her some, he explained in detail.

The chef continued to tell his tale: "I walked into my kitchen to fire up the stove and grabbed a small sauce pot to warm up the beer cheese sauce I had made a few days before. I got that started on the stove, then grabbed two medium frying pans, one to warm up the pork, and added a special ingredient. As I reached into the fridge to grab the container of my original canna-butter, I knew it was going to be my time to shine, and I held nothing back, as I was not only a candidate for Governor but also a fellow cannabis activist. I grabbed the last pan and tossed a spoonful of canna-butter in the pan and added 3 handfuls of chopped smoked pork. Once the pork was warm enough, I tossed a tortilla in the warming pan and sprinkled on approximately one-half cup of Cheddar and Gouda, added 5 ounces of pork on top of the cheese, then folded the tortilla in half. I wrapped the quesadillas in aluminum foil and poured the beer cheese into a pint container to take over to her.

When I arrived, I knocked on the door and waited for her to answer. When she opened the door, she was greeted with the delightful smell of the warm quesadillas. She said how wonderful they smelled, invited me in to talk, and told me to put the food on the dining room table, and asked me to join her. I said that I had eaten before I left, and it was all made for her. She smiled and offered me a drink. After she finished, she said it was one of the best quesadillas she had ever eaten and told me that she was highly interested in my ideas.

I told her that I'm an avid activist for the legalization of cannabis for adult use and said that I would like to open a cannabis-based restaurant in a country store type environment after it was legalized in order to share its many health benefits and also have a small gift shop where for things like infused sauces, cookies, cheeses and cookbooks. The restaurant would have indoor and outdoor courtyard seating and a separate smoking area.

The decor would have been leaning towards the wild west medicine cart theme. The menu would be seasonal with daily specials and offer a nice variety of international comfort foods. It would be supplied in part with produce from its dedicated small farm and other local farms and orchards as much as possible. The ideal location for the restaurant would be near the beach, with my farm no more than 30 - 45 minutes away," he went on.

"She said that she had an upcoming private party and asked me to bring smoked pork. Naturally, I jumped on that opportunity and catered the affair, so here I am today living the dream!" he exclaimed, ending his story.

Did you ever get your cannabis farm down at the beach?" I asked, as I signed the last of the papers and put them back in the envelope.

"I'll make a settlement in two weeks, and the rest is history," he said, as he lightly tapped the table with his hands, "thanks for listening." He smiled, glad at the chance to tell his story. "Now, you better get some sleep," he said softly, "you have a big day ahead," as he cleared the table, and I headed up to bed.

The Captain has me again.

Delirious in his illusion

The pen is in my hand

The Oval Office

Was part of the plan

The first woman president

He whispers in my ear

You can do this

As he drives his intentions one more time

Sign your name on the dotted line

You can make a difference

You will see in time

All my doubts

my insecurities

Just like that

Washed away

With his liquid sea

As he deposits

His plans inside of me

Closing my eyes

One more time

As the Purple Carpet

Unrolls in my mind

Crawling on the floor

The oval office some more

The power was not what I will do this for

My convictions are strong

My faith in my plan

You bet your bottom dollar

I will win this thing

CHAPTER 28

SHIPS, DIPS, AND CORRECTIONAL FACILITIES

The sun was just beginning to rise in the morning sky as The Governor, Clinton, and I got into the back of the car and made our way on I-495 up to where the Port of Wilmington was to the right. Clinton opened the trunk, handed the Governor and me hard hats, and carried a long metal cylinder and a folding table. We walked to an area near some shipping containers where he set up the table. We overlooked the waterfront as nearby stacks released their smoke and fumes. "What is that?" I asked, pointing up ahead, as I watched the bulldozers and circling seagulls playing tit for tat.

"That is the dump, Clinton answered, as we looked up to see a plane taking off from Philadelphia Airport. "Remember," he said, "you will have a test on this later," as he pulled out the blueprints and put them on the table.

The first thing that I saw, scanning the prints, was a big ship. "Holy cow, Clinton… you're building a boat?" I asked, in utter surprise.

"Technically no," he said, I'm not building a boat, that's what shipbuilders do.

The Governor stepped into the conversation and said, "This is the future home of the first of three luxury liners. We are calling the first one *Temptress of the Sea*, in the **Center of Love** cruise ship theme; the second one is the *Immaculata of the Sea*.

Flabbergasted, I interrupted the Governor, "You have got to be kidding me," I shrieked with delight, jumping up and down as I looked through the plans.

"Hold on, Charlotte, there's more, and we're calling the third vessel the *Charm of the Sea*," Clinton said, as he laid out another blueprint.

The Governor unraveled yet another set of blueprints. "This is the terminal, planned for this site with over 200,000 square feet, with restaurants and retail space. We'll have a shuttle from Philadelphia International Airport and Wilmington Airport to bring guests who are flying in from out of town; and with New Jersey, Pennsylvania, and Maryland so close, this is a great location for the base of operations".

Clinton chimed in. "We are also looking at ports in San Diego and Long Beach that will be for Hawaii and the South Pacific, as well as plans for another one in Texas that will tour the Gulf of America, over the span of the next ten years, as each ship is birthed," he said

The sheer magnitude of everything blew me away when I looked at him and said, "You're way more than just an entrepreneur, you're a tycoon," as I put my hands over my mouth.

Clinton looked at me with a bright twinkle in his eye and winked. "Now, Charlotte, I want you to look at this. We have a plan where the Temptress of the Sea will leave from here, stop in Lewes for two days, then head off to Bermuda, then Florida as she makes her way to the U.S. Virgin Islands, where a new resort is being built. On the way back, she will dock in Puerto Rico as well as Dominica before heading back up the Atlantic in a three-week excursion package featuring our healing retreat theme," he elaborated.

"Wow, this is simply amazing!" I exclaimed, as my thoughts began to materialize. "I have been seeing islands, boats, coconuts, pineapples, and birds of paradise in my dreams and just didn't realize what it all meant."

I said joyously.

"I would say so," he replied, "you see. This is just another reason I want you on my team: you're more than a wife, and a chef, you're my chief advisor – one that I can trust to tell me what I need to hear and one that I know can go into the Hall of Records or what we call the Archaic Hall," he said, as the Plan unfolded further.

"Is that why you asked me to marry you, because I can do things that others cannot do?" I asked.

"Yes, it was, as not many people can get inside of there, but I knew you could, and I wanted to see what you saw when you were in there," he intimated, "so, tell me, Charlotte, what else did you see in there when you were reading the books?

"Well, I saw that I would run for President, but I did not see where I would win," I said.

"Perhaps, you didn't look in the right book to see that, you don't run a race with the intention to lose, so we're going to have to work on making sure you win," he said. "You're not quite ready yet, and I get that; however, you will be meeting all kinds of foreign diplomats, and I'll be making sure that you study hard on geopolitics and bring you up to speed on whatever else we need to win this race," he stated.

"Aye, aye, Captain, I salute you," I said with a laugh, "and I am ready for all of this,". Then, I walked around the cement pad, looking at everything and seeing it in my mind's eye. "It may even give us a whole new twist on the acronym 'IPOTus'," I quipped.

Clinton, deadly serious as usual, couldn't help chuckling as the Governor giggled. "That's POTUS," he said, "get it right," he responded. "I know, and do not worry about what people say, do, or think. Just follow what I tell you to do, and you will have what you need in the palm of your hand. That is my job; I am the one who handles logistics. I just want you to listen carefully when I give you your marching orders, do you understand?" he explained.

I turned around to see two men in suits and ties walk up, wearing hard hats. As they reached out and shook our hands, the Governor introduced Jack Betterman and Jarden Durrell and said that they are the ones running the operation. "I will be formally introducing you to the whole board once the paperwork is all drawn up and we're bringing you in as Regional Vice President, for the time being," she said.

"Congratulations, Charlotte", they said, as they reached out their hands. "So, tell me, what do you think of the plans to bring a luxury liner to the Port of Wilmington?" asked Jack.

"It's brilliant, with Philadelphia International Airport to the North and Wilmington Airport just south of here, I like the retail and restaurant, and with the hotels in Wilmington not even ten minutes away; if there are issues, we have some other options, just in case of tropical storms and whatnot causing delays," I answered.

"Clinton looked at me with a twinkle in his eye, "She's got this gentleman, not bad for one day's notice," he said, as he rolled up the plans. "What do you say, Charlotte?" he said, "you in on this deal?".

"Oh, man, am I ever in on this deal, you better believe it," I replied, "how soon can I sign the papers?".

The Governor spoke up. "The lawyers are drawing everything up now, we will have them ready in two days, expect a call no later than Friday," she said energetically, "no worries, you are already in". The deal was done as we all shook hands and headed back to the waiting car.

"Now, we were off to our next destination, and we headed down Route 13 towards Smyrna, Delaware. The car pulled into a large fence-lined piece of property with large towers placed all around. I stepped into another realm as the multitudes of gardens gave way to a glistening pond. The orchard and gardens were meticulous, and beauty beamed from every inch as I watched as each man tended to their chores and smiled, when I realized that the plan had morphed into fruition.

I was led down a hall where rooms opened to my left, and the scent of essential oils filled the air. I looked in to see rows of counters with men in while lab coats wearing goggles and rubber gloves, measuring ingredients and pouring them into bowls. I stepped in and was introduced to the men of the *Vaughn Healing Facility* when I turned to the Governor and said, "You did it!".

She smiled back at me and said that everyone is healing in their own ways, as she led me to another part and showed me a classroom of people building something that I knew was so familiar. I walked up to one man as he smoothed out the leather he was adhering to the board. He smiled at me and said, "We make the **Moon Energy** bed here. It gets tested for weeks to make sure each grid works as it should, and as you can see, we are healing immensely," as the teacher came up to us. As her long hair caught my eye, she smiled back at me and said, "Advocacy!"

The Governor went up to one of the residents and marveled at his work, "I am so looking forward to you being back on the outside," she said as she held up a piece of paper, "now, you're free,".

The tears fell from his eyes as she held his hands. "It's OK, I have a plan". They walked out of the room as the rest of the class clapped.

We spent the rest of the afternoon visiting with all the groups and had lunch outside on picnic tables in the gardens, as we watched family members come in with their kids. The swing sets were filled with both the parents and kids as they got to visit their daddies, while they healed from the world's disasters.

The visit was over, and we all walked back in. When I got to sit down with the Governor, she turned to me and said, "Write it, then watch it unfold, but realize it is all in God's hands, the timing of things". She took my hands into her own. "Charlotte, you are going to be inheriting a lot of things, and you will be beyond blessed with what is coming for you," she said as she looked me in the eyes, "thank you for believing".

Stammering, I asked Clinton, "What, wait, wait, how did that happen?".

"Once you shook their hands, you accepted the deal, the primary paperwork you signed last night set the ball in motion for all our dreams. For starters, expect twenty million right off the top, securities as well as stock options. Then, a salary based on everything else you do. You are being offered another seventeen million when you sign the agreement for an eight-year contract down in the US. Virgin Islands, where you will be stationed. This does not even include the merchandising, which is another whole level, as well as commercials," he said with a wink.

Clinton opened his briefcase and pulled out some more papers. "The rest of the year, you will be in Maine as well as flying back to Las Vegas for other preliminary things. During this time, you will be gaining a wealth of knowledge that will set you up over the next eight years, making you one of the most eligible candidates for the next President of the United States. Mark my words, you will be on the cover of *Forbes Magazine* as one of the wealthiest women in the world. All because you dared to dream big!" he explained.

I sat there in utter shock as everything he said to me began to flutter around my head.

Clinton turned back to me and said, "A fantasy is something your mind thinks up, and a business plan is your fantasy written down; so, I was just a poor boy with nothing but dreams, but in time, I turned my dreams into reality by sitting down and writing a plan".

"Where do I fit into all of this?" I questioned him.

"You," he said, as he looked into my eyes, "are one of my biggest fantasies come true, and when I placed this ring on your hand, it was a fulfillment of a promise I made to myself the very first time I saw you".

"And what promise was that?" I asked, quivering with bated breath.

"The one I told Kennedy about when he asked me what kind of woman I wanted," he said.

"And what type of woman did you want?" I asked, as I slid closer to him.

Laughing, he asked, "Do you remember when you almost fell face first into me that night?".

I blushed and answered, "Yes, I do.

"Well, after you left, I asked Kennedy, 'Who is that woman that just fell into me wearing the chef jacket?' whereupon Kennedy scratched his head and asked, 'Who do you mean, the cook, Charlotte Bennett?' and I answered, 'God… YES! Set me up with her," he said.

A look of worry came over my face when I thought of the night my washing machine went on the fritz and what Kennedy and I did. "So, let me ask you something, why did it take so long for you to contact me again after that night?" I inquired.

Clinton took a deep breath. "I had fantasies, too, ones I did not think included you and you had fantasies I knew were not about me, but I saw something in you that night in the restaurant," he said, "and you intrigued me, so that was when I looked at Kennedy and said, 'I am going to pay you handsomely if you can make that woman my wife, but she must not know anything about me or who I really am".

"Who really are you, Clinton?" I asked, as I looked into his eyes, "What are you?"

He looked back at me as we pulled into what was once the GM plant on Boxwood Road that now houses the Amazon warehouses and asked, "What if love exists and it just takes a long time to find?". My mind was blown away at the sheer poetry that came out of his soul.

The Governor looked at me and asked, "Are you ready for the race of your life?"

"You bet I am, Governor," I replied with a broad smile, "let's do this thing, we're talking cars, right?" The Governor and Clinton warmly smiled back at me as the glass partition came down. "Where to next, Governor?" asked the chauffeur. "Dover," she directed.

A Fleet of Three

As the wind blew in me

Immaculate in its conception

Was a part of the design?

As the baby swells in me

The lure of the Sea

The Love Boat is calling me

To my destiny

Immaculate display

A Seaman's Hideaway

As the smoke swirls in

Destiny is calling

Trust the process

Is all I can do

Immaculate conception

Is inside of me

The third `is the charm

Of the sea

A fleet of three

Make love to me

CHAPTER 29

THE MONSTER MILE

The Delaware State University plane landed just south of Dover, surrounded by corn fields. The president of the university was waiting in a separate limousine as he stepped out to shake hands with Clinton, as Kennedy and Karissa exited the plane.

Standing next to with a stack of papers was his secretary Bonnie placing the papers in Clintons hands she says "The grant money is on its way in, and the food truck is stationed in position; now, do not forget that before the first lap starts is when the car is unveiled," shoving more papers into our hands, "Kennedy, have you ever driven the Monster Mile before?" she asked.

"No," he answered, "but I am certainly looking forward to it," as he picked up the pace with Clinton.

The party that has been racing all over the country was ushered up to the VIP stands at Dover Downs to a packed stadium. The whole crowd rose and placed their hand over their hearts as they recited the Pledge of Allegiance, the invocation was said, and the Star-Spangled Banner was played.

"Oh my God, there goes Kennedy", shouted Karissa as the 1979 Pontiac Trans Am rolled out on the concrete in front of the other race cars. He waved his hand out the window as a team of ladies that looked like a pit crew started blowing him kisses from the sidelines. There was even a large sign of the *Center of Love* logo and the cereal box with a picture of Kennedy in his racing suit holding onto a box of **Weedies** cereal saying, "This is how I get my start!".

The veteran announcer of races long past handled the microphone with ease: "Ladies and gentlemen, start your engines!" The cameras flashed and video rolled as news reporters buzzed around the track. When the green flag was dropped, the 1979 Pontiac Trans Am blasted off, with Kennedy behind the wheel. He took one lap as he went around the mile, then dipped down into the pit road. Bridgeman then got into position, looking to take the lead from Clinton.

"Oh, my God!" I screamed, "Is there nothing this man cannot do?" As he took the lead away from Number 36, Number 2 came back in, trying to take the lead away from Clinton. "Wait … car number 57, isn't that the number of the car on the Center of Love car?" Karissa shrieked excitedly.

Karissa started going through her phone, scanning the pictures until she came across a tall, handsome man waving, and showed it to me. "Well, I'll be, now I know what Kennedy has been doing," she said, "no wonder he has been so uptight, he pulled off a dream of a lifetime!"

It only took a few minutes for Kennedy to appear. "What do you think now, baby?" he said, as he kissed Karissa, "I bet you didn't think I was up to this".

"No, I didn't… but DAMN, Kennedy, I'm impressed," she said.

"You just wait, baby, you ain't seen nothing yet," he replied, "our sample cereal is being distributed to the grandstands, the Cannabis Freedom Act was passed months ago, and this is just pomp and circumstance". 'Now, it's twirling around the floor, and the buzz on the street is that Clinton and Charlotte are getting married in Delaware!

"You're kidding me," said Karissa, "why Delaware?"

"You'll see… we're not so sure about the details, still a few 'I's to dot and 'Ts to cross and all that, but we're almost there, baby," he said warmly, "and thank you for believing in my love club."

"I'll always have Kennedy," Karissa said, as she looked up at him.

His blue eyes filled with wonder, sparkling with delight. "It has been years that I've been working on this," he said, as he took her hand, "I have something for you". Kennedy handed her a box of Weedies and told her to open it. As Karissa opened the little box, with the oatmeal and walnuts that had that familiar crunch. Kennedy asked, "What do you think?" Kennedy says to her

"I think you're brilliant," said Karissa, as she poured the cereal in her hand and out popped a new diamond ring. "Oh my God, Kennedy, I can't believe you did this," she said, as she held the ring up to the light.

"Thirty-three Karats in total," he said, "here let me see your finger". He slid the ring that was encased around six rows of diamonds over her knuckle and then pulled his hand out to show her his matching band.

The diamonds sparkled and fluttered as Bonnie grabbed her hand. "Oh, my Lord, that is a massive diamond, and I hope you took my husband with you," she said, as she laughed, "congratulations". "Are you kidding me, you know who you paired me up with last night?" she said, as Karissa laughed. "I cannot wait to take him to Mississippi and start the next class with you guys," she said, as the Governor's Chief of Staff came in and gave us all a hug.

"Well, I can't wait to teach you how to fly," said Karissa, as she shook the Chief of Staff's hand.

Kennedy just laughed. "I believe you met Big Willy from Philly," he said, "what do you think?"

The Chief laughed right back at him, "Oh my God, he has magic hands!" he said.

"I taught him everything," Kennedy said with a wink.

We watched as the cars kept rolling around the bend with the stadium roaring, as the boxes of **Weedies** were passed down the rows. Karissa looked over at me, smiling. "This is amazing," she said. As the checkered flag was waved, the final lap came fast, as Clinton took the win!

Charlotte started jumping up and down, utterly awestruck by all of this. "I did not see this coming," I said, watching as his car made donuts on the track, and the pit crew popped champagne.

Bonnie and I started hugging and jumping up and down, and Nadia was screaming to take her to the pit, thinking that maybe her future husband was down there.

I looked at her and said, "Where did you come from?" as G'anacia turned the bend. "Girl, you know I was not missing this for the World," she said, as we all started laughing and hugging each other tightly.

"There are more ladies, this is just the beginning," Kennedy chimed in, "you know those cars we all love so much?".

"What, my old Pontiac still sitting up in Maine? I asked.

"Yes, and we're meeting with the executives sometime in the next week," he said, "we are working on jobs."

Karissa started jumping up and down. "We've got a lot of papers being drawn up and we're going public".

"What, wait, you're kidding me," said Karissa, "we're going public, what does that mean?"

"It means we're in the game, baby, we're in the game, listed on the stock exchange," as he held her tight.

Just then, an usher came up to us. "Come with me and I will take you down to the floor," he said. The crowd of people screamed and shouted with excitement as Winslow walked around, rounded the bend, surrounded my men in black suits, dark shades with wire pieces in their ears, as he fixed his gaze on Charlotte and walked towards her. Standing in front of me was the most manganous man I had ever met when I said, it was not Clinton I was trying to impress," as I began to laugh.

Laughing back at me, he explained, "No, you had to do that too; however, I was the one behind all of this". "Let me introduce myself, my name is Winslow," he stated. "Winslow," I said, looking directly at him, "you mean, the King of the Racing Industry?" as everyone around me started to laugh.

"Something like that he laughed, just one of my many attributes he replied warmly, "it's been a long time since we had a Pontiac in the game and you guys in Maine have been creating a lot of excitement in racing – enough so, that I am hungering for you guys to be a part of my team," he stated. "You got brains, kid, and I like your visions," he said as he reached out to shake Kennedy's hand. "I hear you can cook, too," he said with a laugh, as we came closer to Clinton. The cameras flashed as Clinton pointed to me.

"What do you think, Winslow, can I pick 'em or not?" he said.

"I must admit, Clinton, I was a bit worried that you could pull all of this off, but you got my attention, and you got yourself a sponsor. I'll have the papers drawn up".

Clinton's arms wrapped around me, and the hum of the crowd's cheering became a distant drone: "Are you really a race car driver, Clinton?" I asked.

"Nah," he said, as we walked back to where the racing crew was celebrating, "I always wanted to do this, and life is too short not to do what you want to do".

"Oh, I can see that," I said, as we made our way to where the plane had come in earlier.

"I have got another driver I am grooming for this, and he is waiting on that 2025 Pontiac Trans Am to come in," he said.

"You are so amazing, Clinton," I said again, "what are you?"

"Have you not figured it out yet? He asked, as he looked me in the eyes.

You got one, use it

I must admit

I like it like this

Writing a masterpiece

In the middle of the night

It's just me and God

In the moonlight

I'm on a mission

Suffice it to say

A culinary symphony

You could say

Laced with love

All along the way

That is my equation

In my fantasy

I am an author, you see

Writing poetry

There is so much more to be

Don't fret when God speaks to you

He's only trying to steer you too

If you study history

The great minds working in the night

DaVinci, Tesla, and Einstein

A beautiful mind Is a beautiful thing

Everyone gets one of these

Please understand

You're not like the rest

You are brilliant

In your design

Just misunderstood

Most of the time

You don't conform

You're not supposed to

Don't let the trials and tribulations of life

Extinguish your flight

Behind every failure Is an even better plan

Study your history

You know the way

Just because they are not like you

Doesn't mean something's wrong with you

We are all unique

We have our own path

Your story is yours

And it's amazing

Free your mind from its traps

Write, paint, create music

The arts are where it's at

This is my testament

You can do anything in this world

Let your imagination soar

The stars have aligned

Never shall you fret

Just believe in yourself

The God is you

Chapter 30

Pontiac Dream

Karissa's sensuous hand wrapped around Kennedy as he opened the door to the beautiful Trans Am for her. He shut the car door, ran around to the driver's side, and hopped in. The fine-tuned engine immediately roared to life when he turned the ignition key and fired her up. Knowing he needed to confess about the mistress he's been spending money on, he turned to Karissa and said, "I must tell you something".

He banged the gears through the 6-speed Tremec Magnum XL Transmission as his hand dropped each gear into submission, via the Hurst shifter. The tension of his confession must have been playing havoc with him when he slammed down on the 4-wheel disc brakes and let the motor rev. He looked over to Karissa and said, "I fancied her with Moser Engineering 12-bolt rear ends with 4:11:1 gear" as the car took off, making his snowflake wheels squeal with delight as he did a few donuts in the rear parking lot. The breeze blowing through the T-tops had Karissa's hair blowing in her face when Kennedy hollered out, "She's Running on Year One 17"X9" Gold Snowflake wheels wrapped by Nitto 285/40R17 rear tires and 275/45R17 front tires," as Kennedy squealed out of the parking lot and hit the back roads as the hit the first bump Kennedy announces 'Karissa your riding on a Pro-Touring F Body GEN II suspension system".

"Good thing," she said, "with the way you're taking the turns".

I had her wires upgraded by Painless Performance as he looked over to his bride and gave her a wink with his eyes.

"Oh, I like that," she said, looking directly at him, "how much money have you spent on your mistress?

Kennedy fumbled for a second, not sure how to answer the next inquisition, when he blurted, "The cooling system is handled by Be Cool Aluminum Radiators with fourth-generation F-Body GM electric fans as he flipped the switch, hoping to calm her down. "What do you think of her paint job?" as he touted the original Phoenix Graphics on top of factory Solar Gold paint, when he hit the Route 1 South bypass to the Virginia Beach coastline, as the dream came to life.

"So, do you think this is enough pressure to put on General Motors to bring their lineup of racing cars and bring them back to Delaware for manufacturing," as Karissa hollered above the engine's sound. She held on to the "oh shit bar" as the fuel injection kicked in with her hair waving out of the T-tops. "I'm hearing something about Dearborn, Michigan," she said loudly. Kennedy looks over to his wife, "I think you might be right, all of this in time for 2025, if General Motors is willing to bring it back. Can you imagine Bonneville, Grand Prix, Grand Am, and the Trans Am on the showroom floor?" Kennedy shrieked, knowing he was speaking it into existence.

"I can," said Karissa, as she began to build her own car as she hollered out the specks, "I want the 2025 Trans Am to be based of the 79-81 body style. It will have the all-new Pontiac 400 aluminum engine with round aluminum port heads, high flow manifolds, 2 1/2" exhaust with hi pro mufflers plus direct injection for the most optimal fuel mileage utilizing hemp fuel technology and WS6 suspension to tame the wildest curves!"

Kennedy ogled as she reached over and rubbed her leg. "Oh my God, will that make the car so fast?" he said, giggling with delight as he rubbed the steering wheel. "Is this what you are seeing, Karissa?" as he pulled into a gas station that doubled as a chicken joint. Let's get some fried chicken," he said, "we've got a long drive ahead and are bound to hit the traffic in Georgetown, before the split".

"So, what else is the car going to have?" he asked Karissa as they walked into the store.

"Well, this is just my best guess, but I am thinking it will be mated to the all-new Tremec 6-speed manual transmission matched, with the 4:11:1 rear gear for faster acceleration, boasting a whopping 650 Hp @ 7000 rpm and 700 Lb of torque @ 4400 rpm with Brembo 6-piston calipers applying pressure to the 14.5" diameter cross-drilled and slotted rotors to stop on a dime. It will incorporate Pontiac's all-new Bluetooth capability, featuring Apple CarPlay and Android Auto, a SiriusXM radio 10-speaker Premium sound system, and GM's OnStar navigation system!"

Kennedy looked over at his wife as he excitedly exclaimed, "Oh my goodness, Karissa, there is not a man alive that would not want that car," he said, as he opened the cooler and grabbed a few drinks. "I can tell you that you have put a lot of thought into this".

Karissa punched the order in for the fried chicken. She retorted, "Oh, I have"!

Kennedy gave her a look that let her know that he had one up his sleeve, as he took a long gulp of soda. Wiping his mouth, he handed the order to the cashier and said, "Be patient, she is coming my dear: She will have Dual two stage airbags, front side and knee and passenger side, front and side; daytime running lights, HD rear vision camera, LED headlights and turn signals," as Kennedy paid for dinner, winking at the cashier as she smiled at them and says "OH wow, that sounds hot, hot, hot"! As Kennedy hands her a tip. Karissa's eyes and ears perked up when she squealed, "Oh, Kennedy, what color did you order for me? "As they walked back out to the Phoenix Rising as Kennedy opened the door and made sure she was in.

"This is the real kicker, Baby; this one is going to fly off the showroom floor and get the ladies screaming for that torque in between their legs".

"Oh, Kennedy, you are so bad, do tell me what it is," she said as she buckled up her seat belt and pulled out a piece of world-famous fried chicken and bit into his leg.

"Introducing the Firebird with Purple Passion on her lower panel morphing to White Pearl," replied Kennedy, as she climbed her way up. "The roof's exterior color mated with Ebony leather interior that opens all the way up into a convertible, with 8-way power seat driver and 6-way passenger heated and cooled seats, the Diamond Edition in three shades of purple with diamond accents around the whole bird, with 18X9 billet snowflake wheels in the front and 18X10 in the rear, and diamond girdle center cap adorned with a new Pontiac crest in the center that looks like a woman with wings, flying.

"Oh, my goodness, Kennedy, I want that, I want that, when will I get her, I can't wait for her to be on route 13 with her wings opened up, this is going to be the ride of my life!""Yes!" exclaimed Karissa. "A convertible… That's exactly what I want! "Where do you think it's going to be made?" she asked eagerly as she tore into the thigh of that Delmarva chicken.

"Would you like to see the property that the Governor and I looked at when I was down here last month?" said Kennedy, as he pulled out onto Route 13.

"Oh, Kennedy, you are so bad," said Karissa as she squealed with delight, "yes, take me to the spot where you're looking to build it".

It only took a few turns, and they were on Loockerman in the heart of Dover, as he made his way into the country, overlooking a large field by the train tracks. "This is where we are thinking of building the plant," he said, as he opened a bottle of lemonade.

Karissa looked over at Kennedy and said," I'll be squealing with delight when General Motors comes back to Delaware," as a tear fell down her cheek. "Delaware took such a hit back when they left, and I remember how much it affected our economy, and

Dover needs this, Kennedy." She stated as she looked up at him, "Can we pray for this to happen right now?"

"Of course, why don't you lead the way.

"Oh, Lord, please bring General Motors back to Delaware, bring the blessings of jobs for her residents so that prosperity can begin again and please, Lord, let the city of Dover be the place that ignites a nation to believe in the power of your might and mercy!"

"Amen," Karissa said, as she started to jump up and down, looking out to the fields with the FOR SALE sign. "This is a lot of land," she said as she looked at the large expanse of farmland. "What are you going to do with it all?" she asked.

"Grow the hemp for the panels, my dear replied Kennedy. "The Governor wants to bring the company that turns hemp into the quarter panels, hoods, rear decks, et cetera, and have them manufacture them right there," he continued, as he pointed to the Western sunset.

"Wow, Kennedy, this is going to be awesome," she said, "can you imagine all the economic development and employment opportunities that will come out of this?"

"Yes, I can, Karissa," said Kennedy, as he opened the door to the 'Dream of Pontiac' coming back to life, as his wife sat down in the front passenger seat. "How about it if we spend the night in Rehoboth Beach, on the Boardwalk tonight?" he asked, as he sat in the driver's seat.

"Lead the way, Kennedy," she said.

The car took off in flight as it hugged the curves of Kent County down Route 15 until it reached the Route 1 South interchange. As they pulled into the resort, the salty air and breeze from the ocean caught Karissa off guard, reminding her of what was still lingering on her lips, as the 'Dreams of Pontiac' came alive in her mind. They pulled under the building into the parking area, waited a while until Olivianna and the rest of the crew showed up. "I really love vacation places where the crowds are quiet," she said, "off season is my season".

As they checked into the 11th-floor suite, they were greeted by a panoramic ocean view. The king-size bed faced the sea and a series of sliders that opened to the balcony. They put their clothes away and drew a bath located in the corner of a garden bathtub that overlooked the ocean and filled the tub with a bath bomb made of Jasmine and Lavender filled with gold shimmer. How Karissa loved the **"Goddess Within"** bath bomb from **Foobellas**. The gold reflected off her skin and the scented oils that soothed her flesh, as the aphrodisiacs conjured the Spirit of love within.

She looked out the window, and the sky caught her attention, as the gold and pink rays shone through the clouds. The longer she stared towards the sky, the sooner the bright burning bulb of the moon caught her eye as she let the warm waters envelope her. Kennedy came in and lit a candle. He began to play their wedding song as he slipped into the golden water.

Her eyes glazed over at the Moon, as her mind churned with desire. She ran her legs up and down his thigh, gently caressing with her toes. Karissa was excited, knowing that her order was being filled, as images of cars raced through her head. As the moonlight bathed the tub's warm water, she felt like she was in the ocean itself, drifting off to some erotic car dream in a wave of flawless synchronicity. Karissa ran a bar of soap over her breasts, imaging herself driving her very own new Made in Delaware Pontiac when Kennedy slid across the tub and began to kiss her.

No sooner than she had hit the bed, there was Kennedy, nestled between her legs, rooting for her dream like a baby roots for milk on mama's breast. Karissa began to scream.

She hit pay dirt as the gates opened and her dream began to unfold in direct connection to her entire being and took copious notes, as visions of Firebirds danced in her head.

Her carriage ran at full throttle as her hips writhed in the thrall of Venusian delights. Her voice cracked, and she spoke in tongues long forgotten in the recesses of her brain. Her body shook, and for a moment, as she turned into the motor and shaker of the Trans Am.

In an explosion of light and sound, the car morphed into a super galactic love machine with wings for doors that flapped like an eagle in the sky, flying out to sea. Faster and faster, it flew to Atlantis as the 1979 Pontiac Trans Am called out to the rest of its fleet to wake up. The drumbeat rose as they were lifted higher, with wings flapping, watching as the bubbles began to surface on the ocean. Then, like a shooting star in reverse, out from the sea burst forth the craziest thing she ever saw: a car so sleek that she burned with desire.

She raced to her new task in her Mayan red dress with the 1994 Pontiac Grand Am on fire. The passion inside Anastacia took a sharp right, with the back seat filled with child seats and a play pen. Karissa got a feeling that they would be in a new location as she looked over at them.

It appeared that she was planning on a family with all that stuff, when Kennedy pointed to the right and said, "Look at that". Traveling faster than the speed of sound was the Pontiac Solstice, as Nadia burst forth through a giant wave wearing Brazen Orange and took her top off. Dangling from her carriage was the man of her dreams as Jaxson held on for dear life, trying hard to keep everything in place, as she awaited her healing space while he fixed the muffler, then landed in the passenger seat. Flying low to the sea, she handled like a dream. "No babies for us if you know what I mean," she said as he kissed her on the lips and said, "It is just us".

As Karissa's mind wrestled with the meaning of the visions unfolding, she gave in to the higher waves of light and let them take her over. The golden shimmer that glistened on them reminded her of the Golden Trans Am, as it flew out of the water at alarming speeds. This was not what she was expecting, as they and the car became one. All her mind could think of now was of God, and all that she could speak was the name God. All that her voice could even command was "O, God!". That is when it happened, and she let the power compel her without a doubt as she hit the pedal, and they shot out into the air.

Flying down the coast, the fleet of cars did barrel rolls as they pierced the sky. The Verdoro green machine with Kevin with an unidentified passenger wearing a pink bridesmaid dress, took the Pontiac GTO for a new show, transforming in the blink of an eye. As the heart of the car came alive, they virtually heard the voice of God, as their radio transmission came in clearer and the static in their head faded away. The New Life promised was coming his way as he hit the throttle and drove down the coast, heading for Mississippi.

The "Wildcat" was about to explode as the jet fighter hovered close. Circling around, scanning the sea, they heard the transmission as he commanded his transformation and turned into a Star Chief. The fuselage ignited as Officer Wilcatta came roaring to life, as he turned to Mayfair Blue and looked for his bride off the Bermuda Coast.

As if this were not enough, the roar of the Bonneville burst forth from the sea. Wearing her Purple Pearl, Charlotte took the wheel with Clinton to her right. The rumbling of the engines was like fireworks as the waves of the ocean hit the shore. Their radios crackled in some gibberish language that reminded them of a one-year-old, as the waves came into sync and the fleet raced further down the coast to the Florida Keys and the white sandy shore.

Not to be forgotten, Jason appeared in a pearl white Pontiac Grand Prix with his wife by his side and her belly swollen. His white wings with gold lining flew higher than anyone could have ever predicted, as he joined them in their fight to survive, with their radios tuned into each other, hearing the commands. They raced around the Keys, heading back up to Mississippi, where the race of a lifetime was getting ready to flourish.

As Karissa's body began to flow back to the bed, only comprehending a few fleeting thoughts, Kennedy knew that he was taking her over the top. The only words he heard her speak were "Oh my god, oh my god, oh my god", as her head shook back and forth. I had mounted the throbbing dream deep inside her as he released every idea inside, pumping his gas pedal with maximum velocity as the fuel injection opened, sending a load of fuel up her intake. "The Dream of Pontiac" was alive as they collapsed back into the dream of a lifetime.

Kennedy woke up to the picture of a 1979 Trans Am on his cell phone with her motor purring on the front page of the newspaper, then hit the remote on the television, as talks of GM bringing the Pontiac line of racing cars back, bringing manufacturing back to the United States.

Karissa looked over at him, beaming with excitement. "I am so proud of you, Kennedy," she said, "and I cannot believe you've been working on all of this". The afterglow still lingered on her face as she leaned in closer. "No wonder you have been so tense lately, and when we get to Mississippi, I have a special treat for you," she said, before nibbling on one of her Purple Kush cookies.

CHAPTER 31

SHAPE SHIFTER

My ears tuned in to the sounds of birds chirping, though I wasn't willing to open my eyes. The last thing I remembered was kissing Clinton, when I curled down deeper into the bed, pulling the thin blanket around me, wondering where I was. I opened my eyes enough to see the spindles of rich, dark Mahogany with a draping of fabric suspended like clouds in the sky over me. I knew I was in a canopy bed with a chandelier up above. The fabric making it look like stars were twinkling the way the wind blew the crystals throwing shadows on the bed. I looked across the room, where an antique dresser was facing me. A green and yellow *"Gone with the Wind"* lamp, adorned with pink and white roses, up against the yellow rose walls that made up the house in Natchez, Mississippi.

I looked out the windows to a field full of peaches, where off in the distance, horses were gathering as bales of hay were lined up. I also saw juicy melons and strawberries like they were a fruity river, sweet and delusional all at the same time, and wondered how they all could grow like this. I could even smell the scent of hay and taste the salt lick on my tongue, daring me to take it all in this time.

I looked further and followed the dirt path that led to a wrought iron gate. I struggled to adjust my eyes as men with full beards and hats stood by the fence as they smoked their cigarettes, calling me with their money. Suddenly, I heard a scream, "This is no life for me, I'm not someone's property!" as the door to my room slammed shut! I felt a wave of panic flood over me, and this time I bolted out of the room, racing down the hall, screaming for Clinton!

In a flash, he came out of nowhere. "Whoa, Whoa, Whoa, hold on!" he said, "What's the matter?".

"I saw another ghost!" I shrieked, "The ghost that lives here".

Clinton wrapped his arms around me and hugged me tightly, telling me. "It's going to be alright," he said softly. "It's Sarah, she comes in some nights". "You do hear and see them, too," he said with delight. "Oh, how I love that you do, you speak my language, and that's why I am so attracted to you".

"What about the men at the gates?" I asked, as I made my way back to the window, pointing to nothing but a cloud of smoke dissipating.

Clinton looked back at me and said, "Charlotte, all our properties are haunted. I am sure what you saw were men of the past. No doubt it was old Doc and his gang. They were banished long ago from the property. Their spirits cannot enter here, but you will feel the others as they show themselves". No other pick-up line in history could ever beat that. As the violins played out, his wings opened over me. The sparks flying out of his fingers were like nothing I had ever seen before. I could see him transform. "I knew it, he's a superhero," I thought, as I wrapped my arms around his neck. The King of the World was in my arms as I succumbed in his bed. All I remember next was a fireball of explosions as a wild heart darted in mine, and the wind blowing the sheets as the four-poster bed encapsulates me. Once again, I began to wonder if I was dead. It's like being in heaven when he is on top. Each thrust bursting inside my body sent exotic hues of colors, as he took me over the edge. Elixirs dripped off his lips, like honey suckle dew drops, as I reveled in its taste, quenching the thirst in me. His tongue engulfed my own in a duel that took us down each other's throats. Forcing me to see that fate has cast this spell, I feel another presence filling up my well. It was "The Jockey" running through my hair, as his stripes dared me to eat him one more time. "Oh, Clinton," I hollered, just when I think you cannot top what you do, then, damn if you don't see another one through," as I circled back on top of him, mesmerized by his presence as my hands clasped his magic stick. Just like that, I saw Beef Wellington, and oh man, I couldn't wait for his stuffing! The Filet Mignon as it rolls on out. I simply am not one for pastry wrapped around my meat. I like to roast it whole if you know what I mean. Starting with his leg, I use my own stock to rub up and down his shank as my hands explored his vessel. I felt free and light as I danced over his head with the thoughts of his buttery spread nourishing me again. I eagerly took all of him into this enchanted facility.

At first the pony was so unsuspecting as he came up to me and let me pet him as I fell into his wrap running my hands through his mane as he drew me into his trap. The stain of the cigarettes on "The Jockey's" teeth meant that the little pony was no pony at all, as I crumbled at his feet. Knowing he could take me at any minute, and I would let him. As my mind let go, all my fears exploded as I let my insecurities go. I felt his pull upon my hair as the pony turned into a stallion.

My hips shook with excitement, as the thoughts of running my love down on him intensified, wanting him so bad to just take me away to his secret stable and show me what his hands really can do. I nearly lost my mind as wave after wave of releases surged out of me. The pounding of my heart as the gates come undone, The Jockey in my mind beating my rump, slapping me with his whip as he takes me from behind, barreling down hard on the finish line as I hear him neigh – Grunting as his nostrils become larger with each gallop – Riding me harder as he sees the finish line. The closer he got to the win, the more the rain came pouring down, and I started screaming again.

I shrieked as he took the lead, beating me harder as I picked up the pace, screaming out God's name as we both exploded over the Finish Line! There we were, spent, lying on the bed in a crumpled heap, with the sweat of his body dripping upon me. "That was some horsey ride," I said, panting for air, trying to catch my breath as I rubbed my head into his chest.

"Did you like that?" he asked nonchalantly.

"I do not understand what you are, Clinton," I replied.

"I told you; I can be anything I want to be," he replied.

"Yeah, I know. I thought you meant that you could be a doctor, a lawyer, or whatever, I said, "and I did not think you could turn into another person or an animal".

"You did not answer my question," he stated flatly, as he continued to kiss my neck.

"What question was that?" I asked, feigning ignorance, as I continued to spiral inside his spell.

"Do you like it?" he whispered again.

Blushing, I buried my head into his armpits and admitted that I did.

"You are going to have to do better than that, Charlotte, if you're going to get the stallion to come back out of the stable and dance for you," he said.

"Oh my God, Clinton, why do you make me admit these things?" I asked him as I tried to get out of his grip.

"I need to know if you can handle all of this," he said, "not too many women can".

Rolling back on top of him, I could feel my own cougar pawing to get out. "I must be good with you, I am the same thing," I replied, as I sprang from the bed, I turned into The Black Cat, and ran down the hall and the flight of stairs. Then suddenly, I felt like I was starving, looked around at the new kitchen overlooking fields of greenery, and quickly morphed back into me.

"Yes, now I understand," he said, "You are not so much into French Pastry around your meat," as he put the phyllo dough back into the fridge, "how about some Baklava instead?"

I handed him the pistachios and walnuts, still wondering how I did just shape shift the way I did.

"I have some rose water that I made last year," he said, pointing to the walk-in. "It's on the top shelf in the back," he yelled, as he looked for a large pan, "some canning jars marked *Damask*".

I was impressed as I walked back out of the cold box along the side of the kitchen and placed the jar of flowery water on the countertop. "You can make Baklava?" I asked in amazement.

"Woman, you are in my kitchen now," he said, as he snapped a towel out of the drawer and wrapped it around his neck, If you think you can cook, just wait till I get through with your ass!".

"Plan my wedding, you say," I said, as I squeezed the towel sitting on his neck. "I can start planning," I thought as I looked up into his eyes – not knowing if I should marry a man I hardly knew. "Dare I ask when this wedding is?" I spoke. Something inside me already knew the answer to that question when he dared me with his eyebrows to answer him.

"Do not worry about the date, it will come when everything is ready," he declared. I did not know why I allowed him to have so much control over my life, but for some reason, I kind of liked it. I got this strange thought in my head, and it occurred to me that I had no idea what day it even was. I hadn't even looked at my phone in what seemed like days, and I wondered where it was. Turning away, I began to wash the dishes sitting in the sink.

"You must face your past, Charlotte, then let it go, and you need to set him free," he said, as I looked out the window onto the garden and wondered who he was referring to.

"I am going to level with you," he said, as he pulled my hands out of the soapy water, whereupon I cringed, "This is it, he knows all about me," as I waited for the ball to drop.

"I am sure I served with the Bob you knew," he stated, as he reached for a glass and poured in some mint iced tea.

I was so relieved, as I thought for a moment that he was referring to Kennedy.

"He was my best friend on the submarine, but I always called him Bobby," he said, "as we were kitchen mates, he told me everything and said that you were the one that got away".

I nearly froze, wondering what all he knew about me, as I tried to bury my memories into the recesses of my brain.

"He should have forgotten about the whole Navy thing and should have never re-enlisted," said Clinton, "he fell ill one night, vomiting all over the floor of the sub so, I held him in my arms, to keep him from drowning on his own regurgitation, but he died the next day, blood poisoning was what the ships doctor said".

"I knew I recognized his face that day in Rhode Island," I stammered. "Why didn't anyone tell me the truth back when I questioned everyone about the captain?" I asked.

"I wasn't sure of who you were describing," Clinton said, as he placed the meat on the tray and rubbed his dry seasoning in, "and didn't realize you could see them, back then". "It all makes so much more sense to me now," he said, "spirits like to cling close to those they loved on this earth. How did you meet him?" he asked.

"It was Valentine's Day, and my friends set me up on a blind date with him and I cooked him dinner. We kissed and fooled around a little but nothing that would make me think we were any more than that"."As far as I knew, he was doing his thing, and I was doing mine; then; I left for school that summer in Rhode Island and never gave him a thought again," I concluded.

Clinton looked up at the wall as if he were writing my words on a chalkboard, when he asked, "When did you see him again?".

"I had started working in the kitchens all around Newport. Once I learned what I thought I needed, I went on to something different. One night, while we were short on waitstaff at a small private club for officers, I delivered a meal to the dining room, and there he was, sitting at one of the round tables and drinking a glass of wine. When I got off work, he was outside waiting for me. I was older by then, not a virgin anymore, and I found myself down by the shore with him," I told him. I looked out onto the back porch as the air called to me. "Clinton, I do not want to talk about him anymore," I said.

"Fair enough, and I think the pork is calling for you, anyway," he said as he made his way back into the walk-in. The hot breeze wrapped around my hair with the lure of the smoked meat calling me to check on it. "Tell me more about your upbringing," he asked, as we walked out the back door.

I looked down at the dirt as I moved between the grass with my bare feet. "It has been years since I was in Mississippi. My dad stayed here, and my mom went more North. Then, I stayed in foster care once she passed until my friend's mom got me out. A car accident started it, but the pills finished her up. I never looked back again and just kept my eyes on moving forward," I told him, as I pulled on the silk of the corn and walked past the stalks. So, there I was, telling all my secrets to this man who seemed larger than life.

"You've got to deal with the past, so it does not come back to haunt you again," said Clinton, as he took the ear of corn out of my hands. He stripped one side of the husk off with a gentle pull, revealing its pearly whites. I loved the silky blonde hair, clinging tightly to the husk, stripping more of it off and revealing its pearly perfection. "You need more training," he said flatly, as he pulled the husk off and bit into his obsession.

The creamy juice dripped down the cob as he placed it into my mouth. I tasted its fresh, creamy sweetness and asked, "How much more training"?

I bet

I bet you didn't notice

I'm as sharp as a tack

My humor is my weapon

Hiding words is my task

I've kept this secret hidden

Only for the few select

I have a naughty humor

And I'm not afraid to act

One drip off my sword

With a cut of my eye

I can cut you down

in the Blink of an eye

You see, I've been holding

All this far back from you

I've let my secret weapon out

while you were worried about blues

You see, it's my humor

I'm as sharp as a tack

Only letting it out

To the few very select

Blackmail is something

That I always counted on

political pawns clamoring

Until the end of dawns

In a nation full of greed

This was easier to see

What was really hiding

Underneath those little sheets

I bet you didn't notice

That I caught you in those lies

I wonder what else you're hiding

in those crystal blue eyes

You see, I have legions, an army of my own

Think you can destroy me

As my soldier suit comes on

I'm as sharp as a tack

My humor is my weapon

It was my last attack

You see, I have legions

An army of my own

Think you can dethrone me

As my soldier suit comes on

Hiding behind the billboard lies

A snag bag of bricks

Every politician lies

It's all part of the risks

CHAPTER 32

WINNER TAKES ALL

Kennedy's phone rang in its distinct tone, awakening him to Olivianna on the other end. "Hi, Kennedy, I'm just about an hour away from picking you and Karissa up, and Aunt Mabel is all fired up," she said.

"Great," he mumbled as he rolled out of bed.

"It's just a few more days, Kennedy, come on, you need to admit Aunt Mabel is funny," Karissa said, as she got up, too.

"What, funny? Are you nuts?" asked Kennedy, as she began to chuckle. "Oh, yeah, she is a hoot all right," he said, as they got dressed and packed up their bags. They checked out and made their way down to the basement parking area of the hotel and fired up the Trans Am. "Did you have any dreams with the Trans Am last night?" he asked her as they drove out for one last look at the beach.

Karissa stared at the ocean in a brief contemplative moment before turning her full attention to her husband. "Yes, I had this dream that I was flying in the Trans Am over the ocean, and my wings were making the car fly," she said. "Why do you ask?"

Just then, the motor home with Olivianna, Kevin, and Aunt Mabel pulled up. Kennedy looked to Karissa. "I'll talk to you about it later," he said as he drove the Trans Am up the ramp and locked it into position on the trailer.

"Rummy 500," called out Aunt Mabel, as she slammed the deck on the table.

"Best out of three," Kennedy called back as he pulled out a thousand dollars and threw it on the table. Take it or leave it, Aunt Mabel," he said sternly.

Aunt Mabel wryly smiled back had him as her hands caressed the deck and slid the cash to Kevin. "I will take that bet, Sonny," she said, "and where are we staying tonight?" she asked with a sly look on her face, as Kevin started shuffling and handing out the cards.

"Nowhere, we're driving straight to Mississippi," Kennedy replied, as he picked up his cards.

"Really, Kennedy," Karissa responded, "isn't there someplace we could stop?" "I get this motor home has everything, but I could use some extra space," she said.

"Look, Babe, I have got a lot riding on this, and I cannot afford any more hiccups," he said, as he played his next hand. "Beat you, Aunt Mabe!" he exclaimed, "I've got three Jacks of Hearts, and a spread of spades," he said, as he laid his cards down.

"Negative 95," she said, "you may have won the battle, Sonny, but you will not win the war". Aunt Mabel

Broke into hearty laughter as she shuffles the next hand.

"How many more hours until we get to Mississippi?" asked Kennedy with a growl.

"According to the map, sixteen hours is our best bet," as Olivianna informed him, as she plotted the course on the GPS.

"I have got a stop in South Carolina to make," Kennedy said as he put down his next play. "Count 'em up, old lady," as he laid down four Aces, a Jack, a Queen, and a King of Hearts. Kevin counted his cards and wrote down the score as he went further in the hole. "We are picking up some more of Charlotte's family, Kennedy said. "What do you have, Aunt Mabel, negative what?" as Kennedy laid the cards down as the sarcastic grin erupted on his face.

"What, Kennedy?" Karissa stammered in disbelief. "Where are they going to sit?" she asked, with a look of utter confusion.

"I do not know, Karissa," he crackled back," I did not think about all of this … there is a bed in here, maybe it will work".

"Don't worry, Karissa, it's one of Charlotte's cousins," Olivianna explained, "she wants her at the wedding". "G'anacia and Nadia are already on their way down, and she's doing the soul food that Clinton wanted she elaborated, "so, we'll just blow up that air mattress I brought and put it down by the kitchen".

"You brought an air mattress?" Karissa said, knowing we look like we're smuggling in illegal aliens," Karissa laughed with a snort, "plus, I thought the rumor was that the wedding is in Delaware".

"It's just an easy insurance policy – you know what I mean?" said Olivianna.

"Dammit!" shouted Kennedy, as Aunt Mabel took the lead.

"Your wife's looking better already to me," said Aunt Mabel as she laughed some more, "count 'em up, Kennedy", she said with disdain.

"Olivianna, I need a bathroom break, and can you find me a fast-food place?" said Kennedy as he slammed his cards down on the table and got up.

"You got it, boss, she shouted back, as she plugged in the command, "it's twenty minutes to the nearest place".

"Screw it!" he replied, "just pull up to that rest area up ahead, they usually have bathrooms in there.

"Ah, Kennedy, are you sure about this place?" asked Olivianna as she pulled in.

Kennedy made a run for a tree with Aunt Mabel just a few paces behind. Kennedy pulled his water-logged flog out and began hosing down the tree when he saw Aunt Mabel come over to him as he stared back at her. "What, you can't find your own ditch to squat in? Kennedy said sarcastically.

"Why aren't you using the indoor toilet of the motor home?" asked Aunt Mabel. "Why aren't you?" she reiterated as she pulls out her own fire hose in an attempted to squirt him with it.

"What the HELL, Aunt Mabel?" Kennedy stammered as he nearly fell to the ground. He looked up at the woman standing over him, in shock. It took a few moments to register. Finally, Kennedy blurted," Oh man, you're not a woman, you are a man!". "Great, great," he said, utterly confused as he attempted to pull up his fly. "I can't believe this!" he screamed as his hair got stuck in the zipper. "I wonder if Clinton knows this," he thought, as he sprinted back to the motor home.

"Ma, ma, ma… my poker face," said Aunt Mabel. He gave it a little shake and laughed all the way back to the motor home. "Aw, what's the matter, Sonny, you didn't know I was he? I sure fooled you," he said, as they climbed back into the seats.

"Karissa, you won't believe this, Aunt Mabel's got a willy!" he announced as he pulled up her dress.

Kevin scanned the room like he was locked in some bad dream, wondering what he had gotten himself into as he surveyed it all.

"Geez, Kennedy, what's the matter with you?" Karissa shouted back, "I thought you knew".

"Knew what?" he said, "that she was in a dress with a hat? "I'm not playing another round with you, ever!" he hissed.

"What's the matter, aren't you up to the challenge, Sonny?" asked Aunt Mabel.

Kennedy fell silent. "This just keeps getting better and better," he thought to himself, as he pulled out another candy from the jar.

"How much money again, Kennedy?" asked Karissa, laughing out loud.

"It's not about the battle, it's about the war," Kennedy reflected as he pulled the cards out of the box and shuffled some more. "Fine, Aunt Mabel or whatever your name is, you think you can handle my wife's ass?" Kennedy was livid with frustration at having just been made a fool of. "Go ahead buddy, I triple dog dare you to do it," he blurted, and I've got twenty years on you that says I can give her what she likes".

"I have got twenty million, she just might like," said Aunt Mabel as he laid his cards down, "Full House with no discard!"

Kevin just shook his head, as he just could not believe that he was even hearing all of this. "And I thought I had problems," he laughed under his breath.

Olivianna's and Karissa's mouths just dropped, whispering "twenty million".

Kennedy shot back, "My wife is NOT For Sale as he grabbed the deck. "Fine, we'll get a hotel room, are you all happy with that?" he grumbled, "I can't believe this… where are we at?

"Virginia, boss," Olivianna said, "where do you want to stop?

Karissa interrupted. "Wait, ladies and gentlemen, I think we need to take a break," she said. "Tonight, it's a full moon, and it's obvious we are losing our cool, so how about we ground ourselves for a moment or two?""Olivianna, find a place to pull over and let's all go outside and do a little bit of earthing".

Kennedy shook his head and said, "I know you're right, and I really don't know what's got into me today".

"I do, but it's OK," Karissa said, "you're letting money take you over again".

"Is it that obvious?" Kennedy asked, as he faced the group.

"If we are going to do portable catering, Kennedy, from one tip of the country to the next, you might want to figure out a better plan," said Karissa... "I understand what you are trying to do," she spoke plainly, as she put her arms around him. I love that you are trying to get us brand recognition. However, money cannot be the reason we do it, she stated.

Karissa instructed everyone to come together. "Let us all take a hand: Father God up above, we are asking for your blessings. Place a white light of protection around us. Help us to see the illumination disguised as frustration. Help us to shine in all your glory and deliver a feast for our dear friends Charlotte and Clinton, for this is what The Center of Love is about, marrying the couples whose love we helped sprout. Thank you, dear lord

For your divine protection and guidance. Amen and Amen," she implored.

"Now, let us all take a deep breath and get back on the road, we have got a wedding to attend to, we can do this, Kennedy, as I believe in your mission and I have faith," she said.

"Amen. Thank you, Karissa, I really needed to hear that," Kennedy said as he hugged his wife. "I'm sorry for being such an ass," he confessed, as he composed himself, "it's just that I have had a lot on my mind and wasn't thinking straight".

"I know, I am no picnic either," said Karissa. She focused her attention on Aunt Mabel. "Trust me," she said, "no more funny business, you hear?" "I am running the show, and do not forget it!" she declared, as she pointed at his chest.

"Yes, ma'am," he acknowledged. Aunt Mabel then looked over at Kevin and asked, "What gives?"

"Don't look at me, bro. I just met them last week," he responded.

"I will drive," Karissa said as they all piled back in. "You boys kiss and make up".

"You have got to be kidding me, Karissa. I'm not kissing him," said Kennedy.

"Really, she said with a stern look in her eyes. "I am not asking for tongue, you know, just a handshake will do, "Geez, sometimes, men are like boys fighting over a toy in the play pen," she said as she put the car in drive and pulled out.

CHAPTER 33

TRAINING FOR THE REVOLUTION

"This is the last standing Greek Revival structure this side of the Mississippi," Clinton explained, as we walked up the stone steps of the antebellum mansion. "I'm telling you, Charlotte, this is what I'm seeing in you, "he said, as I followed him into the kitchen, "that's why you are here with me, my job is to keep you safe while we condition you for the campaign".

Cringing at the thoughts of what was coming next, my mind began to think of every excuse I could imagine getting him off this tangent. "I'm going to have to get in much better shape, you know," I said.

"Oh, that's going to happen," he said, as he handed me a bag of trim. "Here, Charlotte, process this for me," he directed, "and I want to see your recipe".

"So, tell me about this allegiance again, the Purple Party you were telling me the other day". Then, I weighed out 3 ounces of the trim onto a large baking sheet, covered it with tin foil, and placed it in the oven at 270 degrees for 35 minutes, and set the timer. "What makes you think the voters want to elect a cannabis chef for President, anyway?" I asked, as I closed the oven door.

"It's not now, not yet; however, you will know when the time is right," Clinton stated, "and I promise, there are many other people who see this in you, too". Clinton pulled the pork out of the walk-in refrigerator and rubbed its skin with his special blend of seasoning." You must be a protégée," he said

I investigated his bowl of spices, sizing his ingredients up. "Protégé, you say," I responded, crossing my arms over my chest.

"You need me, and I need you," he said, as he continued to rub his spices into the pork loin, laying them down on the baking trays. "Come closer to me," he suggested. As I walked up and stood beside him, he looked me over thoroughly. "You will be meeting with lots of foreign diplomats, heads of state, and other leaders. The world tours with your cookbooks are just the beginning. However, you have a problem with listening and doing as you're told," he said seriously.

Rolling my eyes, I wondered what I had done right this time, as the thoughts of going back to my former life crept inside my head. "Yes, I understand all of that, but what is the point of the Purple Party?" I asked.

"Glad you asked," he said, as he got back to rubbing his pork down, "It's a blending of the two sides of disaffected people who no longer vote because they're sick and tired of being the pitted back and forth against each other while arrogant, greedy, short-sighted, incompetent, wasteful and corrupt politicians are running our beloved country into the dirt. The IPUS is the party of Peace, Liberty, and Prosperity. Freedom for all, where all people truly get a chance to rise, where "all people are created equal" is more than a platitude they spout off while they steadily stack the deck against the People in favor of the insiders and special interests at public expense. Kids making mistakes when they are just eighteen, then being told that they have no right to vote, are punished for their entire lifetime, without the possibility of a second chance; as well as regular citizens being spied upon for no other reason than increased government control over our very lives. This is not the Republic for which the flag stands, under God, with liberty and justice for all, for it has become a nightmare under their sway. The ruling two parties and their polarization are wrecking America. That's why we need a New Awakening, a New Beginning, a renaissance of the American Spirit and regeneration of the American Mind! There can be no power shift without a paradigm shift, and WE the People are the New Paradigm. We shall reclaim our freedom and destiny from the false elites, with a new party, a party of creative methodology instead of divisive ideology, a party that develops people to be future leaders instead of indoctrinating them as blind followers. Accordingly, the Party of the Paradigm Shift is the IPUS!"

Clinton now had me thoroughly under his spell, as his address came to its crescendo. My legs became weak, and I closed my eyes and felt like I was already inside his plan. I took a deep breath and knew exactly what he meant.

"I'm not blind to this Clinton, I just don't think I've got what it takes to win an election," I responded as I finely chopped three large Vidalia onions.

"Yes, you do," he said as he grew more passionate. "You have been successful in every other avenue of your life. You have dedicated yourself to not only write but publish all your books, and there is no doubt in my mind that you can write a plan for the country".

I smiled back at him, in utter amazement as a thought that he was nuttier than a fruit cake momentarily went through my head. Then, I started sautéing the onions in a Center of Love cannabis butter infusion and waited for them to get golden brown before I placed three pounds of tomato sauce in. Letting the three lemons drip down my arms as my fingers interlaced around the fruit. I squeezed the juice into the pot and added four heaping tablespoons of dried mustard, one pound of clover honey that was freshly drained from its wax, together with a pound of brown sugar and one-half bottle of Worcestershire sauce in a new cast iron pot with removable rubber handles that was part of the now-famous Center of Love Club culinary collection.

"You know, Clinton, I have had my own thoughts about a lot of things," I said as my fingers rubbed the emblem on the cast iron pot. "Why is it so hard to be in business?" I asked, "We live in a country where kids cannot even have a lemonade stand without costly permits". "How can we teach our youth entrepreneurship if we cannot even do that? It's just a shame, together with a system that incarcerates people for using cannabis. Didn't they get the memo that our bodies have an endocannabinoid system?" I continued.

"Oh, I think they know all that," Clinton said, but there is just so much corporate greed in keeping people sick by managing symptoms instead of finding cures. "That is why the first order of business is to make it legal and free to the people by taking it off as a scheduled drug. Then the reintegration of anyone in prison so they can have their lives back, reversal of anything that has to do with cannabis or mushrooms, for that matter. Research is showing how it can help people with depression. So, what kind of sense does it make to not let people have something like that, yet let them have alcohol and tobacco?" he continued.

"Not that alcohol does not have its benefits," said Charlotte as she opens a bottle of whiskey and smashed some mint leaves into a glass, "we would never be able to get the essence out of plants if it were not for grain alcohol, it just makes no sense, if it harms you then you will find it on any street corner under a flashing neon sign, but if it helps you well, nope, sorry you cannot have that" she added.

"The Purple Party is about that and so much more. It is about loving all people and seeing people for what is on the inside, not the color of their skin, how they were born, or their perceived disability. Look at the people who work for us; they are the ones this world has thrown away, but look at what we do with them. We can do better than this. Charlotte and I personally feel that with what you have gone through, you are the perfect person to resonate with the People. You have some rough experiences. You can see and feel things that most people can't, and for that, you have been labeled. When, in all reality, you are beyond what they can perceive and conceive, for, in all honesty, you have a naturally higher operating system. They do, too, but they just do not know how to use it, so they are caught up in their programming. You cannot save everyone, and you will go crazy trying. You just must show up being authentically you and let the people choose if they want to support you and your message of freedom,". Said Clinton.

I thought about what he was saying as I pulled my toasted cannabis out of the oven. Placing it in a large crock pot, I smiled back at Clinton. I did mine the old-fashioned way, as I crushed the dried herbs up in my hands and put four bay leaves in the crock pot, along with ten black pepper seeds. I then stirred in two pounds of butter and one pound of virgin coconut oil into the crock pot, set the dial on medium, then filled it to the top with spring water and covered it.

"That's your secret recipe?" he said.

"It's not much of a secret anymore," I laughed.

"Are you sure you want to give it out, then?" he asked.

Smiling, I laughed, "They don't have my best secret cookie recipe, or these hands", I replied, as I fluttered them in his face, "this is where all my magic is, anyway, that's what the secret is, it's me".

"See, I told you, Charlotte, look at what your cookbooks are doing, you have a following there, and I believe when you get deeper into your heart and soul and let your true self shine, that you will find you are much more than what you thought you were".

I looked up at him and asked if he ever thought of being a motivational speaker.

"All the time, I just do it one on one most of the time," he replied as he loaded the meat on the tray. "Come on," he said, as we headed out back, "we'll never get this food cooked".

I got halfway through my walk when I turned back to see the majestic twenty-two-room Inn that was once a former plantation, now a romantic Bed and Breakfast destination. I walked out to the outdoor kitchen as Clinton placed the different meats all over the grates. As the sizzle of the pork hit the hot flames, I knew that this was going to be my spot for the day. Of all the places I had ever worked for, I had never seen a man with such passion and determination to see a project through. Once all the meat was loaded, he hit a switch, and the trays of meat began revolving like a Ferris wheel. Smiling back at me made it easy as we walked back to the kitchen. The scent of the cannabis infusion had already started to perfume the kitchen, and I decided to give it six more hours to cook, then let it sit in the fridge overnight. Once the fats hardened, I strained out all the water and discarded the cannabis tea water in whatever plant was needing it. Then, I strained my fats through a cheese cloth to get the sediment out. "Then, it will be ready for anything you want," I said, as he went through a large stack of papers in his office. I put a pot of water on and went through the jars of dried teas until I saw the small jasmine pearls I was looking for, and gathered some dried pineapple, mango, rose buds, and lavender, and let them steep inside the boiling water. After about twenty minutes, I put in some clover honey and stirred up my herb infusion. I poured it into a sieve over a large pewter pitcher of ice and walked into his office, placing it on the table beside him.

"Thank you for that," said Clinton as he took a sip.

"How do you do all of this?" I ask him in utter amazement.

Looking up at me, he said, "It is simple, I am an angel".

"I understand that," I said, as I rested my hands on his shoulder. The large leather chair was worn from his endless nights where he orchestrated his next masterpiece. "Are you sure you think I can do this?" I asked,

"Run a country, you mean?" he asked, "have you just been trying to butter me up for some other trick?"

I wrapped my arms around his neck and massaged his shoulders with my elbows, and wanted so much for him to just take me to the desk, but I knew better to even ask. "Oh my god, he is reading my mind, again", I thought, as I contemplated his next move. As he cleared a spot on his desk, one folder marked TOP SECRET caught my eye. "Take your time, I said, I'm going to water the back gardens".

I walked back out to the kitchen and out to the porch, where the smell of the smoked pork was starting to fill the property. Then, I heard the pen as it fell on the desk and was secretly delighted when I heard him yell, "Get back in here!" I turned with a mixture of fear and excitement when he said, "You have not heard your instructions yet".

I was not able to read the lines in his face, as he pulled his chair out from the desk and placed it in front of the large window. "Open the curtains and windows and let the light in for me," he directed.

I stepped back into his office and did as he commanded. The large window must have spanned six feet wide when I again spied the folder that said TOP SECRET. I opened the windows by turning the cranks as the scent of the pork started wafting in. Standing next to the window, waiting for my next instruction as he motioned to me to get down on my knees. For a moment, I began to tremble as I slowly made my way to the floor. Part of me was excited at the way he could command me, yet the other part was so scared that he had this much control over me.

The excitement was overwhelming as I nestled myself in between his legs. So many times, I had imagined this, and now it was happening, yet I did not seem to know what to do with it.

He looked at me and said, "You seem like you have a question for me, what is it?".

"Well," I perked up, "I was working on something for you".

"Really, tell me about it," he said as he adjusted himself in the large wing-backed chair and put his finger up against his cheek and pointed to his eye.

"Do you remember when you said something to me about an edible cannabis infused sexual lubricant?"

"Ah, you do listen to me, continue," he said, as he readjusted himself in the chair.

"Well, I have been working on one that I am curious to try," I continued.

"Really?", he said, "go get it".

I quickly got up and stumbled into the kitchen, wondering where my suitcase was, when I ran up the steps and down the hall. I find the glass jars that I had labeled The Naughty Fig and Hot Peach. Then, I walked back into his office and got back down on my knees. I knew the oil would stain his clothes as I asked him, "Do I have permission to remove your garments?"

I could feel his mood change as he stood up before me like he was a God. "Take them off me," he directed as he pulled his shirt off. I got up on my knees as I unbuckled his belt, letting his pants fall to the floor as he stepped out of them. I moved them to this desk and placed them over the file marked "TOP SECRET," then I crawled back in between his legs, as he sat down in his chair and leaned back.

I opened the jar and scooped some of my concoction out, and had the strangest feeling that we were not the only people in the room. The more I slid the sweet emulsion up and down his shaft, the more my mind started to wonder if his seed held the information wrapped up in its DNA. All I would need to do is swallow it to get to know his plan, and I wondered who was talking in my head. The more I caressed his bulging meat, the more I wondered if I was going crazy.

At least that was what I told myself as I began to lick the peachy dream, wondering if it would be that easy to get out the information. I looked up to him as the tension started to melt away. The man I fell in love with was inside there somewhere. What if he was not kidding me? What if I am supposed to be the first woman President? The more I thought about it, the more excited I became. Then again, maybe I was just the front woman, I thought to myself.

As my mouth continued to please him, my mind went back years ago to when I was in Rhode Island. There were parties at all the big mansions with entrepreneurs and political figures all around. Deals were being made as each course hit the table when I placed each tray of food on the buffet, pretending that I did not hear a thing, when I knew what some of them were planning. That is when it all began to make sense, the **Purple Party**. The blending of the best ideas of the Republicans, Democrats, and Independents, and the discarding of the rest.

The more I thought of the nation rising, the more I realized who this man was. I could see every plan in his bulging head, but did not understand why he did not run himself. It did not matter, for now, I knew the information was getting ready to come in. As he grunted and let all his plans in, I struggled to take all of it in, knowing that I needed not to miss anything.

I pulled up his pants and buttoned them back up. "Keep this a secret, you understand?" he said as he handed me the tea and the folder marked "TOP SECRET" and told me to wash it down.

"Why do you keep this a secret?" I asked in bewilderment.

He smiled back at me. "Honey, I know you are a spy". A look of horror came over my face as I tried to backpedal out of the office and escape. Before I knew it, he was at the door. "Not so fast, Charlotte, I have more to tell you, "He said. I cringed as I fell to the floor.

"All the secrets I knew that I thought I would never have to tell, all of them hidden inside me, I thought I hid so well. "I told you, sweetie, that I'm here to protect you because you have a higher calling and all you need to do is put your hands on somebody to get information out of them," he continued.

I trembled knowing he really does know me.

"I told you, you have a file, and I found it on you years back while I was investigating a murder of someone that you were attached to back then".

"So, what are you going to do, arrest me then?" I said, as I sobbed out in pain, "You know that I didn't do anything, Clinton and I just, for some reason, can see what's happening with them, and it's so scary".

"Tell me what happened that night on the beach with Bob," he interrogated, as he pulled out a recorder and hit the button.

"OK, we had gone down to the cliff walk at about maybe 2:30 in the morning. We were making love on the rocks, as the water sprayed on us. It was so exciting, and I was all caught up in him, and the more I looked at him, the more I could see files in front of me, things marked Confidential and TOP SECRET. I did not think anything of it, and I let it filter out of my head. Two days later, one diplomat I was seeing started asking me questions about him, and I was very curious as to why he was inquiring. I had been secretly sleeping with him for several months. It wasn't love or anything. He was just good in bed, and that was that," I explained.

"Did you see Bob after that night?" he questioned.

"I did and continued to see both men for a while. I knew I had missed my period, and didn't think anything of it at first, because I was exercising a lot back then, and it was not unusual to miss a cycle now and then. One night, I had a dream. In the dream, I saw Bob, and he walked up to me and said he had to go, but he left me a present. I never heard or saw him again".

"And what about the diplomat?" asked Clinton.

"I closed my eyes, not wanting to see him in my head. I saw him when he came back to town. By then, it was obvious that I was pregnant, and he questioned me about who the father was. When I told him I was not sure, I felt the sting of his hand as it went across my face. My instincts were to fight back, and I clawed at his face. The next thing I remember I went down a flight of steps. My leg was broken, and I was screaming in pain. He called an ambulance and told them I had fallen carrying a load of laundry down the steps. The rest is history," I explained.

"I am sorry, Charlotte, I did not know he beat you. Sometimes, diplomatic immunity really sucks," he said.

I grimly smiled and said, "It was only one time, but he made it count".

"He never hit you before?" he asked.

"Well, not like he did that day," I answered.

"But you did see a pattern in him?" he said.

"Well, sort of, I did not see him all that often; he traveled a lot for his job, or so he told me. Honestly, I don't even know if he was really a diplomat or not, and he could have been undercover. People lie a lot, "I said. "Why? Do you think he may have killed Bob or something?" I asked.

"I have always suspected that there was something behind Bob's death. His file said, 'blood poisoning,' but I have never believed it. He would talk about this woman whom he said got away from him and then told me one day about how he caught up with her again and how they made love on the shoreline," said Clinton.

This is so embarrassing, Clinton," I said as I wrapped my arms around my body, trying to protect myself.

"Charlotte, I am not judging you or what you did years ago. The only way we truly ever get to know someone is when we share ourselves with them. It is incredibly beautiful to be honest, especially in this age of duplicity and deception. The way you make love to a man, I feel glad for him that he felt you that night. No man should do without that, even though millions will in just a few more days. As I told you before, I will not let any man ever get to you again".

"Just the ghosts?" I questioned back at him.

"Well, you can control them," he said, surprised at my response.

"How?" I asked

"All you need to do is ask," he said.

"But what if I like the ghosts making love to me? What if I find it exciting?"

I was hoping you would say that. It's one of the best parts of being with you, and I really like to watch it," confessed Clinton.

"You're so weird, "I said back with a laugh.

"It beats another man having to share my bed with you," he said, as I cringed, thinking it was him that day back at Jaxson's house with Kennedy. He looked back at me and asked, "Did you get it out of your system that day?" he asked.

"I could not go through with the whole thing," I muttered back.

"I know, he said," and I was watching," whereupon I felt about as small as a pea as I had just realized my worst nightmare. "Don't worry about it," he said, "I really wanted you to have your fantasy, you will just not get that with me, and I expect the same," he stated.

"It's OK". "I smiled back, I was hoping for the same mutual respect".

"There is nothing wrong with anyone doing that, I have no judgment at all," he said, "it is just you are going to be around a lot of particularly important people: Presidents, Members of Congress, all that jazz".

"Congress," I laughed. "We both know what the *Kama Sutra* says about' Congress' and its different positions," I responded, "in fact, when they're in session, we all get screwed!" "So, Clinton, have you ever wondered why so many people in such high positions have such a high sex drive?" I asked curiously.

"I have thought about that a lot over the years," he said, "and I believe it is a part of the power we have".

"What do you mean by that?" I questioned.

"Well, it is our Sacral Chakra that oversees our sexual desires and reproduction. For People who create things, those ideas of creation begin there, even if what they create is largely just myth, ideology, illusion, and apparatus. The next chakra is the Solar Plexus, and that is our powerhouse. It is just logical that with powerful and driven people, you are going to have powerful sexual desires. Couple that with exercising a natural endorphin booster, then you're bound to have a person who can work for hours".

"Well, the exercising explains your sexual desires, but what about mine?" I inquired.

"Well, that, my dear, is because you are a creative powerhouse. You are like your own supercomputer in the way your brain thinks. Anything conducting that type of energy is bound to have a high sex drive –it comes with the territory".

"Oh", is all I could reply.

"Come on," he said, "enough of all of this, you are going to be getting some heavy downloads with what I just gave you," Clinton said with a broad and triumphant smile. "G'anacia and Nadia will be here tomorrow, helping in the kitchen, preparing for our wedding".

I asked with bewilderment, "What, I'm getting married here?"

"I have been planning everything for you. This place here we have been using for the meet and greet while the Jamestown house is under renovation. Our wedding is just another extension of that, with a few other guests whom I have invited. It is your celebration into the family of angels, so to speak. I love this property here; it is by far one of my favorites. It's a bit haunted, which I'm sure you already felt, and given the display back there, I could tell The Jockey was here," he said.

"So, you really don't think it's odd that ghosts have sex with me I asked, blushing again.

"No, not really, ghosts exist, and from the way they handle you, I think you like it too, so why deny it, Just accept it, plus, it happens to me too and you can't catch any diseases with them – no casing on my meat with a ghost," he said as he slapped my ass again for effect. "It is the only way we will cheat," he added, "you hear me?".

"I do not want to cheat, Clinton, and to tell you the truth, you're so damn good, so why would I want to?"

"That's my woman, I like to hear that," he said affectionately.

"I seriously have no desire for any other man and they've all been floating out of my head," I said, laughing, "even Putin!".

"Well, that's good and it's a safe bet that you'll be negotiating with him, and I would really hate to think it would be under the sheets".

"No, not me, I waited too long for this and cannot believe it, but I am head over heels in love with you," I said, as I reached around his waist.

"That's good, Charlotte, I have been in love with you since the first night we met and have done nothing but think about you and plan everything I could do. I knew you had fantasies, and I did too, which is why I had them orchestrated. I did not want you to have any regrets and just wanted to make sure you were ready for all of this. Now, go take a bath and freshen up and meet me out in the crepe myrtle grove."

CHAPTER 34

KING SIZE BED

As dawn approached, the roar of the planes taking off and landing gave Kennedy a good indication that they were in North Carolina. "All I could get us for an early morning check-in was the motel on Route 6," he hollered to

Karissa. "We're about twenty minutes away from Charlotte, North Carolina," she said informatively.

"What time are we picking up our guests? He asked as Olivianna yawned, "damn, I've got to get a shower, and I feel so yukky," he said just before they pulled into the parking lot.

"I told them no later than three in the afternoon, Karissa replied, "now, let's check in, get some breakfast, and then we'll take a nap. The little diner next to the motel wasn't half bad as they ate breakfast and walked back to their room. As they opened the door, the split pea soup green color that covered the walls greeted them, along with the one and only King-size bed up against the wall.

They looked at each other as everyone shrugged their heads, thinking, "Is this all they had?" Karissa began to laugh. "I don't care, I'm going to bed", she said as she took off her shoes and pulled down the sheets. Karissa quickly plopped her head down and was fast asleep in a moment.

Kennedy kept looking at Aunt Mabel and their pending sleeping arrangement, until I figured out how it would work. "Okay, this is the plan: Karissa and Olivianna in the middle, and you and me on either end. Kevin is staying in the motor home. Got it, Auntie M"?

"You got it, Sonny," Aunt Mabel replied as he took his edge of the bed. Steam came out of the bathroom as Olivianna slid inside the middle. As all four bodies were vying for a spot, the humming of the air conditioner made a droned throughout the room, and it was music to Kennedy's ears as Aunt Mabel's loud snoring vibrated against the walls. Kennedy tossed back and forth, unable to get any rest. He even went through Karissa's purse looking for an Indica blend to help him get to sleep. Kennedy hit the music button and loaded the music from the Reiki station. It soothed his restless soul as he wrapped his tired arms around Karissa and hugged her closely. "You smell so good, honey," he whispered, as his hands caressed her hips. Kennedy kissed her softly on the lips and felt his body begin to relax. Before he knew it, he was fast asleep.

It felt like hours had gone by when he rolled back over and stretched his legs. Kennedy ran his hands along Karissa's hips as I pulled her tightly to him. The more he felt her thighs, the more something just didn't feel the same. "I think you're losing weight, honey, he whispered in her ear, "and you're feeling smaller to me". Kennedy rolled on top of her, nuzzled between her legs, and began kissing her on the neck. "Honey, I'm so confused," he said as he began feeling her breasts.

Suddenly, the lights came on with laughter that could be heard from miles around, as Karissa and Olivianna stared and pointed at him. Kennedy sheepishly fumbled for his glasses and put them on. There he was plastered all over Aunt Mabel.

The sheets and pillows flew in a flurry of consternation, as if a huge family of spiders had just moved in. Kennedy, trying desperately to get the taste of his breath off his mouth, sprang up and bolted for the bathroom, spitting and gagging, trying to get the taste of Aunt Mabel off his lips while everyone else was cackling.

Karissa doubled over with laughter, trying hard not to pee on herself, as Kennedy bellowed hysterically, gargling and brushing his teeth frantically before hitting the shower full blast. He then took a good look at himself in the mirror, as the howls of laughter continued.

Kennedy barreled out of the bathroom, "Let's go," he yelled as he stormed out of the motel and into the mobile home, with the rest of the group in tow. He hit the pedal on the Interstate with such fury as he had never felt before. The muffled giggles still came from under Karissa's breath, as the three kids in back kept erupting with laughter. Annoyed with what was arguably the most embarrassing moment of my life, Kennedy, with one hand on the steering wheel, beat on the door with the other and started yelling out the window. "I kissed a man! He screamed for all to hear, "Are you happy now?" Suddenly, he paused. "Great, now that we could take that off the list, and I would appreciate it if you all kept this to yourselves," he said, as the laughter subsided.

A faint hush seemed to come over the motor home as muted breath dared not creep out. The harder they tried to squelch the voices inside, the more the convulsions came in, as howls of crackles flying out, spurting at the windshield.

"Fine," he said, pointing a finger to the sky, "just remember one thing: Only YOU Can Prevent Wildfire" as the motor home exited the interstate. Kennedy was still fuming with rage as he pulled over and ran into a convenience store. He opened the freezer, selected a box of ice cream sandwiches, pulled his card, and told the cashier to set the pump at one hundred dollars. On the way back, he downed two of the frozen vanilla dreams as lactose-intolerant thoughts steadily crept in.

"I will get back at them," he snickered as he filled up the gas tank. The ice cream was melting down his arm as the gas kept pumping, when the smell of the taco truck, up ahead, hit him. Kennedy sniffed in the air and hollered out to Karissa, "Go get some dinner from that Mexican stand!".

Karissa gave him an "Oh, really" look as she and Olivianna headed over to the little taco truck and placed an order.

Within a few minutes, it becomes abundantly clear that Kennedy had launched a full-scale counterattack with fumes everywhere. It was more than anyone could bear, as the truck rolled around the block to Charlotte's cousin's place, the exiting passengers just narrowly escaped. Knocking on the door, they met Taylor and Darren as they grabbed their bags and hopped on in.

"What died in here?" Taylor gasped as Karissa frantically sprayed a can of **Deck the balls potty** deodorant. Ironically, it was one of Kennedy's Christmas Creations that we never leave home without, she recalled as she sprayed the entire motor home down.

Hours passed as we barreled South to Mississippi, where the wedding was at. Then, it suddenly hit Kennedy that the ice cream sandwiches were launching their own attack! It all happened so fast. His stomach gurgled loudly as toxic fumes came out of his exhaust with a terrible sound effect that could have topped any science fiction movie. Just then, his inner voice said, "Oh-oh, Kennedy, this must be crap!".

Trying discreetly to hold it all in, he knew that he needed to get to the bathroom quickly, or else. He had no choice but to use the inside bathroom, as the voices in the home grumbled, "Oh NO!" He literally made it was two seconds to spare as he sat upon his new 'throne', as each greenhouse gas explosion matched a wave of groans that were coming through from the other side of the door.

As each successive gut laugh sent another splash down with a stench so vile that it almost made him vomit, Kennedy knew that he would never have to share another motel room again. Yet, despite it all, he was genuinely thankful that the Summer Solstice had long been passed, and that the darkness would cover it all up as the laughter from the crew was now being drowned out by the hum and whoosh of the passing cars and trucks. I need some toilet paper!" he screamed to Karissa.

As the motor home pulled back out on the Interstate, this time Olivianna was at the wheel. "We've got to get to Mississippi, Kennedy. I am taking it from here," she said, determined to safely reach their destination. Kennedy through his hands in the air, not caring anymore who was driving, for he had grossly miscalculated. The tacos and ice cream plan and 'special military operation' had backfired on him. He was thoroughly exhausted and humiliated and needed a break.

Kennedy came out moments later, as the munchies took control of his brain. Olivianna said that there is some veal and cheese ravioli in a tomato cream sauce for dinner. "Really?" said Kennedy. As he put the fork into his mouth, a straight new look suddenly came over his face.

"Are you kidding me?" said Olivianna, "this has been the best comedy all year," she said, "and you really do make me laugh, Kennedy". "Now, go to the back and play cards with the rest of them. Karissa and I got this," she instructed.

Heading back to the reclining chair instead, Kennedy drifted off to sleep in hopes of putting the night behind him.

Trapped

Watching her walk down the steps

her long train of flowers in her hair

I cringe at the thought

I would never get another chance to kiss those lips again.

I close my eyes

Her hips as they penetrate me

Her ruby nails as they cast her spell

As she runs them down my back

Why did I do this

She wanted me

I cast her away

Now she is marrying him

The fire Roaring in the night

The best love I had never felt

Is marrying someone else

As my heart cries out

Charlotte my love

I am sorry I sent him

Sorry, I could not do the fantasy

You asked me to give

Now I watch you

eyes blue as the sea

Walking away from me

Can you not feel my heartbeat

Make love to me

Like you did that night

I still remember

Like it was yesterday

The way your eyes

Seduced my thighs

I tremble feeling you inside

Crawl back to me

Down on your knees

As you kiss my feet

Ever so slowly tantalizing me

As you make love to me

How I wish I had not done this

The ring in my pocket

I bet money you would not marry him

Panting in my breath

Your hair as it dances on my chest

Teasing me with your breath

Release this curse

Come back to me

Chapter 35

The Cannabis Effect

"All I want you to do is to lavish me every day while you're here," said Clinton, as we walked along the tomatoes, "then, I promise you your biggest fantasy".

I looked at him through squinted eyes and asked, "How do you even know what my biggest fantasy is anyway?"

"Oh, I know what your fantasy is," he said, as he ran his hands along my shoulders.

"Oh yeah," I teased back, "guess what, I do not even know what my biggest fantasy is, so how do you know what it is?"

"Picture this," he said, with hands outstretched, "I want you to imagine Palm trees, birds of paradise, and crystal blue water".

Already, my mind was in Hawaii as I boarded a ship that looked out to the *Queen Mary* in Long Beach, California. I was already drifting out to sea when he brought me back to reality.

"I want you to feel the white sugar fine sand as it pours through your hands," he continued.

Suddenly, I was in Florida looking out, as he dangled the keys to my new Jaguar in front of me. I was totally mesmerized by the new big shiny cat that caught my attention as it purred at me. With all of that, I was lost in his grace. I took a deep breath, turned to him and said, "It's not the promise of some fantasy life I'm seeking, and I'm not the type of woman to just leap and marry some man I don't know".

"I understand Charlotte, and I feel your hesitation, it is in trusting in faith that this is my next place, and I have always just known when it was time to make a new change. I am scared, however, that the voice in my head is telling me it's OK to proceed, which is why I asked you to marry me. I am looking for a commitment, Charlotte, not a one-night stand, as I am not the type of man to share my woman," he said.

My legs trembled as the thoughts of investing came over me. "I never stayed in any relationship, either culinary or human, longer than three years, Clinton", I said. "What if I can't stay in one place?" I begged the question, as I looked up into his face.

"Would you feel better if I told you I was counting on that?" he said with a wink, as he tapped my behind and lead me inside an arboreal ring where crepe myrtles of white, purple, and fuchsia lined the space in a giant circle. In the center stood a weeping willow whose branches lavished the ground. The sun peeked its way through the leaves, as its rays landed on the round massage table that was set with sheets. A white wrought iron table and chairs stood close to the base of the tree, with two glasses filled with ice with a pitcher of Mint tea. The closer I got, I could hear the shift in the ice as the cannabis honey whiskey made its way down its cold cascade.

Condensation lined the pitcher as the refreshing minty infusion filled its glass, and I could see it all coming together from the sheer hands that seemed to handle these types of things here. I swallowed and accepted that I did see another ghost again, as the fall heat beat down upon the grove. The sugar cane stalks stood tall in the fields as he put his crops to the test.

"All I am asking is for you to trust me, put your faith in me," he said, as he stood, looking down at me. "I am a Godly man, and I will protect you. You will see, just take a chance on me and let the Power of God inside me guide you to the ultimate place of your destiny," he continued.

"How can any woman resist that?" I replied as he climbed onto the massage table. I looked down into his head, at this Superman hiding in disguise. "I will cook for you, my King," I said softly, as I sank my nails into his back. A man who prays for me. That is what I lacked. "I'll marry you, Clinton, because I trust the same God you do", I said as I closed my eyes.

"Well, Charlotte, I have another little hiccup," he said as he cleared his throat, "I have moved our wedding date up," he stated.

"What, when?" I stammered back, "And I thought you said I had some time to prepare".

"I did, but things have changed, and we're moving it up," he said.

My body began to tremble as I took another deep breath, "trust the process, trust the process, trust the process," I kept repeating under my breath with my eyes closed. "I am OK with this, Clinton, and understand the Plan". m When I opened my eyes back up again, it felt like, for once in my life, that God had taken the wheel and all I needed to do was succumb to the image of God standing before me. "So then, Clinton, what's happening in six weeks?" I asked him, as my eyes looked off into the distance.

"The race of your lifetime, my queen," he answered.

I closed my eyes and let the oils glide down his body, not knowing anymore who I was or what had become of me, and thought I was so strong, as I dug my hands into his flesh.

He sat up and took the sheet off himself, letting it hit the ground. "Nothing has happened to you, Charlotte. You're in training camp," he said. He stood there naked in the afternoon sun, and he walked closer to me. As he reached down my hips with his right hand, I felt the fabric as it slid up my skin. My breasts were bursting outside of the purple lace push-up bra as his lips kissed my flesh. I am trembling as the last bit of clothes landed on the ground, as he instructed me to get on the table. His tongue tickled as he whispered in my ear. "I have a limo coming for you," he said softly as he climbed up in between my legs and let the oil run down my back.

I cringed at the thought of who else could be watching me. Paradoxically, the more I was instructed to just relax and breathe, the more I tried to hide myself under his body, when he placed a series of stones around me, all connected by a string. I could feel his expert hands scanning my system, as brilliant shades of red burst through my eyes could feel this sensation deep inside my groin. At first, I felt like a giant presence was looming in front of me. My legs trembled as he commanded me to open myself to him. The more I obeyed the command, the more I could feel this energy expand in me. In my mind, I could see the red ball of light and knew that, as soon as I saw it, we would be counting down. His voice echoed in my ear when I heard 'number three, and I felt an expansion that opened my rose petals up.

As my legs began to shake harder, I felt the vibration as he spoke 'number two' in my ear. His right hand now hovered over my sacral, and I felt a burst of orange light come in. The sensation was so powerful that it sent me rippling with laughter, as the yellow aura hit my solar plexus and expanded out past my physical body. In what seemed like wave after wave pounding against my soul, I was lost in its delirious tryst. My breath was panting as I felt my full heart expansion as rose petals fell from the sky. I breathed in its sweet scent as the Damask toner splashed my face. My body writhed as I watched his hand slide further up my throat and saw the blue lights as they scanned through my neck.

"I want to hear you reach a higher note this time," he said, as he placed his hands on my brow and throat. In what felt like the Colorado River during the spring, there came a surging of fluid as he hit my well. My voice peaked at a pitch I had not ever intoned, as waves of notes sang out in the air. I have no way of knowing how long any of this really went on, but it all seemed like hours to me, as I watched the sun glide over the afternoon sky.

I could feel the warmth of his hands as he placed them over my Third Eye. Varying shades of purple were glowing in my eyes, as images, all in perfect unison, began to form. They danced, well-choreographed, around my eyes in perfect rhyme and harmony, when I felt his hands move to the top of my head. A chill came over me, and the sensation went into my head, then down to my feet. Millions of goosebumps formed over my flesh as I felt the spirit flow in. The bright white light seemed to engulf my whole body as my soul left me. A sense of peace and joy fell over me, and I knew I was in the White Light.

It was over as quickly as it started when I felt my soul come back to my body and took a deep breath. I closed my eyes once again, as the sugar scrub emulsion with the mint from the garden invigorated my skin as his hands scrubbed it in. He started with my feet, ran his hands up my calves, rounding up to my knee, and slid his hands back down. He scooped some more of the sugary temptation and glided it up my thighs, working his hands slowly in a circular motion as the friction sent my skin tingling.

Just then, my elixir spurted out onto the grass as the sudden sting of his hand slapped my buttocks. "You like that?" he whispered in my ear. I feel another slap as he scrubbed my legs. "Answer me, my dear," he demanded, you are going to listen to me, right? I promise you, if you do as you're told and follow my commands, you will be the first woman President in the New Revolution of the Mind". Standing there in the middle of the greenery, all I could do was say YES as I wondered what was happening to me.

"The Cannabis extract in this blend is raised between the sugar cane and Jasmine," he whispered, "you are going to grow the cannabis for the Naughty Fig line, then heal the planet with it".

I shrieked with delight! "That is what I really want to do, Clinton, let me do that," I begged on his arm, as his body dripped with perspiration, and the linen on the table.

"Shhh, we cannot talk too loud," he cautioned, "You never know who's listening".

Once again, I was lost in his grace, as he took care of me, rubbing the grains of sugar up my abdomen and rounded out my breasts as he gilded down to my hands. The mint sent thrills all around my body as its coolness sent shivers down my spine. The heat of the afternoon persisted in the air as I felt him scrubbing my neck. With his mighty arms clinging close to my skin, his hands slid down my rear end. In my mind, I was so excited that I couldn't wait to feel the powerful slap of his hand. I was fully expecting another sharp crack when I felt him enter from behind. The force of his body sent ripples into my core as I struggled to break free and get on top. I was no match for his strength, as I felt my muscles shake. I knew I needed to train harder if I was going to be any match for my "opponent".

Not to be outdone, I call a truce. "Let me scrub you," I whispered in his ear.

"I would like that, take care of me now," he said, as he leaned in closer.

"So, you really think I could be the next President of the United States, after all? I asked, as I gazed into his eyes.

"Not only do I think it, but I also know it, and it's my job to prepare you for it," he answered.

"Wait, what do you mean by 'job'?" I questioned.

"Just do as I say, Charlotte, we've already gone over this," he said, "you need some skin in the game."

As the proverbial bucket of water fell over my head, it was then that I realized this was all an arranged marriage. I closed my eyes and saw my life flashing before my eyes. I knew what was happening and have known it all along, as I have tried so desperately to outmaneuver it.

"You can't outwit your destiny, Charlotte," Clinton said, as he tried to comfort me, "what is meant for you is coming, no matter what you do to try and stop it".

I knew what he was saying was true as I tried to close out the thoughts and concentrate on the task at hand. The sun and sky threw a range of hints of shades, and the breeze rang the chimes, as I ran my fingers all the way up his behind. "Damn, his skin is so fine," I thought, as I made my way up his back. I ran the sides of my hands along the length of his spine, gliding the oil past his traps, along the sides of his neck, out to his fingertips, then circled back down, while releasing my breath. Then, I ran my whole body down the length of his shank, starting with his feet, as I sent my love in, repeating the sequence. As I lubricated his essence, I began to vividly imagine myself becoming the first woman President on the Purple Party ticket in the New Revolution of the Mind. I could see it all now: the rallies, faces in the crowd, the stump speeches, the election, inauguration, the balls, the White House, the Oval Office with a fountain pen, the Lincoln Bedroom, the Cabinet, press conferences, the dignitaries, Air Force One, and going head-to-head with Putin! It was all I could do not to jump on his back, as I let the oil slide down his crack. Going back down to the other leg, I squealed again when his muscles expanded as the Eucalyptus and Lavender made their way in. I slowly started to trace his dark skin as the slurry of oils roasted his gastrocnemius. My fingers danced all the way up his legs, along the length of his back, rounding the shoulders all the way out to his biceps, then down through his fingertips, and ran my hands the whole length of his canvas, as notes of Geranium and Chamomile poured in. My hair grazed his legs, tempting my lips to kiss his hips, as I ran my elbow down his lower back, sliding off the hips as my fingers traced his back. I couldn't help but let my arms come back in, digging my way deeper as I climbed onto the table, nestled between his legs as the Clary Sage enticed him, massaging his back with everything I've got and using my elbow to get the big knot out. The Juniper oil delighted me with its pungent hints, keeping the mosquitoes far away as the beehives were buzzing, tempting me with their honey. As I glided my hands up his back, the afternoon sun heated up his flesh as his perspiration slurred with the oil, making the glide that much more exciting.

I applied my full weight as I put each rib back into place. His skin shimmered under my fingers as the babbling water beckoned me. I opened the jar of scrub and scooped some into my hands. Longing for the honey to come down my neck and tempting me as it ran off my fingers, as I licked the sweetness off his lips. Starting with his feet, kissing each toe as my fingers pressed into his arch, hugging his foot, as it rubbed my heart; then down back again with the sugary scrub with its mint and honey. Using both of my hands, with his leg resting in between my breasts, I massaged the sugar and mint into his lower extremities. The sweet emulsion sprayed me, as I glided it along his hamstrings and loved the way it worked in my hands, creamed with beeswax and the essences of various plants. The further I glided up his calf, the more sugar I rubbed into his back, as my hands engulfed his traps and his fingers came alive, sending me a signal back that he was also on fire. "Damn, this man is getting to me," I thought as he moaned in pleasure. As I rubbed his arms, I imagined taking his filet of beef out and running my fingers up its flank while making sure every ounce of fat is removed, as my forearms bore down on his shoulder. My breath panted increasingly, as the pain, mixed with pleasure, took him onto the next level.

"That is, it's Baby, breath with me," he said, as I licked my lips and came down with all my might, making sure his back was properly adjusted as we breathed out the pain of our releases. His back was just too tough for all that, so my elbows were going to have to do it, as I made one more run down. "Breathe with me," I said again, "take a deep breath," as I went back in, all the way up to his shoulder blade. "Hold it for a count of seven," I said, as we rode each election. Pondering what I just said, I could tell that my new programming was already happening. One - as a rib pops into place, Two - as the next wave comes on in, Three – as the next election cycle hits, Four - as the reality comes in, Five - as the momentum takes over, Six - as the country makes a shift, Seven - the Revolution is happening. "OK, how was that?" I spoke.

"Oh God, yeah!" he exclaimed as he lifted his back. "That is the spot! Yeah… Yes, again… Say it again with more conviction this time, let me hear that you mean it," he said.

I get myself into my next space, feeling my own momentum gathering, as I saw the face of the children I would be serving. "Now, take a very deep breath," I said, as I felt my new voice coming in, "slide one more time, from the small of your back up into the nape of your neck and take a deep breath". "On the count of five. We're going to release that again, breathe deeply: One – as my elbow dug in, two – breathe with me, and let's release, ahhhh, three – I know it hurts, keep breathing, four – Here we go, Five. Ah, that's it!" I said, as I heard everything fall into place in my own spine as well as his. "How do you feel, now?" I asked him as he got off the table.

"Fantastic!" he said, "like my meat is falling off the bones". "Oh, how I cannot wait for you to taste my ribs," said Clinton, as he rubbed his hands together, "you suck the meat right off the bone, don't ya," as he placed his hand on my head and brought me closer.

"Mississippi didn't raise no fool, and I know how to suck the meat off a bone!" I said, blushing.

My mouth was watering as I watched him taste his meat with his simmering barbecue sauce. As the tomato base started to crystallize around the fat of the pork, I just couldn't help myself. I quickly sliced a rib off and put it up to my nose. The scent was like the Fourth of July meets Labor Day, as he dropped a rib on my plate.

"Here, try this," he said.

It was not hard licking that bone dry, even though I knew it would be in between my thighs. My whole body was beginning to electrify as I licked my lips. "Ummm, I can't wait to taste that sauce you got," I said as I let his bone slide into my mouth. Oh, how the sweetness of his tender meat melted in my mouth, with my brain picking up on his molasses and stout.

"Some corn bread muffins with honey butter, baked beans, and potato salad were all this was missing," he said, "you should head back in the kitchen".

I grabbed his hand. "Not yet, that pork needs a little more smoking," I said as I slapped his butt, "you ain't done yet, get your ass back in the groove and up on that table".

"I like the way you talk," he said, as he sauntered himself over the table, larger than life, letting his clothes fall wherever he liked.

"You ain't seen nothing yet," I teased back at him as I made one more run, from the heels of his foot, with my forearms on his calves, up to his thighs, and rounding his gluteus maximus. Taking a deep breath again, I made my way to the small of his back, following the spine, as I heard each rib fall back into place. Rounding his shoulders, then down his arms, I slid my whole body down to his palms, and repeated the sequence, three more times."NOW, how are you feeling?" I asked him confidently.

"It feels awesome, all but this one more place, right here," he said as he reached around to point out exactly where he wanted me to place my thumb.

"OK, let's go in deeper: I want you to breathe with me, and I'm going to put my elbow all the way in so. It's OK to holler as this stuff hurts me just as much as you and that's why I am going to holler with you". "On the count of three here we go: One – take a deep breath, two –hold that breath, three – Here we go, hold it, hold it, now release," I instructed as we pushed our breath out together How are you feeling I ask?

"It was very strange, like I was massaging Kennedy," he said, coughing his name out.

Oh well now, that makes sense," I replied, as I asked him to roll over, squeezing the oil into my palms, "it's their recipes, right?".

"You know, Charlotte, you are right, that is good, you are feeling the energy of him then," said Clinton. I watched as each drop came squeezing out of the head, as I so the flip top lids way better than pumps. I lavished more oil around his hips, my love began to orchestrate as the violins cascaded in, and the oil continued to glide up his chest. Ever so slowly as I poured the oil around his flesh, I felt the call of Maui as the coconut oil rounded out the muscle blend, taking me far away to some tropical island. It was all I could do now not to lead him to the gorge and let the water run over his glistening head.

I turned to whisper in his ear, "I want you to imagine the blue-green water as it laps against the beach. I want you to picture the sugar fine sand as it encases your feet as I massage the sugary emulsion into your toes. Slowly running my fingers inside your digits. Washing your soul with my hands. Making love to your legs as my hands circling around your knees as I glide the emulsion up your length".

The need to blow into his solar plexus became readily apparent, as I massaged the scrub up his chest and the heat of the sun beat down upon his flesh. Beads of perspiration glistened on his skin, as the Honey and Mint and the scent of his hormones tempted my lips as they mixed with the oil when he exfoliated his underarms. The sweetness of the mint reminded me of the Julip sitting on the wrought iron table as I offered a sip to him.

"Damn," that's so refreshing, he said gratefully, as I watched it slide down his gullet.

"Flip over, please," I whispered softly in his ear.

"Oh, wait," he said, "do that again, just one more time," he said.

"I smiled inside, knowing he really does love me, as I rubbed the scrub in my hands and started on his back. As my hands rested upon the nape of his neck, I made a giant heart with my palms, by spreading my arms around out from his traps and made my way down to the small of his back and massaging the scrub into his gluteus maximus. The calves of his legs glittered as the sugary emulsion penetrated the back of his hips.

As his sculpted body glistened under the hot Mississippi sun, he appeared like a God, standing in the light, and I couldn't help but bow down to him. He was more than an angel, and I knew it, as we rounded the corner back to where his pork was smoking.

CHAPTER 36

THE KING OF LOVE

The traffic jam was miles long as he started to think about all he had done. The voices of everyone in the motor home were singing stupid show tunes when all Kennedy could think about was "What did I do? How had I let this woman get to me as he fumbled with the ring inside his front pocket? "What was it about her that I could not break myself free from?" he asked himself, as he curled up into a ball, pulling the covers up over my head. "Just a few more hours and we will be there," he reflected. Kennedy checked his phone, hoping to get a message from her.

"Of all the women I had ever wanted, this one somehow had gotten away," he sighed, thinking of what I did not do. Kennedy faded off to sleep, and there she was, center stage, in his dreams. Her dress of gray and pink silk flowed around her breasts as it opened below her knees, then cascaded down to where the veneer of her love called out to him. Her hair was fashioned up with sprigs of gold, rounding her face, and the white crystal embedded knitted earthing shoes gave her a hippy girl look. She wore a crown of Jasmine and Rose petals on her head, embellished with crystals, gems, and baby's breath. The bouquet from the garden was most delightful, with leaves of Cannabis, some purple butterfly sprigs mixed with Lavender Lantana, tied with hemp string. She flowed down the enchanted steps into the back garden. The Full Moon shone brightly into the clear night as the moon flowers began to bloom.

"Who gives this woman's hand away in marriage?" he heard in a boom from above. "I do," said Clinton as he slipped the ring over her hand. "Oh, Kennedy," he could hear her swoon, as he tightly kissed her lips. Would not have missed this for the world, love as a tear falls from my eye. My arms wrap around her waist as we walk down the aisle. He looked down the runner to where Clinton stood in a black tuxedo with a Purple Kush and baby's breath tucked into his vest.

His wings sprouted out as the look on his face caused my own wings to emerge. "We will share her then," he said to him, silently. The wind picked up the flurry of fabric as it billowed in the breeze, with that most glorious woman standing in between. From a corner of his eye, he spied his friend, Jaxson, standing nearby, and telepathically he heard "Don't ruin this, Kennedy!".

Next, he saw himself floating in the ceiling of their master bedroom. "Is that when it is happening?" he asked the seamstress with a laugh, as he didn't even know. "Clinton is handling everything, I guess, and I'm usually the last to know anything," he felt, as he watched her take her dress off and her beautiful breasts called out to him. "Oh, how I want to make love to her," he wished, as he watched her put her night dress made of shimmering pearls back on and walk down the red carpet with nothing but her crystal earthing shoes adorned on her feet with her wings protruding wildly, as the golden hue filled in.

"Come on down to the kitchen and get something to eat, we have a feast cooking," he heard her voice say. "I would like that clam chowder again, Charlotte," he said, as his hands reached out to her.

Suddenly, the dream ended abruptly when the driver slammed on the brakes, and the mobile home nearly missed the exit ramp. "I guess this is what I get," Kennedy said, abruptly thrust back into reality.

"You can't have everything," said Kevin.

"What about when you want them all?" Kennedy said back. "I knew this was for the best as she deserved a man who would not put her second on a list, and I am a womanizer," he thought more about it. Kennedy walked up to the front of the motor home, where Olivianna and Karissa batted their eyes at each other. "Hot Damn! Karissa goes both ways, he saw. "Oh, yes, there is a God," he shouted out.

"I guess we used each other," he realized. "Hello, Karma, how do you do? My name is Kennedy McCormick, but they call me 'the Fingler,'" he thought, as he fluttered his fingers in midair and watched as the woman spurted out their juice on the dashboard.

As he wrapped his arms around both women in the front seat, he felt his gray feathers begin to get a little lighter. They let me know that they loved him by taking the two hot dogs that he had made for himself and stuffing them in their mouths as if they had not eaten in weeks. Watching this made his own pork roll plump up a few more inches as they stuffed their faces. In that moment, he felt his robe of silk descend upon him and knew that he would be forever known as the 'King of Pussy', in the Land of Milk and Honey, as he planted a seed in the special one's belly.

CHAPTER 37

MISSISSIPPI WRITHING

I was lying in bed, buried deep in his chest. I could not help but think about the ring I saw out back. "Clinton," I said, as I crawled in between his legs, tell me, have you taken the mud class?".

"Taken IT," he said intensely with a matching look in his eyes. "I invented IT!" he exclaimed, as he pulled me back to his chest.

The excitement was indescribable, as I begged him to take me behind the woodshed.

"What, you would like me to teach you a lesson?" he asked eagerly.

I could hardly contain my excitement as I hopped out of bed and peeled off my sarong. Then, I took off running, begging for that appointment. On the way, I checked on the potatoes and eggs that I had cooling and whipped some mayonnaise with yellow mustard, a splash of vinegar, honey, salt, and pepper with some fresh parsley – all while watching as he rearranged some things in his office. I cut the celery stalks sprouting up from the ground. "The Vidalia are over there," he said, as he pointed further down. "I'm in love with this garden," I shouted with joy, "it so reminds me of when I was a kid,". A trail of natural stones leads the way to a large round opening with a wooden arbor with its posts placed firmly in the ground, covered with moon flowers and honeysuckle cascading their way down. I looked out at the Doric columns that made up his next show. Twenty-two bedrooms were a lot to manage, but I understood that he wanted to make sure that I could run this operation, as I made my way to the swing. The Red Canna caught my eyes first, as the hummingbirds darted back and forth. Tiger Lillies of all different colors nested between the butterfly bushes, and a line of variegated Hostas bordered out the entire arrangement. Magic virtually happened as I walked inside its confines and stepped into the mud pit. As its chocolate mineral offering oozed around my flesh, relaxing me further, he massaged it up my neck. I was lost in his embrace as his hands glided up my flesh. I could not resist touching him back and massaging the mud into his shank, whereupon the slow dance of love continued as we mutually gave and received pleasure. It was like nothing I have ever experience before. As we reveled in the moment, never had I suspected that mud massaging could be so much fun until you've wrestled with the absolute best under the hot Mississippi sun.

Rainbows of colors appeared before my eyes as the mud washed off his massive thighs along with the minerals that had encased us. "We match," he said, as he made passionate love to me. Suddenly, I felt the onrush of a storm brewing over in the sky. I did not care as I watched the lightning flash in front of my eyes and felt the rain as it further pelted the mud off our skin, as we rolled around in ecstasy, washing away our sins, lingering in the dusk. His wings spread wide as he took me on his back, ready for a horsey ride.

"Oh my God, you're Pegasus," I gasped, as we flew off into the night sky. Clinging tightly to him, I watched as his eyes changed to those of an Eagle coming in for a landing.

I couldn't even look as he swooped on down. "Damn it! I just don't know at all who this man really is. How can any woman not be in love with him? He is a stallion of the highest degree; he is everything, so how can any woman not fall head over heels in love with him? "I thought, as I massaged his neck. "Tell me more about you, Clinton," I said, as I clung to his back in flight.

"You tell me, "He said, as we landed in the garden. He gently sat me down in a chair as he swung in the hammock. "Tell me about me," he beckoned.

I took his hand, as I rubbed the lines in his palms, closed my eyes, and asked the first question in my mind. "I want to go back in time, tell me, where did it all begin?" I called out silently to my guides to answer his inquisition.

As I took a deep breath and began to probe deep inside him, I started to see the ocean, and I began to swim in the coral reefs as if I were a mermaid. The more I asked the question, the more I saw Neptune and his staff, and a chill came over me as I began to think of the statue in Rhode Island. I looked back up at him, afraid to answer the question as he gazed upon me intently. The increased pressure to deliver an answer further pounded into my soul when I blurted out, "I think you are a God".

"A God is what you think," he said, as he laughed. I felt naive if not stupid with the answer I gave him, but in truth, it is all I ever see when I look at him. A burst of excitement came out of me when my voice suddenly clarified. "Yes, that is what I think, Clinton, "honestly, I do think you are a God of some sort". I looked down at him as his skin shimmered in the moonlight. He looked back up at me with the light in his eyes and replied, "Well, if I am a God, then what does that make you?".

I thought back to the night when I was flying in the sky over Virginia, when my wings came out for the first time, and to the day when I flew across the lake, not even knowing that I was doing it at the time. Then, I got back down on my knees and said, "I do not know anymore, all my life I have had this drive in me, a thirst to be something bigger than what I originally started with. I thought I was a chef, but now, I feel a Brave New Spirit inside of me and really don't know what's happening. Somehow, I know that I changed the other night by morphing into a cat and haven't got a clue about how I did that. I cannot sustain the energy and in truth, I just feel like I'm gradually going crazy".

"So, what if you are a cat, or some tropical bird?" he replied, "What if you're all of that and more?" "If I am all of that, then I do not know where I am, too," he said as I looked up into the sky, hoping for answers that would explain it all.

"Have you ever thought that perhaps you are not one hundred percent human, Charlotte?" he asked deeply.

I closed my eyes and took a deep breath. "That is exactly what I am beginning to fear," I replied as I felt my back, waiting for my wings to appear, when the scent of ripe figs began calling me, begging to be added into the sauce that was still simmering." Let's go for a walk, Clinton, I said, as I pulled him off the ground, "I smell a fig and need to find it".

He stood beside me with his body towering over me, leading me around the bend, and opened his hands wide. "Your wish is my command," he responded, as he twirled his hands in the garden. "The sweetness of our plump and juicy fresh figs, ready to be picked – man, are they ever so delicious!" he declared as he put one to my lips.

With my eyes closed as I made my wish, I felt his breath next to mine as he placed a fig between his teeth.

"Take it from me," he said as he flashed his pearly whites.

Reaching up on my toes, I danced with my lips ever so close. "As my gloss touched his teeth, I felt the fig explode out of its sweet pink flesh in between our tongues. I picked a few more, peeled the skin, and brought some more for him to taste.

As we made our way to the brook hidden in the trees, a plethora of ferns as the water greeted us, and we made love again in all its majesty. "I swear if this man were not a God, he surely could have fooled me," I thought, as we walked back to the house with the bundle of fresh figs and vegetables in my hands. He shucked the Silver Queen corn while I chopped up the celery and onions.

He said that his magnificent obsession still needed another week as he tossed the tiny pearls in with the potatoes, eggs, onions, and celery; slowly spreading the dressing on his salad, giving it a toss and a sprinkle of fresh parsley, "That should hit the spot," he announced, as he placed plastic wrap on top of the silver bowl and headed for the walk-in.

Oh, now for that lovely pork smoking on the rack, those sweet baby ribs, and the beans in the cast iron kettle as we made our way to the outdoor ovens. The fire was still smoldering as he tossed on some peach limbs, and it got me thinking to add a few more ingredients to the mix. "Which ones?" I kept thinking to myself as I placed my fingers to my chin.

Clinton interrupts me and says, "Why not put it in both?" he suggested as he poured Jasmine tea over the frosted glass, "and of course, some peaches." As his meat was marinating in the sweet and spicy barbecue blast, I sprang to action down the rows, looking for the perfect peach to place in my baked beans. I might have to fight off a few wasps to do it, but in the end, it's worth every sting.

"That is why leftovers are so much better," he said, as he opened the ladder under the trees where the yellow cling peaches were still being harvested. Do you not remember all the fighting it took you to get it to this, just to taste the sweetness?" he asked rhetorically.

Buried deep in the freezer, I forgot all about it as he pulled out a frozen tray of macaroni, made with Jalapenos and Monterey Jack cheese. We were in Hog Heaven with those sweet baby back ribs with a peachy glaze, the caramelized onions in a dried mustard base, and the sweet tomatoes fresh off the vine, simmered with the peaches and figs in a cast oven roasting design. "One that works wonders in your backyard ovens," I said with a wink. Dinner was ready as we loaded the refrigerator out back. "I am falling in love with this place, Clinton," I said as I loaded the last rack in.

"I knew you would, once you got a taste of it," he said, "you will love it here, that I can almost guarantee". The summer is very hot, which is why we stay mostly up North during the thick of it. Our fine staff runs most of everything and I have a few more tricks up my sleeve," he said. "Take your time," I said, as I fell into his warm embrace "every day here has been like Hanukkah and I am not even Jewish,". I cannot help but be in awe of him. It is like he is way beyond what I first thought. "I want you to teach me everything you know, and I promise that I will be a good student," I said, as I washed the last pot.

"What if you disobey?" he said as his eyes glared hard at me. "Oh, you can spank me, too," I said as I threw a dish towel at him. Soon, he was chasing me off the back porch, stinging me with his whip.

"The problem is you would like it," he said, as he grabbed hold of me.

"Oh, you're so right," I screamed. "What do I have to do to get it?" I asked as I snatched the towel out of his hand. I ran through the rows of his obsession, not ready to be picked and doubled over with laughter as he caught up to me.

"What am I going to do with you, woman?" he asked. Clinton quickly threw me over his back and royally spanked my ass as he took me around back, "I think you need a good lickin', running through my fields like that!"

Emerging from the pole beans suspended by smaller limbs, I continued laughing as my hands slapped his ass, "Oh, I was hoping for that," I said.

CHAPTER 38

FALLEN ANGEL IN MY DREAM

I floated down the steps of the Antebellum mansion in a shimmering gown of red pearl satin with ruby rhinestones sewn into my cups. When I stepped to the entrance of a hidden garden, adorned by the stars that made up the night sky, as thousands of angels flew into witness, descending into the field. They sparkled with a kaleidoscope of lights, and all one needed to do was mentally ask who they were, and, in an instant, you knew them.

The little bunny rabbits that were nibbling on the clover also watched with intensity as I straddled the ground on my knees. Time stood still now. I felt myself begin to illuminate, as the scent of Neroli blossoms got my attention and I floated deeper into the heart chamber of the Secret Garden.

Blue Holly Hocks blossomed, and hundreds of butterflies flapped their wings as they perched on their stalks, while the hummingbirds' beaks poked inside the red and orange Canna that acted as the backdrop to the entrance. I sniffed each flower as I walked down the winding red brick with my scissors, burying my nose in its stamen as I collected their perfume. Using a Rose Quartz crystal bowl that was crafted into the shape of a heart, I snipped the French Purple Lilac off its bush, placing the branches into the oasis until I had them secured on all fours.

As each Pink Peony nestled its way in, the Yellow Roses blossomed into place. The **FooBellas** Cannabis plant filled each nook and cranny, as spikes of Lavender and Rosemary came out in explosions from the sides. The green ferns, red and orange Lantana, and Neroli blossoms filled in what was left of the space. Three cannabis-infused tapers lit up the eight-place settings, making the energy even calmer, as each table glowed well under the moonlight.

I was immediately drawn to the gold chargers that are floating in the air as they were placed down on the round tables, dressed in a hemp and cotton finish. The dinner plate of white with gold trim danced in the air. The cup and saucer went whizzing by me as they landed on the table filled with hot coffee. I watched in delight as the ghosts of the property scurry about. They all seemed to be oblivious of my stares when one of the younger girls came up to me with a crystal chalice, handed me a drink, and winked. She giggled with laughter as she spun around the table, using her right index finger to fill the champagne flutes as the sparkling bubbles floated up to the top of her fingernails like dew drops.

Just then, a storm of rose petals blew through the breeze, landing in the sherbet glasses that were filled with a lemon and spring water slurry. The wine glasses appeared out of nowhere as they danced their way through fields of grape vines. The straggly-haired ghost did his magic with a wave of his hand, as he turned the grapes into wine and placed them on the table. Gazing into his eyes, I stepped back further into his world. Even before his phantom silhouette emerged, I could sense he was here.

The black wrought iron dome-shaped trellis was embedded in its veneer with lotus petals with tiny lights that shone like stars twinkling in the night sky. Trumpet Vines and Moon Flowers opened as the Night Blooming Cirrus blossomed on a rotating pedestal in the center around the musical instruments. I took off into the garden, running faster to him until I reached the *Center of Love*. I hadn't noticed the Red Roses before, as White Jasmine clustered down from the trellis. I closed my eyes and began to take a deep breath. With each moment that passed, I could smell his scent closing in from behind me. I felt a tingle as his tongue danced in my ear. My legs squeezed tight as his fingers slid up my femur. Then, I heard the command, "Open your legs".

I rubbed my right thigh with my hand while his hand slid ever so close to my vulva as I unquestioningly obeyed his command and opened my knees. He taunted me with his words as he massaged my lips, "You like it like that? as his tongue lapped at my opening. He lifted my dress as my hips succumbed into the grass, my white pearl finish as he took me over the edge. I cannot tell if that was the tongue of a serpent the way he thrashed and writhed upon me, but it wouldn't matter if it was, as I'd still let him lick me.

The darkness of the night blinded me from his face as the gray-winged creature's feathers fluttered all around me. I was so frantic that I could hardly bear it as he suckled on my milk and honey. Barley able to say a word, I felt engorged as his wings began to flutter once again. Then, I felt my own wings emerge as I took his hand and stood on the platform. My wings were sparkling with a myriad of colors as gold sparks shot off in various directions. Taking me further down into his dimension, as I laid back down on the wet grass, wrapping my hands around the woody limb, that is, when I saw it. A large diamond ring came encased with many more diamonds all around its band, and I gasped when I beheld it.

I saw flashing lights and heard thunderous claps and felt the intensity as his vitality came in, propelling my soul out of my body as he recalibrated every chakra. I felt my whole system light up as his fingers trailed up the center of my body, lighting up my root chakra, as his fingers reached inside of me. In what felt like milliseconds, my whole body was lifting off the ground. I gazed up as the stars circled around me, as flashes of orange light beams went through my Sacral Chakra, as I knew this energy. Electrical currents burst out of his fingertips, sending spams that riveted my pelvic floor as he connected my Solar Plexus, releasing streams of gold into the earth's crust.

If I did not know any better, I would be thinking that I was having a seizure, as my limbs contorted to the sky. The bright lights flashed before my eyes as the sparkling diamond ring went all the way down my ring finger. I dared to look back up into his face, wanting so bad to peer into his eyes and see if it was Kennedy. It was no use. The waves of petals were all falling from the sky, as my heart filled with a love that I could not deny.

All I could feel was the beating of his heart as he breathed into me with his spirit so broken and raw that in that moment my soul reached out to his. I was so delirious as his tongue quenched my thirst, as his spirit filled me. The once gray feathers began to take on a new hue as I witnessed a collision of colors attempt to break through.

I reached out to touch his heart, and in doing so, it connected with my own. I felt the anguish and rejection in his soul. I felt the pain of neglect as he fell from his star. The bruised and battered soul only wants to be a part of the show. I feel my own wings emerge as I wrap my love around his body and nurse the fallen angel in my arms.

I wiped away the tears that were now dropping on my cleavage as my soul heaved into his. I watched as his feathers began to show off more colors. The more I caressed his silver hair, the more I felt this fallen angel come back to life. Within seconds, I was standing under the black dome with the winged man to my right. I felt the band go up my hand and knew I was his bride. I turned back to look at his face when he disappeared into thin air.

Later, I awoke to the sounds of laughter coming from down in the kitchen. The voices were so familiar, and I knew in an instant who they were. The sheets around the bed billowed in the breeze as I wiped off the crust that had formed around my eyes. I looked down at my left hand, and there was the ring Clinton had placed on my finger. I twisted it around my finger, wondering if the dark-winged man was really Kennedy in disguise.

I then heard the cackles of laughter as G'anacia and Nadia's voices hollered from the back kitchen as I made my way down the servants' steps. I ran around the stove and reached out to G'anacia and threw my arms around her. "I'm so excited that you are here," I said as I fluffed her skin down. "When did you get here?" I asked.

"Girl, what are you talking about?" she replied, as they laughed back at me, "we've been here for a week now." "Also, the pork necks with cornbread stuffing and mashed red potatoes rounding out this wedding reception are already here, too," she said.

"Oh my God, you have been here for a week?" I said, as I checked the clock, wondering how long I was even here".

Nadia chimed in. "Um, girl, I do not know what you did, but this man can orchestrate things with a snap of his finger," she said, swaying around the kitchen like silver flying fish. "He really is dreamy, and if you're not sure you can handle him, I'll take him off your hands if he's too much for you," she mused.

I was just so confused as to what was happening and how it happened so fast when I reached inside the refrigerator and pulled out some tea.

G'anacia and Nadia spoke in unison, "Trust the process, trust what God is doing in your life!".

The more those words rang in my head, the more I wondered if Clinton was a God. For a fleeting second, I let it all come in. What if he were a God, and I have been trying to convince myself he is human? The more I let the thoughts roll around my head, the more I decided to just let him in. What if he were a God? What then?

"Go on, get out of here, Charlotte," G'anacia said, as she cued at me with her hand, "it's your wedding day!".

"Wedding Day," I thought to myself, as I stood there frozen in time, until the sound of the front doorbell ringing got my attention. I walked to the front door in a daze to see a woman with eyes as seductive as the Crescent Moon. She had long, jet-black, wavy hair and was accompanied by a young man standing behind her with a basketball in his hand.

"Can I go play now, mama?" he asked as he bounced the ball around the courtyard.

"You must be Stephanie, Clinton told me all about you," I said, as I put my arms around her and invited her in.

"I have a few bags I need to bring in," she said as we walked back to her car. She returned, carrying dark, long bags with a hanger sticking out of the top.

I led her up the steps and down the hall to the room facing the courtyard.

"Clinton sent me your measurements some time back, and I made a few dresses that he had picked out for you", she said, as I opened the door.

"Really," I said back, with a look of curiosity when I asked, "How long did it take for you to make these dresses"?

"Oh, I have been working for almost a year on them".

"You don't say," I said, as a broad smile beamed across my face. "He did know on the first date," I thought, as a tingle came up my feet. I walked to the window where I knew I could see him out in the field. A smile came into my heart, so, for whatever is happening, I am happy with it. As I walked back into the kitchen, G'anacia and Nadia were at the center island, chopping up some vegetables. I looked over at them, not sure of what I was seeing, when I asked. "How long have you guys been here, again?".

G'anacia gives me a very strange look as she tilts her head to the right. "We've got all this, plus Kennedy is only a few hours away".

"Kennedy! I exclaimed, "What is he doing here?".

Nadia gave me a look of great concern. "Charlotte, you really need to go get dressed, because you have a lot of guests today".

I reluctantly turned around and headed up the steps. Waves of terror came over me as I wondered what I had gotten myself into. The way the vibration of his name came out of her throat made my hair stand up on end, and I wondered why I wasn't over him. I walked down the hall to the room where the strand of windows opened to the courtyard. The round tables were all decorated. When I saw the pink quartz sitting in the center of the table with the flowers I had picked in my dream.

I stood under the arbor in my mind as the purple velvet crush dress went over my body. Surveying myself in the full-length mirror, I liked the way the cut came so low on my cleavage. The trail that fanned out like fins made me think of the water fountain back in Rhode Island. I can do this, I kept telling myself, as I walked down the steps, "I am not in love with Kennedy anymore, I am in love with someone else," I thought as I walked back up the steps.

Just then, I froze up in my mind. "I closed my eyes and looked up to my right from the small window, and I spied the arbor with all its twinkling lights as Kennedy stood there under the moonlight. I closed my eyes again as I walked back down the steps into the Enchanted Garden, as Kennedy called out my name.

The excitement grew as I felt his kiss on my lips. Then, I looked up and he was gone. I cringed as I fell back under the lights, as the cascade of ivy swirled around the design. I held my eyes tightly as a little whimper came out.

"Charlotte," I heard, as I looked up ahead, try this one for size and see how you like it", as I unzipped the dress. As I took the next one in my hands, its white panels had a much simpler feel, sort of hippy meets 1920s, as the straps, hand sewn with gold and black panels, were revealed. I can do this, I keep telling myself. "Can I really do this?" I wondered to myself.

Chapter 39

A Symphony in Me

As I walked back into the grand kitchen that made up the Natchez Estate as the crew from the *Center of Love* assembled. I knew deep in my heart this was where I was supposed to be. Could I pull off a wedding and deal with all the stress, then walk out of the kitchen wearing my best, as if nothing had ever happened with Kennedy? As we held hands around the countertop, we all knew what this was about. This was not a one-cart pony show; this was a massive undertaking that would lead to world-class administration of a major hotel chain, or so I thought.

As we continued to breathe, I thought about all the things I would need as I felt G'anacia's breathe on me as she prayed over my soul. As the words flowed out of her, I was dancing in a sea of fruits and vegetables, wild-flowers, animals running free, tropical foliage, banana trees, and pineapple fields as far as I could imagine. Off in the distance, there were huts over the water in the lagoon – another part of the *Center of Love,* I presumed. That is why I am giving him my house; I am investing in this too. I stood spellbound as her words poured into my very being. I could see it all now. This was only a test.

Nadia gave it a stir as the pungent balsamic vinegar reduced in the pan. "Yes, chef! What's next?" she called to me.

As I stand in the kitchen, my spoon is my wand, as I raise my hands up to the culinary Gods. I am the conductor of my symphony, with G'anacia my cello, Nadia my violin, Karissa my viola, as David's flute flowed in, Olivianna with the sweetest of treats when she harps at me, Kennedy's base beat in my ear, and Kevin with castanets, as he strikes such a cord of familiarity. We even made a cannabis wedding cake that was nothing short of a dream with mango filling and rich butter cream, just like the one I had seen the other week in Delaware.

Aunt Mabel picked the flowers that will garnish her base. Off in the distance, I saw Clinton dancing in the smoke pit as he put the finishing touches on his baby back ribs, as the wind instruments blew in. All I was missing was my pianist. As the breeze flowed in, I felt Sergei as he breathed down my neck. He was the Russian from way back when I was just twenty-seven. I had not thought of him in so long, as I heard his fingers dance along my spine. He played my rib cage like it was a piano, and he would pound on my back, as the xylophone twinkled in the air with my angels dancing all around, as my crescendo gets ready to play.

G'anacia, let's get on with the corn bread stuffing; Kennedy, slice the baby red potatoes in half; hey, Kevin, make some Plutskies as an appetizer and a bowl of sour cream with some chives for dipping! "You got it, Chef, "Hey all chimed back.

A flurry of notes comes under my nose as Iran out to the garden in my mind. I kept seeing corn fritters and I just couldn't help it as I pulled this obsession off the stalk, gathering the

Zucchini and squash, as I plucked a fresh Vidalia from the ground, to round out my basket, as I ran back in. Slicing my squash into thin little strips, I added the onion and tossed in some butter in my big cast iron skillet. The corn was steaming in the pot on the back burner as I grabbed a bowl and poured in some full-fat milk, a few cups of flour, a few eggs, a generous handful of sugar, and added salt and pepper to taste, and I tossed in some baking powder. "This is for Sylvia," I thought.

The mini pie pastry was being pressed in as I envisioned the lemon, pecan, and cherry pie fillings. I took a deep breath as the kitchen heated up. The love of my family is in each dish I cook. When my veggies were all translucent, I took them off the burner to cool. My corn looked delicious as I husked its shaft, and rubbed some butter on it – who wants some lunch? "It's traditional to make corn fritters with the leftovers," I chimed in as I continued to run around the kitchen, inspecting everything.

Aunt Mabel came in with a bouquet of greens. "I found these out back," she said as she poured the water into a pot. When G'anacia hollered, "Hold up, I've got a smoked ham hock for those greens!"

"Oh my God, you made it," I said, as the rest of the crew fell in.

"We'll get these later," she said to me with a twinkle in her eyes as Clinton came in with a handful of his ribs slathered with peachy barbecue sauce.

"I added a splash of bourbon while it was simmering," he said with a wink.

Just then, I heard a voice as Jaxson walked in, with his briefcase, filled with his palette of colors. As we gathered around the center island and tasted all our creations, Clinton swayed in the air.

"How do you like the new *Center of Love*, dear?" he asked. "After the weekend's festivities, we have a new class coming in. Kennedy and Karissa, I have to hand it to you. You helped me find the woman of my dreams. Together, we are going to make history! Now is the time to take the *Center of Love* to the next level

Looking over at Clinton, I asked, "What is the next level?"

He looked over at me and asked, "What have you been seeing, Charlotte?"

"Well," I said, "I have been seeing tropical forests, and seas of blue, I've been seeing Birds of Paradise everywhere I look. I see new vegetation and lots of rebuilding".

"Where do you think you are, Charlotte?" he asked.

"I am not sure," I answered, as my wings began to emerge, trying hard to contain myself as I fluttered about the room. "The Dominican Republic, I responded.

"Close, very close," he said, "you'll see, let some things be a surprise".

"Jaxson interjected, "Come with me, chef, we've got to turn you into a bride".

"I do not even know what I'm wearing," I said.

"Don't worry about that now, everything's in perfect timing," he said.

"We got this, Chef!" the group shouted out in unison, as they hurried me out.

As I ran up the steps of the antebellum mansion, I gazed out over the scene as the Mississippi Orchestra was rehearsing.

Not understanding any sense of the time, the chorus of angels filed in. "I can't believe all of this is happening," I said, as I fell into his chest, "and you did all of this for me." I looked up into his eyes one more time

He picked me up and placed me on the bench. "You are my Queen, and you will have the very best," he said, as he placed a crown of jewels on my head.

Trembling at the thought of everything, I fell into his arms again. "I knew you were a King," I said softly, as I melted in his embrace.

"I have a bath of Rosewater and Jasmine waiting for you, my Queen," he said.

I walked into the bathroom as the sun was starting to make its way down. The candles flickered all around as the tub was filled with honey and cream. "You are my dream," he said, as he washed me down. The heart-shaped soaps are filled with Honey, Jasmine, and Lavender. As he ran them over me, the shimmering of the soap glistened on my skin, cascading his love all over me. He handed me the soap and I washed him.

I massaged his back with the creamy lather, washing away the smoke, as the scent of sandalwood and rose permeated the air was engulfed in his eminence once again as he made the sweetest love to me. My mind wanted to forget everything, to just be lost in his embrace and make more love to him. I was almost lost again when I heard a knock on the door.

"Um, excuse me, Chef, what are we doing with the filet?" asked Nadia.

"This is my masterpiece, and I should go back to the kitchen," I said as I pulled away from him.

"No, you are the grand conductor, just tell her in your mind," said Clinton.

Smiling back at him, I understand. "Nadia, listen to me, I want you to go back downstairs and just channel my energy," I said, "you will know what to do, just trust the voice inside of you".

"Yes, Chef," she said as I heard her retreat.

The olive oil flowed from Jordan as she drizzled it over that filet, carefully massaging the crushed garlic, honey, and salt into its flesh. The reduced balsamic was next, rounding out the Rosemary, encasing my love. Leaving it whole, bathing in its aromatic bath, a nice Italian Gorgonzola that looks like the sunset will be topping it.

"Yes, chef," I heard my head, as a flurry of sheets unruffled the bed. I was lost once again as I ran my hands down his back.

His ribs flexed as he engorged me again, wanting so bad to shout out his name, while trying to be quiet is just not the same.

"Then don't be," said Clinton, as he went deeper inside of me. "I love it when you scream my name," he said, as his hips started churning in a circular motion. As it hit the 90-degree mark, he drove back in again, taking my breath away as he reached up into my chest. "I have got your filet," he said as I laughed at his candidness. "No pastry either," he said as he pushed deeper into me, each thrust sending me over the edge as my elixir spurted out of me. "It's almost time, my Queen, I'm going to give you my seed," as he released its full measure within me.

Kissing me gingerly, he carried me back to the tub. "Go get ready, my love." The creamy bath still awaited me as the cream and honey nourished my skin. Still, I tremble as the orgasms keep fluttering in. As I looked out the window, the sun had all but set, the guests were arriving, and I heard the orchestra play. I looked out the window as the tiniest of angels flew around in the night sky, laughing as the lightning bugs took them all around the garden.

"Jaxson is waiting for you," I heard in my mind, as I ran down the hall.

I walked in and saw my dress hanging on the hook. "This is like a fairy tale," I said as I looked up into his blond hair and thanked him for everything.

He dabbed my face with some cream. "Close your eyes," he said. In a flurry of brushes and colors, I was transformed. My hair was fashioned up with little sprigs of curls running down my face.

As the wedding dress came over me, I realized that I had never seen one like this before, as I basked in its glow. "I feel like an angel, I feel like a queen, I feel like everything," I thought as I marveled back into the full-length mirrors. It was a truly surprise as he did not want me to see, as the flurry of fantasy came over me.

Tear drops of Amethyst dangled off my ears as Clinton placed the necklace of gold and gems that matched my earrings around my neck, as he kissed me and locked the clasp.

CHAPTER 40

YOUR TIME TO SHINE

As I looked out deeply into the night sky, the crickets chimed in, and the violins began to play. It was as if Rachmaninoff himself were here, as I could hear *Rhapsody on a Theme of Paganini* being played as the youngest violinist took center stage. The harpist was off to the right, as her fingers played. The little angel with dreamy chocolate eyes and a myriad of petals in her basket sprinkled them around as she danced through the hall with delight. Her wings protruding out of her little body as she called to me, "Come on, let's get married,".

I took her hand as we danced down the hall like little minnows at the edge of a lake and out the doors to the grand staircase. At the base of the steps, another little angel named Luna was waiting to take her hand. Together, they flew around the night sky as they dusted the petals like raindrops, giggling with each handful they dropped. The French horns blew, and flutes took flight, as the cherubs danced up and about in the moonlight.

My culinary team came in painted toes, each wearing dresses of different colors as their wings all emerged.

Approaching the man in splendor from his head to his toes, I watched as Anastacia flowed in her red dress and took the pilot's hand and saw, by the way he kissed her, that he took command. Then, I saw Jaxson's wings emerge and knew, by the special way he faced Nadia and that he had found his blazing soul. Olivianna was in her yellow dress with rose petals as the mystery man took her hand. Kevin's wings expanded as he took the hand of his new love, wearing cannabis greenery. G'anacia lit up the walkway in salon sapphire blue as Big Willy took her hand. Karissa's purple dress, clinging to her breasts, nearly stole the show. Standing beside her was the man of the hour. Kennedy stepped in.

I walked down the steps with my long gown trailing with each pace, glistening in the moonlight, as the diamonds encrusted in my breasts with golden wings of petals that caught the stars' eyes, as my barefoot toes shinned in the starlight. My Amethyst tears hung from my ears as the violins silently called out to me. The whispering of the oboe called me ever so closer to the man of my dreams.

I saw my future as I rested my arm over Kennedy's. I looked up into his crystal blue eyes as a tear fell down his cheek, and my own eyes began to blur with tears now forming. I scanned his eyes for what felt like eternity as I begged him in my mind to take me away. He closed his eyes and said silently, "I can't, the dye has been cast," as he kissed my forehead with his lips. Then, I closed my eyes as I felt a surge of energy whirl around me and asked him, "Why not?" as I felt a tingle in my nose.

"I'm doing my job," he said as he took my hand.

"What job is that?" I questioned him back.

You hired me to deliver you the man of your dreams, now go marry your King," he said as he patted my hand.

I looked back up at Kennedy. "How could he not have known that he was the man of my dreams," I thought as he gave me one last kiss on my lips, then handed me over to Clinton Tuckerman.

I watched intently as Clinton took my hand away from his, his wings emerging as the sparks flew out, as the tug of war began between the two men. I stood there, secretly knowing I wanted them both. Aunt Mabel's wings emerged as she flew up on the table. I heard the gasps as I looked back out to the crowd. There were celebrities, dignitaries, heads of state, and Kings and Queens from different lands... Then, the piano begins to play harder as they led me up to the altar.

With a booming voice and a wide-open gesture, the ceremony began. "Ladies and gentlemen, I am Reverend Lickalattapuss," he announced as the laughter rang out and the Burning Bushes exploded. This is the first wedding I am officiating in the Grand State of Mississippi, a spiritual union for Charlotte and Clinton," he said as the final cords played. Clinton kissed my hands as the orchestra faded, and I wondered what he meant by 'spiritual union'".

The White Crystal spun over our heads in the sacred bond between us, uniting our spirits into one. The feeling that the secret hand gestures no one knows the meaning of, as each one is unique in blessing from the Universe, now came over me. As the piano and strings invited me in, my wings fluttered as the ring slid over my finger, the diamond band that matches Clinton's hand. The stallion flew, as I rode his back throughout the Mississippi sky, as the dancing of cherubs floated over the sugar cane, making love in the fields of grain, as Kennedy and Karissa celebrated another successful collaboration.

As the buffet of culinary delights took center stage, with every type of food imaginable on display. I saw veal raviolis in a tomato cream sauce, moussaka, pierogi, bulgogi and Korean pancakes, chicken Tikka Masala, paneer, beef teriyaki beef on a plate of mixed vegetable as crawdads flowing over the jambalaya and finally, the lamb gyros in bite size appetizers, as they make their way around the room on platters with winged angels. Every nation and tradition was represented here, from the dessert to the appetizers to the wines. I saw the melting pot, this is our nation, as every man, woman, and child of all tribes gather to give praise to the Gods that make up our world, and every person is respected for their beliefs. I look over at Clinton, marveling at what I am seeing, when my eyes met Kennedy's again, and I wondered why nothing ever happened with him.

I picked up my little cherub and put her on my hip. I saw her mama off in the distance, with her eyes taking a shine to Kevin as he put his arms around her hips. I watched as he flutters his wings and took her for a ride around the garden. "You are getting so big now," I told her, as she told me her stories. Down by my feet, her little boyfriend was in tow, before they bid me goodbye and took flight.

Scooping up the desserts from off the table, I can hear him say that he loves grapes, as he popped each one in his mouth, as a platter of cream puffs caught his eye with a bright little smile. As his dark chocolate eyes twinkled in the sky. I danced around the room with my angels from up North. The ones that create all the *Center of Love* potions, when Angel Rose comes up to me. Smiling, she put her arms around me, and we danced under the stars for all eternity.

Clinton made up to Kennedy, "I knew you would not let me down, and how hard this was for you. Thank you for being a gentleman with her," he said.

Kennedy smiled back, "It wasn't easy, Clinton, but it is ultimately for the best," he replied as he played with the ring, still sitting in his pocket, "and this time I didn't eat the cupcakes".

"The *Center of Love* did amaze at Dover Downs, and the food trucks are in position with sample boxes of our new cereal making their way around the nation, so, you got your deal, Kennedy," said Clinton as he heartily extended his hand.

"We are making our debut in the race," Kennedy said with a broad smile, as the two firmly shook hands.

"I'm using the Trans Am to put some pressure on GM to be ready by 2025 with the new their new model at the Dover, Delaware assembly plant," as Clinton gave a nod to the man pulling the strings.

"I also have my sights set on Mississippi and Tennessee for the Grand Prix and Chevy Monte Carlo to be built," said Kennedy, as the two partners each took a shot of cannabis whiskey and celebrated their next victory. "All of this just in time for Pontiac to come back to racing," said Kennedy as he rubbed his hands together, "and I will not let down the American people, Clinton".

"I know we have a good plan, Kennedy," replied Clinton, as another round of whiskey slid down Kennedy's throat, "The Kennedy Plan". "I know they are wanting on the Trans Am, too," he added, "but the whole fleet is coming back real soon!".

"This has been amazing, Clinton," said Kennedy, as he brought it home for the win, hugging and shaking hands.

Clinton declared: "After the honeymoon, our next mission is to have the United States take down its awful and abominable anti-Cannabis legislation!".

"So," Kennedy asked, "when do you think you will start the next bid"?

"As soon as Charlotte realizes she is it to win it", Clinton said with a twinkle in his eye, "anytime, now".

"You really think she'll do it?" Kennedy asked as he turned his eyes to Charlotte, who danced in the field. "She will have no other choice, with the People's frustration with dirty two-party politics and the economy, it's only going to take a pen stroke to write her in," said Clinton as he turned, raised his shot glass, took another sip of whiskey, and saluted her. "To Charlotte Bennett, our Next President!" he declared.

"I've got to hand it to you, Clinton, you know how to pick 'em!" said Kennedy as he raised his glass. "To Charlotte Bennett, the next POTUS, and to Clinton Tuckerman, our first and future First Gentleman," he toasted.

"Thanks, buddy, she is one hot ticket, in more ways than one!" said Clinton, moved by Kennedy's gift of gab.

"That she is, sir, that she is," as they raise their shot glass for the third time. "To Charlotte, Mother of a New Nation! "Write her in!" he exclaimed. Suddenly, as if by hyper-dimensional mass media, the crowd shouted, "Write her IN, write her IN!" as Clinton waved to them with a radiant smile and Charlotte approached. "Keep it up and you'll be the White House Press Secretary," Clinton jabbed, giving Kennedy a hearty elbow.

<conraddemail.com

Standing in the center of the field was Karissa. A round table filled with glass flutes and carafes of her finest tart cherry sparkling cannabis wine, when she says, "let's make a toast". As Olivianna fills the flutes, she hands two to Kennedy. Kennedy hands each person a glass just as Jaxson comes to the center of the group. Jaxson takes a glass and gives a nod to Benny the Big Tuna Cohen and Clinton, "So do you think Charlotte Bennett will run for President? Clinton takes a slow sip of the cannabis wine, letting it dance on his lips as Aunt Mabel and G'Nacia step into the center. Clinton cocks his eye toward Charlotte Bennett, who was dancing in the field with the crew from FooBellas House. Raising his glass to the air, he says, "She will have no choice, the people will write her in as President". Kennedy's eyes flicker, a lightning bolt of information downloaded into his head when Jaxon looks to the group forming and says, "Who would be her Vice President"? Kennedy reacts with hands in the air and excitement in his voice "the woman who wrote all of this, Kathy

DeMatteis" Clinton smiles and says, "Kathy DeMatteis, I like the sound of that" Bennet DeMatteis the Big Tuna says as he wraps his arms around Clinton and Kennedy "sounds like a winning ticket if you ask me" as he takes a sip of Karissa's wine. He looks to the center of the field where Kathy DeMatteis was singing, tipping his glass towards her, he hollers and salutes out, "Madam Vice President. It was a small sound at first, a low mumble as the sounds of clicks could be heard, as the collective hum of the tracker on Amazon kept going up. As the word began to spread, it was like wildfire. Within hours, millions of copies were sold around the globe, making Lewis a millionaire with his last wager. With their pens in the air, the people shouting, "Bennett DeMatteis for the Win Were Writing you in"! Before anyone could even figure out what happened, Bennett DeMatteis had garnished the top two positions in the land. When the papers settled and the last vote was stacked and counted, the auditor general looked up at the Senate floor and said, "Holy Shit, they won!!!" And just like that, Bennet & DeMatteis made history. The first woman to be President and Vice President of the United States of America was written under the Revolution of the mind. All because "we the people" collectively, with a resounding 57 percent of the vote, said enough is enough, it's time to give the women a chance, and they wrote Bennet DeMatteis in. After all, a Fantasy is just a lie on Steroids until you have the courage to write a new plan and execute it!

Diamonds in my Sheets

by Kathy DeMatteis

Diamonds in my sheets

Diamonds in my sheets

I'll be wearing robes of gold

With diamonds in my sheets

Diamonds in my sheets

Oh, Diamonds in my sheets

I'll be wearing robes of gold

With diamonds in my sheets

You see, I am the trump card

I've yet to final play

You can bet your bottom dollar

I am here to stay

They watch us as we suffer

And laugh as we take heed

For all they have been feeding us

From the flower to the seed

Oh, Diamonds in my sheets

Oh, Diamonds in my sheets

I'll be wearing robes of gold

With diamonds in my sheets

Diamonds in my sheets

Oh, Diamonds in my sheets

I'll be wearing robes of gold

With diamonds in my sheets

I see our future clearly

As we thrust upon its wake

Dancing in the Milky Way

A mighty world to take

I do believe it's happening

The tides' about to turn

Every object ever wanted

Is forever in your earn

Oh, Diamonds in my sheets

Oh, Diamonds in my sheets

I'll be wearing robes of gold

With diamonds in my sheets

Diamonds in my sheets

Oh, Diamonds in my sheets

I'll be wearing robes of gold

With diamonds in my sheets

We have ruled the jungles

And the mighty ships of sea

We have tamed the lions

On the sea of Galilee

We have soaked in the stars

Highly upon the hills

We have traveled in the stars

To the galaxy of wills

Oh, Diamonds in my sheets

Oh, Diamonds in my sheets

I'll be wearing robes of gold

With diamonds in my sheets

Diamonds in my sheets

Oh, Diamonds in my sheets

I'll be wearing robes of gold

With diamonds in my sheets

[Repeat 3 times]

"All my life, food was always the centerpiece to any family function; some things will never change."

Kathy S. DeMatteis

CHAPTER 41

WOULD THE REAL CHARLOTTE BENNETT PLEASE STAND UP!?

The plane landed in Kent County, Delaware, as a nearby farmer plowed the field. The leaves had all but fallen, and bales of hay still dotted the front porches as November ushered in. I watched the dust as it whirled around the land when my first assignment came in. I got into the car knowing I would be back in the kitchen next to the real **Chef Bones**, and this time the stakes were even higher when we pulled into the driveway of Woodburn, the Governor's official residence.

Clinton patted me on the shoulder. "Are you ready to face him again?" he said

"Oh, you have no idea," I replied, as the excitement welled up within me.

"Are you sure that you're not upset about your honeymoon being postponed?" Clinton said, eyeing me up and down.

"What, and miss a chance to go head-to-head with **Chef Bones** again? "I replied. "Oh, no way… I'm on it, Clinton! I replied firmly, as I squirmed in my seat and punched my fists in the air. "I got him this time, he's mine!" I added for good measure.

Clinton took a few playful jabs at my side. "You ready to get back in the ring?" he asked, already knowing the answer.

I'm not going down without a fight this time," I said, as I vividly imagined my recipes beating **Chef Bones** in a fight of a lifetime. "No way, Clinton. I'm not intimidated by him. I got this! I got my own spin on things," I went on. I put my hands on my hips and said, "What, you don't think I can take him?"

"Oh no, I think you can, but you're seeming awful cocky, and I like that," he said.

"I am awful cocky," I said, as my hands went back on my hips, "and that's just the way I like it".

"OK, Killer, calm down, I just want to make sure I got the right woman for the job," said Clinton with a hearty laugh.

"I can beat **Chef Bones** because he thinks he can take me down easy and I got a few secrets up my sleeve, too, ya know," I replied as we walked into what appeared to be another *Center of Love Inn* dream.

Before the car was even in Park, I saw Kennedy and Karissa pull up in the *Center of Love* Mobile food truck as Aunt Mabel and the whole crew stepped out. I ran up and hugged Aunt Mable, burying my head in her chest. I love you, Auntie Mable, you always have my back," I whispered softly, as Kennedy and Karissa came up to me and gave me a hug.

Aunt Mable began rubbing my shoulders. "Sweetie, you are way too tight," she said, "and you better schedule some massages, so you are ready for this fight".

Clinton took my hand and said, "We will take a day to rest and walk the Delaware Beaches and take in some sights, then it's time to take **Chef Bones** down in his own shack!"

Aunt Mabel put her hand on the front of my shoulders and looked me in the eye. "OK, Charlotte, you know he is a master at his craft," she said. "You've been in Maine for some time pumping out Lobster Bisque, but those ribs you made the other day were mighty tasty and with Clinton and Kennedy at your side, "I believe in you, girl, you got this!" she exclaimed, as she choked up, holding back her tears.

"You got as good a chance as anyone," Kennedy said, as he grabbed my hands, "now, go put on those pork picnics and let's get this show down started.

"What pork picnics?" I asked.

"The ones I just picked up for you at the butcher," he answered, "now go make me some Southern-style Pulled Pork Sammies".

"You got it, Kennedy," I said as I took the order. Then, I ran like a linebacker into the mobile kitchen and began to rub the pork shoulders down with Clinton's secret blend.

"Don't forget the Cole slaw this time!" Clinton yelled.

I rolled my eyes mockingly, "Don't forget the coleslaw." I mouthed back, parodying his voice. "I don't like coleslaw, but I'll make it for him, anyway," I grumbled under my breath, as Karissa and Olivianna began pulling fresh cabbage and carrots out of the fridge.

Kennedy came in right behind me, pulled his pink meat out, and placed it on the counter. I looked over to him and asked, "You up for this?" I asked, pointing over to a bag of charcoal and wood chips.

"I guess so," he said as he hoisted the bag over his shoulder and headed out to the back of the Governor's House.

In just three days, I was going to be up against the biggest name in Delaware. Film crews and judges from all around the country would weigh in on their opinion of who the winner is: Chef Bones of **TenderBones Rib Shack,** or Chef Charlotte of the ***Center of Love Club***.

Grabbing the largest pot I could find, I began chopping up four large onions, placed them on the six-burner, and sautéed them up in some olive oil. Adding in 12 cloves of garlic that I had finely minced, ½ cup of dried mustard, a few cups of apple cider vinegar, a large can of tomato sauce, a bottle of Worcestershire, a pound of honey, handful of celery seed with two cups of sea salt; and filled the rest of the pot with some water and let it boil for an hour. Before I was done, there were two hundred half chickens stuffed inside the refrigerators of the Governor's Mansion, and I set my sights on my sweet sauce.

It was almost ten o'clock at night before the last of my dishes was all lined up. I had yet to try his dessert when I began to slice the skins off the peaches and sugar them down for the iced tea that I had brewed. When I set my sights on my trays of peach cobbler with fresh peach ice cream, I knew I was going to bring Chef Bones to his knees! It was almost midnight before I had crawled into the guest room at the Governor's house and set the alarm for 8 am.

Meanwhile, Chef Bones was in his Dover location of **TenderBones Rib Shack** at 617 East Loockerman Street, stoking up his fire. As the first flame kindled, he gloated profusely, knowing he was taking Chef Charlotte down this time and there wasn't a damn thing she could do about it. He knew her weakness, or so he thought, as he rubbed his hands on his meat and massaged in his special secret blend of herbs and spices. He laid his prized possession on the grate, as he breathed in deep the scent of his win. The smell of his provisions enveloped the Shack, as the fat crackled under the fire. "Can't touch this!" he said, as he headed back to the kitchen to make more of his secret sauce.

His staff was busy preparing for the crowds, with tickets ringing up all over the state. He knew he was getting what he bargained for and, maybe more, as the publicity surrounding this cook-off was garnishing national attention. "Who's bringing Cannabis Chef Charlotte Bennett to her knees"? he bellowed out, leading the cheer.

The crew's chorus yelled back, "Chef Bones, Chef!" in unison.

"That's what I want to hear," he said. He then inspected the pork, which he had previously hand-selected for this Tuesday's match-up, with an eye that would leave even a USDA inspector envious; surveying each piece of meat, as he pulled out his select cuts and prepared them himself. The look in his eyes turned sly as he conjured up an image of Charlotte begging for mercy, as his succulent meats melted in the judges' mouths, and giggled to himself, that smack-talking Clinton Tuckerman was sending in a rookie woman to do his bidding. He could picture it now, as she crumbled to her knees. Chef Bones remembered her from back in the day when they had their last match in the kitchen. "This time," he said to himself, "I'm going to take her all the way down, and that trophy and check is as good as mine".

The days flew by fast, and before she knew it, the mobile catering truck was at **TenderBones Rib Shack** on Route 13 in Dover. Walking in with her crew flanking her side. The 124-seated dining room was filled with loyal patrons chowing down on his food. From the looks on their faces, Charlotte knew that this was going to be a tight win when she heard the voice of Chef Bones holler her name.

"Chef Charlotte, hey, I never thought I would see your face in my kitchen again," he said. Turning to Clinton, he said, "What are you doing, sending a girl to fight your battle with me?" he jabbed. "You too scared to take me yourself, Mr. Tuckerman," he added for good measure, as the two men began talking chops.

Clinton looked over at me and smiled, then looked right back at Chef Bones. "I am not scared, and I know she can take you and that, my friend, is what I'm here for," he said.

Scoffing at the thought, Chef Bones opened his hands and said, "Come on in, Charlotte".

There I was again, face to face with him. As his warm hug embraced me, I knew not to get too cozy with him when he turned to shake hands with Clinton and Kennedy. I already knew that I was coming here to beat him, even though he graciously shared half his kitchen with me. I walked into the back like I owned the Shack myself and took control right away as I sized up the kitchen.

Our mutual passion for barbecue came through all the hype and bluster when Chef Bones announced that my meat had just come in. I went to the back and hoisted the bins of smoked chickens up on the counter.

For the audience, the smack talk between Chef Bones and Chef Charlotte was the real show, as tongues began to wag. It soon became clear that Charlotte was not going down as easy as he thought she would. Chef Bones smiled as the fire began to grow outback, and he knew he was going to have to bring his Big One in. With a sly look on his face, He told his sous-chef to call in an order for another thousand rolls for the big match-up as he began to shave his rib-eyes down.

The sous chef just looked at him and asked, "Are you sure that's not too much?"

The knife came down hard on the table. "Am I sure?" hollered Chef Bones, "just do as you're told and place the damn order!" as he upped his game. He grumbled as he looked at the numbers. "You're going down, Charlotte," he said, "we just sold over 700 tickets to this event over the last two days, and with all the chatter happening on Facebook and Instagram, it should bring in a few more stragglers to watch you get burnt to the stove".

"I laughed right back at him. "Oh, is that what this is all about?" I replied, "and I take it you're using your big bad steak sandwich to put some more heat on me".

Chef Bones snickered under his breath. "I don't need my steak sandwich to take you down," he said, "and I just heard that every hotel within a 50-mile radius of Dover is booked and y'all know who they are coming to see, don't you?"

"Yeah, me", I shouted back, as I began counting the tickets that already had come in over the past weekend.

"Oh, you might think they are coming for you, but I am wagering my next bet on my steak sandwich taking the show," he said.

I smiled inside, knowing that he had no clue about the chicken breasts that chilled for two days in brine and the roasted red peppers and Kennett mushrooms with Vidalia onions that we smoked at Woodburn. "It's not the size, it's the flavor, Chef," I smiled, knowing that I had a few more tricks up my sleeve.

Chef Bones laughed and said, 'You ain't got nothing on me, and I love watching you think you can beat me".

All his smack talk was revving me up. The more he talked of taking me down, the more excited I grew. This time, I got right in his face and said, "I'm betting my three-cheese blend of mozzarella, provolone, and sharp cheddar, melted over the top of hearth-baked bread soaked with garlic butter, is going to bring the crowds ever so closer to me.

"You think a chicken sandwich is any match for my hot meat?" he said, laughing in my face.

With a sly look, I said, We're in Delmarva Chicken Country, baby! I've been itching for a poultry bomb. You better hope I don't drop some of my world-famous crab cakes with my roasted red pepper aioli down on that chicken and get the Eastern Shore in on this. His spatula trembled slightly in his hands when I got in his face. "Wanna taste, Chef?" I asked as I held a sample under his nose.

Our mobile food truck pulled onto Loockerman Street as the crowds began to show up long before the first pieces of meat would be ready for the plate. The excitement grew as what appeared to be half of the State of Delaware, television crews, and the Governor came to see who would win, as the Battle of Delaware Barbecue took center stage.

The scent of hickory smoke swirled through the air as Chef Bones talked with a newscaster from the local TV 16 station. I strutted across the parking lot as the smokey wind whirled through my locks, and I walked right up to Chef Bones and said, "You ready to go down tonight on-camera?" He grinned back at me and said, "I'll be more than happy to take you down publicly… you ready for a real butt whipping"?

I smiled back as the news broadcaster laughed and began to ask me what I had in store to beat Chef Bones.

"Stick around and taste for yourself," I said. Then I turned and looked at the camera. "So, come on down to TenderBones Rib Shack in Dover, Delaware, and judge for yourself, I said, seizing the moment. With that, the kid gloves came off, and we both raced to the kitchen to pull out our meats. The dining hall began to fill up as Kennedy and Kevin laid the table out for the judges. Everyone could hear the fat sizzle as it hit the steel grates, and before we knew it, the first votes came in.

It was like a dream, as the panel sat before my eyes. Pit master's from all over the world and famous chefs came down to taste our version of pulled pork. I stood beside Chef Bones as the judges took bites from both plates that we laid down. I stood with my hands behind my back as I watched them write down things on a score sheet. Each judge asked us both some questions, and I watched as one of the chefs savored my macaroni and cheese and felt a bit relieved when she slathered more of my honey-butter on her corn bread and wiped her plate clean. The crowds grew wild as they all cheered, and the City of Dover began to swarm, as people traveled from all over the state and surrounding region to be a part of the biggest event in town.

It was not over until midnight, when a panel of judges counted the votes, and my favorite Governor stood up and said, "AND the winner is…

Chef Bones gave me a big, warm hug and a brilliant smile. "It's all for good," he said, "We raised a lot of money for our charities today, and that is what matters the most!" as the crowd burst into cheers.

I looked at Chef Bones and smiled at him. Shook his hand and said, "Shall we go bury the hatchet?"

"He looked back at me with a truly magnanimous glow on his face. "How about we do it on The Green?"

"You got yourself a deal, let's go!" I replied.

The End

Kathy DeMatteis

Write her In

Independence on my mind

Political redirection

Of the third kind

Before we get to the next pole

Let me ask you

What's your elected politician

done for?

Are you paying more at the pump

Lost your home

living on the run

Charismatic as they lite

The stage Making promises

Designed for the grave

You gotta choice

We can change all this

Tired of the diplomatic Crock of shit

Dangling $1000 to make you shift

Enough to keep you thinking

They got you on this

But wait

What's that

Throwing in their hat

A rich man's game

Wasn't supposed to be like that

Read your constitution

Look up the facts

Everyone has the right to run

The establishment

Doesn't want it like that

They like the power

They wheeled over us

Making us hate

While they laugh at us

And we're supposed to accept this shit?

The news tailored to show the right clip

Whatever it takes to raise a fist

To Shame you for not wanting to be a part of an experiment

Carry around a card that violates your rights

HIPAA laws Aint that right

Making a living off our backs

Have no desire to fix any of this

If this were your business, You'd be in the hole, but they got your paycheck on hold

You don't get yours, To Uncle Sammy gets his, And the Govt is pulling on the purse strings

So take that power In your hands. Write the person that you want in.

Drop this two-party system. That's already in bed. Bypass the game they set us up to play

Write Charlotte Bennett in for President of the USA

When they ask who her VP is

Write Kathy DeMatteis. In her

The woman who wrote this thing

The Master's Revelations

Oh, but I am

Always a part of the plans

As he smiled at me

My darling Kathy

Who do you think writes these things?

I look back up

at the God that rocks my nights

and rules my thoughts

wrapped my arms

around him and said

I am ready for the show to start

Then pack your bags

Things are about to be told

How glorious life can be

When you reach inside your soul

You learn that a woman is a brilliant design

She holds secrets to the universe

Programmed in her mind

Take my hand

We will do this together

World peace is on the Horizon

God's always on time.

1. Which character did you resonate with the most inside the story?

2. Which aspect did you pick up on first?

3. Did you learn anything new that you did not know before?

4. Did the sex excite you?

5. Do you see any of the political implications of the Purple party coming true?

6. Did you see it as a movie already in your head?

7. Do you think Clinton Tuckerman will be leading the revolution?

8. Do you want to learn how to have multiple orgasms as the characters suggest?

9. Do you believe you can have the life that you seek?

10. Is Charlotte relatable both to you as a man and a woman?

11. What's your impression of Kennedy?

12. Did you like the feel of the soaps on your skin?

13. How do you see yourself inside this story?

14. Do you think Jaxson will take over the Center of Love Club?

15. Will Karissa indulge Kennedy's fantasy, or will she leave him for uncharted waters?

16. If you could play any character in the story, big or small, who would it be?

17. Do you see G'anacia owning her own restaurant one day?

18. Do you want to invest and purchase a week of healing vacation at any one of our locations?

19. Do you see yourself living in any one of our locations part-time?

20. Do you see yourself as a part of the *Center of Love Club* as an investor or full-time owner?